QUIET SPELLS

Isa Agajanian (they/them) is a writer and illustrator living in the United States. Raised in California and spirited away to Florida, then Oregon, Isa is never writing in one place for too long. They are joined in their pursuit of good stories by a hefty grey cat named Mosse and at least one roommate at a time. *Modern Divination* is their first published novel at the crux of a hundred unpublished stories.

By Isa Agajanian

Spells for Life and Death Duology

Modern Divination

Quiet Spells

Praise for Isa Agajanian

'Lush and atmospheric, full of magic and yearning'

Olivie Blake

'Stylish, moody, with an atmosphere thick enough to drown in, *Modern Divination* is the cosy contemporary fantasy of my dreams. I promise you, too, will be drawn in by its gorgeous and aching warmth'

Ava Reid

'With high stakes, deft romance and intriguing magic, *Modern Divination* is a gem of a book'

Hannah Whitten

'Cosy like a favourite sweater and thick with atmosphere like fog on a winter night, *Modern Divination* beautifully captures the romance of small intimacies, hard-won vulnerability and, of course, academic rivalry, Agajanian's debut had me under its spell from start to finish. Utterly magical'

Allison Saft

'As suspenseful, magical and dangerous as it is tender, indulgent and deeply romantic. A skilful, soaring debut'

Sarah Underwood

'In *Modern Divination*, Isa Agajanian crafts a vivid, delightful world of academic rivalry, hidden secrets and reluctant alliances – all with a delicious undercurrent of magic. Readers will be drawn through the pages like a spell, immersed in a cosy atmosphere of slow-burn romance, endless cups of tea and the sound of rain over cobblestones'

Lyndall Clipstone

'Enchanting. *Modern Divination* casts its spell from the very first page, inviting the reader to dive deep into its academic heart. The characters are breathtakingly tender, their romance stitched tight with lingering glances, guarded hearts and a love that's slow to simmer, but quick to ignite. Set against rain-slick streets, Agajanian crafts a gorgeous world where even the magic itself glitters gold. An absolutely stellar debut'

Skyla Arndt

'This dark contemporary fantasy has a mesmerising blend of high-stakes drama, magic and rivals-to-lovers romance'

Cosmopolitan

ISA AGAJANIAN

QUIET SPELLS

TOR

First published in 2026 by Tor

This paperback edition first published 2026 by Tor
an imprint of Pan Macmillan
The Smithson, 6 Briset Street, London EC1M 5NR
EU representative: Macmillan Publishers Ireland Ltd, 1st Floor,
The Liffey Trust Centre, 117–126 Sheriff Street Upper,
Dublin 1 D01 YC43
Associated companies throughout the world

ISBN 978-1-0350-5005-5

1 3 5 7 9 8 6 4 2

A CIP catalogue record for this book is available from the British Library.

Typeset by Palimpsest Book Production Ltd, Falkirk, Stirlingshire
Printed and bound in the UK using 100% Renewable Electricity by CPI Group (UK) Ltd

FSC
www.fsc.org
MIX
Paper | Supporting responsible forestry
FSC® C116313

Hey Soph. Thanks for being my friend. ☺

PROLOGUE

Water pooled around Alaric's leather shoes, trickling towards the front door of a humble – rather *bleak* – South London flat. It descended from each step of a rickety staircase before him with a faint hiss. The caretaker lowered himself to one knee, enough for the hem of his trousers to droop into the water but not his kneecap. Rolling up his shirt sleeve, Alaric let the water pass through his fingers and made a note to himself: *Clear.*

Then again, diluted with so much of it, he'd miss even the darkest colour of witch's blood.

A soft, distinctly male whimper trickled down from the flooding loo.

So, his witch was still alive.

This, Alaric had not expected. He smothered a spiteful urge growing in his stomach.

Mercy, mercy.

He was bound to this man's survival, to being abundantly forgiving, which wasn't much of a stretch from his general unwillingness to overexert himself on a job. Alaric rose again, throwing his shoulders back to protest against the ache in his body. He'd endured far too many years of this profession. The caretaker role would have long since drained any good man.

Who could blame him for wanting one easy job when his muscles ached as much as they did – when he'd been carrying the weight of this thankless role for as long as he had.

Much of it was tedious. His days consisted mostly of paperwork, inventory, making sure that every borrowed magical artefact was within arm's reach and returned to his care promptly. Sometimes, a low-ranking offshoot of the royal family would call upon him with a hush-hush task like demon banishing or divinatory reconnaissance, and he would have to pretend he hadn't been singing songs about the downfall of the British monarchy every night straight through his youth.

This particular excursion, which had him skulking cautiously around every corner, should have been rarer. But fate had been rather unkind to him lately, and the only person he knew who could have ever truly made sense of it had disappeared eight long months ago.

He knew fate favoured patterns. One peculiar house call became two, then three; and this one, which was not technically a house call because it was a flat, marked the eighth visit of the past two months. Certainly the first that would follow him home.

And spell trouble for all of them.

At least it would be quick. Alaric's silence on the matter of the witch in question meant he wouldn't stand any trial with the council. He'd kept the peripheral details of the shapeshifting witch Leona Sum's case as quiet as he could. He explained with the confidence of a man past the need for concern that Leona Sum had come and gone and left little mess to clean up.

What he did not say was that his town's resident diviner,

Gemma, was still gone, and her family, waiting for her back home, were reluctant to believe that Leona worked alone. He did not divulge the specificities of Theodore Ingram's lying low on account of the accidental shattering of London's Tate Modern museum, though the council had begun to take interest in the influences stealing Alaric Friedman away from his work all the time. He was hiding something – they were all sure of it – but he remained seemingly, *stubbornly* oblivious to any and all inquiries regarding the current instability plaguing the witches of England due to Leona Sum's violent harvesting of magic.

Which was a difficult balance of omission on both sides. The council was eager for Alaric to devote more to them – to give his unwavering commitment, sacrifice his loves, and divulge his dirty secrets, which included the large cover-up for Townsend's new resident reaper. On the other hand, the boy grew restless in Townsend whenever Alaric left for too long, asking for his whereabouts when Alaric wanted to keep him as uninvolved in council assignments as possible.

He'd always had a soft spot for Gemma's family, and Teddy Ingram was no different, woven into the sordid bunch with an invisible stitch. But there was only so much he could give in reassurance that he was doing everything in his power to find Townsend's missing matriarch and bring her home.

Trust me, thought the caretaker as he pushed himself onto the last step, *I'm tired too.*

A limb, hidden past the elbow, poked out from behind the bathroom door. Alaric reached for the inner pocket of his leather jacket, tracing the ridges of two bronze bangles through the fabric.

He cleared his throat. The man's wrist twitched in response, and he choked something unintelligibly.

Alaric answered presumptuously. 'Alaric Friedman. Your resident council seat—'

The witch pitched forward as a mucus-drowned cough leaked out. Bile spilled from the corner of his mouth. He'd been poisoned. Perhaps, he'd poisoned himself. Everything Alaric had learned about the man subverted whatever his former expectations had been, and he turned from villain to victim to *vulnerable.* In any circumstance, he should not have been the type of person who would drink his own draught of destruction.

The caretaker crossed over the body, twisting the shrill tap until the water stilled. Surely, the man wouldn't care for Alaric's title, or his duty, or the fact that he was bound by magical decree to keep the man alive. More likely, the man wanted to curse him for the intrusion, for what Alaric knew that the man did not want discovered.

It was too late for the man to have secrets when those secrets affected his family.

Alaric slipped the bangles from his pocket and shut them around the man's wrist, the pooling over of bathwater back crawling up his trousers fully. Whatever curse sat on the edge of the man's tied tongue fizzled out ineffectively while his dark, quivering wrists were circled in those flimsy bronze bands. They were small enchantments that would stifle even the darkest spells.

There was no struggle, which gave Alaric a stricter sense of urgency. Up until now, he'd taken his time, built himself up for a slow interrogation; the man would live, after all. And from what Alaric knew of him, the suffering in-between was not entirely undeserved. He had been watching, studying him, from a safe distance, the periphery of known existence. From a shadow wedged between dimensions. And though the man had walked a careful path, Alaric knew it was because the man had created a monster.

The caretaker would concern himself with that later. The monster in question was dead now, and her maker was in too poor a state to withstand even the gentlest questioning.

The man forced a response, mustering up the strain of a hundred crushed breaths. 'Here to . . . kill me?'

'No, Mr Sum.' Alaric propped the man against the side of the tub with a groan. The man didn't seem fazed by the sound of his surname in a stranger's mouth, though Alaric suspected he lacked the energy to *seem* much of anything at all. The caretaker clasped the man by his chin, examining his eyes, then his teeth, before delivering his verdict. 'You're not going to die today.'

CHAPTER ONE

Ingram –

It dawned on me about a week ago that you might be trying to text me, or call me, but can't, seeing as I have ten plus messages denoted on my phone in red as never having reached you. Then again, you could have written to me if you'd wanted to. You're the one with the other's address. I might have sent this sooner if I knew where to send it, but it seems Martin's address is just as difficult to remember as the cottage's – without the quick identification that comes with being 'the cottage at the top of the hill'. I'm not even sure if this will get to you.

I can't remember the last time I wrote a letter to anyone.

Do you miss me there yet? Using up your room, rifling through your cabinets for tea? Pembroke's campus is different without you. Better, but in a worse way. No one strikes me as insufferable and thought-consuming the way you were. However, I'm partial to spite as a motivation for greatness.

You already know that, don't you? Aside from Ryan, you were the only person who knew me, faults and all. Faults, especially. You could spin them in a way that made me palatable. You were always better with words than I was. I used to hate you for it. Mostly, I hate how much I still think of you every day.

The other night, Ry invited me to this party. It was mostly uneventful, but I left feeling uneasy, which is the tempered way of saying I hated myself. I wanted to be alone, or at least, I thought I did. I keep your copy of *Sir Gawain and the Green Knight* on my desk beside my bed, and I thumb through it sometimes, whenever things get particularly bad. You're with me still, but not enough.

Write to me if you'd like. It's getting embarrassing, having to read the same things again and again. But I do read them – your letter and your notes. I'll read anything you write to me.

I'll resort to your papers if circumstances are dire enough.

Aurelia J. Schwartz

Ingram,

Teddy,

I wasn't sure if you got my first letter. It's been a while since I got any messages from you. I assumed it was the lack of cell service up there, but obviously, I can't be sure. I wish I didn't have to wonder so much. I wish you were closer. Sometimes, when Ryan gets late-night package deliveries, I think it might be you showing up unannounced. I get really excited, and a little nervous.

Have you been OK? Have you read anything good lately? I picked up *Middlegame* by Seanan McGuire about a month ago, but I've been so busy that it's still sitting on my desk untouched.

Write back to me. Tell me something. The only thing worse than you telling me off for the intrusion is sending these out into the ether just to wait and wonder. It's eating me alive.

Aurelia J. Schwartz

Teddy,
Please say something.

Ingram,
I wrote your name down on the page knowing I wasn't going to mail it. It's clear to me that your magical wards must have incinerated everything I've sent to you before; that, or you've seized the opportunity to ice me out completely now that you're not stricken by my presence every day. Still, some of your texts have come through. Mixed signals don't sit well on the ego, but you probably know all about that.

I had a great cup of tea today. It's not a blend I've put together before. I tend to err on the side of sweetness, because what's the point of having a drink if it doesn't taste good? It's why I could never be a coffee snob. I made a cup for myself, then one for Ryan, but I had some leftover water and couldn't bring myself to dump it. So, I made another cup to put the excess in since mine was full and set it on my desk in case of emergency.

I didn't always have this issue; I was good with my water estimations. Never made too much, and sometimes didn't even make enough. Lately, I've been trying to fill this space I brought back with me with excesses of everything. But the extra tea, I save for you.

I'd taken sips from each this morning without realizing it. Ultimately, they were the same drink, so I wasn't going to notice by taste. (I put saffron in it, which spiced it pleasantly, just on the cusp of too much.) By the time I was full, both mugs were nearly empty, and I could see the white ceramic on the bottoms.

As I write, I'm compelled to apologize to you for it, as if you'd known a cup for you was sitting on my desk, and you would have gotten to it eventually. I cling to a hope that that might be true. To think that what we had might never happen again scares the shit out of me. I can feel that absence inside me growing large, calcifying.

If it's yours, there is a part of you that I can still have. It's much easier to think that way.

Talk soon. x

CHAPTER TWO

Ghosts passed through the cottage sitting on the peak of Townsend Hill like passengers in a train station. Some, Teddy Ingram knew, stayed longer than others. They arrived too late or came too early, forced to linger and – even worse – inclined to attempt small talk with the station's resident reaper.

He ignored them. But some, Teddy also knew, were more persistent than others.

Teddy was thinking of Aurelia again. Not quite a ghost but a haunting all the same. Late summer sunlight touched down on the grassy hillside, blanketing the sun-bleached grass in rays of orange and violet. In his hand sat an uneaten peach, plucked earlier that day from a stall at the Townsend market. Teddy brought it to his lips and bit, grazing the short fuzz with his thumb as he chewed. Everything made him think of her nowadays, but this was perhaps the most pitiful catalyst for his memory.

Bright in his mind was the peach fuzz that he'd kissed high on her cheek, just beneath her eye. Yesterday, it was her laugh, a sound he kept safely in his memory, locked in a vault so it could not be sullied by hands other than his own. The day before, it was her silly orange puffer coat and how she'd said her father called her *pumpkin*.

Wind forced his hair into disarray. In the months that had followed his part-time mother Gemma Eakley's disappearance – a period that he saw as a pause in time – finding a new barber had been low on his list of priorities. His hair had grown to unruly lengths, sticking to the back of his neck and curling around his ears. It embraced its reddish hues beneath the sunlight, and made him, in collaboration with the altogether romantic premise of summer, look softer. *Kinder.*

Ghosts were drawn to him, just as his peers at Pembroke had been before, and every now and then, a new one would slip through the wards and sit beside him at the kitchen counter. If his unresponsiveness didn't deter them, they would make themselves at home.

The cottage kept him surprisingly busy. Sometimes he wondered if he was so desperate for something to do that he created unnecessary tasks for himself. He'd applied for some jobs, but in the surrounding area to the cottage, where he was bound by the responsibility of raising Gemma's young daughter Louisa, there was little work not already spoken for, much less for a medievalist with an emphasis on translation. So, he often found himself looking after Alaric Friedman's two-faced bookshop, or outside the cottage, hanging another batch of wet laundry on the wire, then hidden in the grass with a book in his hand held up to the sun to shield his eyes.

Which reminded him that today's clothing was likely to be dry. Rather, one of the many ghosts crowded within their fortified wards reminded him by yanking on the edge of one of his buttoned shirts. They could be helpful sometimes. More often, they got in the way of what little time he spent relaxing – *truly* relaxing – to urge him back into his household tasks.

It reminded him of Gemma a bit. But none of them were her, and thus he derived no comfort from it, only a perpetual irritation by unexpected noises and changes in the atmosphere.

He rose from the grass, silent and slow, accosted by the heat. Above the curtain of long stalks, Louisa waved to him, leaning out from the open doorway of the cottage.

'Teddy, look what I did!'

She'd be turning eight soon. Teddy hadn't quite figured out *how* to celebrate her birthday while her mother was still missing, but he was adamant that they would mark mark it somehow. They deserved a celebration for something, for anything. It seemed as if every small force in the universe wanted Teddy to fail except for himself; but he was hopeful, even if he didn't know what he was aiming for. They searched for silver linings every day. The current drew him somewhere, yet he was convinced he would not drown.

Louisa held one of her books high above her head as she ran to him, legs pushing through the grass with vigour. He pulled each garment from the posted clothesline, folding them over his arm while the girl flipped to a page and displayed it openly for him to see.

'Hmm,' he assessed. 'Perfect.'

She smiled brightly, clapping the book shut again, sealing her newfound love of annotations between her fingers. Her notes were frivolous and inconsequential, but she had taken interest in Teddy's defaced margins; and when Louisa Eakley asked something of him, Teddy Ingram could not object. He bought her new fine line pens in all of her favourite colours. The task kept her busy, stimulating her burgeoning mind between school terms whenever Teddy no longer could. What more could he ask for?

'And the rest of the series,' he suggested.

'How many are there?' asked Lou. She was effervescently joyous. Through his magical gift of empathy, Teddy Ingram couldn't help but feel similarly gleeful.

'How many do you have?'

She thought hard. Her mushroom-coloured curls had been easier to maintain after her recent trim, and she wore them in neat braids. 'Four.'

'I'll see if Al has the rest.'

Louisa beamed, hugging her book to her chest. 'Maybe we could go back to Heffer's.'

He pulled a shirt of hers from the wire and hung it over one of her small shoulders. They could only go to Heffer's once they had made the journey back to Cambridge. Teddy would have left her with Alaric and gone on his own if he could; he'd texted Aurelia Schwartz before he left just to watch the message bounce back instantly. Mobile service in the town remained bleak and unpromising. He used to think the wards were particularly affecting his attempts at messaging her, but he rarely succeeded in sending something over text at the local cafe too. Besides, it was a wishful thought to indulge. There, Lou had helped him pile the remnants of his academic life into his car and tidy his old flat just enough for someone else to clean it. And sell it.

'Maybe,' he answered.

'Ugh.'

'Put these away,' he said softly. 'Not on your floor this time.'

'I hate laundry. Why do I have to fold them every day if I'm just going to wear them again? What's the point? I'm not *that* dirty.'

Teddy shook his head, his voice a fond crooning of exasperation. 'Hate to ruin your fun, but you are quite honestly the filthiest child I know.'

She groaned, tucked both the book and her dried clothes beneath her arm, and left towards the cottage again.

For the most part, things were all right in the cottage at the top of Townsend Hill. Lou had spent her whole, albeit short, life learning to keep busy by herself, but Teddy had taken to it too. The slowness, the quiet, the repetitious days that never seemed to end as the seasons shifted around him . . . The change had been kind to him.

Winter had passed, then spring. Heat collected in red patches on his cheeks, black T-shirts gathering beams of sunlight from above the tall grass wherein he so often reclined. The wards around Gemma's cottage should have prohibited anyone but the other magical townsfolk to stumble up the hill and discover him there; the wards that Alaric Friedman cast eight months ago made it impossible for any human – friendly or hostile – to see the cottage at all. But sometimes, when he heard a rustle in the grass, he'd turn his head, thinking Schwartz would be there beside him, weaving her bitten fingers through his hair the way she'd done in her dreams.

Teddy was envious then of that version of himself that he thought she could love. But that one was not real. Had not been struck through with a knife and left with rough, mottled scars. That version of himself was not monstrous; it would remain forever untrue.

He took the last garment from the wire, folding it over the growing pile on his arm, and followed Lou inside. Soon, he hoped, something would come to drag him out of Townsend too.

He ordered a chai latte and an orange juice from Katie at Petro's – the cafe in the heart of town – who flirted with him yet again. She had an admirable persistence that Teddy normally wished she would direct elsewhere, but his ego had been particularly deflated by the touch-memory of that peach, so he'd said nothing when she delivered an open invitation to do whatever the hell she did after work with her.

'One more thing,' he added. Lou tugged his sleeve and whispered for him to add a croissant, which made him correct himself to, 'Two things, then.'

He ordered a coffee for Alaric Friedman. Townsend's resident bookseller never seemed to mind the bitterness of Petro's signature brew.

Katie raised her brows and asked, 'You expecting company?'

'I *am* company,' he said. 'Rather not arrive empty-handed.'

'You don't strike me as particularly social,' she said light-heartedly.

Teddy lowered his head and paid. He'd been social, once. In Cambridge, he'd been admired, even if he hadn't been on the giving end of that admiration. He'd been coveted, a treasure to be kept hidden, or a prize to be set upon one's mantlepiece.

That was not love – or even friendship – but it was worth something to him, to be wanted.

Here, he was nothing. He was no monster, but he was no man either. It was something he'd once liked about Townsend, among other things – how easy it was to disappear.

Louisa reached for the croissant that Katie passed over the counter in a takeaway box, and Teddy couldn't shake her words. When their drinks came, Lou took hold of her cup of juice and drank eagerly. Teddy brought his lips to one of the unlabelled paper cups in his hands and tasted Alaric's bitter drink inside of it.

Upon arriving at the bookshop, Alaric Friedman thanked him wordlessly and took a large swallow. Al was preoccupied these days, always called away on some business that Teddy could only catch muttered words on here and there; but when he returned to his dingy Townsend bookshop, he always asked to see Lou.

Injured ego aside, Teddy cared about Lou more than anything else. Alaric never had to voice his care for Teddy Ingram aloud for him to know that he was loved too, but Teddy couldn't help feeling jealous sometimes of the fragile way one was cared for when young. Alaric asked him how he was, but not as much as he should.

Then he was thinking of her all over again.

Her face pressed into his chest after she'd asked him to come to bed with her.

Where does it hurt?

Everywhere.

Maybe it was common decency to ask a question like that, but they were anything but common – and no one else ever did.

Even now, Alaric Friedman was attending to Lou, squatting low onto his haunches to grasp the young girl's shoulders while she recounted the past week to him in excessive detail. Al nodded eagerly, encouraging her with a cycle of rasping hums and wondrous *ahhhs*.

Teddy perused the shelves for dust, as if he hadn't spent most days at the shop tending to them since he'd moved into the Townsend cottage. Al was frequently called away for secretive business, and Teddy had needed something more to focus his attention on. They'd struck an easy bargain for Teddy to take care of the dingy shop while Al took care of . . . whatever it was that Alaric Friedman took care of.

It was more than magical texts. More than whatever was written in the pages of his grand library's prized tomes – but Teddy knew it was not his place to ask. He'd been made clear about that years ago.

Al tapped his knuckles on a shelf behind Teddy, alerting the boy to his presence. 'Looks good,' he said.

'Hmm.'

'Has it been quiet here since I left?'

'Quiet as ever,' Teddy answered, thumbing over a spine that had been marked with something sticky. 'Eager to leave.'

'Think you'll visit Cambridge soon?'

He didn't want to say no. 'No' quashed a sliver of hope that Teddy tried so fervently to sustain. If it were up to him, Teddy would be boarding a train back to Cambridge tomorrow, texting his friends to meet him for drinks. He'd immerse himself in the traffic of the crowd, follow the steps of his old routes to Pembroke for the sake of reminiscing. For the most part, he'd kept to himself, but there were alcoves of the city that he had found solace in while his studies pulled him in different directions. If all that day accomplished was resurrecting the buried body of his life's work, it wouldn't be lost. Pity, he thought, how work became so sentimental. How academia became ritualistic. To sit behind his desk or beside his window, poring over digitized manuscripts until the early hours of morning, was such a simple thing to want.

'How much was the coffee?' asked Al. 'It's quite good this time.'

'It's on me,' Teddy said.

Al took another large sip and gave a throaty hum. 'Has Lou been all right?'

'Perfect.'

'Yeah,' the caretaker agreed thoughtlessly. 'Perfect.'

The girl in question was on a makeshift scavenger hunt in another aisle, searching for books from a list that Alaric kept handy for every day that she came to visit. On it were eight books that he knew would be on his shelves and one that would not be.

'I don't suppose you've heard anything about Gemma,' Teddy said softly.

Al shook his head, black and silver curls hung messily over the crest of his brow. 'You are the first person I'd tell if I had something new.'

He said that every time, but Teddy was always hopeful that Al had simply overlooked a forgotten piece of information that'd tell him Gemma Eakley was coming home. He clung to the possibility that she was not dead – rather *missing*. Teddy

Ingram hadn't prayed since before Kenny Eakley died, and even then, it'd been empty words syphoned out from Celia Ingram during church services; but he held on to the thought with the steadfastness that Catholics held on to homilies and made it his religion.

It became harder every day to convince himself of that possibility. Gemma would have come by now if she were alive.

'Teddy,' Al said sharply, pulling the boy from his stupor. 'Do you remember anything more about what happened in London while you and Aurelia were at the Tate Modern?'

They hadn't spoken about that night in months. Teddy had shunned the finer details in his memory. He remembered Schwartz's hands beneath his jacket outside the museum before the New Year gala began. He remembered taking their empty champagne glasses downstairs, heart in his throat, wondering how terrible it would be to confess his infatuation with her there. He remembered thinking, *awful, awful idea, Teddy,* then downing another glass of champagne whose effects he wouldn't feel due to his inhuman constitution.

And he remembered a lot of darkness. A desperation to save her. Botching a blood oath. Within it were all those nightmarish memories he chose not to uncover again.

'What do you need to know?' he asked.

Al pursed his lips, his hands on his hips atop his weathered black belt.

Teddy listened for the sound of Lou, then added, 'I could tell you if I knew what it was that you wanted.'

'Involving you in council discussion isn't something you need on your plate. I want you as far from this issue as possible.'

'Seems like I'm already involved in something,' Teddy reasoned.

'I need to know what Leona Sum discovered by stealing magic. If it brought her success at any point.'

He remembered Leona Sum's knife slashing through his wings, and the inferno his body had become as a last-ditch defence, but few of the words she'd spoken. 'I . . . I don't know. To my knowledge, none of her blood oaths were sworn willingly. It was obvious she'd been suffering from the forcedness of it.'

'Hmm.' Alaric's lips twisted asymmetrically while he debated what else he could admit. 'That's unfortunate. It seems that another witch in Argentina has a similar thought. Better execution, but with a little damage of their own. Some breaking and entering. What matters is that someone is meddling in the survival of witches.'

'Trying to ensure their survival?' Teddy asked, raising his brows.

'Going about it the wrong way.'

How many *wrong ways* were there to preserve a civilization? Surprisingly many, as Teddy was learning, and the surplus of desperate witches gave him reason to believe that the end was nearer than he'd imagined.

It was impossible to pretend that a reaper like him could be human, but Teddy forgot it sometimes. What purpose did he have to think objectively about his livelihood while he spent his days stretched out on the hillside, out of reach from the world beyond Townsend?

He was simply *there*. Nothing more. Years after the death of

Kenny Eakley, he had finally made magic another replaceable facet of his life, like his clothing or his bedsheets. Tucking his fatal gifts in a shadowy, untouched corner of his mind left him with the safe, palatable kinds of spells that fixed their faulty taps and dusted shelves and harmed no one.

Magic didn't weigh so heavily on him any more.

'Nothing else?' asked Al.

'Not that I can remember.'

'Would Aurelia know?'

Teddy swiped a finger across the topmost shelf to his right. *Dust.*

'Dunno.'

Al sighed, fisting his hand through his curls roughly. 'Have you spoken to her lately?'

Teddy couldn't be sure that any of his messages were delivered when he sent them. She'd sent him texts. He'd sent some back. He'd cursed the rural town endlessly for its lack of connection, whenever a week's worth of messages delivered to his phone all at once.

So, that didn't count. Not really.

'You seem to think we were good friends,' said Teddy.

'No,' Alaric Friedman replied. 'I thought you were keen on her.'

'And you just assumed that she would feel the same? She's not that kind of girl.'

Al tensed. 'Maybe you should see her. You're miserable when you're like this, Teddy. Do it for my sake. Resolve something. Be a big boy.'

Teddy exhaled deeply. 'She's busy.'

'Would it make you happy to see her?'

He scoffed. 'What kind of question is that?'

'I'm trying to understand why you're acting like such a twat right now. Grow up.'

Teddy's voice rang musically through the quiet, ashen shop. 'Lou darling, where are you hiding?'

'I want you to be happy,' Al interjected. 'I want good things for you, Teddy, but you have to want them too.'

Teddy turned on his heels, arms folded over his chest, and with a clipped tone, he said, 'How would you know that I'm unhappy? Honestly, Al, give it a rest. I'm tired. She's probably busy.'

Moving on, he thought in what was a manufactured recollection of Aurelia Schwartz's voice on their last night together. It'd been Teddy that said it though, sprawled out across his mattress with her, half-clothed and flushed for post-sex pillow talk. Teddy, who suggested they both would move on once they parted ways, even if he didn't want to.

He could think of little else sometimes except her, and yet he'd put up such an indifferent, armoured front willingly to keep the distance from hurting so much. And now, they only ever talked if the stars aligned and the weather was ideal and they were both somehow in the right places at the right time for the mobile network to push messages through . . .

Idiot.

Al said nothing, squaring his body toward the younger man confidently. His dark brown gaze searched through Teddy Ingram's for a pressure point, and Teddy scoffed, turning away once more.

Louisa reappeared with eight books in her arms and a

flustered expression. She rose onto her toes, heaving them up towards Teddy, and said, 'I could only find eight.'

'I'm sure Al can find the rest.'

'Are you sure? It's just one more.'

Al assured her, 'I'll find it, little bug. Let me take it from here.'

The girl heaved the pile of books into Alaric Friedman's arms and inhaled sharply, catching her breath. Teddy couldn't meet Alaric's eyes as he gave the part-time bookseller a debriefing of the shop's recent occurrences. Al nodded passively, not really caring. Nothing happened in Townsend. At least, nothing before Leona Sum and nothing *after* her.

Teddy hadn't yet succumbed to the idea that Gemma Eakley might not return, so there was no *after Gemma* to point to.

The bell above the shop door announced Teddy and Louisa's exit.

The girl, with her new book in hand, nudged Teddy with her shoulder and asked, 'Can I have a piggy-back ride?'

'Maybe,' he said softly. 'If you walk a bit first.'

Lou smiled. From the bottom of the hill to the top where the wards of the cottage kept the dwelling from view, Lou amassed an extraordinary amount of weight. Teddy could have denied her outright but, *no.* He was physically incapable of doing that. She had become his world once Cambridge fell away. It took a conscious effort to keep himself from becoming hers, the sole recipient of her attention the way her mother had made herself. Gemma had called it safety, but Teddy understood in the aftermath of her abandonment that Louisa had been denied the potential to make friends with the other young children in town.

Because of Gemma.

Having lived so many years under the neglect of his own mother, Teddy made certain that Louisa was loved. He told her often, but made it clear through more than words that she would never be without care again. If Gemma couldn't do it, he would; and it would be for more than Louisa's sake that he succeeded. There was a young, unloved, and unnurtured version of himself inside his heart that begged him to be patient, to make right of all the absence he'd been subjected to.

In the sway of the tall grass ahead, it seemed as if daylight had dug its fingers into the rolling earth so that the wind would not blow it away.

'Go ahead, Lou,' he crooned. 'I'll be right behind you.'

Louisa Eakley gazed upward at him, a question in the pull of her pale brows, and then she hurried towards the shaded grass boundary of the hill without him. Teddy held himself back from the journey home, slipping into the narrow corridor of brick between two closed shops at the end of town.

He unearthed his phone from his pocket. No texts. No calls. On a whim, he found Schwartz's name and dialled, but it didn't even ring. He drafted another text, traipsing over the remnants of their last fragmented conversation.

I know I'm shouting into the void, but I'm thinking of you again.

He couldn't bring himself to send it. Would she know any better? Would it get to her tonight or in two more weeks, whenever the service in Townsend decided to relent and deliver his message?

Teddy sent it before he could question himself, stuffed his phone into his pocket, and continued towards the hill, chasing the last threads of gold. By the time he entered the wards of the hidden cottage, daylight had begun to unhook its claws from the hill and retreat in fear.

In the basement, Lou sat with her knees tucked to her chest in front of the couch. A television show played quietly on the old box TV. Teddy was hardly paying attention, but it sufficed for background noise as he turned the page of one of Gemma's grimoires.

He'd discovered a collection of unevenly bound grimoires in a cabinet upstairs that had been buried underneath unfinished quilts and fabric squares. There were spells and rituals penned in them, but journal entries spanned most of their pages, from the year of Kenneth Eakley's birth – Gemma's son and Teddy's first love – to last December.

Teddy didn't have the heart to read anything from the year of Kenny's death. He avoided entries from the adjacent years as well; he'd made the mistake of letting his gaze bleed over too many pages and found the limit to be staunchly drawn.

Does it ever get easier? Gemma wrote. *Will I stop crying?*

I'm sorry for him. I know he lost a friend, but I lost my son.

Sometimes I imagine him standing just outside the front door, saying he's sorry he left school late. I'd forgive him without question.

The last was only two years old. It never got easier.

Teddy gritted through mentions of his own name if only to keep some part of Gemma alive in his mind while she couldn't be there in person, but reading her intermittent entries meant that all her years of assuring him he wasn't to blame for Kenny's death were undone.

She still resented him. She'd loved him like her own.

Of course, Teddy suspected this conflict living inside her already. Words made it real, but he'd wondered for a while if he had cost the Eakleys not only a son but a mother as well.

Tonight, like most nights, he paid those pages no attention and dialled into her scratchy penmanship for a spell, perched on the edge of the couch cushion with his forearms on his knees and a pen between his teeth. Gemma's script was jagged, words abbreviated in ways he couldn't always understand. At uni, he'd been well versed in dead languages, and he considered himself well versed in the living ones as well; but he'd stumbled across language in her grimoires specific to magic and enchantment that he was still sorting out with help from Alaric's library. Not all of it made sense, but he'd been able to rewrite most of the information from Gemma's grimoires into something more palatable to someone like him. A witch without aim.

Lou kicked her legs onto Teddy's lap, her head craned up on a heap of mismatched decorative pillows. 'Teddy, they're hurting again.'

'Again?' He straightened her knees over his lap and began to massage the persistent ache of growing pains from her calves. She sighed, folded her hands on her stomach, and glanced towards the TV once more.

'It's not *as* bad as yesterday,' she said.

'Hmm.'

'Why is it always just my legs?'

Teddy shrugged, attention ceded from the illegible script before him. 'Dunno. Maybe you'll have disproportionately long legs and be two metres tall.'

She's the size of Townsend Hill, Alaric had said.

Larger than life.

Lou was happy, and that gave Teddy enough hope to rise early every morning, learn a new recipe or two, busy himself enough to forget that something was missing from the house, and admit that he needed to become a better witch. He'd confess, being studious over anything satisfied an itch that his departure from Pembroke left him with, but never completely.

'Teddy,' Lou repeated, 'what if I have to come home again?'

His brows pulled together inquisitively. 'What do you mean, darling?'

After Gemma had gone missing, he'd made the decision to enrol Louisa in a proper school again. It'd been two years since she was prematurely withdrawn by her paranoid mother over the consequences of an unintended spell. At the time, Teddy hadn't questioned Gemma's decision to remove her; it was clear to all of them how much it hurt Louisa to be so violently misunderstood at such a young age. From his present vantage point though, Teddy resented the fact that she had not since been allowed to re-enter human society.

She seemed to deflate more and more with every confessed insecurity. 'Well, last time, Mummy pulled me out of school because the other girls didn't like me, and I didn't get along with the teacher. What if the new kids don't like me either? What if I can't make friends?'

Then, there were moments like this where Teddy remembered he had a *kid* now, that he was newly twenty-four years old with full, unofficial custody of this bright young girl who was neither related to him nor bound to him by law; and sure, she was mostly happy, but he had no fucking clue what he was doing. They were getting by. Nothing seemed to be glaringly amiss in Townsend, but there must be more to raising a child than the unending prayer that the world wouldn't turn to shit overnight – right?

His best never seemed like enough here. There were no marks to be given for saying the right thing to soothe a temperamental child or mastering a new spell in the isolation of his bedroom. No one to tell him he was on the right path.

He stared at Lou, frowning, not knowing how to respond. As she stared back at him, he felt through that empathetic bond a twinge of shame which she didn't show.

Shutting the grimoire over one of his pens, he angled his body towards her and spoke softly. 'You know we're *different,* yes?'

Lou nodded.

'And that most people don't have magic like we do?'

Again, she nodded, gaze naively intent.

'Magic,' he began, 'will always be something special about you, Lou. Something different. Try as you might to keep that hidden, you're never going to be the same as the other kids there. You don't have to try to be, either. There's nothing wrong with what you are. *Who* you are. The way you think. They'll . . .'

He paused, considering the grimoires before him. What would Gemma say?

Would Gemma have allowed her to start school again? Leave the perimeter of Townsend without a chaperone? When Kenny Eakley's life ended as a result of Teddy's destructive magic, had Teddy spoiled that free-spirited love Gemma felt for her son and diminished Lou's chance of freedom in consequence?

The cottage, wondrous as it was, could not give her the tools she needed to grow. He knew this. Had known this from the beginning. But Gemma *wouldn't* have allowed it, and it was with great paranoia of his own that he filled out the registration paperwork for her enrolment. Was he doing right by her if he was defying Gemma's plans for her? She lacked friends, conversing mostly with her mother and Teddy, and now the ever-present ghosts that'd leaked out of the walls with Teddy's permanent residence.

'They'll always take issue with you. Keep your magic tucked away, and they'll tease you for your clothes or your *freckles*. Cover those up, and they'll attack your cleverness. The way you think and the way they'll expect you to think are entirely different things. But there is *nothing* wrong with it, Lou. Nothing wrong with *you*. Trust me. You're wonderful as you are.'

'You don't think I'll make friends?'

He sighed, kneading her other calf. 'You will. I just want them to be the right ones. I want you to look out for the right things. You're so smart, darling. I want you to love school. And loving school comes with tolerating the people, unfortunately. Can't really predict how they'll treat you.'

'Ugh,' she said. 'It's always the people.'

Teddy pinched her leg, and Lou yelped. 'God, Lou, you're starting to sound like me. Miserable.'

'You pinched me.'

'Wash your hands or I'll do it again. I don't even know how you can get that filthy.'

'It's just ink.'

'Yes, but it's nearly dinner time. Go and wash,' he ordered gently. 'And those clothes better be in your drawers by the time I get up there.'

With another despondent groan, Louisa clambered off the couch and disappeared up the basement staircase. Teddy listened to the sound of her footsteps disappearing. The running tap. Her bedroom door. The grimoire open on the table in front of him shuddered for attention, a ghost of Gemma's magic. He could spend minutes lost in a daze if he didn't have something to snap him out of it.

Teddy closed his laptop, then his eyes, fisting his hands in his hair for support.

What was he doing?

He needed a haircut. He needed a different job. He needed to stop thinking of what could have been, needed someone to hold him, to stop *wanting*.

Out of all the things he never expected to miss, Schwartz's constant white noise was the most jarring. He reckoned she was always considering a hundred things at once, but she managed it somehow. After a while, Teddy found it soothing to listen to.

He waited for the moment his own clutter would become that comforting. Less overwhelming.

Does it ever get easier?

He was hopeful, the way Louisa was happy – only notable because of adversity. The way loveless people valued touch. The well of their wishing could have drowned them months ago.

Lou sang his name from the kitchen. 'Teddy!'

'What is it?'

Before she could respond, Teddy heard a knock at the front door. It had to be their neighbour Martin, pushing himself through the violent resistance of the wards to deliver the old post since no postman could rationalize a torrential journey through the wards. Poor thing, Teddy thought, gathering himself off the couch. Martin was one of the few inhabitants of the town who possessed no magic of his own, and the new wards that Alaric erected packed enough punch to make a human ill.

Alaric himself had a key. He didn't lose things, and he didn't knock.

Louisa rocked on her heels beside the counter, following an instruction to keep the doors locked at all times. Something Gemma had ingrained in her early on that Teddy no longer contested now that Gemma had been missing for eight months. Some precautions he could afford to keep.

The wind hummed through their open door like breath in a flute. The doorstep was vacant. Teddy turned to Louisa. 'It's loud tonight.'

She frowned. 'I don't hear anything.'

At least, they had both heard the knocking. Unease crept up his sleeves, raising the hairs on the back of his covered neck. All his familiar ghosts were accounted for. 'Wait here.'

He closed the door behind him, sheltering Louisa inside.

Out of the countless things Teddy had absorbed during his years as an empath, grief was most potent. It manifested differently for everyone, but Teddy's magic had summoned those ghosts. It was cruel magic that positioned him in front of them, like an eternal reminder of the consequences of his wretched reaper magic.

He didn't know which outcome he preferred as he searched the slope in front of him: spirit or passer-by. The town went dark in the evening, save for a single light in Alaric's upstairs window. Ghosts, he knew, didn't abide by those wards, but that didn't mean they were more pleasant as guests.

Maybe it's Gemma, coming home.

He dispelled the thought as quickly as it came and spotted the dark silhouette of a person leaving for the town again. Equipped with a tote bag that swung at her hip and curls that whipped from her neck in the wind, a figure that looked too much like Aurelia Schwartz for his liking was walking away – *leaving*, in a manner that haunted him just the same.

The words stalled in Teddy's throat. *Come back.* From where he stood, she shouldn't have been able to see him. Humans and witches alike had been blinded to the cottage's existence now; and one had to know, and believe through the duration of the journey upward, that the cottage would be there to see it.

Schwartz saw him anyway, turning at the catch in his breath as if she could hear it. Otherworldly enough that she, too, could be a ghost. She smiled at him, tucking a dark, curled strand of hair behind her ear. He wondered for a moment if he'd been grieving *her* too – feeling enough to manifest Schwartz's ghost on the hillside while she was still alive several hours from him.

Out of all the cruelties his mind had made him suffer, that might've been the worst.

'Are you—' *Real?* He couldn't finish. Couldn't let the apparition confirm his fears, that she wasn't there and wouldn't have come back.

Her jaw tightened visibly, fingers curling around the strap of a tote bag. 'Looks like we're finally even for late-night visits. Are you going to let me in?'

CHAPTER THREE

She'd been unwinding after a shift at her recent waitressing job when she got the news. Her housemate, Ryan, who she hadn't spoken to in more than a handful of days due to their conflicting schedules, surprised her with a late-night knock on her bedroom door. 'Something came in the post for you today.'

Languishing on her tiny bed, Aurelia Schwartz perked up. Had he finally sent her something? She'd been waiting for mail from Teddy Ingram. More specifically, a return address. She had sent a letter months ago to what she hoped was the correct address but received nothing back. It was possible that it'd touched the magical shroud around the cottage and burst into flames, or that Alaric Friedman's dog had found it on a walk and torn it to shreds with his teeth. She devised a hundred reasons for why Ingram didn't write back to her to ignore the reality that he was probably just not as invested in maintaining a thread of connection with her.

Besides, Google Maps was no match for a house shrouded in wards that didn't want to be found. Tens of written and rewritten letters covered the bottom of her desk drawer, addressed to a name. Only a name.

But they were all filled with things she regretted writing the day after. It was best she didn't know, best not to have sent them.

Ryan dropped the envelope onto her desk and took a seat at the foot of her bed. 'What'd you eat today?'

'I stole a bit of gnocchi that got sent back,' she told them, swiping the envelope from her desk. She pulled her knees to her chest, which gave her housemate more space to unfold backwards onto the mattress. Aurelia flipped the envelope over and frowned. No name. Most of the return address had smeared off; her own name barely legible. Softly, she added, 'A few slices of garlic bread too.'

'That's not nearly enough, babes. You want a sandwich, if I make some?'

Her finger slipped under a gap in the glue, wriggling the contents of the envelope free. The trifolds of the paper were furred and worn as if creased and unfolded over and over again. 'Um.'

'Um?'

'Yeah,' Aurelia replied, returning to herself. The words were the least interesting part of the page, struck through by scratches of ink and other shapes. They warped before her eyes. The outer curves of letters melted into the ones beside them.

She blinked at the page, spreading it out between her fingers until the words settled into place. Ryan cleared their throat.

'Yeah, sorry,' Aurelia stuttered. 'If that's OK with you. I'll be down in a second.'

Satisfied with the response but wary nonetheless, Ryan stood from the edge of their housemate's bed and left for the kitchenette, shutting the door behind them.

They were alone then – Aurelia and her letter – yet she could feel a presence unspooling from the ink. She kicked her feet off the bed and peered out her window where she saw only the distant lights from other people's windows, no more curious than she was.

Her skin prickled from the sensation of being seen from some hidden vantage point.

The letter had not come from Ingram. It had not come from her father or sister in Vancouver, Washington. The most legible words on the page, and the words to which her eyes first snapped, were a name and a farewell at the bottom:

Meredith Albert

Forever your mama

Time seemed to cease around her.

CHAPTER FOUR

Schwartz approached him again timidly, picking at her nails with her hands against her stomach. 'I tried to call, but the service here . . . I know I shouldn't have turned up uninvited. I just thought . . . I don't know what I was thinking. I didn't have anywhere else to go.'

'Come here.' His legs were already moving, taking him past the wards of Gemma's hidden cottage. The door shut behind him on a magical cue.

'Ingram,' she said. 'What are you—'

Teddy threw his arms around her midsection, raising her onto her toes, where she huffed out a shallow, '*Mmph.*'

He buried his nose in Aurelia Schwartz's hair, breathing her in. 'For a moment, I couldn't tell if it was really you.'

Even as she looped her arms around his neck, Teddy wavered in his conviction. He remembered the floral scent of her conditioner, but it smelled deceptively strong beneath his nose. It would have been easy to conjure her image like a spell – she kept her hair in the same short crop since the day they met in Latin I, and he doubted that, wherever the real Aurelia Schwartz was, she had decided to change it.

Besides, no one touched him this way, held him so surely.

Not any more. They'd been allowed such a short moment in time to hold each other like this, and it had looked much different with a backdrop of wintertime. She had shed the barrier of her puffy, orange coat for a pale blouse that exposed her shoulders and the warm flesh of her inner arms.

'Very real. Very much *me,*' Schwartz assured him. That soft flesh pressed to his ears as she surrendered to his hold.

'And you're here. Why are you—?'

His gaze dropped to the place where Leona had left a scar and found it covered. In the dark, he made out the tattooed shape of leaves. His fingers twitched as he loosened his grip. He was too eager, too afraid of letting go, as though she would fade into his imagination the moment he took his hands off her.

'I needed to see you,' she said simply. 'I figured you were here, and I—'

'Are you OK? What's happened?'

She opened the tote bag on her shoulder, sifting past notebooks and spare toiletries to find an envelope. He accepted it, catching a glimpse of his copy of *Sir Gawain and the Green Knight* among the spines in her bag.

'Nothing,' she lied. 'Not really. I had this *idea,* and the realization that . . . Well, it *could* be nothing, but I thought, since you were still here, that it was worth a shot to share it.'

'Plainly, Schwartz,' he said.

'I'm still trying to figure it out myself, OK,' she said, lowering her voice. Her eyes flickered nervously to the front door, looking past the wood as if she could sense Louisa behind it. 'It's about Gemma. Sort of. There's something I want to try.'

He shut his mouth immediately. What more was there to say about Gemma Eakley that they hadn't already said? What more was there to try that he and Alaric hadn't already done? Nothing he said would be optimistic. Schwartz didn't need to hear it.

Teddy pushed the front door of the cottage open, ushering her inside.

She asked, 'Is Louisa here?'

The girl in question threw her arms around Schwartz's hips at the first sound of the door. They stumbled together, Lou's laughter breaking loose. Schwartz discarded her bag beside the staircase to embrace the girl with an equal ferocity.

'Where've you been?' Muffled against the fabric of Schwartz's blouse, Louisa then looked up with wide, devilishly innocent eyes. 'I thought you'd come and visit me sooner.'

Schwartz smoothed a hand down Lou's hair, none the wiser to Lou's charm, and tugged at one of the girl's braids. 'I missed you so much, Lou. You have no idea. Trust me, I wish I could have.'

Not to his surprise, that answer sufficed for Lou, whose only follow-up was, 'Are you staying again?', which Teddy wondered too. 'Oh please, please, please stay? I need to show you all my new books!'

Teddy looked to the bag tilted over by her feet, wondering if she'd brought clothes or a toothbrush. How many times had she tried to call? Sent him texts that he never got?

'You can stay as long as you need,' he assured her. 'Whenever you'd like.'

She nodded curtly. 'Just the night. I need to get back to Cambridge soon. Get ready to leave.'

'Leave?' asked Lou. 'Leave where?'

'Washington, to see my dad and my sister.' Schwartz offered him a warning glance: *Don't ask. Not yet.*

'You have a sister?' Lou asked.

Teddy left them to catch up, gathered what few belongings of his were strewn about on his bedroom floor and tucked them into the armoire or beneath his bed. Books, he rearranged on the shelf behind his mattress, a copy of *La Vita Nuova* lurking on his nightstand. He swiped his fingers over the blinds for dust and pursed his lips at the thin coat of it on his skin. He'd worry about it later, worrying enough as it was already. Feeling exhilarated by Schwartz's presence, yet filled with an anticipatory dread that she would leave just as suddenly.

His skin buzzed with an anxious heat. What could Schwartz have found out about Gemma that would have compelled her to come? After months of silence and missed conversations, a discovery lured her to return to Townsend – to the memory of Leona Sum's pursuit.

Schwartz knocked, even though he'd left his door ajar. 'I told her I needed a second. She's getting something out of her room to show me.'

A soft creak in the wood told him she'd leaned against the frame and made herself comfortable as a spectator. She didn't move from within the doorframe – simply watched him, quiet and unobtrusive, her gaze flickering to the unopened envelope on his bed. Teddy frowned, smoothing out creases in the sheets.

'I'm usually very clean,' he explained.

'I know.'

'It's been busy around here lately.' He didn't know why he

felt the need to defend himself. He'd seen her flat before. Character and clutter were two different things divided by a pencil-thin line, and she had plenty of both.

'Do you need something? Are you hungry? I could make you something,' he said. 'What about water? *Tea?*'

She wrapped her arms around herself and said, 'Maybe later. I could use a shower.'

He nodded and fetched her a fresh towel from the linen closet. She stood unyielding in the doorframe, watching with that familiar, flustered expression.

'Do I need to find you something to wear?' he asked.

'I have pyjamas. I actually brought your old shirt with me too.'

He hummed to himself. His shirt. *Sir Gawain.* Maybe she'd come to give them back, get rid of his things like closure with an ex – not that that's what they were. What they'd had was ephemeral, locked in a moment that they rarely acknowledged except when (he assumed) Schwartz was lonely. The knot between them was plenty frayed. Maybe this was her way of cutting it completely.

Teddy forced the thought from his mind and took enough satisfaction that she was there again so that he could ignore it might be for the purpose of returning his things.

'I'm sorry,' he said. 'You're tired. We can talk about this later.'

He nodded to the letter, but neither thought excited him.

She nodded back. 'I'm always tired. Honestly, if anyone could help me make sense of it . . . I mean, Alaric's probably the one I need to go to, but you—'

'Ah.'

'I wanted to see you too,' she assured him. 'The last thing I want is to get your hopes up over Gemma. But I wasn't sure if I needed an excuse to come back.'

'You should know better than that, Schwartz.'

'As if it wasn't so bizarre for you to see me here that you had to question whether or not I was real. I'm trying not to assume things with you any more. Obviously, that got us into a pickle beforehand.'

'Point taken.'

'I'm trying to be careful.'

He shut the armoire, encircled himself with his arms, and leaned his shoulder onto it. *Careful.* A word which promised at least one degree of separation between them. A word that affirmed his hesitation to reach out and brush a curl from her cheek.

'So, I assume Ryan knows you're here this time?'

'Yep,' she said, popping the *p*.

'And that you don't have . . . I dunno, someone *else* who'd have an issue with you being—'

She snorted cynically. 'You know me better than that, Ingram.'

He pursed his lips. 'Guess so.'

'Your hair is getting long.'

'Oh.' His hand flew to his head, and he ran his fingers through it. He could shove that mop of hair aside into something that vaguely resembled one of those 1990s Hollywood ingenue-heartthrobs, but only if he could catch it in time. Regrettably, Schwartz caught it in its natural, currently unwashed state, where it looked more doggish and limper than anything. Which was even more unsettling, considering she'd been studying and socializing and *existing* that beautifully for months he'd been made to miss. What a misfortune to know how pretty she looked to everyone else in Cambridge all this time. *Christ.*

'I'm going to, um . . . take that shower now.'

'Right.'

'Maybe cool off a bit.'

'Yeah.' They hovered in an uncertain moment, neither moving away nor moving towards one another. Her tongue darted out from between her lips. He looked to the nightstand.

'You've been good here?' she asked. 'You've been OK?'

It'd been a long time since anyone asked him that, and up until now, he would have answered that question with a resounding *no;* but for the first time, he thought he might be. Having her there seemed like enough.

Teddy smiled softly, but Schwartz took his silence as an answer of its own, left her towel on the bed, and pressed herself into him, fitting her head beneath his chin and her arms around his waist. He felt the rise of her chest and the subtle, secondary shift of sinking into someone else once you'd already got close to.

Something had rattled her enough to bring her back to him, and to Alaric Friedman; and knowing that Schwartz leaned on him made him stand a bit taller, fortify himself. Like a column on the steps of a great pantheon. A knight at the hand of the king. He was good at building himself up when it became necessary. He'd done it for Lou after the disappearance, and for Gemma just before it.

But being held by his old rival felt incomparable. It was like opening his arms to the rapture of a star, letting her consume him. Her warmth touched him everywhere, even the places her body couldn't. Her heartbeat raced so thunderously, so *close* to his that it moved his to a similar rhythm.

They melted into one another perfectly. Teddy had the distinct feeling that he would fit to her however she was. It was possible that he'd already done it.

'Better,' he said.

'Yeah,' she answered, as if he'd posed that word like a question. Teddy pried himself free, placing the towel back in her arms where he had just been. He smoothed one of her curls behind her ear.

Once she left, Teddy recognized the rhythm of his own pulse as something startling and uneven. She wouldn't have had to be an empath to feel that.

Teddy assigned Lou the task of peeling apples and potatoes for a warm curry dish he'd perfected in all his time at the cottage. The girl whittled at the skins though means of a common spell until they were ribboned into piles on the cutting board. It kept her occupied enough while she waited impatiently for Schwartz's return. Within a few minutes, the tap croaked.

Once it was ready, Teddy spooned some of the sweet curry into their bowls. 'Take these downstairs for me, darling.'

'Shouldn't we wait?'

'I'm sure she'll be out soon.'

Lou set the coffee table in the basement, and Schwartz joined them after, wearing a cream-coloured pyjama set, wet coils of her hair grazing her shoulders limply. Exhaustion was running her into the ground. Teddy felt the heaviness of her eyelids through his magical tether, a numbness that clouded her emotions. She sat across the low table from him, on the ground with her feet tucked beneath her, prodding softly at a diced piece of chicken. He wasn't used to Schwartz making herself small.

He took a chance at Lou's first yawn and said, 'Time for bed. Help me tidy up.'

'Fine,' said the girl, grabbing her bowl. Lou's striped socks disappeared up the iron staircase, and Teddy followed her with the rest of the dishes. He washed them, set them to dry, gave Lou a quiet thanks, and sent her to bed. He didn't have the heart to share, didn't know if he could manage Lou's excitement while he was trying to suppress his own.

Maybe that was sad, he thought. Schwartz had come here with a specific purpose, and held him only because he'd given her reason to suspect something was wrong. Surely her motivations ran deeper than desire for a social visit. It'd been over a month since anyone else had stepped foot in the cottage, and that person had been Alaric.

A small squeak captured his attention as he wiped the stovetop clear of splatter. Then music.

Not sad at all, he decided. He could have spent the rest of his life missing her face, missing the sound of music he didn't turn on. When Lou badgered her with questions through mouthfuls of curry and rice, Schwartz cast glances to him in amusement, fielding the girl's enthusiasm with unparalleled patience. *Admirable,* he thought. She was wonderful in every possible way. He forced back a smile as if someone might catch him.

Something about being so unabashedly smitten with her felt wrong; perhaps he was destined to fight himself on his feelings for her forever.

The fear of certainty pressed him on all sides. Things he loved tended to disappear.

Teddy set a full kettle on the stovetop and lit the flame.

After Gemma's disappearance, the cottage's collection of tea had dwindled significantly. On the rare occasion that Gemma had ventured out of Townsend for an errand run, she'd returned with boxes of tea to stock her shelves for the future. Once, she'd had a collection that rivalled Schwartz's, but it was mostly depleted now. Teddy hadn't realized how empty Gemma's kitchen cabinet looked until he had to choose a bag for someone else.

One bag of ginger chamomile left – Gem's favourite. He tore the bag from the foil and wound the string around the handle of Schwartz's cup, which Lou had adorned with paintings of various leaves just over a year ago.

He placed their mugs beside each other on the coffee table and watched Schwartz rifle through the records in her hands. From the turntable on the other side of the basement, she asked, 'Are those Gemma's grimoires?'

They'd been pushed into a pile by the arm of the couch to make room for their dinner. 'I've been transcribing them,' he said. 'She's got decades of her magical practice in them, and half of it is unreadable due to her particular brand of shorthand. I'd say I have about three more to get through.'

She smiled to herself, turning a record over in her hands. 'I'm guessing you picked up a thing or two.'

He summoned the record from her hands. It rocketed into his grip with pinpoint accuracy. 'You'd guess correctly.'

'Cheeky.'

On the hillside, he'd called it child's play. He had also taken Schwartz's grimoire to his gut minutes afterward and nearly cracked one of his ribs. She didn't need to know how long he'd been waiting to show her that simple piece of common magic. It made him terribly proud.

Between them, the air was light. Schwartz's white noise fell to little more than a buzz. She asked, 'Did you read the letter yet?'

Teddy shook his head and watched her slide the remaining records into their hatch. He sent his off with a flick of his fingers, curving it around her path to nestle in beside her records. With a nod towards the leaf-painted mug, he said, 'That's for you. Thought it might help you sleep tonight.'

She lifted it to her lips and blew softly. 'It's still hot.'

He held his breath as she shifted onto the couch beside him, then promptly resented himself for it. He wasn't fourteen any more. He wasn't fumbling his way through first dates and clumsy, tooth-addled kisses. Then again, he never really knew where he stood with Schwartz. He felt the way her pulse sped up with his eyes on her, but it was possible that, after she had been allowed to settle back into Cambridge again, she didn't think of him any more. Maybe, he had become a stranger – an accomplice at most – and being examined so closely by anyone new alarmed her. Maybe, without the neat sophistication of his hair and his sexy uniform of turtlenecks, she'd remembered why she'd hated him in the first place.

She swiped the envelope up from the table and opened it.

'How long have you had it?' he asked.

'About a week,' Schwartz answered, unfolding squared pages of small, sharp words. Dread spilled through her as she scanned the top page. She relinquished it quickly and averted her gaze.

It took him two seconds to realize that Schwartz's mother had written a suicide note.

The intent was so darkly obscured by frantic, nonsensical strings of words and crossed-out passages that he found himself reading it over again and again. She had written words over other words like a typewriter punching out its old mistakes, spare letters floating in the in-between spaces of wide-set lines. Creases bent each page into unusual directions, into quarters and corners.

He could make excuses. Say that her mother's mind wasn't sound, and theorize that she was worse off than either of them could ever imagine. Schwartz wouldn't be able to disprove it. She hadn't met her mother – not in any way that mattered.

A knot formed in his throat, and he looked up at Schwartz, with her pinched brow and her hands picking at one another feverishly in her lap. Of course, she knew what it meant. At least, she had considered it, only hoping that he'd dispel her fears and convince her otherwise.

'Is she . . .?'

Her answer was small, and she tortured her nailbeds while she spoke. 'I called my dad the day that it came, but he couldn't tell me anything. The last time he saw her was probably the last day *she* ever saw *me*. So, it's been a while.'

'And you wanted Alaric to read this.' Teddy folded the pages in on themselves again. He didn't know if letters like these were meant to be preserved; Kenny's was somewhere that he hoped he would never stumble across. It'd give his buried grief too much of a voice, one that'd whisper to him in the dark and make the blinds shudder above his bed.

But Alaric . . . What words could the caretaker offer her as comfort that Teddy couldn't? Some sage wisdom that could only be invoked through suffering? Teddy didn't think it existed, but if it gave her peace of mind . . . He said nothing.

She swallowed and told him, 'Because there's something else. Another message that I'm not getting. Something she wants me to know that I just can't . . . I can't understand it.'

Carefully he said, 'I know it isn't something you want to hear, but I don't think there's anything else.'

Schwartz snatched the pages away, spreading them flat. 'You're not getting me, Ingram. It's not about what she wrote. Although, I'm not saying that what she wrote isn't jarring on its own.' She began to fold the pages differently. He watched closely, eyeing the creases that she followed, then watched Schwartz herself, noting the taut determination in her stream of consciousness. She pressed her edges sharply, making the shape smaller and smaller with each fold. 'Maybe you've already picked up on my nervous habits, but if not, I have about two dozen. And somehow, she knew that I'd have this one too.'

'Origami?'

'To keep my nails out of my mouth,' Schwartz scoffed, but there was no humour in her eyes. She held up the finished shape – a simple crane – then lightly gripped its tail with her thumb and forefinger.

She pulled, and the wings extended.

Again, and its toughened, paper body breathed in some of their air. Teddy blinked once, twice, questioning the slow, automatic movement of its wings until she released it altogether. It kept itself suspended in the space between them.

'I'd have to charm it to make it fly on its own,' she said. 'But she had already done it. And I hate how clever it is, because a suicide note is such a fucked-up intention to make a spell out of, but . . .'

It flew to Teddy's nose, cocking its head to eye him curiously. He lifted his hand to pluck it from the air, but it sped from reach.

'You made it a bird,' he whispered.

'It's just the one I know best.'

He hummed softly. Schwartz reached for her mug of tea and sipped it cautiously.

'You think it means something?' he asked plainly.

'It's quiet now,' she answered, 'but when I was folding it in my bedroom for the first time – just wanting to hold onto it – it opened its mouth and said something to me.'

The crane fluttered to the turntable and perched on the base of the needle, watching them from afar.

'That's the part I can't figure out. What it said. It was all garbled up. I didn't know the language either, but I can't imagine her voice sounding like that. I haven't convinced it to repeat itself. If anyone knows how to get it to talk, it'd be Al. And I think . . .' She rose from the couch and tutted. The bird came without hesitation, gliding down onto her outstretched palm. 'Well, I suspect Gemma might have hidden an enchantment in her note, too. And if we can trigger it somehow, it might tell us what she intended by leaving.'

Teddy was inclined to agree, if only because she'd arrived with so much conviction, and she was right about most things. Behind that suggestion, though, was an apathetic deflection from the contents of the note.

Schwartz closed it within her hands like a mother shielding the bright eyes of a newborn. 'It's unnerving, isn't it? I'm going to unfold it. Try to stop thinking about it.'

'I'm sorry about your mother, Schwartz.'

She shrugged stiffly.

'I know this isn't the kind of closure you ever wanted.'

'I didn't think it was an open wound,' she said. 'But it must be, if it feels so obscene.'

He caught her hand gingerly from where he still sat on the couch and brushed his thumb over the ridges of her knuckles.

Schwartz asked, 'What's it been like here without her?' As if talking about Gemma wasn't like talking about the dead.

Cyclical, he thought. Most days, Teddy went about his tasks mindlessly, tidying the cottage like a dutiful house sitter for Gemma's eventual return. Other days, he'd wake with the soul-shattering realization of the passage of time, all the lost days between Gemma's disappearance from the cottage until now; and it would tether to his heels and weigh him down until nightfall.

Schwartz sat beside him on the couch again, her fingers slipping tentatively from his grasp. He followed the faint rise of her veins distractedly, feeling a perverse, overwhelming urge to take a bite from her. 'I try not to think about it,' he said, 'but sometimes the tedium of living here – managing the way she did, in the middle of nowhere – makes me feel closer to her than ever. I mean, I try to be better about socializing Lou than she was. I take her into the city with me whenever I go, and she seems happiest that way; but really, being inside all the time makes me feel empty. I'm not managing nearly as well as Gem did.'

With a laboured sigh, Teddy folded deeper into the cushions, and Schwartz reclined too, pressing the balls of her feet into the edge of the coffee table. He'd given her some socks to borrow for the night, and they ballooned at the heels, much too long to fit her.

Her mouth turned up at the corners with a sad, hardly visible smile. 'It seems like you've kept busy well enough.'

'With her grimoires, you mean?' he asked. 'Somewhat. It's the closest thing to study I have left.' Teddy shut his eyes and pinched the bridge of his nose wearily. 'I miss Pembroke. I miss living in Cambridge where there were a hundred things to do at any given time. I haven't even been able to say it aloud, because it's just me and Lou here, and I can't give her a reason to think that I'd rather be anywhere else but with her. She's *tender*, you know. Comments like that grow with age. They never stop hurting.'

They were talking about trauma, but his side was warm from the closeness of her body, and he hated himself for the places his mind was wandering. He could feel her eyes tracing his cupid's bow and that a similar, regrettable sense of yearning wanted to pull her hand towards his cheek. She turned onto her shoulder, facing him, and asked, 'What about me?'

I miss you more than I can stand. Teddy folded his fingers together on his stomach. 'Yeah.'

Almost beneath her breath, she replied, 'I wish you'd told me.'

'I didn't think you'd want me to. I thought it'd make things too—'

'Complicated?'

He angled his head towards her and scanned her features intently. *I miss you even now.*

'I'm not disagreeing with you,' Schwartz said. Her gaze wandered lower, resting on a wrinkle in his shirt which she traced reverently with her forefinger. 'Just curious.'

'Hmm.'

She retracted her hand, tucking it into her chest with her fingers curled in a fist like she'd taken a fraction of his heart. She wiggled nearer to him, resting her cheek against his shoulder in a more platonic way. 'Forget it. Been a long day. I'm probably delirious.'

'Right. Long day.' He searched through the part in her hair. She smelled of floral conditioner. Felt serene like Arcadia. The pale sliver of skin was close enough to his mouth that he wouldn't have to reposition himself to kiss it.

'I'm going to try to sleep now,' she told him.

He nodded, already too cosy to give up his portion of the couch. 'Rory,' he said. 'D'you still have those nightmares?'

The couch's frame creaked as she made herself more

comfortable on it. 'Sometimes. It's a little better when you're around,' she added. 'If that counts for anything.'

She replaced her tea on the coffee table after taking one last sip of it. Teddy noticed it was still half-full.

'I don't know what you want from me right now, Schwartz.'

She took a deep breath, smiling to herself. 'God, you sound just like yourself.'

Schwartz wrapped her arms around his midsection. Teddy, failing to find the right words, simply played with her hair until her pulse slowed and her fingers loosened on the fabric of his shirt.

CHAPTER FIVE

Her touch stirred him awake the next morning. Warm yellow slats of light fell over his rumpled duvet, curving around Schwartz's moving wrist.

He'd awakened the previous night with his neck bent into an uncomfortable angle and shifted out from underneath her as she slept beside him on the couch. For a moment, as he had unfolded a blanket and spread it over her body, Schwartz opened her eyes and tracked his movements with the astuteness of a hunter.

Should I stay? he thought to ask. *There's space for you on my pillow.*

It was indecent to want so much when her heart was so torn. She mouthed, 'Thank you.'

So, he left and kept his thoughts to himself.

By the time he woke up in his own bed, she had changed into that old T-shirt of his and brushed her teeth. Her bag lay beside her feet, and she sat at the edge of Teddy's bed, her fingers splayed over his ribs. Slivers formed in the corners of her eyes. She retracted her hand from his body as Teddy came to, folding it in her lap.

'Hey.'

'What time is it?' Teddy tucked his hands beneath his pillow, cheek buried into it.

'Almost eight thirty.'

Too early. Not early enough, however, to get more sleep, since Alaric had scheduled him to work at ten.

He couldn't remember what time he'd fallen asleep again. He felt her stir through the tether, through the floorboards, a buzz against his cheek which he couldn't ignore.

The bed was noticeably cold without her.

Then again, it had always been cold. He managed it, or perhaps he worried too much about other things to mind the cold sheets. With Schwartz stuttering in and out of consciousness a few floorboards away, all he could think of was her heartbeat. When did it slow? When did it catch?

Had she dreamed of him again?

In the kitchen, Louisa ran the tap. Schwartz followed the sound with her gaze, granting him access to the sleeve hiding her new tattoo. He propped himself onto his elbow, lifting the hem with his fingertip.

'When did you get this?'

She worked her bottom lip with her teeth in thought. 'March, I think. Just before Ryan's birthday. They'd come into some extra money from an art gallery feature they did and wanted me to get one with them.'

'Hmm.'

Full, etched stems of lavender followed the path of her scar, drawn over the place where Leona Sum had ripped her open. His fingers met the raised skin, memorizing—

No. *Remembering*. He'd already learned her. Teddy had made

a mental map of her body, knew where his hands could fit, and where their spaces would align. He wondered if she had been trying to write over not just her scar but the kisses he'd placed there too.

'You want to come down to Alaric's with me?' she asked.

Teddy let the sleeve fall. Simple pleasures like that gave his mind permission to want treacherous things. Normality. Steadiness. Teddy had no intention of denying his witchcraft, but he coveted the small, human practices that people like him and Schwartz weren't allowed to have.

Not yet. Not without the time. Not in this place.

He sighed and swung his legs off the edge of the bed. 'Give me a minute.'

'I *do* have things to do in Cambridge before I go.'

'And I thought you might be enjoying my company. Besides, Al's probably out right now.'

'I'm riveted. Get up.'

'Fine,' he murmured. 'You want to grab something to eat? I've got . . . fruits.'

'I stole an apple earlier.'

Slipping into a pair of iron-grey trousers, he asked, 'How long have you been up?'

Then came that signature expression of thoughtfulness that Schwartz often conjured up: the twisted lip, wrinkled nose, and tightened brow. It came and went in mere seconds, lost like the scent of wildflowers on the wind. 'Just over an hour. I keep busy.'

'Wouldn't have guessed,' he responded, tugging his boots

over his heels, then the ankles of his trousers over those boots. 'Let me wake Lou.'

She looked at him for permission – an anomalous expression, really. Teddy would never get used to it, even if the mere *awareness* that she'd hesitated for Lou's sake tugged at something vulnerable and soft in his heart.

'I suppose . . .' He could ask one of his resident ghosts to keep her entertained during his brief outing. On the rare occasion he had to drop her off at Alaric's for an errand out of town she didn't want to join him for, there was one spirit – an Edwardian governess in her later fifties – who reluctantly donned the mask of her old profession to keep the girl occupied with schoolwork. 'I'm sure she'll be OK for the morning,' he said, more of a self-assurance than anything. 'We won't be out long. And we've been safe here.'

'That's . . . something?'

'I think so too.'

Teddy shrugged a light jacket over his shirt, fussing with the collars so they laid neatly beside one another. Schwartz's hand rose shyly, and he turned to give her clearer access, thinking of a time he wouldn't have dared to let her this close to his neck. All the close encounters that resulted in snide insults and a wounded ego. She tucked the bottom collar into its place. Her eyes drifted to the shallow V that exposed the fitted shirt underneath, and he caught the subtle bob of her throat.

'There.' Her palm rested on his shoulder for a second longer, just above his heart, and she pronounced the word as if she'd proven a point. If she had, it was a point Teddy Ingram already knew – that life was better in the most fractional and seemingly insignificant ways when she was around, and the sum of all those parts was a loss he never wanted to feel again.

Schwartz's fingers curled around the strap of her bag, nails scraping absentmindedly over the canvas fibres as they waited for Alaric in the bookshop.

'He should be here,' Teddy said. 'Even if he's busy, he usually comes round before I open to brief me on the day's tasks. Besides, I'm only meant to cover for him until one.'

Schwartz leaned back against the counter, then folded her arms across her chest to stifle the incessant urge. 'Do you think something's wrong?'

Teddy shook his head, but he didn't know. He suspected there was plenty of trouble that the caretaker withheld from him, trouble that he wouldn't figure out until it all came crashing down around them.

'I think he just sleeps in,' Teddy replied. 'It's a nice, quiet morning – *I* would.'

She pursed her lips, unconvinced. 'Since when have you had a key?'

'He gave it to me a week after I moved all my things here,' Teddy answered. 'Townsend's brilliant for a quick getaway but there's not much to do as far as employment goes. It's a job that keeps me close to Lou. Keeps me busy enough.'

Schwartz pressed her lips together, her eyes narrowing in good humour. Leaning back against the front counter, she said, 'It's kind of sexy.'

Teddy scoffed. 'Might be if anyone actually stopped in. The demographic is primarily folks over seventy.'

'Bet you're a hit with single moms though.'

'Hmm.'

She said nothing for a while, and Teddy disappeared down an aisle to locate a second-hand, beginner origami book. He found one crushed into a top shelf with some square practice sheets still glued into the spine. He kept himself alert to the sound – or the shifts – of the girl lingering beside the front counter, but she trod quietly, lost in thought.

'You all right, Schwartz?' he asked.

'Sure,' she replied unconvincingly. 'Are you?'

He shrugged as he rounded the aisle again, tossing the flimsy book onto the counter for later viewing. 'Enough.'

Schwartz smiled at him softly, rummaging through her tote bag to find the flattened paper bird sandwiched between the pages of *Sir Gawain*. 'You'll give this to him for me then? I should get to the station soon.'

Teddy nodded and took the bird from her, nestling it under the cover of the origami book. The letters on it were large and puffed, colourful like a children's book. He turned it over, his cheeks warming to pink.

'My ticket's time sensitive,' she explained. 'And I leave for Heathrow tomorrow. I still haven't packed anything.'

'I'll make sure he gets it, whenever that is. I can't guarantee when he'll be back, but he's never gone too long. Just sporadically. It's a pain in the arse, honestly. Let me walk you out.'

The door whined as he swung it open for her. Quietly, she asked, 'Will you call me if he finds something new from it?'

'Of course.'

'Or write to me.' This, she said with an uncharacteristic

shyness. Schwartz stepped down from the pavement, folding her arms around her body. A soft gust of wind swept her curls from the back of her neck. 'It's just a hunch, but if you end up finding the same kind of enchantment in Gemma's note, I'd want to know that too.'

'Yeah,' he said. 'I'll let you know.'

It was wishful thinking, and he, who felt as wishful as the worst of people, never expected that kind of rhetoric from her. She lowered her gaze, and he wondered if it embarrassed her to hold onto hope when it was so distant. Did she think about Gemma often? Did it follow her home to Cambridge the way Kenny Eakley's death followed him to Townsend?

'Why didn't you write back to me before?' she asked. 'You must have gotten my letters.'

'I didn't even know you wrote.'

'Figures.' Her gaze landed on something in the stones, and she leaned forward to pluck a severed weed from between the cracks. With a sigh, she turned it in her fingers, then searched the path towards the hillside again. A distant, distracted smile tugged at the corners of her lips. 'You know, it's exactly how I remembered it. From my dream.'

Teddy had seen the seasons change so many times in Townsend that he overlooked how beautiful it was when summer cast the hill in its vibrant embrace. Just before the waist-high stalks of grass lost their colour and fell victim to the English downpour, they crested over the hill in layers of olive and sage, red with the sunlight at its back, and indigo in the night. Pale white flowers grew from delicate stems, all the way into the town, reaching up from beneath their boots.

He knew that dream, recalling the strange heat on his skin, the solidness of her mouth. He thought of it often. The one where she had twisted her hand into the fabric of his shirt and kissed him hard enough their teeth knocked together – before she had come around to her senses and given him an inch that he took without hesitation.

She was thinking of it too, now. To what extent, Teddy would probably never know. He turned over every possible idea that she might have been writing to him about, another mystery she'd leave for him to solve. If those letters had crossed the threshold of the cottage, he would have seen them. He would have tucked them into the drawer beside his bed and memorized them like poetry.

Schwartz shielded her eyes from the sun with her hand and gazed up at him, stifling a smile. 'Can I ask you something?'

He lowered his head and scoffed at that dreaded question. 'You've got to stop prefacing with that. You can ask me anything, Schwartz. You should know that by now.'

'Do you ever think about coming back? I mean, *seriously* consider it?'

'To Pembroke?' he asked.

'To Cambridge.'

There was a fine line of difference between those things. With Lou in his care, returning to Pembroke was out of the question, and he couldn't have Pembroke without Cambridge.

But the other way around? What else did Cambridge have for him if not his studies? A more expensive flat and a hundred familiar faces that could easily find the inconsistencies of his story with Lou. Rumours took root with the virility of weeds, without any of the pretty, pocketable consequences. When one of the many rich sons of his stepmother Celia's old colleagues travelled home to London on holiday, they'd mention the strange kid at Teddy's side. And word, which travelled fast already, travelled even faster in the mouths of British socialites. Celia would come next, knocking rapidly at his door like a woodpecker, just as sharp and just as infrequent, to give him an earful about the impropriety of it all. About how Lou wasn't really his family. And Gemma hadn't been the one to raise him.

Celia had a number of excuses that she pulled to justify her rage, but never came close to pinning down a reason for Teddy's absence.

'I can't go back,' he said plainly. 'It's not that I don't think about it, Schwartz. It's not like it doesn't kill me to see everything I worked for slipping out of reach. But things with Lou . . . They're delicate. I can't bring her with me without fielding unwanted attention. And there isn't a version of this story where I get out of taking care of her.'

Shrinking into herself, she replied, 'I get it.'

He had more to say, words on the tip of his tongue yearning to be set free; but he looked at her and said nothing. He forced that unnecessary swell of emotion aside. Some might've called it giving up, but he didn't. If only to remain wishful and hold fast to the goodness the universe gave him in return for his compliance. If he was quiet, trouble wouldn't seek him out. If God saw him like an obedient dog who wouldn't bite at his hand, he'd offer Teddy another bone to chew.

Another chance.

'But it's quieter now,' she told him. 'Less exciting.'

'That's because there are few things more exciting than medieval theology, Schwartz. Hard to believe you're making this discovery so deep into your studies.'

'You really think I'd change so much? You're funny, Ingram. But I swear, sometimes you look at me like you've never seen me before.'

Because you look prettier every time I see you, he thought. He didn't know when it had started. Maybe that fateful night at King's College or on the first train to Townsend when she wrinkled her nose at his taste in music. He knew that by the time she had found one of Gemma's ill-fitting dresses to wear to the Tate, he was already hopelessly enamoured with her. But everything up until then was a tangle of yarn on a scarf he would never finish weaving. He didn't see a point in finding the stitch where it had all begun to unravel.

'Sorry,' she said. 'It's just that – I don't know. We're not strangers, Teddy . . .' She trailed off as if she had more to say, but nothing came after, and he wondered if *she* knew what they were, if not strangers.

'No,' Teddy assured her. 'We aren't.'

The caretaker came stumbling up the steps behind the counter seconds after she'd left, toothbrush in his mouth, glasses hanging off the front of a rumpled dress shirt. He paused, blinking confusedly at the sight of Teddy Ingram in his shop, as if his presence hadn't been predetermined days ago at his own request.

'Sorry, am I late?' Alaric asked.

Teddy lifted his hands in surrender. 'I dunno, mate. It's your shop.'

'Yes, but I usually don't have folks gathering this early. Or at all.' The caretaker then raised his finger and stole a moment to spit the foam from his mouth in the sink downstairs.

'It's past ten,' Teddy called.

'Is it?'

'Technically, *I'm* late to open. Shame though – you just missed her.'

'Who?' This time, Neil bounded up the steps in front of him, tail wagging. He rose onto his hind legs and gave Teddy's trousers a flat-tongued lap.

'Schwartz,' Teddy answered flatly. 'She came to see you.'

'What'd she do that for?'

'She's had a . . .' Teddy waved his hand flippantly. 'A family emergency. There's this bit of magic she came across in a letter from her mother that she needs help dissecting.'

Alaric frowned, working his jaw between bony fingers. 'I would have loved to see her.'

Teddy hummed to himself, disgruntled. Alaric ran a hand through his hair, keeping it unkempt and shaggy as ever, but he didn't seem as if he'd been recently awakened. His clothing, although slightly wrinkled, seemed well worn for the day, and a spot of what looked like aftershave had seeped into the front of his shirt.

Teddy said, 'You could have if you'd been here to open shop yourself. Where've you been? Had a long night?' He caught the hint of irritation that momentarily moved across the caretaker's features, and it stuck like a stain. 'Let me guess, you can't tell me. *Council matters.*'

'Bit early to be starting with this again, isn't it? Look, it's not that I wouldn't like to—'

'But that's exactly it. No one's stopped you from sharing anything with me except for you. I doubt your beloved council cares as much as you think they do.'

Alaric made a scornful '*Ha!*' and shook his head. Teddy sucked his gums, trying not to feel like a shunned child. To say aloud that Alaric was patronizing him gave truth to the fact that Teddy felt like, with enough of Alaric's attitude, he could be confined to a little box and silenced. The caretaker pushed his glasses onto his nose and began to unlock the drawers to the counter, ushering the argument to a close.

Teddy made no further mention of Alaric's council, but his eyes found the puffy letters of the origami book lying on the desk again and he wondered what made him unworthy of Alaric's honesty. Could Teddy not be trusted? Had he not done enough – proven himself enough – to be Alaric's confidant?

Schwartz's arrival had left him with a hugely hollow sense of dissatisfaction. Everything in her wake felt colourless and annoying, and Alaric's condescension put him in a fouler mood than usual.

The caretaker fidgeted in discomfort, his hands on the rims of his glasses, his shirt buttons, his pockets . . . He shielded his gaze from Teddy's, hiding an answer with it.

'Tell me about that piece of magic,' Alaric said.

'Do you have time?'

'Not much,' he replied. 'Enough to consider it at least. That's the first step to taking action on anything. Can't bypass it.' The caretaker removed his hands from his pockets, massaging his wrists with twitching fingers.

'What's wrong with your wrists?'

Alaric dipped his hands back into his pockets and removed two narrow, bronze cuffs. He offered them to Teddy. 'Cast something.'

Brushing off his trepidation, Teddy slid the bangles onto his wrists and flexed his fingers in the direction of a distant shelf.

Then, the intention shone through. He summoned *Persuasion*. Common magic came almost instantly for him with all the practice he'd devoted to Gemma's grimoires.

Schwartz would be proud, he thought. Or pissed off, depending on how competitive she was feeling.

But nothing on the shelf moved. Not even the soft rattle of books wriggling free from their tight, perfect spaces. Teddy flexed his other hand, a subtle *crack* jumping through his fingers, but the next attempt brought the same lack of results.

'It's not you,' Al explained. 'I don't think I'll ever get used to them. They're suppressants. We're made to wear them when deliberating on more pressing matters.'

'Is it not all pressing?' Teddy asked, eager to rid himself of the strange, bronze jewellery. Alaric took them again and closed them inside the now-unlocked drawer of the shop's front counter.

'Some matters are more pressing than most. If it's particularly divisive, we've sworn to surrender our magic for the sake of discussion. Supposed to promote civility . . . Unclouded judgement.'

'Doesn't seem like something that should be necessary for people with so much power.'

'Doesn't it, though? Take away the humans' bombs and tanks, and they'd come to very different conclusions. Now,' Alaric continued, 'tell me about Aurelia's dilemma.'

Leaning against the counter, he twirled the flattened shape of the bird within his fingers and told Alaric everything. The weight of bronze circled his wrists even as he spoke and didn't ease until he left for the cottage hours later.

CHAPTER SIX

Alaric then disappeared for several days. It should have worried Teddy Ingram that the caretaker's disappearance followed so quickly after the last, but Teddy stored his resentment much closer to his heart than his worry. At least, when Lou was looking.

The girl remained mostly unbothered by Alaric's absence. Teddy brought her to the shop with him while he found new corners to clean and cobwebs to clear, and she occupied herself with the books. She never grew bored of them, fixating on stories of faraway places with such palpable immersion that Teddy couldn't help feeling almost bitter. Most of the stories he'd loved at her age had lost their wonder. He had been searching throughout his fresh adulthood for one that made him feel that awestruck and naive, that made his world as vivid and consuming as the ones he'd seen in Gemma's dreams while wind flurried through her wings. Magic, he knew, was not always the shiny, glorious thing that fairy tales made it out to be, but Teddy wanted to believe in its goodness too. When it hovered, gloomy and miserable, over his small corner of the world, stories were where he sought the silver lining. Lou found it every day. Teddy wished he could find it again too.

They would walk to Petro's. Teddy would order himself tea, and if Katie felt chipper enough, she would give Louisa's orange juice to him for free. He tipped the price of it, curbing her enthusiastic non-invitations to visit her after work. He sifted through old mail, the bulk of which was sparse already now that Gemma couldn't maintain her usual correspondence. Martin, the kindly baker who lived at the bottom of the hill, offered Teddy the most recent mail that had arrived, but nothing interested him.

For those several days, Teddy thought tirelessly of Aurelia Schwartz. They passed in a muddy whirr of familiar images but stretched forever. He didn't count his days, but remained painfully aware of every one wherein he wouldn't see her.

His desperation had reached unprecedented levels when he decided to send her an email via her university account.

Schwartz,

Nothing to report as far as your mother's letter. Alaric has been gone for a few days now, but the issue is on his radar. Hopefully I'll have something more promising for you next time we talk. I figured an email would reach you quicker than a text. I'm writing to you from Petro's, and they're spotty on delivering anything else. Lou misses you. I'm sure you already know how I feel. I'm re-reading *The Lais of Marie de France* and there's only so much I can find that doesn't remind me of you.

Yours,
Teddy

Every step in the routine remained in its place. Why he ever thought he could break from it, Teddy didn't know. Hope led him stumbling forward, if not blinded by some lax sense of duty; everything he did, he did for Lou.

He stole a few moments for himself too. He ran more often, set his alarm early every other morning to walk down the hill and begin his run to the next town over where it was flatter, and return by the cock's crow covered in sweat, ablaze with the rush of endorphins, nursing the dormant ache in his leg. Teddy would shower off the grime of exercise by the time Lou woke, make breakfast, place a record on the turntable, and work again.

The hardest work was making it feel new each day – persuading himself that life at the top of the hill could still foster some excitement. Teddy used to consider the charming cottage from the town below with a sense of wonder, back when Kenny's death had first slaughtered all his faith in magic and witchcraft. The quaintness of it had embraced him warmly, smothered him in a gold haze that he'd maintained for years up until Gemma's disappearance.

Still, he clung to it – the fragment of beauty that Gemma had left them with when she disappeared.

Louisa helped him dry the clean dishes after breakfast. She kept her head down, quiet as a mouse, a deep furrow set between her pale brows as she turned a thought over and over in her mind.

'Chin up, Lou. So grumpy this morning.'

'I'm not grumpy,' she insisted. 'Just tired.'

'Couldn't sleep?'

Louisa shook her head, standing on tiptoe to reach the overhead cabinet and tuck a plate inside.

'I'm going into the shop today,' said Teddy, to which Lou released a discouraged sigh.

'Can I stay home today? To sleep?'

'I'm not supposed to leave you here alone.'

'But you do it sometimes,' she noted.

'I leave you with Agatha,' Teddy corrected, referring to the spinster, who he could vaguely make out the lurking shape of through the window over the sink. Drawing out the shape of spirits was a distortion, a warping of light at their edges. When the view was clear, Teddy could see as much as the slotting of Agatha's fingers into each other, held over her stomach demurely. What was she looking at? Teddy often found her there, staring at the vacant descent of the hill opposite the town, as if there were ghosts of places in the grass abstract enough for only her eyes to see.

Stubbornly, Louisa said, 'That doesn't count. She's *barely* there.'

Agatha turned sharply, offended.

'Fine,' he said. 'But give Agatha some credit. And doors stay locked.'

She shrugged and said, 'Well, yeah. I was just going to nap.'

'It's not you that I'm worried about, little bug. You're always good.'

'Mummy used to say that, too,' said Lou. 'It's "not you. It's everyone else." In that case, everyone else would be scared too, but it's just me that has to stay inside.'

Heat rose to Teddy's face. This wasn't supposed to be his

conversation. He hadn't prepared, nor had he wanted to say things the way Gemma would say them. Did Louisa really believe that they were so similar? Were they?

'Lou, darling,' he murmured, 'it's not you. Truthfully, it isn't everyone *else* either.'

The girl squeezed the rag between her fingers in an attempt at ambivalence, but heat swarmed up beneath the surface of her skin, and Teddy felt it vividly. He leaned back against the counter, arms folded across his stomach, mulling over every word in his mind with trepidation.

He had to say the right thing. Mostly though, he had to believe it himself.

'I'd say I spent about twelve or thirteen years of my life completely human. From the time I was born, I was raised by humans – only humans. I knew there was something off about me but didn't know what. Odd things happened that I couldn't explain. My mother's houseplants never lived more than a week or two. Rodents came around to our house just to die on our doorstep. Things that people told me weren't normal enough to ignore, but weren't *ab*normal enough to question. Accidents that I was punished for. I spent every year up until I was thirteen thinking there was something wrong with me,' Teddy admitted. 'By human standard, I suppose that was true.'

Lou spoke up, clinging to his words, 'What happened when you were thirteen?'

Your brother, thought Teddy. 'I met someone. Someone like me – like *us*. Someone who knew what being a witch entailed and gave me room to grow. Someone who loved me. I met your mother too.'

'Whoa.'

Teddy smiled to himself. 'Yeah. *Whoa*. It was nice to have someone who understood. I hadn't realized until then how lonely I'd been surrounded by humans. There had been a disconnect between me and my parents. Me against them and me against the other kids at school, except that I was the only one who knew we were in conflict. They'd never understand me, not the way you or your mum understand me. The hardest part was that I knew I couldn't tell anyone. Humans never have to be the ones to change. Sadly, the world will never belong to us the way it does for them.'

'So, what did you do?'

Teddy shrugged. 'Nothing. There isn't much we can do, Lou, except carry on. You'll do better than I did at your age.'

'You think so?'

Teddy gathered Louisa into his arms and held her tightly. 'I'm sure of it. You have *me*. Everyone else is temporary. You and I are indefinite.'

She nodded, pressing her face into his stomach. 'And Alaric, right?'

Teddy brushed strands of silken ashy hair from her forehead and said, 'Sure. Al too.'

In the shop, Teddy busied himself with the origami book – *busied* being a generous term. Late afternoon had crept onto him, casting a warm orange light through the curtained windows. An older woman from the neighbouring city wandered the aisles, humming to herself in a way that Teddy couldn't ignore. He pressed the book open flat to display the pattern for a bird that didn't quite look like the one Schwartz had made. Its neck and tail were more stout, its body made of more obtuse angles, but he didn't know where to begin with folding. If the augur of Townsend Hill had hidden an enchantment in her letter, she would have been deliberate with what kind of bird she chose to bear her message.

By then, more than half a year had come and gone. Teddy could spare a few hours, or even a few days, to practise folding birds until he figured out which one she'd chosen – if she'd chosen one at all.

> Northern cardinals, symbolic of loyalty, strength. Indigo buntings carry messages of self-discovery, listen closely.

He had assumed that Gemma's musings on birds would point him in the right direction, but he'd also overestimated the number of folding patterns specific to birds.

As for Schwartz's paper specimen, it remained flattened beneath the page with the corresponding crane pattern, waiting to be pulled apart by more experienced hands. Alaric hadn't yet returned in the flesh, but Teddy had opened up shop to find a hastily scribbled note taped to the edge of the counter:

> Haven't had time to fetch a new bag of food for Neil. There's some money underneath the lid of the record crate for you to use. Take an extra fiver for some coffee, or flowers for Lou. Send her all my love.

'Excuse me,' the old woman said. 'Do you have a shelf for thrillers?'

'Thrillers?' Teddy echoed, finding the shelf label just above her blanched, white hair. Teddy rounded the counter, and asked, 'What are you looking for?'

She curled her fingers around the strap of her handbag. 'Oh. Silly me. Let's see . . . Dorothy L. Sayers is good. Would you know if you have any of her books?'

Teddy hooked a short stepping stool with his foot and climbed to the beginning of the *S*'s. From it, he pulled *The Five Red Herrings* and *In the Teeth of the Evidence*.

'Is that all?' the woman asked. 'It's just, I've read *The Five Red Herrings* already.'

'I could order something for you, if you have a title in mind.'

She shrugged. 'No need to bother with that. I don't come round here often.'

'There are few inhabited towns that are as quiet as Townsend,' Teddy agreed.

'Yes. It's quite wonderful, isn't it? It's so peaceful.'

'I find myself terribly bored most of the time. Did you want to get that one?' Teddy rang her up for a single used paperback and a recipe book on Scottish pastries. She remarked on the pleasant warmth of summer outside and that he must have exciting plans for the season outside of work. He shelved his discontent and smiled faintly, counting her change.

'When you're young,' she said, clutching her paper-wrapped books with sun-spotted hands, 'the world seems inexhaustible. You ought to go outside and chase it, before it chases you. Before you're my age, begging for a moment of peace and quiet.'

The bell on the shop door rang with her departure, and Teddy felt it reverberating through his head long after it had stopped ringing. He resumed his folding in silence, saying nothing.

Most days, he said nothing at all. No one stopped in. Asked how he was doing.

Out of a squared sheet of Alaric's notepad, Teddy folded two birds with dull points, posed them beside each other for a photograph, and attached them to another email for Aurelia Schwartz that he wrote during Petro's last hour of business.

She responded minutes afterwards.

Ingram,

It's bold of you to think I know how you feel, but I can't imagine it's too bad if you're sending me pictures of paper birds. They're good by the way, but those creases aren't sharp enough. Flatten them with the edge of your thumbnail. Be gentle with them, or they'll tear.

Are you bored to death out there? Tell me a story about your birds. Give them a name. Send them on a journey. Unless you have something more productive to do with all your free time like learning how to cobble shoes or laundering money for overseas tech moguls.

Either way, write me soon and keep me posted. My sister's getting married soon, so I might not get back to you as quickly as I'd like to, but I'll see it ASAP. It's sweet that you emailed me, if not a little geriatric. I can't say I wouldn't have done the same.

Aurelia J. Schwartz

He smiled to himself and wrote her a response.

Schwartz,

Oddly formal tone, using your full name as a sign-off. What happened to 'we're not strangers'? Seems rather estranged to me, but what do I know? It's hard enough to read you as it is, but impossible to read you through a screen. Maybe that's where the disconnect comes from – I always assumed my feelings for you were perfectly clear.

If you need it in plainer words, I miss you, Schwartz. I miss you always. Out of all the things that living in Townsend deprives me of, I feel your absence worst of all. Imagine that these paper birds were me and you – I'd have folded us together.

With sharper creases,

Teddy

CHAPTER SEVEN

When long-buried grief came for him in his bed, it was a cold, ghostly hand sliding up his back. If it took more than one caress, he could delude himself into believing he had developed a tolerance for it.

Maybe one day he could forget it was still there. He wrapped his arms around himself and nestled closer to the wall, swathing himself beneath the duvet; but the hand persisted, stroking his spine gingerly. He wished he found it comforting. Perhaps gentleness was what Kenny had wanted for them all along.

It unnerved him, regardless. He wanted different things now, had grown into a different person. He'd spent years trying to make peace with the finality of Kenny Eakley's death, and now his ghost wanted to rip that peace from his hands.

Except, it wasn't Kenny beneath his bed this time. A different voice sung into his ear, a woman unlike anyone he knew, except *maybe* Schwartz. Teddy jolted underneath his sheets, pushing off the unfamiliar presence. It scrambled to the foot of his bed, blue and translucent like crystallizing ice on a windowsill. He sat up, reaching for the nightstand as if he could swing something at it. As if it wouldn't go right through her.

The woman held her finger up to her lips, casting a sidelong glance to his bedroom door; and at the thought of Lou nearby, a deeper panic overcame him. Kenny never mentioned Lou, never asked about the sister he'd never met. Kenny was merely a shadow on the back of the boy Teddy Ingram had been several years ago, stuck in time and his old form; harmless, overall.

To the spectres, he – the beacon – was the only thing worth reaching out to.

'Who are you?' he hissed.

She mouthed her name like it was a curse: '*Meredith.*' It sat on a breath that the spirit couldn't have possibly possessed.

'Schwartz's mother,' he muttered aloud. 'Why can I see you?'

She cocked her head to the side in reply. '*Why shouldn't you?*' Her words had graced the cottage, her memory unfolded in the basement under the very place he slept. There was magic in the pages of her letter collecting before his very eyes.

Meredith rounded the side of his bed, approaching him with caution like a wounded, feral creature caught in a trap. The dead never hurt him. Not physically, at least. Up until now, Teddy had been lucky enough to know only benevolent ghosts – grief that settled like dust instead of hardening like a knife – but Meredith could be the first.

She gripped the knob of his nightstand, pulling it open slowly. Teddy watched her retrieve one of his dying pens, click it, then spread the pages of Kenny's old copy of *The Hardy Boys* that sat behind his bed frame.

'I read your letter,' he whispered. 'Why did you do it?'

Meredith shook her head, pressing the open face of the

book flat with her translucent fingers. Her hands were built like her daughter's, slender and fitted together with knobby knuckles. '*It isn't permanent,*' she whispered.

'What's not permanent?'

She ignored him, pressing the tip of her pen to paper. He followed her first strokes impatiently, cursing the lines of ink that failed to stick.

'They won't let me rest.'

By the time Teddy threw on his shoes and locked the front door behind him, Alaric would have been asleep, but Teddy didn't care. The shopkeeper could spare one inconvenience in exchange for the several he'd given Teddy.

He needed to get out of the cottage, or better yet, out of Townsend; but getting out of the cottage at this hour terrified him enough. Leaving Townsend without Lou would do more to his nerves than he could imagine. His hands shook in his pockets. His steps struck the ground hard. Every unexpected shift in the grass set him on edge, and his breath congealed in his throat.

He brought his shop key to the door, then deigned to give the caretaker a warning to his presence. Teddy brought the flat of his hand to Alaric Friedman's shop door and pounded. He paced on the pavement, waiting for the caretaker to wake, feeling that hand on his back and the sound of Meredith's scratching pen in his mind. The words seared into his mind on a brutal, unending loop. *They won't let me rest.*

Neither do the ghosts, he thought.

He knocked again. The door swung open, revealing Alaric's

dishevelled face full of unruly curls and Neil's figure curved around his legs.

'You realize what time it is, don't you?'

'I saw her,' Teddy spat. 'I saw Meredith. Aurelia's mother.'

The caretaker took in the sight of Teddy Ingram on his doorstep and his lip curled with disdain. He sighed, stepping aside to let him pass through. 'Were you dreaming?' he asked.

'It wasn't a dream,' said Teddy, manoeuvring past Neil's curious, wet nose. The library clicked corner by corner into being, lazy and half-hearted as Alaric was to cast its spell. The shelves rose with a sense of lethargy, aching to lie dormant. Teddy sidestepped the coffee table that sputtered into shape near the fireplace, collapsing on the dark leather couch.

'You can keep talking,' Al said, slogging up the staircase. 'Give me a minute.'

The hound gave Teddy's knee a comforting lap with his tongue, and Teddy scraped his nails underneath its chin graciously.

Teddy didn't know where to start if he didn't know what the visitation meant, but he trained his breaths as Neil tucked his face into his hands, and picked something. An affirmation. Something with consequence. 'She was real. Not alive, but . . . *there*.'

Alaric stalled at a half-opened door at the top of the staircase, peering at the boy over the railing. Teddy almost added that it couldn't have just been in his head, but who could say? If anyone was capable of validating his stories, it was Kenny Eakley, the boy at the forefront of most of them; but Kenny served the role of tormentor more than a testifier. Only ever with Teddy at the worst of times.

'They're like ghosts. Have you ever seen a ghost?'

The man rubbed his eyes over the frames of his glasses and sighed. 'What do you mean "*they*"?'

'Well, she's not the first. I doubt she'll be the last. They show up whenever I think I'm comfortable and try to start something up again. Not fear, per se, but a remembrance. They don't want to be forgotten. First, it was Kenny, and then—'

'You've seen Kenny?' Alaric was behind the door now, joined by gentle clinking noises.

'Y-yes,' Teddy said. 'I've seen him for years now.'

'Have you told Gemma?'

Teddy had thought about it the first few times Kenny's form appeared in the spare bedroom, when Teddy had woken her up with his incoherent stammering. He could have told her then, but the weight of his gift was a burden only he could carry. Excuses were easier to conjure up than courage.

'I thought it'd hurt her more if she knew,' he told Alaric, not loud enough that he could be sure the caretaker heard it. 'It didn't seem necessary to tell her.'

Nor did Teddy want to share this version of Kenny that appeared. The memory of Gemma's son was much different in his mind than hers. They'd shared things that Kenny would have hated for him to divulge to his mother. Al said nothing, leaving Teddy in total silence. He sat still on the couch, wondering if treading too lightly fixed him into more harrowing situations than admitting things plainly. Someone was always angry with him – Celia Ingram, Gemma, and *especially* Alaric Friedman. Then, in Cambridge, he had Aurelia Schwartz to deal with; and hers were issues that tipped a completely different scale.

The caretaker returned in a minute, carrying a dark green bottle and two cups. 'You look shaken,' he said frankly. 'Have a drink.'

'What's in there?' Teddy asked. It'd take a keg of those to get him drunk, but how much to calm his nerves? He hadn't tried.

'Absinthe. Brewed specifically for people like us.' Alaric poured a few centimetres of it into his own cup, then gave the same to Teddy. 'It's generally called *witch liquor*.'

'I've never actually been drunk before,' Teddy said.

'And you're not going to be drunk tonight. This is just enough to make you drowsy. Lower your inhibitions.'

Teddy slipped his fingers through the loop. Alaric held up his cup for a toast, clinking it against Teddy's with a groggy utterance: 'Cheers.'

Swallowing the first, fiery sip, Teddy said, 'It wasn't like seeing Kenny, though. He doesn't talk. He doesn't . . . ask for anything. He's just there. Stuck to me. I don't think he wants to be.'

'But you still see him?'

Teddy nodded. 'It seemed like Mer— I mean, Schwartz's mother was looking for me. Like she wasn't tied to anyone but lost, and *searching* . . .' He reached into the inside pocket of his jacket and unearthed the page he tore from *The Hardy Boys*, scanning it first to ensure that the ink was still visible. Flattening it on the table, he said, 'The first word is *they*. Faulty pen. Message seems a bit on the nose, doesn't it?'

'How so?'

It had made perfect sense after being roused from his bed

in the dead of night. Now Teddy only shrugged. 'Never mind. Have you taken a look at her letter yet?'

Alaric thumbed through the pages of the flattened book, his response delivered low and distant, as if from behind a locked glass bookcase. 'Only briefly. I've asked someone for a second opinion. The enchantment seems simple enough to break, but I don't tamper with another witch's magic on my own.'

'Another caretaker?' A deeper sip of absinthe dissipated in his bloodstream, warming him underneath the skin. The feeling was . . . *Pleasant,* he thought. He couldn't imagine how it'd feel to down the entire bottle beneath Alaric's arm if a few shallow sips could give him a buzz.

'You can meet her if you'd like,' Al said.

Never before had Alaric introduced him to one of his colleagues. The divide between the human world and the world of witches was one that Teddy had learned to cross without seams, but Alaric's world of magical politics was completely foreign and off-limits. It seemed too good of an offer to be true.

Maybe it was just the witch liquor talking. Either way, Al's offers were always time-sensitive. 'I'll be there,' Teddy said. 'Just tell me when.'

'Right.'

'Is it something I need to tell Schwartz about?'

'Not yet,' Alaric said. 'I'm not promising anything. I'd hate for her to get her hopes up for nothing.'

'Hmm.'

'Why do you call her that?'

Teddy shrugged, leaning back against the pillows of the couch. 'Habit. Does it bother you?'

'Doesn't matter what I think. What you say to each other in private is one thing, but she calls you Teddy when she talks to me.'

'I didn't know you were such great friends.' He hated the bitter edge in his voice. The words had rushed out unbidden. Alaric uncapped the bottle and drank directly from it, swallowing more than what he'd poured into Teddy's cup.

'She's *good*,' said the caretaker. A small word that carried such incalculable weight: good, as in kind. Good, as in deserving. Not flippantly satisfactory like what one would deem a distant colleague, but rather someone who warranted more delicate consideration.

'I know,' Teddy replied begrudgingly. 'She's wonderful. I can't stand it sometimes.'

'Because she's too good for you?' Alaric's voice held a note of mischief.

Teddy deflated, thinking of the care she'd shown for his collar – his throat. Such an easy place to sink one's teeth into, or hide a kiss. 'Because it gets to me now. It never used to be like this when all I had was Lou and Gem. It spreads me thin – all this feeling. I wish I could get rid of it.'

The caretaker's prickly, peppered brows pulled towards the crease above his long nose. 'You don't mean that.'

'It does me no good when I'm surrounded by people who are unhappy; and what else do I do but continue to try and fix that, knowing I'll never be able to do that on my own? All this time, I believed my reaper's gift was the one to get rid of, but the empathy is what makes me hurt more. That isn't magic people ask for. No one ever wants to be an empath.'

The caretaker tucked the capped bottle on the ground beside his ankles. He stared at Teddy in an unfinished way, and Teddy thought Alaric might punctuate that silence with a hug. Saying nothing, still as death, Teddy wondered what it would feel like for Alaric Friedman to hold him. The thought alone made his skin burn.

Teddy had grown accustomed to making discoveries in retrospect. He didn't understand the weight of his family's wealth until a boy at his school asked about the frequent pressing of his uniform. Didn't realize how much he lacked in a mother's love before he witnessed that same boy, Kenny Eakley, wiping Gemma's kiss from his freckled forehead in embarrassment. What Teddy discovered in the aftermath of Aurelia Schwartz's brief visit was that he hadn't been touched in months. More than just her hands on his shirt or her gaze on his skin, he missed the casual, careful brush of shoulder against shoulder as they walked. The simple, yet incomparable feeling of contentment that came when someone put their arms around him and squeezed.

Alaric never did that. They were twin pillars of the same crumbling building, and the moment they veered toward one another for an embrace was the moment that a monument collapsed. The caretaker simply looked at him now, questioningly.

'We all have it, Teddy,' he said. 'Or at least, most of us. We all feel, to some degree, the weight of everyone else in the world on our shoulders. If it's too much for you – if it's too heavy for you to carry on your own – that doesn't make you weak. I . . . I haven't done a good job lately of sharing that burden with you. I need to be better about that.'

That admission alone eased some of the pressure from Teddy's shoulders. He sighed and kneaded his eyes.

'Meredith came from that letter,' Teddy mused. 'I can't tell you why. I just feel it. Opening it in the basement must have, I dunno, *released* it. But not completely.'

'We can look at it this week. Thankfully, I have some time.'

Wiping his mouth, Teddy rose from the couch and coughed to clear his throat. 'I should go back now. It still makes me a bit uneasy to leave Lou there for very long. My mind goes to the worst.'

'You're just looking out for her,' Alaric assured him. 'There's no harm in worrying, as long as you don't let it build too much. Try to get some rest.'

Like a child expecting to see monsters beneath his bed, Teddy asked, 'What if Meredith comes back?'

Alaric gave him a weary, glassy-eyed smile and answered, 'You give her a better pen.'

Before witch liquor, it had been a cigarette, plain and ineffective. The first time they'd commiserated over some self-destructive substance, Teddy was just shy of sixteen years old, which, following Kenny Eakley's death, happened to be the longest year of his life.

He only knew the caretaker in passing up until that point, as a shadow sliding beneath the crack under Kenny's door. He knew that Kenny was not Alaric's son, nor did he ever try to be; and also that Kenny didn't seem to mind it though. His mother hovered like a gull on the wind. Kenny never knew what to do with all the extra attention.

Gemma and her son lived in a shabby flat in Croydon, where the windows were always shut and the door was always locked. Teddy visited often during the school year, praising her dinners, and slipping copies of his favourite books to Kenny. It took little for her to see through his pampered upbringing. She took him under her wing and, in doing so, set him free.

Not that she would ever admit to it. Teddy's magic had always been volatile, but if she hadn't given him the security – the *freedom* – to explore his magic, her son might have still been alive.

The flat never seemed so dreary until the day he died. Kenny enshrouded their home in a light that only his death could extinguish. No home had ever looked greyer.

Teddy came with flowers, holding bouquets that swallowed him up as if she might not recognize the boy behind the gesture. Gemma was nothing if not forgiving to him, but she didn't have to be. She kept her mouth shut whenever he came. Teddy kept his head down.

They both knew it was no way to keep living.

The flat would have devoured her in time; the piles grew and dust accumulated on every surface. Surely, one could lose oneself in a labyrinth, but Teddy learned one could lose oneself to a box too – by becoming the smallest thing in it.

His bouquet was smaller that day. At eleven in the morning, Teddy should have been in school, but he was struggling beneath the weight of his backpack up the flight of stairs towards Gemma's flat. The broken bones in his leg had healed but the injury was still fresh. He couldn't play football any more. He didn't really want to.

Before Kenny had died, during the worst of Teddy's pain, Kenny would jokingly hoist the taller boy into his arms and carry him up. 'Stop laughing,' he would say, bowing under his weight, 'or I'm going to drop you down the stairs.' He would come back for Teddy's bag on a second trip. Their arms were always full with the weight of each other.

Teddy didn't have the chance to knock before Alaric Friedman, former spectre, tossed the door open with his knee, preoccupied with cardboard boxes. Alaric took one look at him from above the glasses slipping down his nose and yelled, 'You have a visitor,' before rushing past him to load his box into a van.

Alaric never looked twice at him. If he had spoken to Teddy before, Teddy considered it insignificant.

Teddy stepped into the empty flat. 'What's all this?'

Wiping her nose of dust, or tears, Gemma scurried past him with a smaller box of her own. 'I wasn't expecting you. It's a school day, isn't it?'

'You're leaving. Why are you leaving?' Teddy let his arm fall back by his side, petals tilting to the ground.

Gemma shook her head. 'I figured it was time. It's expensive here. Without Kenny in school, I just thought . . .'

'You didn't tell me.'

Her hands shook as she added knick-knacks from the shelves to her box. 'I shouldn't have to explain myself to you. You should be in school right now, not here. You wouldn't understand.'

Teddy didn't think he had any tears left, but they formed triumphantly. He steeled his expression; this small, defensive gesture became automatic for him over the years. He could be anything to anyone with enough confidence, so he covered himself in different skins: a sheep, a wolf. Mostly, he wanted to be strong. He wanted not to cry in front of Gemma Eakley for the thirtieth time.

Alaric returned. Teddy hated him then, this stranger passing in and out of Kenny's life, taking Gemma away. His glasses were smudged, and hair was unkempt. He gave the first impression of a person who didn't know how to take care of himself, or simply didn't care to. Teddy remembered thinking this man couldn't have taken care of Gemma, even if he'd wanted to.

'What if *I* helped?' Teddy asked. 'I've got enough money to help with rent, and I'm sure my dad would help, since he knows how much time—'

'Don't ask your father,' Gemma hissed.

'*I* could get a job. You can't leave,' Teddy pleaded. 'Not without me.'

Gemma's jaw clenched. She avoided his gaze masterfully, tucking back hair that had already started to grey. She made herself into a wall, though even Teddy knew it was unformidable. He could try to tear it down . . . What good would that do?

Alaric's hand fell onto Teddy's back above his backpack. Teddy remembered his initial surprise at the caretaker's softness. His expression certainly didn't suggest niceties. His features were sharp, and everything he wore, including his unruly mop of hair, looked as if it'd been dyed in the most severe shade of black imaginable. Teddy met his touch with disgust, pushing the hand from his back.

'Walk with me,' Alaric said.

'Why?' Teddy looked to Gemma, but she couldn't meet his gaze.

Alaric rolled his eyes. 'Don't be daft. You're not in trouble. It's a quick chat.'

Still, Teddy felt as if Alaric was evicting him, as if he could see Teddy for the wicked, cursed thing he was and wanted to remove him like a parasite. Leaving his flowers on the counter in a huff, he left with the caretaker, brimming with resentment.

No sooner did the door click shut behind them that Alaric nudged Teddy with his elbow and whispered, 'Light me a cigarette.'

Teddy's fingers curled around the straps of his backpack, his lip curling in disdain.

'You don't have to be coy, Theodore. I know you've got them. My stress is astronomical these days.'

Slowly, Teddy twisted to dig up his buried L&B pack. 'They don't really do anything,' he said.

The caretaker chuckled to himself. Of course, he'd know that. It was stupid, arrogant oversight for Teddy not to think a skilled witch wouldn't know something like that.

Alaric took one gingerly from the pack and decided, after awaiting the procurement of a light, to light it himself with a flick of his fingers in broad daylight. They were far enough away from the only other person who could see them, an elderly man reading his paper behind a distant flat window across a communal space.

The tobacco did nothing for Teddy's nerves. He'd done it for the social aesthetic at first. Self-destructive tendencies were less concerning when shared with others. The caretaker took a deep drag, then passed it to Teddy. 'Let's walk.'

Commiserating could feel like relief if he wasn't alone.

Teddy paused outside the shop and leaned back against the brick exterior, the cool summer breeze skating along the nape of his neck. Townsend was hardly lively in the daylight, but at night it was dead altogether. Save for the reach of a dim bulb in the back of Alaric's shop, blue covered everything in sight: the stone pavements, the grassy hillside, the leaning buildings . . . Mostly, Townsend left him wanting, missing Cambridge and the way things had been before.

Teddy couldn't find this kind of quiet anywhere other than Townsend, and that was certainly worth something. Distress bore down on Teddy's chest, and he slid onto his haunches, hands clasped around the back of his head, to regain his breath. If anyone stumbled across him, they wouldn't think twice about him.

Teddy had always imagined he'd end up here at some point, after he had got another degree or two and translated as many texts as his scholar's brain could allot. One day, he thought, when he'd seen enough and done enough to feel accomplished.

But not today. Gemma's disappearance had done more than leave him with a new responsibility. It left him with the grief of missed opportunities. Following every week's holiday or quiet summer in Townsend, he'd return to his flat in Cambridge, having missed the steady buzz of his phone in his pocket. Texts from Lawrence Kressler, asking for a friend to kill the time with at the college pub, forty photos taken out of Tricia Werner's back pocket as she got too drunk for a weekday with her phone on. He knew things would never be the same as they had been before he'd left, but his friends were still there. Curriculum was being written and rewritten and debated. And to his knowledge, Aurelia Schwartz was still usually walking across the greens to get home with her nose pointed towards the ground so no one felt the need to approach her.

Life carried on without him, a passing train that wouldn't stop to let him on. Sometimes, Teddy thought that he and Schwartz were watching each other disappear through the glass, and he'd lose track of time wondering if he'd eventually get on or if she'd get off.

He rose to his feet again, stretching and aching. His phone buzzed as he paced towards the hill, catching an echo of someone's internet connection, and another email came through, missing a signature altogether.

There's so much I have to tell you when I get back.

Can I see you again?

CHAPTER EIGHT

Earlier that night, she had gone to see a witch burning.

The frequency of witch burnings as acts of violence was largely mythical, outweighed by the number of burnings done in celebration. Aurelia couldn't say she had been to many – at least, not on purpose – and everyone had been drunk on something, writing hymns in the dark, more jovial than morose. Witch funerals were loud, electric gatherings to be beheld by the gods, performed under new moons and star-speckled skies.

Or on county-approved burn days. Whichever came first.

To her knowledge, her father didn't know that she'd left just after eleven. The engine of her old car sputtered loudly. She kept the headlights off until she reached the end of her street, hoping that was enough to set out undetected.

Tony Schwartz had been answering her guardedly, deterring each question about her mother like it was a web, a trap to fall into. She could forgive his reservedness to some extent. She knew the feeling of abandonment from a different perspective, as a distant, hazy thing that only took colour when something reminded her of what she was missing. Like Gemma Eakley pulling pills of wool from Louisa's coat. The augur's warm embrace in the warm, yellow light of her kitchen . . .

Aurelia knew her father's wound was deeper. He kept it covered masterfully, but it took one guarded person to know one, even if it meant witnessing each other from a distance. Tony Schwartz rarely said that he loved her. She and her sister, Annette, had grown up loved, but never aloud – always through subtle acts of service, a language that she'd spoken throughout her adulthood thus far. Aurelia rolled Annette's joints and lit them between her sister's teeth whenever she was visiting her in Vancouver, because she loved her. She soothed all of Ryan Jena's preventable hangovers and encouraged their artistic endeavours, because she loved them too. She'd been deprived of Teddy Ingram for the better part of a year, and so she spent a few seconds too long toying with the collar of his shirt before she left; Aurelia could only admit that love to herself, and not even all the time.

But she, like her father, kept the admission of love buried behind thorny branches and rough tree bark, with a sharpness that kept princes from the towers of their beloveds by gouging out their eyes.

She was trying to be better about that.

Still, she tried not to picture the curtains of Tony Schwartz's front windows pulling open as she drove. The radio hissed, teetering between classic rock stations that her father must have been listening to in her absence – until she hit a red light, found something more distracting on her phone, and let the album run for the rest of the drive.

Witch burnings had never been inconspicuous occasions, except when performed by other witches. The wards they cast granted them a capacity for reverence, privacy to mourn as they pleased; and that usually meant with witch liquor and dance. Under the wards, deep in the evergreen forests of the Pacific Northwest, witches laid their own on the pyre and set the blaze, burning the bodies and the magic held within them.

To burn a witch was, in some way, a form of protection.

Tonight, Meredith's coven would make her untouchable, even to her own daughter. It seemed only appropriate in their theme of parental abandonment that the first time Aurelia would meet her mother was the last time she'd have a shape on earth, be more than dust or charred flesh for the coyotes to pick through the next day.

Aurelia mouthed the words to a song in her car soundlessly. An inch of negative space remained before she hit her threshold, and she could fill it with something other than Meredith's unevenly penned words if she caught it quickly enough. Louisa's face came to mind, those two thin braids beginning at the nape of her neck that didn't catch her baby hairs; so Aurelia started another braid in her mind. Another pattern. Strand over strand, thick and unending. A braid that she would never have to tie off, that wouldn't leave another empty space she'd need to fill again.

Her phone began to buzz in the cupholder: *Annie*.

With a clammy, fidgeting grip on the steering wheel, Aurelia debated answering, donning a sleepy, slurring voice to assure her sister that she was fine, exactly where she was supposed to be. Better yet, she reasoned, she should simply not pick up the phone at all.

In her rear-view mirror, someone flashed their brights at her. When the initial blindness subsided, she squinted hard into the reflection. In Washington, a Subaru logo meant nothing, but she knew her sister drove one, and it was enough of a lead to make the hair on the back of her neck stand to attention.

Before the buzzing ended, Aurelia clumsily swiped her phone screen and accepted the call.

'Is that you?'

'What are you doing, Rory?'

Dread seared up her throat, bitter and heavy over Annette's grave tone. 'You don't have to come.'

'I wasn't intending to,' said Annette. 'But I can't have you walking into trouble without at least trying to stop you.'

'I'm not looking for trouble.'

'Then why were you sneaking out of the house?'

'Those aren't – I mean . . . How did you even—'

'I was sitting outside,' Annette said sharply. 'Working up the courage to come in and have a chat. I even brought a game for us to play.'

Aurelia's voice was quiet, her tone shaped by a habit of speaking through gritted teeth. Annette's had been much higher than hers growing up, louder and confident, unavoidably present at the worst of times; but it'd become raspy due to frequent cannabis smoking. They barely talked on the phone any more. The difference in her voice was starker when she wasn't looking at her sister's virtually unchanged face.

Aurelia swallowed, itching with guilt, before she remembered the first hints of accusation were lobbed by her sister and not her. 'What game?'

'Phase 10.'

Aurelia glanced up to the dim reflection in the rear-view,

smiling to herself. It was a long card game. They would have had ample time to catch up privately while their dad slept in the other room. Girl talk. 'You want to drive with me?'

'I want you to turn around and come back home,' Annette noted. Aurelia heard the softest trace of a sigh. It was a battle Annette had to come to fight knowing she wouldn't win. For that, Aurelia had to give her credit – and wonder why she came anyway.

'I know you don't want anything to do with Mom, but I just need to be able to see her before it's too late.'

Silence bled through the phone. Aurelia hit a bump in the road as cement shifted to hard, packed dirt, and the only lights she could see were her sister's headlights and the stars overhead.

'It's not that simple, Rory,' Annette said solemnly. 'And I'm not going to leave my car out here in the middle of nowhere to save a little gas. Just tell me where we're going.'

Where they were driving, the cover of smog from nearby cities parted to make way for stars. This was unusual, a sign of hidden magic at play. It shouldn't have been so clear here; the farmland was still wedged between populated cities.

She parked the oxidized red nose of her car beneath low-hanging tree branches, Annette following suit behind her, and locked her doors. They regarded each other with a clearing of throats. If they talked, it would be to argue over whether Aurelia had made a terrible decision coming here, and that did no one any good. She had made up her mind. Annette knew not to get in the way of her little sister's determination.

Aurelia looked up at the dark sky – deceptively clear, freckled with uncommonly bright stars, and beautiful. She hadn't seen this many stars since Townsend.

From where they stood, it looked like an empty field, covered in flattened brush and fragmented wood, but Aurelia felt it like a pulse beneath skin. She kicked a littered snack wrapper off her boot and took a burdensome breath.

Seconds passed between them in silence, punctuated by the sound of their steps on the dry, tawny grass until they reached the invisible ward. A shimmer unfolded over their bodies and the world lit up in flames.

Within the boundaries of the ward, at least fifty witches gathered around its circumference, watching a pyre burn in the centre. The heat of the growing flame left no witch untouched, their faces aglow with white heat. Aurelia passed her fingers through the boundary again as a reminder. Quieter worlds were on the other sides of witch wards, and though she'd chosen this side a long time ago, she could leave just as easily. Their father Tony had done it, and though it never seemed deliberate, Annette didn't care for magic either.

The presence of it in such grandiosity seemed to discomfort Annette, who fidgeted with the leather bracelets around her wrist. Her light brown hair, whose natural strands of blonde had spread around her scalp, was gathered loosely into a ponytail at the nape of her neck. Like Louisa and unlike her own sister, Annette's curls were concentrated at the ends; and her lighter brows looked thin over her dark eyes. Their eyes were, perhaps, the only point of similarity between the sisters, inherited from their father so that every time their gazes met in avoidance of the bright flame, they were reminded of how disappointed Tony might be with them if he found out where they were.

Aurelia bristled at the sudden appearance of a woman at her side, blonde with bright blue eyes and crusted black mascara. Aurelia sidestepped evasively into her sister.

'You're late,' the woman said, wrinkling with a mild-mannered smile. 'We lit the fire about twenty minutes ago.'

'We're fine, thanks.' The abruptness in Annette's voice spelled out warning. She was just paranoid, thought Aurelia. Desperate to impress enough gravitas to drive her younger sister home.

Annette's hand curled around Aurelia's, keeping her close when she tried to recover the space between them.

'I'm sorry to interrupt, but I don't think we've met,' the woman said. Her skin was loose and tanned with age framing crystalline eyes. A wide smile pulled across her face. 'I'm Julia Chaplain. One of Meredith's co-practitioners.'

Aurelia's eyes widened in spite of herself. 'You were in her coven?'

'*Rory*,' Annette whispered.

'Well, most of us are,' said Julia. 'Or *were* at one point. We've been fractured for a few years now, but most of us keep in touch. Are you not with one of the covens?'

Before Aurelia could respond, Annette said, 'Just here out of courtesy.'

Riotous laughter broke from a cluster of witches to the right of them. In their hands were short, empty glasses, glinting with firelight.

'I belong here,' Aurelia amended with what sounded like petulance. She made herself taller, more assured. 'She is my mother.'

Julia's eyes flickered back and forth between the pair, from Aurelia's dark furrowed brow and Annette's pale-rimmed eyes, trying to find the points of connection.

'Strange. I thought she only had Annie.'

'Because she means mother-*in-law,*' Annette lied, shaking their clasped hands. 'We just haven't gotten our rings yet, is all. Now, if you'll excuse us.'

Aurelia resisted the urge to wriggle her hand free from her sister's. She would ask later about what made Annette so cagey and get an answer that probably made no sense. But it could be something, too. She could think of no other reason Annie would resort to an unnecessarily incestuous game of house.

'Well, it's good to see you here anyways. I know it gutted her not to be more involved.'

'Sure, it did,' Annette said. 'Gutted her so much she never came back. I'd like to grieve alone now, thanks.'

Julia's eyes dropped in apology. 'Yes, of course. I'm sure this is difficult for you. But you should know that Meredith's wish – your *mother's* wish – was for this to be a celebration. Not a day of mourning.'

When Aurelia thought they'd heard the end of Julia Chaplain's intrusion, Chaplain's hand rose to the youngest daughter's face. 'You look so much like her though. Same eyes . . . same curls . . .'

Aurelia struck Julia Chaplain's hand away swiftly. 'Don't touch me.' She took this opportunity to slip her hand out from her sister's and wipe it on her side. Chaplain didn't seem to notice, too busy reckoning something within herself that reeked of danger.

'Shed your grief into the fire before you leave,' she instructed, 'or else it might stay with you forever.'

Aurelia nodded passively. Annette's mouth tipped downward at the edges.

'She was brave, you know. So brave,' Julia echoed softly. 'If you're anything like her, there is a place for you in our practice. Visit if you'd like. I'm sure you can find us.'

A card materialized between the woman's wrinkled index and middle fingers: a blank, grey slate with small, silver text. A name. Annette took it first, then handed it to her sister. As Aurelia accepted the card and turned it in her hands, an address gleamed to life in silver beside it.

The woman left with a wave and added, 'Take care.'

Aurelia whispered once Julia Chaplain was out of earshot, 'Why are you being so weird?'

Evasive, Annette replied, 'They can hear you, you know. They hear everything inside the wards. It's like an echo chamber.'

Aurelia blinked up at her, stunned to hear a word of familiarity with magical knowledge coming from her sister's mouth, let alone full sentences.

'What? I'm not an idiot. And neither are you. You should say your goodbyes fast. Something isn't right about all this.'

Aurelia clenched her jaw, staring at the flames even when they blinded her. No one paid her attention as she approached the funeral pyre, though a few followed her sister, who trailed several paces behind her.

Whether it bothered her was beside the fact that she was grateful not to be watched.

The fire, caged within wards of its own, still burned her as she neared it. Tears welled in her eyes at the realization that she hadn't just been something to abandon – she was something to forget. Was she another stranger to them? Hearing her sister's nickname in Julia Chaplain's mouth sent a pang of envy through her body in the form of bitter bile. Pressure seized her chest, and she felt her heart splitting open little by little.

Softly, Annette squeezed her shoulder. 'Did you bring anything?'

Aurelia sniffed and gave her nose a quick wipe with her wrist. 'It's not my grief,' she muttered to herself, 'but it's something.'

She held the card in front of her face, an act of spite to anyone who might have spared her a second glance. *They don't know me,* she thought. *Why should they care?*

But she cared. As long as no one was watching her, she cared a great deal. She cared about her friends and her father. She cared about Annette and her housemate, Ryan Jena. She cared about Teddy Ingram far more than anything she'd ever let on to him aloud.

More than anything, she cared about her mother. And the pain she felt while standing at the funeral pyre was unlike anything she had ever imagined.

Past the dancing flame, she caught the outline of a woman swathed in the shadow of the treeline. She was far enough from her to linger on the other side of the first ward, and from the look of it, she intended to go no further.

Aurelia knew her face. Even from afar or in her dreams, and despite the lack of similarities, Aurelia recognized it as easily as if it were her own. Years later, past the new wrinkles and without the lipstick, her old tutor's face was present as ever.

Gabrielle stared back at her, unblinking.

'Rory,' Annette said darkly, her eyes catching on Aurelia's line of sight.

Aurelia flicked the enchanted card into the flame, the heat propelling it upward before it cascaded back to the centre and disappeared behind the blinding light. She raced toward the opposite end of the ward. Past witches with green-tinted bottles and cups in their hands and blithe smiles on their lips.

Instead of waiting, her old tutor turned fast and disappeared behind a wall of trees on the other side.

Her pursuit, which had been a brisk walk up until that point, became a frenzied chase. Emerging from the protection of the ward, Aurelia lost sight of the jovial, drunk witches of Meredith Albert's old coven, but Gabrielle was nowhere to be seen either. She stopped, scouring the expanse, craning around large tree trunks into darker, midnight corners. An abysmal ache festered in her stomach at Gabrielle's absence and the silence of the woods. She knew her eyes hadn't deceived her; but her love, her adoration for the older witch gave her reason to believe that their eagerness was mutual. What was she missing? Had she forgotten something?

A twig broke beneath pressure somewhere nearby. She opened her mouth and asked into the darkness, 'Is that you?' Before another word could leave her mouth, a shrouded hand clapped down over it, silencing her. She tried to shout and felt her tutor's warm breath against her ear, consoling her.

'Shh, shh. I am not supposed to be here. Neither are you.'

Annette crunched through the dry brush behind her irritably, unperturbed by Aurelia's old tutor, which only seem to frustrate her. 'And *you,*' Gabrielle scolded. 'You ought to know better.'

'Hey, I don't know shit,' Annette said, 'but I tried getting her back home.'

Aurelia pried Gabrielle's fingers from her face with a strangled gasp. Her racing adrenaline made her hot and triggered a reactive spell that sparked around her fingertips, which she tightened into fists underneath her arms to hide.

'My mother just died,' Aurelia hissed. 'Why wouldn't I be here?'

Gabrielle ran her hands down her jeans, wiping off the heat of Aurelia's saliva and the bite of her teeth. She cleared her throat, pacing to put some distance between the rest of them; and with any amount of space, Aurelia could notice that Gabrielle was dressed for the sole purpose of going unnoticed.

'You are a sweet thing, but your father – bless his soul – never told you that all issues concerning Meredith should be left alone.'

'He did,' Aurelia explained, 'but I thought that was stupid advice.'

Gabrielle rolled her eyes and huffed nervously. 'What am I going to do with you? Stubborn as always.'

Aurelia's brow furrowed. As if she didn't have the right to ask for more. All her life, she'd been given so little and forced to take things for herself. She wanted an explanation, an apology for whatever had just happened; but standing in front of her sister and her beloved tutor now, she felt like a child again, vulnerable and stripped of all her authority. Did Gabrielle see her as any more than an awkward, silver-toothed teenager? It might not have been so bad, Aurelia thought. She wanted to be treated just as gently, folded into the woman's embrace, and told that she was missed.

She caught her breath and pushed her hair behind her ears. 'I didn't know if I'd ever see you again.'

It was such a vulnerable admission that Annette stuffed her hands into her pockets sheepishly and looked away.

'Has anyone seen you?' her tutor asked.

Aurelia simply nodded, lowering her gaze to the forest floor. Her boots were filthy. Sharp dried stems endowed the leather with new scrapes – a parting gift from the north-west. 'They don't even know who I am.'

'I told someone she was my wife,' Annette explained.

'Which was weird, by the way.'

'It felt warranted!'

Even in the dark, Gabrielle's dissatisfaction was plain as day. Aurelia bit down on her lip, keeping the words in and her chin from quivering. She wished Gabrielle would stop looking at her that way, as if she'd committed a crime. As if her grief kept taking shapes that didn't fit the mould.

Her father should have told her. Gabrielle should have told her. Instead, everyone had given her the leftovers of Meredith Albert and scorned her for wanting to feed from them.

A holler emerged from within the wards. The field around

the ward was empty and dark, but Gabrielle gave the girl her hand and tugged her further from it. 'Come with me. I've overstayed my welcome here.'

Aurelia hadn't taken two steps into her tutor's quaint home before Gabrielle sprang another inquiry upon her. 'How many people saw you tonight?'

'It was just one person. She was friendly enough.'

'Too friendly,' Annette clarified.

'She might've been drunk for all I know,' was Aurelia's half-hearted defence. 'You saw their glasses. They'd been drinking before we showed up.'

She didn't really care about defending Julia Chaplain's honour, but she was keen not to assign danger to something that might only be a little social awkwardness. The alternative was that she'd gotten herself into something she wasn't prepared for, which would prove everyone right about her: she was foolish, naive and out of her depth.

To her old tutor, Aurelia asked, 'Why aren't you welcome there?'

Gabrielle sent her jacket to the coat rack by the door with a flick of her fingers. Like Tony Schwartz's home, the humble, wallpapered place that Gabrielle had taken up residence in fell victim to sickeningly blue lightbulbs. Aurelia turned, fingers pinched between one another in front of her ribcage, looking for every artefact of Gabrielle's old house that she'd catalogued in her memory. Photographs of Gabrielle's parents, washed out with age, hung sparsely on the walls, their frames shining blue light right back to her.

Gabrielle disappeared into the bathroom, then re-emerged with a jar of pink salve in her hands. 'Because I am not one of them any more. It's one thing to stay on the outside, looking in, but another to leave once you've had a taste of what they offer. To them, it is betrayal, and they haven't forgiven me.'

Gabrielle collapsed into a faded velvet seat, uncapped the jar and placed it on a coffee table in front of her. Aurelia eyed the salve, waiting for Gabrielle to dip her fingers into the glass, but her old tutor's eyes were fixed on her.

'Is that why my dad doesn't practise any more either?'

'Dad doesn't practise because the *real* world keeps him busy enough,' Annette said, her taller frame sagging against the arm of a couch. 'Not everyone can afford to maintain both.'

The implication that magic was something less real, less sophisticated, roused a defence within the other two. It embarrassed Aurelia, as did most of her older sister's bold behaviours.

Gabrielle sighed. 'That's somewhat the case. His story isn't mine to tell. *Sit.*'

'But you're the only one who will tell me.' Aurelia rested her weight on the edge of the coffee table between the others, knee to knee with her tutor. In the light, or perhaps with the distance, Gabrielle's expression wasn't nearly as severe. 'It seems important – this is all very grave behaviour.'

The woman took Aurelia's hand firmly, lathering a dense layer of salve onto her fingers as she spoke. 'Your mother had . . . It's such a strange time to tell you, with her being gone so recently. Your mother would have these visions – these *premonitions* – that she would give to the coven. When she was pregnant with Annette, they were more vivid, more precise;

and everyone wanted to know what they were: good career prospects, ritual magic success, and whatnot.'

'She was a diviner?' It was more than Aurelia had ever been told by her father, and still nothing at all.

Almost reluctantly, Annette said, 'She was.'

'A badgered one, at that,' Gabrielle continued. 'She hated the way the coven would hound her for answers. After she gave birth to your sister, she couldn't give them such precise prophecies. She told me once that it was like "the waters had gone murky". Your father had been trying to get her to rest for months – anyone could see how much of a toll the first pregnancy took on her. He took it as a blessing that she couldn't give them anything else. But two years passed, and Annette had been such a good baby that they wanted another. Not long after she told me about this, she got pregnant with you; and the coven members wanted to know what she would say this time.

'You may not think that I like your dad, but I do,' said Gabrielle. Her full lips turned up at the corners in recollection. 'If I ever disliked him, he loved Meredith so much that it was impossible to stay in conflict. We both urged her not to practise with the coven for her health. To stay home and disconnect her landline so no one could reach her. She was so lonely that she let the others overstep their boundaries time and time again just for a bit of company while Tony was working long hours and all she had was Annie. I came around as much as I could, but I wasn't enough. I had other things to do too. I had a life of my own to juggle. I tried my best.'

Annette pushed herself off the couch and stalked toward the nearest window. Gabrielle's eyes followed her curiously, dropping Aurelia's hands back into the girl's lap. The curtains were pulled shut. Annette hooked her finger round one and peered through it, watching for something in the dark that didn't show up.

Letting the curtains fall shut, she asked, 'And then what?'

'About seven months in, something happened to her. She'd had another fairly healthy pregnancy up to that point, and that was all we could ask for with how much time and energy she'd given to the coven and their demands. I came around more and more. I brought them both food and new groceries. We played card games most nights of the week, so I got her new decks of cards with designs that she loved. I thought everything was good. But on one particular night when I'd been too tired to start my car and drive home, I spent the night on her and Tony's couch; and she came to me in the middle of the night, asking me to take her somewhere. It was the beginning of February, so I told her, "No, it's too cold outside." But she had this . . . this dazed, frenzied look in her eyes. And she kept saying she had to go, that something in her mind was hammering to get out.

'She got into my car without a jacket, so I had to find one in my trunk. She kept telling me, "The river is changing, just go." She wanted me to take her to the Willamette. Said her divination was more accurate in rivers and natural bodies of water than in her scrying dish. This was important to her. I don't know why.'

Aurelia brought one of her hands to her neck, massaging the back of it with her fingers, and asked, 'Do you know what she saw?'

The scent from Gabrielle's salve thickened as her fingers

neared her face; her tutor had soaked her bitten fingernails in repellent.

'None of us will ever know exactly what she saw. But I can tell you now that it scared the shit out of her. She leaned over the water, looking for *you* and told me I couldn't tell anyone from the coven where we had been, or what she saw. I'd never seen her look so scared. She knelt down by the riverbank, and I kept asking her what she was looking for. It was so cold. I wanted to get back in the car. She was going to get sick, and I couldn't let that happen, you know. She said she needed to get closer, that it wasn't enough. She stuck her head into the water and fell in. You know how disgusting the Willamette is? There was no way she didn't catch something. She came out drenched and shaking, and then I had to take her home. Tony was furious with me. I'm sure he must blame me a little for what happened.'

'But what happened? Did she get sick?'

Gabrielle shook her head again and took on a wistful expression. 'Somehow, she remained healthy through the rest of her pregnancy, but something was off about her. She spent the next two months inside and made me tell the rest of the coven she had . . . well, that she had miscarried. Something about that vision from the Willamette gave her reason to believe that you would be in danger with them. But it was a *healer* she spoke of. A healer that the coven would take advantage of. And you are *not* a healer . . . Still, we swore to her terms that they would never find out about you, and not long after, she vanished.'

Aurelia had started to speak at some point, to share the news that her gift had changed its shift and that she was, in fact, a healer. When Gabrielle didn't hear her, she kept her mouth shut; and Annette shot her a look from the window that left her with the distinct impression she should never voice that gift aloud again.

'That's what we all thought,' Gabrielle continued. 'She'd left us signs, but they were all so vague that we couldn't have anticipated what she was trying to do. The thing about diviners is that they assume we know as much as they do, that our fraction of knowledge is much larger than it really is. For years, we assumed the worst. She couldn't have been dead. We refused to believe it. Your father tried so hard to find her – he really did. I don't know if anyone was more torn up about her disappearance than he was, except for me, but we both knew that he had to be a dad more than he had to be a husband. You and Annie needed him. So, after some time, he let her go. I thought that was the end of it.'

'It was my dad who told me she died,' Aurelia said. 'How'd he know?'

Gabrielle's brows raised. She massaged her hands, considering the possibilities. 'I can tell you how *I* found out. I can't speak for Tony. I still haven't spoken to him. It surprises me that he told you anything – especially *now*.'

'He would have told you if you asked,' Annette said. 'There's nothing he loves more than having you back home, Rory. Having us all together.'

'It would have been nice to hear from you,' Gabrielle added.

Aurelia's heart gave a violent pang. 'You never reached out to me. Or asked how I was doing. You wouldn't believe how much shit I've had to deal with.' She pushed her jacket down her shoulder and pushed the short sleeve of her shirt up to expose the scar. 'I could have used the guidance when I had a witch hunting me.'

Gabrielle leaned forward, lifting her fingers to the raised skin on Aurelia's arm. All eyes narrowed on the mark. Annette's stern expression melted into something that looked like guilt. Some things Aurelia hadn't felt the need to share. Her family's rejection of magic had felt too much like a rejection of her.

'If you needed me,' Gabrielle said slowly, 'my door was always open for you. Not far from where I used to teach you, either. But you didn't seem to need me any more, and that's a good thing, too . . . Whoever stitched you up is clumsy with their needle.'

It was the first incision Aurelia had ever mended as a healer, and it showed. They didn't need to know that though. Covering the mark, Aurelia muttered, 'You didn't see the wound. It was deep.'

Gabrielle grimaced before diverting their conversation back to Meredith. 'I hope your father didn't find out the way I did. I hope his discovery was kinder. Hopefully, he made it kind for you.'

As kind as any dead parent discovery could be, she thought. Even the gentlest words from her father had sent her deeper into a spiral of loss. She cried. She felt nothing. She felt everything. She went to Tesco. She didn't tell her peers. She submitted a paper she wasn't proud of. She cried again only for the guilt of not having cried enough. Tony Schwartz had been *so* kind and forgiving while she was starting to devolve, and yet it made no difference while she tried to figure out the correct way to grieve.

'One of my fellow practitioners – or at least, she'd *been* a practitioner at the time I was involved – slipped a note beneath my door demanding my cooperation with questioning. I believe she's a high priestess now. Doesn't matter much to me; I never went. She thinks I knew something about Meredith's death, thinks Meredith was hiding something. Of course she was hiding something.' Gabrielle rose from her chair, shifting past Aurelia's knees to retrieve a large book with photographs hanging from its edges. She stood above the girl, rifling through it pointedly; then, with a hissing separation of glue, she ripped out a photograph to give to Aurelia. 'Your mother had more secrets than anyone I ever knew. But she also had her reasons. I didn't pry. Even if it killed me every day.'

In the photograph, a heavily pregnant Meredith Albert reclined on a couch with her head in Gabrielle's lap. Annette's toys lay scattered on the low table in front of them. Meredith's eyes were ringed in dark, sallow skin, much like Aurelia's always were. Gabrielle, tired as she was, looked happier with Meredith in her lap than Aurelia had ever witnessed before. 'You can keep that,' Gab said with a sigh.

'You won't miss it?'

'I was, at least, there. If I had more to give you, I would.'

Aurelia stood, compelled by the late hour and Annette's impatient, too-close stance to return home. With the photograph wedged between her fingers, she wrapped her arms around herself, tapping her heels on the ground. She wouldn't ask for more, but she wondered if Gabrielle truly had nothing else of her mother in the house. She eyed the picture frames in her periphery and saw a face she didn't recognize. A tall, thin woman with short, golden hair. 'Are you married now?' Aurelia should have asked earlier, not just about the marriage but about all the things that she'd missed being separated from Gabrielle.

'My wife, Robin,' said her tutor. 'She works nights. She would have loved to meet you.'

'She looks kind.'

'She's quiet,' Gabrielle said. 'Gentle. Wouldn't hurt a fly, though I wish she would sometimes. She can reach the spiders that I can't.'

'Is she . . .'

Human. Aurelia didn't have to finish for the meaning to sink in. Throughout their lessons, Gabrielle warned against the cruelty of humanity, so much that it was sometimes paralysing to consider. Sure, they could be cruel, but not completely. No crueller than a witch could be, and much less powerful on their own.

Gabrielle squeezed her arm, leading her to the door unhurriedly. 'Perhaps it was best for you to miss those years with me. I said so many things I regret. I'm learning, the same as you are, that there is so much I don't understand. But she loves me, magic and all, and that's a gift I can't forsake, *ma lumière*. I try my best to deserve it. You'll visit us before you leave, yes?' Her gaze fluttered between the two sisters, which surprised no one more than Annette, who had never really been close to Gabrielle at all.

Aurelia nodded, compartmentalizing every word that Gabrielle said so she wouldn't forget them. They spun like skipping records in her mind. Meredith, the river, Robin, a healer . . . Gabrielle had looked at Meredith in the photograph the way Robin looked at *her*.

Annette gathered her toward the front door.

A hundred pieces puzzled together in Aurelia's head. Her mother had taken a secret to the grave just to keep it out of the coven's hands. Aurelia's breath grew thick and dry – she was thinking of Teddy again and the scars on his back, the skin reaching over red, bloody gashes to reconvene. What could be so bad about magic like that?

'Did it matter so much that I wasn't a healer?'

'Very much,' Gabrielle said through her opened front door. 'Not enough to put us at ease, but if it was a *healer* that the coven wanted to exploit, they wouldn't get that from you; and that was all we could ask for. Now, drive safely, you two. You never know what's hiding in these woods.'

CHAPTER NINE

For days, Teddy worked with his gaze turned over his shoulder. As he sliced fruits for Lou's morning yoghurt or cleaned the upper shelves in Alaric's shop, Meredith's presence hung on him like a shadow.

He couldn't tell if she was still there or not. She hadn't shown her face since the first night, and when the cold phantom hand fell upon his back a few nights afterwards, he woke to find Kenny there. Still boyish and wide-eyed, in need of remembrance. Teddy gave a relieved sigh but shook his head.

You have to leave me alone.

Unlike Meredith, Kenny never spoke. He simply slithered out of Teddy's bed and disappeared like a monster beneath it, leaving Teddy alone with his guilt and his grief.

Teddy ran in the mornings, just after the sun had come up from the horizon but the sky was still more blue than baby pink. He tried to drown out some of his paranoia with the loud music in his earbuds, but he could still vaguely hear the crunch of the grass beneath his shoes, and Meredith's presence still hung onto his heels. It would have been easier, at this point, if she appeared to him again rather than lingering uncertainly in the alcoves of his mind.

The simultaneous presence and absence of her started to drive him mad. He didn't even know if she was really there or if his anxiety was just a product of the strangeness – but he would be washing in the shower afterwards, probably thinking of Schwartz's bare waist or the curve of her neck, and he'd feel more shameful than ever touching himself.

Where the slope of the hill levelled, he started to run. He ran until Cliff, the owner of Petro's cafe, was turning the sign on the front door to *OPEN*. He ran as far as the neighbouring city, following the trail most worn and flat from the tyres of occasional cars, and then turned back. Today, he ran as if Meredith Albert chased him.

He wouldn't tell Schwartz about it yet. He'd wait for Alaric and his colleague to help him reanimate the paper bird; and by the time he told Schwartz about seeing Meredith's ghost, he would have more to say. Something promising.

Nearing midnight, Alaric Friedman returned. Teddy ensured that Lou was tucked tightly into her bed before making the journey down the hill again. He pulled the curtains over the bookshop window and disappeared with him into the grand library.

A woman pushed through one of the doors upstairs, a pale linen cardigan tied loose around her waist. She paid Teddy Ingram no attention as she entered the library assuredly. 'So late here, Friedman,' she called from the staircase. 'My day is just beginning.'

'Do I seem tired?' Alaric asked her. He then looked at Teddy with a playfulness that Teddy didn't think he'd seen in years, not since he was a teenager. 'Do I?'

Teddy answered, 'Age besets us all, old man.'

The woman – another caretaker – approached them, extending her hand for Teddy to shake, so he did. It was thin and veiny, stacked with creases between her knuckles and wrinkles in her palm.

'We haven't met before. I'm Hye-Jin,' she said.

'Theodore.'

Alaric smiled wearily, and muttered, 'Formalities. She knows who you are.'

'I know a great deal about you,' Hye-Jin said. 'He tells me so much.'

'Now, that doesn't seem very fair, Al.' Teddy raised his brows at the Townsend caretaker in a subtle provocation. 'He doesn't tell me anything that goes on in your realm. Not even with a little coaxing.'

'He must have told you about Carmichael, no?' Hye-Jin asked.

Alaric spoke before either of them could draw their next breath. 'That's not important right now. I want to get this thing talking. Come.'

Hye-Jin nodded dutifully, joining the other caretaker in the vacant space between the sitting room and the library shelves. She clasped her hands in front of her stomach, massaging her knuckles as she walked. When she unclasped them, Teddy noticed a small tremor in her fingers. She kept them fastened around each other or on the waist-tie of her cardigan for support.

In his left hand, Alaric held a small white pouch, which he dipped the fingers of his right into to extract a fistful of salt. It trailed delicately onto the floorboards, and he kept his hand low to the ground to create a clean, closed shape.

'Do you think there's something harmful in that letter?' Teddy asked. 'Binding it in a circle feels rather accusatory.'

'It's just a precaution,' Alaric offered. 'In the council, we have rigid protocols to follow. Rituals that might seem unnecessary in the beginning that become vital later on. Being so large scale, we want to ensure our magical practices remain safe. That being said, this isn't council practice.' He cast Hye-Jin a warning glance, adding, 'I'd prefer the others *didn't* hear about this.'

'Isn't that always the case with you?' she asked, but there was no hint of malice or dissatisfaction on her face. Hye-Jin had round cheeks with dimples beneath her eyes that formed when she smiled at him. Teddy had always felt like Alaric's closest confidant, but there was such fondness and familiarity in the way that Alaric and Hye-Jin looked at each other that he almost felt like a third wheel, spoiling a private moment.

Something about it made his stomach turn. For all he'd done and surrendered himself to, the least he could expect was to feel valued. Alaric kept his gaze averted from Teddy's, leading the tail end of the salt circle to the head and closing it off. Perhaps, the caretaker thought of him as a chore. Someone who brought their baggage back to Townsend not to unpack it but to take up more space.

Wiping his hands down the front of his corduroy trousers, Alaric said, 'Are you both ready?'

Teddy nodded, then Hye-Jin. Alaric took the flattened paper bird from the coffee table in the sitting room, carrying it to the circle openly, as if to invite a final rescission. Neither Hye-Jin nor Teddy stopped him.

Alaric tugged at the bird's tail the way Schwartz had done in the basement, but his hold was more careful. He leaned into the centre of the circle, keeping his feet firmly planted outside the salt boundaries, and the paper bird fell from his hand with the softness of a feather, fluttering to life before it hit the wood.

Alaric uttered something beneath his breath that Teddy could not understand, though he listened closely to catch a word or a sound. Before he could ask, Hye-Jin's fingers curled around his wrist, and she whispered, 'You wouldn't know it. It's an arcane language.'

'Those are the best kind.'

Even if *he* couldn't decipher it, Schwartz might be able to. He had found his strength in language, she in ideology; but an understanding of both was essential in furthering their appreciation of the other. Schwartz took it as an insult that he was there in all the gaps of her knowledge, but the pair of them were more like the teeth of a zip – ineffective on their own, needing the other to fulfil a purpose.

It was wishful thinking, he knew, to assume she would recognize the words when he didn't; but most of the time, wishful thinking was all he had. The least he could do was ask.

From the small paper figure, another shape burst free. A feather on the wing. A heartbeat in its chest. It grew twice its size, then doubled again. The stems of new legs protruded from what was formerly a clean, white edge.

Teddy held his breath, trading quick glances between the caretakers next to him.

'Did this happen the first time?' Alaric asked softly.

Teddy shook his head. 'N-no. It stayed just like that.' The air in his lungs felt thin and insufficient, and his body went cold.

The bird outgrew its allotted space within the salt circle, writhing upwards with no other direction to move in. The boundary was crushing it, holding it in. It beat one of its massive wings against the wall of the salt circle. The paper burned where it struck the circle. The creature cried out, singed and hurting.

For a moment, Teddy mistook it for the cry of a woman, and the inside of his mouth went dry. He knew that Meredith was embedded in those words, designated to the page. It occurred to him that what he'd done was rip her from the letter just to cage her within something else.

Meredith was still there, full of feeling, not quite *alive*.

And just like he could feel the other witches around him, Teddy felt all of her too. The fire on her wings. The horror in her cry. The *confusion*.

'Let her out,' he said.

Alaric shook his head. 'What are you talking about?'

'It's hurting her. The circle isn't big enough.' Teddy couldn't justify his overwhelming sense of kinship with the creature in the circle. He knew they were dissimilar in plenty of ways, but when he looked at the creature – at *Meredith* – he felt the scars on his back reopened and porous with blood again.

'Theodore,' Hye-Jin said sternly. 'What are you seeing?'

He blinked at her in confusion. 'Sh-she doesn't fit in the circle any more. She's outgrown the page, and the circle. It's burning her.'

'*They can't see me, sweetheart.*' The creature, still paper white though her features were more human, wrapped herself in her wings.

Teddy kept his eyes on her as he said, 'She's talking to me.'

Hye-Jin snapped her fingers at Alaric. 'Write it down. Tell us what she's saying.'

But Meredith didn't elaborate immediately. She scoffed rudely, shaking her head before laying it on top of her folded arms. '*It's because I am a manifestation of grief. Imbued into paper and given a voice by you.*'

'Not letting you rest?' Teddy asked.

'*No. I cannot rest if I do not wake.*'

'What do you mean then? Who won't let you rest?'

'What's it saying?' Alaric pushed his glasses up his nose, pen poised within his hand to transcribe Teddy's words.

'*Sweet thing,*' Meredith said sadly. The phrase lacked any of the usual condescension and had the scent of complete sincerity. '*My message wasn't meant for you. I didn't mean to reach you the way I did, but no one grieves the way you do. It's hard to ignore. You called to me like a beacon.*'

Teddy's lips parted, but he didn't know what to say. 'I'm sorry.' He was an intruder. A captor, not a confidant. Aurelia's mother hadn't wanted to be attached to him the same way he had wanted to shed her like snakeskin.

But she smiled warmly. Even through the abstraction of

paper, he could see the origin of Schwartz's smile. '*It's not your fault. This grief is not yours to carry. You seem kind. Where is my girl? Is she safe?*'

'She is.'

'*Is she loved?*'

Teddy nodded. 'Yeah.'

Hye-Jin spoke to the other caretaker in hushed tones. Alaric responded, but his voice was distant too, as if his words were uttered behind glass or underwater.

'*Where did she go? Why isn't she here to receive me?*'

'She's gone home to see you.'

Alaric's voice grew harsh. 'Teddy, what is it saying?'

'*But I am long gone,*' Meredith said.

'She'll be back soon,' said Teddy. 'I can give her a message, if you'll just tell me.'

'*Where did she go?*'

'To your funeral. She wanted to see you,' Teddy explained.

To this, the creature twitched and cried out again. Teddy stepped backwards, as if Meredith might now extend her white, dove-like wings through the circle and beat him; but the circle singed her again.

'*Bring her back,*' she bellowed. '*Bring her back now!*'

'Why?' he asked.

Alaric growled, 'Teddy, what's going on? Tell me what's happening!'

'The circle,' said Hye-Jin, clutching Teddy's wrist to keep him grounded. 'You've disrupted it. Step back.'

'*She can't go to the coven. You have to tell her to come back.*'

'Tell me why.'

Meredith launched herself towards the boundary, shrieking as her paper body struck the boundary again; but a sliver of light slipped through the gap Teddy's shoe had smeared in the salt circle. The gap was small, and what emerged was no wider than the surface of a blade.

Alaric discarded the page and pen at once, pulling Teddy from the circle – not before that sharp spear of phantom energy struck the boy through the chest.

For a moment, everything behind his eyes was white, and his body felt weightless. A ripple scattered across the library, rustling open pages, tugging on the wood until they creaked. His chest burned. He reached for it, half expecting to feel the same silver sword that he'd seen lodged in Margarita Palermo's chest inside the dining hall of King's College. His fingers passed over his sternum as he fell backwards into Hye-Jin's expectant embrace.

Nothing. Nothing but fire and white. He shut his eyes and his body went limp.

'Get him something,' Alaric commanded. 'Quickly, please.' Hye-Jin released Teddy's skull onto the pillow she'd dragged down from the couch. His head lobbed unceremoniously to the side, heavier and more burdensome than ever. Teddy opened his mouth but could do nothing more than groan and gasp. He'd felt the air surge from his lungs when Meredith's being burst, and he struggled to take it back in.

She disappeared up the staircase and through a door. Alaric brushed the hair back from Teddy's forehead and said, 'She keeps potions. She'll have something to help. Can you tell me what you're feeling?'

'Dizzy,' Teddy said. 'Feel like . . . 'm not sure.' Alaric's thumb traced the shape of his temple softly – was he hallucinating? It felt surreal to be touched so softly and by someone that wasn't Aurelia Schwartz that he found himself blinking rapidly to force the exhaustion from his eyes. He was in the library, beside the dormant fireplace – but six months earlier. Alaric and Aurelia had stripped him of his clothing, pressed their dampened rags to the still-bleeding gashes in his back, and spoke softly over the deflated shape of his body. His head was in her lap, her fingers in his hair; and the sound of her voice warred with the one in his head that whispered, *You monster. You hideous beast.*

'She's not here,' Alaric said. 'She's in Washington. You know this.'

'What?'

'You asked for Aurelia. She's not here.'

Above them, the door opened and shut again. Clearing the last of the haze from his mind, Teddy could see Hye-Jin approaching hurriedly, clutching a shot glass and an amber-tinted bottle. She lowered herself to her knees beside Alaric. He held the shot glass while she poured, and then he wiggled his hand beneath Teddy's head to prop him up for a drink.

'Mind the taste,' said Hye-Jin. It was sour and cold. Teddy felt it crawling all the way down his throat and sputtered some of it back up as if he'd drowned in it.

'There,' Alaric murmured. 'Everything's all right.'

'I saw Meredith,' Teddy said. 'She was like an angel.'

Alaric returned the glass to Hye-Jin, and she pushed both things aside.

'And what did she say?' Hye-Jin prodded. 'We didn't see what you saw. It was just a bird, speaking the way that birds do.'

Teddy's upside-down view of Alaric strengthened. The man's brow furrowed tightly, his lips curving severely downwards. Teddy had yearned for his concern, for his attention, but it only embarrassed him now. He'd done something wrong. Maybe Alaric was disappointed with him.

The calluses on his fingers scraped Teddy's unmarked skin. 'You're OK,' the caretaker whispered. 'You can tell me.'

Now, you'll listen, thought Teddy. Only now, but it was better than nothing. It probably took as much trust to believe anything Teddy said as it did to believe that Alaric would take him seriously.

'She didn't want to talk to me. She wanted to talk to her daughter, and when I said Schwartz was in Washington, she tried to break through and warn me.'

'Warn you of what?' Hye-Jin asked. Alaric's fingers traced a path down Teddy's temple again. The caretaker's mercy made him feel so *meek* and obedient. He needed so little to be opened up and picked apart – an inkling of kindness or a soft touch. As little as it was, it didn't manifest itself enough.

It made him desperate. And compliant.

'All she said was that Schwartz "can't go to the coven". She needs to come back. But she'll be back soon – I tried to tell her that, and then she just . . .' Teddy lifted his hands and pantomimed a small burst.

'You're picking her up soon, aren't you?' Alaric asked.

'Tomorrow night,' Teddy said. He looked to Hye-Jin, then back to Alaric. 'Do you think she's in danger?'

It was a precarious position to place Alaric Friedman in. No one knew, least of all the ones who hadn't spoken to Meredith Albert themselves. Teddy could see the wheel turning in the caretaker's mind. At last, Alaric said, 'Not if she is home with us. Let's make sure she gets here.'

CHAPTER TEN

Morning had mostly passed by the time Teddy woke up on the couch in Alaric's library. Lou peered at him across the table where she'd laid and configured the frame (and a large, floating piece in the centre) of a puzzle. The open skylight gave way to the strength of summer light, and it bore directly into his face.

With a groan, he turned onto his elbow and asked, 'Where's Al? What are you doing here?'

She shrugged. 'I dunno. He came this morning and said you stayed over here last night. Asked if I wanted to be here instead.'

'I'm sorry.'

'Why? I like it here.' She pushed the hair from her face, but the fine front bits were less than cooperative. Teddy recognized her pyjamas from the previous night, a hideously patterned set with crude cat illustrations on them.

The least Alaric had done was ensure that Lou's teeth got brushed and her hair got combed, but Teddy usually braided her hair for her in the mornings – the way Gemma had always done. Another routine he'd inherited after her disappearance, one that he rather enjoyed. On the days where the practice was missed, Lou carried on with her morning slightly undone, with her fair brows hanging low over her eyes in frustration, trying to figure out what she'd forgotten.

Teddy never forgot. Some mornings were simply more difficult for him to spend in someone else's company.

For the most part, Teddy could quell the virulence of his empathetic gift and keep everyone else's feelings at bay, but night unleashed the hands of his empathy; and unbeknownst to him, they'd reach for others in the household. His mind was not his own after dark. It fell victim to the dread and the longing that inundated those around him, dragging him through the depths of hell and back by morning. Their dreams. Their fears. Every plaguing thought that kept them awake came to him like pigs to a trough. His magic nurtured it, kept fear well fed.

Waking up had been much easier before Gemma vanished, with Louisa unburdened and the augur still around, but it had never been easy. The day began with the weight of all the night's terrors already sitting on his chest. He started his mornings earlier to avoid it. To run and rid his mind of the grief that got into bed with him.

None of it had ever chased him the way Meredith Albert did.

Louisa coughed into her arm, then continued finding compatible puzzle pieces.

'Lou, darling, are you getting sick?'

'My head just feels stuffy, that's all. Al's going to get me some medicine anyway.'

Teddy kicked his legs off the side of the couch, shrugging off a blanket that Alaric had laid over his body at some point in the night. Every breath squeezed his chest hard. For once, the physical pain overpowered the usual feeling of mental torment. Teddy waved Lou forward wordlessly. The girl pushed a puzzle piece into its partner, leaving them both on the table.

'You have a hair tie?'

She held up her wrist and wiggled it. 'I have two.'

Teddy rolled them over her small hands and muttered, 'Sit,' which she did without protest. Routine comforted her. As Teddy straightened the central part in her hair with his fingers, he felt her relax into the space between his knees, working the puzzle upside down. 'How long has Alaric been gone?'

'Maybe twenty minutes.'

'Ah.'

'Is that bad?' Lou asked.

Not inherently. But for all the attention that Teddy devoted to Lou, either by his own decision or by Alaric's, he'd assumed the caretaker would give the same. He had thought about this frequently, when Alaric went away for weeks without calling or when his mind wandered mid-conversation. Giving him the benefit of the doubt, Teddy had spent months, maybe even years, assuring himself that the thought was unfair. But duty to a family was no less important than that to a job, and the council distracted Alaric enough for Teddy to forgive himself for letting his concerns ruminate.

'No,' Teddy decided then. 'I wish he'd told me though, before he left. I don't appreciate him leaving you here like that. Agatha would have looked after you.'

'But I'm OK, Teddy. I promise.' Louisa tilted her head up to look at him, inadvertently messing up the even sections Teddy had just made in her hair. To Lou, Alaric could do no wrong. His returns were hastily wrapped gifts, a flower that bloomed only under full moons. The girl had been struck by enough hardship at once that Teddy trod lightly to ensure he didn't soil the source of Louisa's precarious joy.

He, too, was part of that. As proud an assumption as it might be, Teddy knew he'd be a fool not to acknowledge his contribution to her joy. But part of assuming the responsibility of what Gemma left meant humbling himself at every turn, keeping himself ignorant of a reward that he might otherwise reap. He let her smile, and he didn't make himself too integral to it.

A door shuddered above him. Tying off the end of Louisa's flimsy braid, Teddy turned to meet the caretaker's glum expression. A dull glint from the curve of his bronze bangles caught Teddy's eye.

'A bit early for important business,' Teddy said.

Alaric found no humour in it, tugging the bangles off his wrists forcefully. 'How are you feeling?'

Lou twisted to face him with curious concern. He didn't think Alaric would tell her about the encounter with Meredith – Teddy didn't see the point in making it Lou's problem. The way he saw it, if Aurelia could have reanimated the paper bird herself, she wouldn't have made it Teddy's problem either.

'Smashing,' Teddy replied, smoothing Lou's parting. 'Like someone's taken a cleaver to my skull.'

'Bad enough to need a doctor?'

Pushing himself from the couch, Teddy said, 'I could manage without.' The caretaker slid the bronze pieces into his linen shirt pocket, their weight pulling it slightly downwards. He placed his hands on either side of Teddy's face, and with the rough pads of his thumbs, tugged at the skin beneath the boy's eyes.

'Your pupils are extremely dilated,' Alaric mused. 'But if you're not feeling any other adverse effects, I wouldn't think too much about it.'

'I didn't hit my head, did I?'

Alaric shook his head, released the boy from his grasp, then offered Lou a smile where she sat. 'It's not the impact I'm worried about. More than anyone else in the council, I trust Hye-Jin to make sure my loved ones and I are given the proper care, but I didn't ask her what was in the bottle she gave you before we administered it.'

'Ah. Lucky me then,' Teddy said. Alaric's hands left whispers of cold on Teddy's flushed cheeks. He blinked a few times in exhaustion, lifting his wrists to his eyes to knead them. 'I don't suppose that was what you were discussing today.'

'Not in front of Lou,' Alaric whispered.

With a huff, Teddy responded, 'Not like you'd tell me anyway.'

The man's lips pressed together sternly. 'I would, actually. Lately, I'd felt you were owed an explanation.' Teddy lowered his gaze and internally chastised himself. He could see the caretaker's expression steeling over his face, his willingness draining before him. Lou cleared her throat, ensnaring them both again. They gave her the same automatic smile, then promptly wiped it clear, ashamed of it. 'Let's take a walk,' Alaric said. 'If you think you can stomach it.'

'Sure.' *A thread of promise*, thought Teddy. It was fragile and pulled taut between them, but he could still hold onto it.

He just needed to keep himself upright.

The doors of Alaric's library were closed to most folks from both sides. Until Alaric led him through the door to Luxembourg, Teddy had forgotten that it existed anywhere else, that it wasn't just a refuge in his mind or an extension of Townsend, absent in time and space.

Midday hung over them but spared Teddy's headache from the bright light. Alaric leashed his old dog quietly. Teddy blinked, blindly following the sound of the caretaker's footsteps as they turned from the entrance of a shaded alleyway into the white of midday.

'Are you coming?' Alaric asked. Teddy stifled a groan and rushed to join him at the other side of his dog.

'Will we be gone long?' he asked. 'I'm not too keen on leaving Lou at the library.'

'The library has been extensively proofed,' Alaric assured him. 'The dangerous bits are warded off.'

'Can knowledge be so dangerous to the impressionable young mind?' the boy deadpanned. 'What do you mean *dangerous?*'

'Never mind that,' Alaric said, leaving Teddy Ingram with more questions than he'd begun with. 'Now . . . when the council was first made aware of Leona Sum, many of the caretakers chose to ignore the motive behind her attacks. What mattered most was that we eliminated the threat of forced blood transferences. Not considering that, in doing so, we were quashing one witch's attempt at reversing the decline of our own kind.

'In theory,' Alaric continued, 'Sum's plan would have accomplished exactly what our kind needed – a rejuvenation of magical fortitude in weakening bloodlines. Think about it: all this secrecy keeps us from forming honest ties with people. We're growing old without marrying, not having children. The children we have are turned down opposite paths. Ones that will eventually lead an entire race of magic-folk to a quiet end.

'We couldn't have allowed her to carry on in her own way, but getting rid of her left the root problem unexamined,' Alaric finished. 'The witch race is dying. I worry that we will only endanger ourselves further if we can't form communities to depend on. I've seen more and more erratic bursts of untamed magic in these past few years than ever before, with effects that we can't hide. Human prejudice grows in the face of the unknown. So, what do we do?'

The boy nodded softly, his eyes scanning over the caretaker's face as he spoke. Al continued, fidgeting with the lead in his hand.

'We are dying, Teddy. Several of the caretakers believed that it was, in part, due to the lack of biological variation, but it's more complicated than that. In past generations, a magical parent and a non-magical parent would almost certainly birth a magical child. Nowadays, it's rare that that pairing will produce something other than human. It's a toss-up now, seeing which genes will prosper, but the point is that we have so little of our magical parentage left in our bloodlines that we won't survive more than a few generations. And frankly, it's difficult to find each other without being open to showing the rest of the world what we are. You see the issue?'

'Yes,' Teddy said. 'But I don't see why that takes you away from Townsend so often.'

Alaric's gaze roved the ground, attention crushed between his dog's staggered footsteps. He scraped his stubble with the flat of his joined fingers. 'I have to ask . . . does it concern you that centuries from now, the world might not have any more people like us in it?'

Teddy was probably the worst possible witch to ask. 'People like us' included him, and he had always hated his gift. The destructive powers that came from being a reaper should have been eliminated long ago. Had it not been for a life of secrecy, someone might have done it for him already. A young, unassuming boy was easier to exsanguinate than a man with two deaths behind him already.

Then there were witches like Schwartz, who sewed the severed skin on the backs of monstrous boys, who could use their gifts to heal the ailments of people more deserving than him. Witches who gave second chances to those the world had all but stripped of their livelihoods, with powers that made frostbitten fields capable of flowering again. Magic-folk could have thrived in the world of humankind if *that* was the face it wore – and not his. If it came in plentiful harvests and cured disease instead of on crows' wings with extended claws, maybe they wouldn't have to hide.

Alaric bumped him with his shoulder once, and Teddy shrugged. 'I'm not sure I'll care much once I'm dead, but it's certainly not comforting to think about. I tried to shed my nihilism when I was seventeen.'

The caretaker pursed his lips. 'I ask because there are others like Leona Sum who are doing everything they possibly can to ensure that it never comes to that. Their efforts are different – meaning significantly less violent – but worrisome, nonetheless. Leona was dangerous because she was reckless, but she was messy, too. A witch at the end of her rope. The others . . .'

Alaric tugged the lead lightly, and Neil stalled by his side. A cyclist brushed past them on the road to their left. Neil lunged, but remained firmly in place by way of his taut lead.

The two men surveyed the street for others before Alaric released a sigh and continued. 'The others are dangerous because they are intentional. *Knowledgeable*. It'll take more than a few ignorant, non-consensual blood oaths to deter them.'

'And they *need* to be deterred?'

Alaric's warning gaze struck him fiercely. 'This is the hardest part to understand or explain. Why would we need to prevent the regeneration of a species? In doing so, are we acknowledging that the world of humankind would be better off without us?' The man shook his head, pushing up his glasses again. 'Of course not. But to someone who isn't privy to the same kind of information that the council is privy to, it'd appear that that's the stance we've taken; and they're targeting us for it. Hye-Jin's collection has already been breached, and we're trying to figure out how.'

'So, you haven't been around because . . . We're a risk to your security?'

'Not exactly. That was more a matter of protocol. No one

outside the council is supposed to know this. As it all unfolds, we are being watched more closely than ever for breaches of privacy. By extension, many of those with families have elected to withdraw from their seats. This is a matter of protected information, you see. I shouldn't even be telling you this.'

Yet he was. Rather tensely, as Teddy noticed. He stepped onto the pedestrian crossing of an empty street corner, but Alaric remained fastened in place, fist closed around Neil's lead without much room for give.

With his hands in his pockets, Teddy asked, 'Are we walking?'

Al glanced furtively at the buildings around him as if there were ears within them all, pressed against the walls to hear them with damning curiosity. 'No. Let's head back.'

So, Teddy returned to the pavement, boots silent against the smooth concrete. 'The council isn't doing anything, then? To reverse the extinction of witches?'

'That's something I can't tell you,' Alaric said. 'I've said too much already.'

'Have you?' asked Teddy. 'I'm not sure you've given me more than a broad concept or a thought puzzle.' Or the feeling of impending doom.

The caretaker cleared his throat. 'You must understand that I am one person standing in a room with almost fifty others, trying to be heard. I can speak my truth, but if that is not the truth of others, they are equally as capable – and just as unchecked – as I am. In the end, my decisions are for the sake of you and Lou.'

'I suppose I should accept a lifetime of cryptic messages from you, then.'

'Luckily, the measure of my lifetime from now will be much shorter than yours. Then you will never have to burden yourself with my cryptic messages again.'

'Stop it,' Teddy said, sharp. 'I won't listen to you talk like that.'

'We should talk about it, though. I expect it'll come sooner than you think.'

Teddy shook his head. 'I'd rather not talk about anything at all if that's what you want to discuss. I have no interest in making light conversation of your death. Besides, you hunch and sulk around as if we're being listened to. Is that a conversation you'd want someone to overhear?'

The edge that Alaric had tried to cover up returned on full display for Teddy to witness. Angles and corners took shape in Alaric Friedman's figure that had all been smoothed over by some semblance of calm. Was it wrong, Teddy wondered, to prod at the caretaker's paranoia when Alaric had forced him to bear the brunt of his own? He thought it fair, if anything, to return some of the worry. If he couldn't put it to rest, Teddy would instil it into the heart of his tormentor himself.

Alaric's voice lowered to a whisper once they reached the narrow alleyway that hid the grand library's door. It cowered in the shadowy crevice between two tall, brutish buildings, only as tall as their knees and wide enough for one person to slip through sideways. Teddy hadn't seen the grand library from outside before – only the Townsend bookshop. Alaric stepped forward, placing Neil's lead in the younger man's hand. He then offered Teddy a wry, twisted grin, standing close enough to the wall to place a kiss upon one of the burnished bricks, and struck his heel into the ground directly beneath him. Teddy lurched forward, his breath catching in shock as the concrete gave way beneath the caretaker. Neil countered him, tugging him from the edge of the concave ground, the lead around his neck meant to rein back the boy instead.

With the door's bottom half uncovered, Alaric twisted his key in the lock and summoned his dog inside.

'One day,' mused the caretaker, 'he won't be able to make that jump down. And at some point, neither will I. We have to worry about these things, Teddy, or that day will come and leave you with another one of my problems to solve. Something like that would spoil my good memory, don't you think?'

CHAPTER ELEVEN

In the burned brush, a sliver glint drew the coven leader's eye. She crunched through the debris to grab it while the others gathered the last remnants of the burning into their arms and dropped them into trash bags. 'Rosie,' she called, and a younger woman to her left hurried to join her, attentive and obedient. Julia Chaplain's name on the card gleamed from within the charred edges. She drew her thumb across it, wiping the soot from the embossing considerately. 'You wouldn't happen to remember someone at the funeral named Aurelia, would you?'

Rosie shook her head, 'No ma'am. But if you told me what she looked like, maybe—'

'Like Meredith,' Chaplain said, crushing the card in her hand. 'Just not blonde. Same curls. Same eyes. Same stupid sense of stubbornness.'

'I think I would have remembered something like that,' Rosie replied.

'It seems I'm the only one who does. Weird, isn't it? Not a single person there remembered seeing her face except for me. Like she came just to torment me.'

Rosie bowed her head in thought and, finding a shred of burnt cloth, went to pick it up. 'Why do you ask?'

'She told me that Meredith was her mother,' Chaplain answered. Leaving the debris beneath her thick-soled Patagonia shoes untouched, Chaplain approached the funeral pyre – or what was left of it. The body in the branches had been reduced to its bones, the woven cage of wood scraps around it now a pile of white ash. 'I think *I* would have remembered something like that, too.'

'Was it *Annette* you saw, ma'am?'

Chaplain's wrinkled mouth pressed into a fine, furious line. 'Well, *Annie* corrected her after that little slip-up. They were there together.' Anyone would be sceptical, she thought. But it was almost insulting at this point for everyone to suggest that she had misremembered the girl at the burning. If she could rid her from memory altogether, she might not have lost hours of sleep. The suggestion might stop infuriating her so much.

Though she said nothing, the irritation in her face was clear enough that Rosie lowered her head once more in apology. 'That *is* strange. Tony would know, though. The treaty must have ended now that Meredith is gone,' Rosie said.

The treaty.

Something sprung to life in the coven leader's mind. She hadn't questioned the terms when they were set – and why would she? The role still belonged to the mother, and she had no reason to believe that Meredith Albert possessed ulterior motives for making a promise like that. They'd been friends once; honest, devoted *friends*. If Meredith claimed to need the coven's protection from another ex-practitioner who'd since abandoned them, why should the coven turn her away? God welcomed all sinners once they were repentant. If disobedient followers could not all ask forgiveness from God directly, the coven would ask it from Julia, who stood one rung lower and served as a liaison. 'Yes, Meredith,' she had said. 'Anything to have you back.'

But Meredith's terms of separation from her family would outlive her. By thirty years, in fact. Julia assumed it was a formality, a clause that simply bound the coven to legality, but Meredith must have known more. Having a diviner's gift of foresight came with wicked, deceptive implications for the rest of them. They'd trusted her to guide them rightfully. To lead their coven toward a rebirth, a *revival*.

Julia reached for the bones, expecting them to burn at her touch. 'I'm not allowed contact with Tony until thirty years from now,' she said scornfully. Mere days had passed since they'd placed another body on the pyre in Meredith's place, excavated from the depths of a forgotten freezer, and the bones were cold under Julia Chaplain's hands. *Poor girl*, she thought. She couldn't even remember when this one had died, nor could she ask. All but a select few knew that the witch in the fire was not really Meredith, and the others had bestowed such sweet memories onto her unsuspectingly.

Money they'd earned through her honest guidance. Fruits they'd grown with her climate predictions. All surrendered to the wrong woman. *A damned waste*.

Chaplain supposed that, if the girl had come on her own, no treaty had been violated. Then again, if it *had* been, such encounters rendered the treaty null and void. The morbid truth was that Meredith Albert died with her secrets. Chaplain examined her hands, forcing the weak pulse of a spell through them, and knew with total conviction that one of those secrets was meant for her.

To be kept *from* her.

They could afford to ask Meredith what it was.

Meredith existed in a trinity of her own making: on paper, in spirit, and in the flesh.

The first resided in the basement of a cottage in sleepy Townsend. The second, bound to no fixed space in particular, had a list of people worth haunting. This included, but was not limited to, a pair of medievalists who had devoted their efforts to deciphering magic from a folded piece of paper. Also, in Vancouver, Tony and Annette Schwartz clung to her spirit like the last drop of oil in their lamp.

But the third, Meredith's body, had been hauled into the sprawling woods of the Pacific Northwest in the sticker-plastered trunk of Rosie Starling's Toyota Camry. With each dip in the forest floor and every gnarled, protruding tree trunk, the body of Meredith Albert gave a hard thunk.

Shit, shit, shit. Rosie gripped the wheel. She'd turned her headlights off. The trees grew in clusters too thick to allow her to take her eyes off the front of her car, but she sent a silent apology toward the back of the car, to whichever version of the diviner that could hear her.

Unlike the high priestess of her coven, Rosie had liked Meredith. The encounters were sparse, but the water scryer's smile, even in passing, left Rosie with a bubbling, acquiescing joy she couldn't shake for hours. Something about her general disposition comforted Rosie Starling, who eyes always passed over and to whom care was rarely afforded. It was easy to forgive their resident diviner's frequent withdrawals.

Meredith visited rarely, delivered her advice, and left quickly as if she'd had the devil at her feet. Had Rosie not found herself beneath Julia Chaplain's hand, she wouldn't have expected Meredith Albert to spare her any time.

So, on top of the *usual* guilt of delivering a dead body for necromantic practice, Rosie was trying her best to placate the body in the trunk of her car.

In the clearing, Chaplain flashed her brights twice. 'Took you long enough.'

'Are you kidding? She still weighs, like, over a hundred pounds. I wasn't going to ask someone to help me load a body bag into my car.'

Chaplain folded her arms over her chest as Rosie's trunk lid swung upward, not keen on helping her lug Meredith's body *out* of the car either.

'I want to try something new today,' Chaplain said.

'Is it safe?' Rosie was panting and subsequently regretting it when the stench of early decay flooded her nostrils through the bag.

'We'll see.'

Rosie embraced the bag, holding it upright before Julia Chaplain gave a passive nod to a spot nearby.

I'm trying my best to keep you intact, she thought to the body bag, *but we're still working out the kinks.*

'All she has to do is talk,' Chaplain said. 'I think she'll tell us the rest.'

Rosie Starling's thoughts were clouded with shame. The

pieces clicked together behind a murky veil of rushing blood and inaudible ringing. 'You think she knows how to do it right?'

Julia Chaplain was not a necromancer; nor was Meredith, for that matter. And neither being predisposed to the gift of necromancy meant that the pride of exacting such magic couldn't fall neatly to either witch.

Surely, the high priestess had gotten close though. It felt perverse and traitorous to help her get any closer. But time was weighing on the backs of every witch in the local coven, and Julia was the only witch proffering any suggestions. If they could not outrun the plague of their demise, perhaps they could cheat death another way.

They needed to get closer.

'I'll bet you anything it's that kid,' Chaplain whispered.

'You're still thinking about her?'

'You didn't see her. Spitting image of Meredith, I swear, and yet I've never heard a single thing about her.'

'Maybe she's just Tony's kid, different mom.'

'That doesn't make any sense, Ro. Besides, the poor man was lovestruck,' Chaplain said, tonguing her tea-stained teeth. 'He didn't remarry. Shame, too. He used to be so handsome.'

'Maybe she's a liar,' Rosie suggested.

'For someone you've never met, you sound pretty keen on defences.'

Rosie shut her mouth, looking down at the body bag.

'Unzip it.'

She did as the high priestess instructed.

'You'll hold her if she gets violent, yeah?'

Rosie nodded. The teeth of the zipper caught above

Meredith's ribs, exposing fragile, greying skin. If Rosie could be sick, she would have been. If she could still breathe, she would have held her breath to guard from the odour of decay. 'How long do you need her alive?'

Chaplain smiled for the first time all evening. Rosie wouldn't have thought too hard about it if it were not sickeningly *true*.

'However long it takes,' the coven leader said, 'to admit that her kid can raise the dead.'

CHAPTER TWELVE

Aurelia typed him a quick text, crouched on the tiles of the Heathrow Airport bathroom: *Just landed, see you soon xx.* She wiped her mouth of spit, stomach still turning.

She was definitely about to vomit again, anxiety and wet greens mixing in her stomach for a sour second taste that'd prove all her attempts to hold down the in-flight breakfast fruitless. Her priorities were elsewhere though, and she considered deleting the kisses at the end. Nervously, she sent the message, tucked her phone back into her pocket and her curls behind her ears, and poised herself over the seat again in anticipation of a reply.

Flying had never gotten easier for her; after the initial move, she made few attempts to return home, stretching the limits of her visa to breaking point. She kept herself bound to Cambridge, never too far from her institution or her jobs, close to her best friend and far from the airport.

Meredith's funeral had been an untimely exception.

Aurelia followed the tile grooves in meditation, counting them up to the ceiling. The disorientation stuck like mould to the bathroom wall. Her jaw felt loose and her body hollow. Sitting back on her haunches, she listened to the sound of final boarding calls and passenger pages from outside made fuzzy by her plugged ears. *One. Two.* Someone stumbled into the stall on her left hurriedly, slamming the door behind them.

The announcements outside ceased suddenly, leaving her with the echo of a clipped word. The shoes beneath her stall walls stilled, one shoe poised on its toe; and save for her own breath, the airport restroom became eerily quiet.

She swallowed down the unsavoury taste of bile and cleared her throat. For the sake of making some noise, she fumbled with the toilet paper dispenser. Had she fainted? Did the flight and the stress leave her delirious?

Aurelia flushed the toilet behind her and unlocked the door, expecting someone waiting in line to rush in and replace her. The woman in the queue stared, unblinking, slack-jawed and utterly still.

'Are you . . . all right?' asked Aurelia.

She had to be dreaming. She lifted her hand to the woman's face and pinched her cheek, a rush of panic climbing through her body.

Please say something.

'I was thinking—'

The words came from behind her. Aurelia gasped, pivoting to the source of a distinctly American voice. A head of silver blonde met her in the doorway of the stall, with wide blue eyes fixed right on Aurelia Schwartz.

'You're so jumpy,' said the woman. For a second, straining to collect her thoughts, Aurelia simply stared at her with her mouth agape, floundering between horror and disbelief. She had seen this woman once in her life, spoken with her for no longer than ten minutes – yet she had been followed to London, pinned with a terrifying blank gaze.

The turn of a card came to mind. Slate grey, silver text. In the firelight of Meredith Albert's funeral pyre, a name illuminated.

'There were only so many places I thought I could find you,' Chaplain said, smoothing stray blonde hairs back into her slick ponytail.

'You followed me?' Aurelia asked incredulously.

'I'd been thinking,' the woman began, 'since we met at Meredith's burning, that you were someone I should have recognized.'

No, Aurelia thought. *You shouldn't have.*

'In fact, I spent the next several days trying to figure out who you were. No one else in the coven remembered your name. At some point, I was resigned to believing that you were just . . .' Julia Chaplain took a confident step forward, until they were nearly face to face, save for the two inches of height she had on Aurelia Schwartz. From here, with the older coven leader's mouth pulled into a wicked smile, Aurelia could see the stain of lipstick on her teeth, the layers of crow's feet beside her eyes.

'Maybe you were just *lying,*' Chaplain finished. 'But why would someone lie about being Meredith's daughter? And not even the one we knew about. I ran questions past every one of my members about you, and none of them could tell me about Meredith's second daughter. Except—'

Aurelia's face fell despite her best efforts to remain a steel wall. Gabrielle would have known. Aurelia had grown up half under her care, following the path laid out by Gabrielle's magical practice. Even if years had passed, Gabrielle couldn't have forgotten her face.

She would have protected her. *That*, Aurelia knew with full certainty.

'I remembered something late one night; I lost a bit of sleep trying to solve the mystery of you, you know. That Meredith had *lost* a child. We all grieved with her, you see. We took care of her when Tony proved incapable of it.'

Aurelia's teeth clenched. She backed into the counter, the sink digging into her waist. 'I think you have the wrong person.'

'Would you swear by your mother's grimoire that you are not Aurelia Jean Schwartz?' Every piece of her name was damning evidence. Had it been Gabrielle that offered up her full name? Aurelia's father? Her own sister? She'd made the mistake of granting Julia Chaplain the first, unaware of the dark vision that plagued her birth, but she hadn't given her anything else. Maybe it was too late.

Chaplain's smile faltered piteously. 'You don't have to be nervous. It's just me.'

'Am I supposed to know who you are?' Aurelia asked. 'I think you've made a mistake about me . . . I think you've got the wrong idea.'

'You'd go against your own mother's claims?'

'What claims? Meredith Albert is dead,' Aurelia said, fear giving way to anger. Her heartbeat was in her ears, a spell beneath her etched palms.

'Not completely,' Chaplain answered.

'She *is*,' Aurelia replied, but the implication made her

shudder. 'I don't know what you're getting at, but if it's information about Meredith you want, I don't have anything. And that's the truth.'

'*She* gave me information about *you*,' the coven leader interrupted. 'Just not all of it. She's like you in that regard – very reserved.'

'Before she died?'

'Death is less exacting than you'd think, kid. It's certainly reversible. You could still talk to her, if you'd like. Give her a real goodbye.'

The restroom lights flickered once. Aurelia gripped the edge of the sink, and like a camera flash, she tried to sear the image of Julia Chaplain into her mind. Evidence. A souvenir to validate that this had ever happened.

She couldn't believe the coven leader's words. Meredith had abandoned her out of fear that the coven would covet her healer magic. To grant them access to her daughter now, after she'd died—

Death had washed Meredith Albert of the blame. What did it matter that the coven now knew of Aurelia's existence when she could not ask for her mother's help? For guidance?

She should have run. The spell teeming underneath her skin was waiting to be unleashed, but she suppressed it a moment longer out of a morbid curiosity. 'What did she say?'

Chaplain's face softened. Had her eyes not maintained that porcelain glaze, she would have appeared utterly endeared to the girl. Aurelia cursed her mother. Meredith had been a ghost for all her daughter's life. Was it not easy enough to let her prophecy die with her?

Chaplain offered the girl her pale, manicured hand and crooned, 'Let me show you.'

But all Aurelia could see was Leona Sum, extending her poisoned arm. Magic could pollute a person in more ways than through sabotaged blood oaths. A witch with one gift was just as susceptible to greed as one who had stolen several. Aurelia didn't trust this one not to carve her open and extract something just as precious as her magic from her. There was a sharp light in the blue of her eyes, a glassiness that Aurelia had only ever seen in porcelain dolls. An unreliable slant in her mouth.

Chaplain waited. Although, at some point, her patience became a taunt, as time was the most effective accomplice of doubt. Every passing second was a destruction of the coven leader's good faith.

'I don't think I have what you're looking for,' Aurelia said. She released the sink's edge from her steel-strong grip and started to move.

Toward her bag in the stall. Past the silver blonde witch. Their eyes held communion while she moved, never straying. The spell in Aurelia's heartlines promised her that she didn't have to be the hunted one. She could be just as dangerous. She could leave safely.

'She misses you, you know,' Chaplain said.

'She's *dead*.'

Chaplain tutted, shaking her head. The lights flickered again, and in that flash of darkness, Aurelia saw gold within the coven leader's hands.

She couldn't afford to wait and see what kind of magic was

brimming at the tips of Julia Chaplain's fingers. Aurelia struck first for good measure.

Yanked by the cross pendant hanging at her neck, Chaplain skittered back in shock, slamming into the sink. Glass broke behind her, the mirror shards lodged in place. In its slivered reflection, Aurelia could only see herself. Chaplain's shape flickered like the restroom lights as she wiped her cheek, pinning her attacker with a wrathful gaze.

Then, she vanished, just as her reflection had done long before. The woman in the queue reanimated like an unpaused film, blinking at the unexpected sight of an empty stall.

'We have to leave.' She grabbed Teddy's free hand and pulled him towards the exit. Louisa, who attached herself to his other hand, struggling to match their pace.

'What?' Teddy asked.

'Why are we running?' added Louisa.

The airport signage melted together in her mind. The announcements reverberated in Aurelia's bones. 'Where's the car? Did you drive?'

'Calm down, Schwartz,' said Teddy. 'Tell me what's wrong. Are you OK?'

The airport bustled around them. Rolling luggage clicked against tiles from every direction. People parted around them like they were stones in a riverbed. Too much noise, too many people – none of them Julia Chaplain. Where had she gone? Chaplain had come and left in the middle of a crowded restroom, seemingly out of nowhere. And for that impossible feat, Aurelia expected to see her reappear again and seek an ending to their conversation.

Teddy pulled her to a standstill, his hands loose around her elbow and Lou's shoulder. What could she say that didn't sound batshit crazy? She couldn't rationalize anything that had just occurred, but it terrified her. It terrified her enough that she couldn't allow herself a moment to pull herself out of the situation and think objectively. She wanted to go home. She wanted to go back to Vancouver. She wanted Teddy to stop looking at her like that. She wanted him to hide her beneath his wings again. He cupped her cheeks in his hands, and after just a few seconds of consideration, the realization trickled into his features.

Of course he could tell. His predisposition for her moods had always seemed so unfair, but she was begging him to let this unspoken fear of hers lead them away from the airport. To indicate to him just how wrong everything was and how imperative it was for them to leave.

'Not here,' she said. 'I promise I'll tell you everything.'

He looked downward and mouthed, *OK.* He cocked his head, leading her to the car park. He fumbled with his keys and unlocked his car. 'Get in, Lou.'

The girl did as she was told, and after she tugged the back door closed behind her, Teddy lowered his voice and returned his urgent gaze back to Aurelia.

'God, Schwartz, can you at least tell me if it's something *I* need to be worried about?'

'I don't know what's happening,' she lamented. 'I feel like I'm losing my mind right now, and I just spent a ten-hour flight without any sleep.'

She tugged the handle of the car door, but Teddy locked it again with the press of a button, locking Louisa in. He stared at Aurelia over the top of the car, his expression hard-edged and straight. Aurelia's gaze flickered around the car park, waiting for Chaplain's face to appear in another place she shouldn't have been.

Nothing.

'Look at me,' Teddy whispered. Her face was flushed and her hair a mess from the involuntary urge to pull it out of stress, but the worst of her panic happened unseen; and that was what he narrowed into. His eyes were wide and round but everything else was a hard line or a sharp corner. It took his sternness to level her, but once he had brought her back down to earth from that high-strung wire, he softened.

It started with a matched breath. A mirrored rhythm. Teddy braced himself on the other side of the car with his hand at the top edge of the door, and Aurelia watched the tension in his knuckles dissolve in a rush of colour. She watched his shoulders rise and fall with the rate of her own, then watched them slow incrementally. The worry was still bubbling up within her, but he had become the fixed variable now, which meant she'd become the mirror.

Her pulse slowed. After another deep breath, which broke whatever hypnotic tether bound them together in that moment, the tight line of his mouth snapped and he asked, 'Better?'

Her gaze darted around the car park, and she nodded. Despite the obvious possibility of Chaplain at her heels, Aurelia did, in fact, feel better.

So much better that her panic seemed redundant and

foolish. She tore her gaze away from his, though another question grew between them. What about Lou? Was Aurelia meant to sit passively in the car and say nothing, even when Louisa could tell something was wrong? Aurelia hadn't expected Lou to come, but why would she not? Ingram would always be bound to the Eakleys with a knot that Aurelia would never find the start to; and his loyalty to Louisa wasn't something Aurelia should be able to forget, however much she tried.

Sometimes, she even loved him more for it. But the reminder seemed to come whenever it was least convenient.

'She's OK,' Aurelia assured him. 'It's OK. I didn't realize . . . I don't know what I was thinking.'

Teddy shook his head. 'Just get in the car. We've got a long drive to talk.'

He unlocked the door, and Aurelia slid into the seat with an exhausted huff. 'To Townsend, right?'

He looked to Lou, who looked at both of them with a dull, bedraggled expression and whined, 'Teddy, my legs are hurting again.' He nodded, twisting his key in the ignition, and started the car.

Aurelia checked the mirrors, half expecting to see something staring back at her. A figure out of place. A woman with a bruised cheek. As Teddy navigated them out of the car park, Aurelia felt the immediacy of fear roll off her, and in its absence remained a question that rocked between them in the privacy of Teddy's car:

What did Meredith Albert leave me with?

CHAPTER THIRTEEN

Louisa's legs were draped over Teddy's lap, and he kneaded them dutifully while Schwartz sat on the bottom step of the staircase, ruminating on the findings of her mother's letter. He hadn't planned on discussing it until they were alone, but her recollection of the funeral in Vancouver and the encounter with Julia Chaplain in the toilets had left her shaken again, with all the panic he'd tried to soothe from her flooding back en masse. He'd spent the duration of the drive back to Townsend gripping the wheel with white knuckles, overcome by her panic and Lou's growing pains, so that he didn't think to turn on the music at all or make an attempt at more pleasant conversation.

Schwartz chewed on her cuticles viciously. Her eyes darted across an imaginary plane which Teddy knew she reserved for her puzzle pieces. She withdrew from his world whenever something unsettled her, fixing a solution together in her mind like shards of a broken vase. He wished he could see what she saw, but all he felt was her confusion. All he saw was the furl of her body, closed in around itself like a fist.

She perched her chin on folded arms and sighed heavily. Teddy loosened his jaw, trying against all odds to pluck his emotions out from the muddle of hers. He'd never been able to manage that task in school, the result of his failure a niggling reflection of her own annoyance. Why he'd thought his attempts might prove successful now, Teddy didn't know.

But he was hopeful. Always hopeful. He couldn't afford to let go of that hope for fear of dragging Louisa through the cracks with him. To lose it might prove disastrous for everyone in his wake.

Schwartz rose from the step just as Teddy opened his mouth to ask her a question, and she disappeared up the spiral staircase without as much as a *goodnight.*

Lou shifted slightly, bringing her wrist to her nose to wipe. Teddy leaned back into the couch cushions, exhausted and riddled with questions. At the forefront of his mind: why could he not shake this feeling of defeat? What game had he fallen victim to that made him feel as if he'd lost something? He felt, even with all the time that had passed since Leona set her sights on him, that he was back at the beginning, plagued by so many questions that he was completely and utterly helpless to stop anything. Back then, he'd turned to Gemma for some sense of normality, of peace; but now he was at the helm of the ship, forging ahead, with a storm pressing him from every direction.

At his side, Lou sniffled again, and Teddy realized she'd begun to cry. She pulled her knees to her chest and her legs off his lap.

'Lou, darling, what's the matter?'

She shook her head.

'Talk to me,' he said. 'What's going on?' Teddy leaned forward and held out his arms for her to fall into, which she did without protest. Her fists curled into the back of his shirt, sobs shaking her. He held her steady to his body, stroking her hair with a languid rhythm.

'You seemed so mad at me,' she said. 'In the car. Like you wish I never went with you. Did I do something wrong?'

'Mad at you?' Teddy shook his head, oblivious to where he'd gone wrong. 'God no. I could never be mad at you. You are my favourite person in the world. None of that was your fault.'

'But you looked so upset,' Lou said, hiccupping into his shoulder. 'And when I said – when I said that my legs were hurting, you just . . . I got the feeling you were angry.' The fact that she leaned on him even as she dreaded him was a painful, isolating thought. Who else did Louisa have but him? She deserved more, he knew. A proper guardian, one who knew what they were doing. One who had more time to reckon with the sacrifices of raising a child, and not some grumbling, ex-medievalist with faulty parentage of his own.

'I'm sorry,' was all that Teddy said to her. 'I wish that had never happened. It wasn't your fault. I promise.'

'But what about—'

He smoothed her baby hairs from her forehead and silenced her. 'It wasn't you. I don't want you to worry over this.'

She shrugged, her mouth still pulled into a quivering pout. 'Is Aurelia mad at me?'

Teddy smiled and shook his head. 'No one is mad at you, little bug. It's been a long night.'

She looked at him for a while without saying anything else, and Teddy wondered if he would have known what to say a year ago. He wondered if Lou would place so much weight on his moods, or if she would take after her mother and disregard them like passing gusts of wind.

Lou wiped her face quickly, her face still freckled with red; and she lifted her pinky between them as an offering, a habit she'd only donned after Schwartz's first visit to Townsend.

He hooked his own little finger gently around hers and gave her a smile, which she returned with some effort. He cradled the back of her head and pulled her forward to kiss her scalp. Although her nose was still stuffy, she made a light-hearted '*Ew,*' and laughed at him for the gesture.

Teddy felt as if he had only narrowly evaded something cataclysmic.

The incident came and went, and within minutes, she'd fallen asleep with her head lolled sideways against a decorative pillow. Teddy gathered her into his arms, which she protested against through unintelligible murmurs, and took her to her bedroom. Often, he had peered inside while passing by, made a mental note of its general untidiness, and left without further consideration. Perhaps it was a product of the dark and the blue left by the slats of her blinds, but he now saw a loneliness to the mess that he'd previously overlooked. Had it always been this way? Was there nothing he could do to give back what Gemma had taken on the day she disappeared?

Teddy pulled the quilt to her chin and brushed her hair from her neck, an old thought passing through his mind for the hundredth time. *Why did you go? Tell me what to do.*

But for Lou, he would have to be better and pray that *better* was, at least, enough to sate the growing pains.

*

The touch of another cold hand woke him up from his dream. He opened his eyes to the sight of an empty room and untucked sheets. Schwartz should be there – if not in his bed, making some noise in the kitchen or the adjacent bathroom. He grabbed his phone and checked the time. It was silent throughout the house. He pushed himself out of bed to check Lou's room out of paranoid habit, closed her door again, and checked the basement, only to see that all the lights were off, and Schwartz wasn't there.

He felt Schwartz's presence though, distant but undeniable; and he soon spotted her through the window beside the front door, crouched in the grass, her head nearly hidden behind the crest of the stalks.

He couldn't place the feeling behind her, but through the tether, he listened for the quickened pulse. It was calm for once, her mind sifting through thoughts with deliberate slowness. He lingered beside the couch, picking at one of Gemma's crocheted afghans, and considered returning to his room. Schwartz's peace was a rarity, one he valued enough to leave undisturbed.

In its periphery, Teddy felt comfortable and warm, not unlike the way he'd felt when Alaric's witch liquor had seeped into his system; and he wanted to be around her somehow, even if at a distance. To stay in her orbit closely enough that he could still feel her light on his surface. Maybe she'd tell him off for it. He could manage. Teddy slipped his boots and a pullover on, then left the cottage quietly.

Schwartz perked up at the sound of the latching door and gave him a soft smile that guaranteed his intrusion was a welcome one. 'Thought I could use some air,' she said. 'Sorry if I woke you.'

'You didn't,' he said, still hoarse from his own groggy slumber. 'Just thought I'd check on you.'

Schwartz shuffled aside in a wordless invitation for him to sit. Teddy hadn't heard her changing, but she'd slipped back into her jeans to save her skin from the rough ground. Most of the grass on the hillside had blanched from the heat and broken in places with some light pressure, but it still reached past their shoulders when they sat, thinning at the tops like the split ends of hair.

Her shoulder brushed the sleeve of his jumper as she shifted – undoubtedly an accident from the abrupt way she withdrew her arm. He wanted to follow, to tell her, *No, come closer.* A stray curl hung from her temple; he wanted to push it back, to tidy it ineffectively so that he'd have more reason to touch her again.

Yes, he thought, it was just like witch liquor. Perhaps far worse, his thoughts even less inhibited.

His magic wanted to lure him past the unspoken boundary of their relationship, a temptation that he'd been resisting for years with other people. Like a starved animal, it needed to feed, gravitating to those that couldn't hide well enough. As much as he tried, he couldn't ignore the loud whirr of Schwartz's head; but he tried nonetheless, to keep her from swaying him too much.

In a low, weary voice, she told him, 'I should go back to Cambridge soon. I keep thinking I know enough about magic and spell craft to know what comes next, but I never do. I can't hide from it every time something goes awry. I can't keep bringing my problems here. It's not fair to you and Lou.'

'I don't think it's unfair,' he replied. 'You were terrified, Schwartz. I've never seen you shaken. And I've seen you at knifepoint before.'

She shook her head and tied her arms around her knees like she could hold herself together. If she would let him, he'd do it for her. He'd been holding Gemma and Lou together for years; he was completely certain he could spare the effort for her too.

'Lou doesn't need to see me like this,' she said. 'If magic hasn't already become a tainted concept for her, I don't want to be the one who spoils it. I should have dealt with this myself.'

'You're being so hard on yourself for not shrugging this off, Schwartz, but that wasn't normal, what happened,' Teddy said sternly.

'I probably just needed time. I'm a big girl. I can take care of myself,' she argued. 'I've been doing it for years. I don't know why it's been impossible lately.'

The assurance was less for him and more for herself, but he couldn't understand why she worked so hard to discount what she saw at Heathrow. Knowing what she felt without knowing *why* was like playing a song through muscle memory without hearing the notes. He wanted to place it. He wanted to understand. But Schwartz was such a masterful study in contradiction, in multitudes, in layers, that Teddy didn't know if he could.

'I'm not sure why you're so adamant about being alone,' he said, more harshly than he'd intended to. For a while, she said nothing in response, and Teddy dug the heels of his boots into the hard dirt, considering an apology.

She broke off a few fragile blades of grass and started to fold them methodically. Teddy could sense her fingertips throbbing with the aftermath of over-bitten nails. 'Well, I'm not sure why you want to shoulder my problems so much,' she responded. 'No offence, Ingram, but you have enough here.'

'My concern doesn't just leave with you. It weighs on me every day. I need you to know that you can call me when things like this happen and not be so stubborn about letting me help you.' Teddy leaned back onto the heels of his hands, opening himself up to the night like a moonflower. 'I know you can take care of yourself, but you don't always have to. It's not a comment on your capability. It's a safeguard.'

Deep down, he knew it wasn't just Townsend that made him that way, but being there certainly helped mould him into a softer shape. It made him into a resting ground, a safe haven. He could be the sword in Aurelia Schwartz's grasp or the shield on her arm, and all she had to do was ask – he was malleable in her hands. He didn't expect her to treat him gently, but he prayed that she kept him intact.

It was better for both their sakes that she didn't see how much control she possessed over him.

Schwartz wiped her nose with her wrist, keeping her eyes on the ground. 'I wish you could have been there,' she mumbled. 'At the funeral, I mean. I saw my old tutor there.'

'Gabrielle?'

She nodded, smiling sadly. 'It's been so many years, but she still looks the same. I wish I'd said more to her before I left. I lose so much track of time trying to manage everything, and then I find myself back here, having said nothing that really matters.'

Teddy couldn't even remember the last thing he had said to Gemma, and the realization made his stomach wind into knots.

'She would have hated you,' Schwartz added with a laugh. 'Or at least, she would have acted like it. She used to tell me I got all the bad parts from my parents to make me angry, but they were always things like *resilience* and *curiosity*. Things that aren't really bad at all when you have enough self-restraint. It used to piss me off, but I miss it all the time. I wish I'd told her that.'

Teddy said nothing, breathing deeply in time with the dulled rhythm of her heartbeat. It had quickened slightly since he first sat down beside her, a few beats more per minute at most. His skin prickled at her closeness, his face warm and abuzz the way it had been in Alaric's library. The fact that he could still discover new things about his magic filled him with hope. Maybe then, he and Schwartz could come together over more than just their troubles. Maybe then, magic could be a good thing.

She angled herself towards him, the hollow of her cheek fitting to the hardest part of his shoulder. 'I've felt a lot of ways about my mother before, but I've never hated her so much until now,' she admitted. 'I don't know what to do with what she left me. God, Teddy, I'm so fucking scared. I thought I could just let her go – let *all* of this go.'

At that, Teddy slung his arm around her shoulder, clearing the last barrier between them. 'You don't have to go back yet,' he said. 'I meant it – you can stay here as long as you want. The wards are strong, and Alaric should be back tomorrow.'

'And then?' Schwartz asked. 'I can't stay here forever. What happens when Chaplain finds me walking to Pembroke or at my next job? What happens if she finds me in my flat, or – even worse – if she finds Ryan on their own and thinks they know something? I still think about how things might have been different if Marga knew I was a witch too, wondering if she might still be alive if she knew she had someone to talk to. I'm going to end up just like her, dead in a crowd of non-witches, and no one is going to bury me the way I want. I don't know what I'm supposed to do—'

She choked on her next words, tears welling in her shut eyes. Her hands curled into fists around her sweater, her collective figure curled even tighter. *Stay forever then*, he wanted to say. The impulse was there, eager on the tip of his tongue, but it was selfish, unwelcome. It'd be dangerous to hope for and rude to suggest.

'I'm sorry,' he whispered into her hair, not just for comfort but for absolution. Did it matter what his reasons were if all he wanted was to fix it for her?

Her body shook with her next breath, tucked into a small shape but hardened like stone. 'I've spent all night asking myself what I did to deserve this,' she confessed.

Curtly, he answered, 'Nothing.'

'I don't know. Maybe I forgot something,' Schwartz replied. 'Why else would these things keep chasing me?'

Teddy closed his eyes, heat gathering beneath his lids. 'In all my life, magic hasn't once been fair to me. I've asked myself that question every day since I was fifteen. It's not you,' he assured her. 'It wasn't me either. Some hardships you can never justify.'

But now, he asked himself if that was what he believed. Did he not shoulder the blame for Kenny's death by giving him the tool with which to end his own life? He could tell himself that Kenny would have found a way without him, if he was so desperate for relief. He could tell himself that death by human method would've absolved him of the sin. But could he ever *truly* convince himself?

Kenny followed him regardless. Those cold, silver hands still reached for his spine in the night to wake him, his first love's young, freckled face tightened in question: *Why am I still here? Can I not be freed?*

Schwartz's pulse echoed in his mind, the thought of magic in their veins present and torturous in his conscience. Even if he managed to convince himself that Kenny's death was not his fault, he never expected to feel the same urge from that first fateful night when he cut through his flesh and gave his blood for someone else. He loved differently now. He knew more. His principles and his priorities had grown with him, and nothing scared him more than to be the reason someone else died.

No, Teddy Ingram was not fifteen any more, but his love was still boundless. If he could not be more than his magic, he would make use of it in the only way that made sense – in defence of someone he cared for. Schwartz's hands unfurled just to find their grasp on his jumper; and for the first time, Teddy considered his gift in a more forgiving light. He opened his mouth, but the fear kept her name from being more than a confessional whisper on his tongue.

'Rory?'

She said nothing, but her head tilted upward slightly in

acknowledgement. In the dark, her eyes were black and mirror-like, her lashes full beneath a pulled-taut brow. The hand she had placed on his stomach slid to his chest warily, as if she half expected him to shrug her off. When he opened his mouth again, nothing came.

'I'm sorry. I shouldn't be laying all this on you,' she said quietly. 'I'm stressing you out. Your heart is pounding.'

'It's because you're touching me, Schwartz.'

With that reassurance, she moved her hand further until it curved around his shoulder. 'Do you ever wonder if it'd be easier not knowing me?'

'I used to. Sometimes, you'd look at me in the dining hall like you wanted to bite my head off. That, I could've done without,' he said. 'I'd rather you still hate me than imagine my life without you.'

She shook her head, but a smile crept along her lips, which she hid in the collar of his jumper. Teddy was painfully aware of all the places they touched, how quickly they found themselves wrapped around each other whenever they had a moment to themselves. Schwartz's breath warmed his skin as she muttered, 'I have to go back to Cambridge. I have to be fine on my own.'

Even if he knew the truth, Teddy let his mind wander. How far would they go if they had more time? What shape would she give him if she held him long enough? Sword, shield, or something else entirely?

If he offered her his magic, what other purpose would he serve?

With his heart in his stomach, he asked, 'How much would you give to know that you and your housemate would be safe?'

She shrugged. 'Anything. *Everything.* If it came down to it, I'd give my whole life for the people I love. You'd do the same for Lou, wouldn't you?'

'I'd kill for her,' Teddy said frankly. 'Would you do that for Ryan?'

Schwartz wiped the wet corners of her eyes with an exasperated sigh. 'Why are you asking me this?'

'Would you?' he repeated. When she didn't answer immediately, he added in a hushed tone, 'I'd do it for you, Schwartz. And I know that, at one point, you would have done it for me too. But when it came down to that before, you and I still had each other to call on.'

Teddy pried himself away from her nervously, baring the hand which still bore the scar from Leona Sum's knife. He offered it to her with his palm upturned and unfurled. She took it uncertainly, raising her brows in question.

'Let's say it gets to that point again and I'm not there . . . Let's say the call doesn't go through, or maybe I can't reach you in time. What do you do to keep yourself alive? To keep Ryan alive?'

Schwartz's gaze lowered to his palm in her hands. Her thumb trailed along his lifeline in meditation, and she answered him gravely without meeting his stare. 'Anything. I'd do anything for them.'

The rest went unspoken, but as easy as it was to decipher, the weight of it was unparalleled. After a minute of silence, of her averted gaze and accelerated pulse, Teddy murmured. 'You know I wouldn't offer you something like this lightly. This magic is irreversible, but it works when it's needed. And if you found yourself alone in a position where you needed it, I wouldn't be able to forgive myself for not letting you take it.'

'But you said—' With a small shake of her head, she dismissed the thought. 'Call me old-fashioned, but those oaths are supposed to mean something. It's not like trading one small favour for another. It's a vow.'

'You don't think I know that?'

She covered his palm with her own. 'It's not that I don't believe you. I think you'd find some way to give me the sun if you could. But this ritual is supposed to be *equal*, and I can't give you enough. Believe me, I'd try.'

'Is it not equal? My magic for yours – the principle is there.'

'It's not just about our magic though, is it?' Without any hangnails left to pick it, she drew her focus to his hand, toying with it mindlessly. 'It's a matter of partnership. Commitment.'

'And you don't want that,' Teddy said. She stifled a smile, a sliver of truth. An antithesis to her words from up above the Thames. He didn't know which hand to play: one for her feelings or one for what she said aloud to him. Could they be equally true?

He folded his fingers around hers and gambled with an answer, while his heart was already bared for her to see.

'We're allowed to have the things we want, Schwartz.'

She nodded, answering him gently. 'I can't afford to give you what you want. Not yet.'

Was he so transparent, even with his walls, that she could see how much of it was her? She peered back at the cottage as if their conversation had carried them farther away from it. But while Schwartz looked to the house for an anchor, Teddy looked to *her.* He charted the pattern of her curls and the crease beside her lips like they would one day lead him home.

Wherever that was.

He used to believe that place was Townsend, but now he wasn't so sure.

'Just think about it,' he said, rising with a creak from the grass like old furniture. 'And stay a while. Lou likes having you around.'

'Where are you going?'

'Back to bed. I don't particularly enjoy being awake at this hour. Are you staying?'

'Just for a few more minutes, I think. I'll come in soon.'

She raised her hand, catching him before he could leave. Her thumb slid delicately over his knuckles, fingers around the palm that held the knife's scar. If she wanted him to stay, she didn't voice it, but he could feel another inclination lurking within her. To ask for something. To confess.

Whatever it was, she left it unsaid. 'Goodnight, Ingram.'

He offered her a small, lazy smile, and raised her knuckles to his lips. 'Goodnight.'

CHAPTER FOURTEEN

Lou was rambling in the distance, hidden somewhere in the grass. Teddy spotted Schwartz's dark curls before anything else, peeking through the curtain of faded green as she flipped from her stomach into an upward sitting position. She took something from Louisa, and they traded in hushed conversation, oblivious to Teddy's presence at the front door.

He'd spent the morning trying not to think of what he'd said to Schwartz the previous night in that same spot, cycling between a fear of her rejection and a fear of her acceptance. He had meant it last night, wholeheartedly. The way she'd looked at him had been enigmatic, and he couldn't help mentally chastising himself for sharing so much. He also couldn't blame her for rejecting his magic, but he still wondered if it was a rejection of him too.

The two girls turned to face him as he crunched through the grass. Lou twisted onto her knees, a folded paper shape wedged between her fingers. 'Aurelia's been teaching me how to fold.'

Schwartz pushed a pair of black sunglasses up her nose and leaned back onto the quilted blanket she'd snatched from the cottage. She opened her book to the place where she'd slotted an old receipt and asked, 'Are you going somewhere?'

'To the shop,' he replied, turning Lou's paper lily flower in his hands. Schwartz had stressed the importance of sharp edges to her. He pictured Schwartz's jittering, chewed-up fingertips pressed tight around the folds in demonstration. Keeping her lines even and her corners pointed. He imagined her curling the petals of the flower over her knuckles meticulously, then passing it to Lou with an encouragement: *Your turn.*

Teddy gave it back to Louisa with a smile, and as he raised his fingers to pass them through her mushroom brown hair, he found it combed back and secured into two neat plaits.

'You braided it yourself,' Teddy murmured.

'No,' Lou said. 'Aurelia did that too.'

He gave one of her braids a soft tug. 'Hmm.'

Schwartz shut the book and sighed almost petulantly, holding it over her face to shield the sunlight. She exuded summer in the best possible way, radiant and freckled in copper. 'Is that a problem?'

He shrugged and tore his gaze away. 'I usually do it, is all. Looks nice.'

Schwartz's nose wrinkled up at him. 'I know.'

But something within his chest squeezed, and he kept his gaze elsewhere. 'You can fetch your mother's bird, if you'd like.'

She eyed him blankly for a second, the directness of her stare stifled by the dark lenses of her sunglasses. He felt its weight intensely, noting the way the arms of her sunglasses pressed her temples at a place he'd longed to kiss. She turned to

Lou and asked her something that Teddy couldn't hear, which made the girl chuckle.

'I'll swing by in a few minutes,' Schwartz told him passively. 'I need a refill for this.' She gestured to the tipped-over mug of tea she'd emptied just before he arrived, on which Louisa had painted a swirl of leaves and left a subtle thumbprint in the same shade of green.

The girl rose to her feet beside her and handed him another shape. A bird. A pattern more intricate than the crane he'd learned to make. Lou added, 'She's going to teach me this one next.'

'Maybe tonight?' Schwartz said.

'When you get back,' Lou replied.

Teddy placed the bird on the blanket next to her, and lingered, bowed over Schwartz's head, to trail his thumb along her cheek before he left for the shop. 'Maybe you could teach me, too.'

He fumbled with his sparse ring of keys for a moment as he neared the storefront, pausing briefly to wipe a finger through the thin layer of grime on the window. He pursed his lips in disapproval, catching a small movement in the reflection.

Schwartz's paper bird hovered above his shoulders, its wings flapping rigidly. It cocked its head and surveyed him as if sentient – and *curious*. On its belly, a line of ink crept out that Teddy hadn't seen before in his study. He plucked it from mid-air, cast a wary glance around the street for unseen passers-by, then began to peel it apart. At his touch, the creature stilled, and he wondered if he'd ruined it. He couldn't help but ask himself if unfolding the crease at its neck was akin to a slaughter.

He nudged the door with his hip and flicked the lights on with his elbow.

I tried to thank you for that copy of Sir Gawain and the Green Knight, but I don't think my letter got to you. It's taken up a permanent residence on my desk next to where I sleep and makes me think of you constantly.

So, thanks for that. Again.

– Aurelia

He smiled to himself, studying the creases he'd just undone, and muttered to the empty shop, 'Not so sharp after all, Schwartz.'

Something in the basement shuffled.

'Al?' he asked, pocketing the note quickly. 'Is that you?'

An array of footsteps sounded from the same direction, but it was distant. Even from outside the basement, Teddy should have heard more. As it was, he found himself questioning whether he'd heard anything at all.

Then a voice broke through, garbled and soft as if speaking underwater, *suffocating*. It had to be coming from the library, a place Teddy couldn't reach without the caretaker's magic. Whoever it was needed to lower their voice or leave entirely. Surely, they knew how thin the veil was between this place and the other. Why else would Alaric have welcomed them in?

Teddy rounded the desk and combed through the drawers

for Alaric's suppressants. Had he taken them? Was it the council in Alaric's library, bickering amongst themselves again? Such veils wouldn't hinder them if their matters were important enough; at least, Teddy assured himself they must have been important. It eased his conscience to think of Alaric as a hero rather than a serial deserter. If he left out of selflessness, Teddy might be able to forgive the long stretches of time in which Lou asked for him and the caretaker couldn't answer.

With a soft shudder, the veil parted and sent through a solid being.

'Who the hell are you?'

The man's head swivelled towards Teddy with unabashed shock. He gripped the rail of the basement steps, dizzy from crossing the divide, as if he hadn't fully intended to in the first place.

Teddy slammed the drawers shut, his hands braced on his hips as the man struggled for an answer. The stranger's hair was shorn close to his scalp, his dark skin aglow beneath the flickering light of the shop basement. His mouth opened. Then shut. Teddy straightened his back and cleared his throat – this wasn't the place for another person with non-responses.

Behind him, Hye-Jin clambered out from wherever he'd just come from. The man looked to her in question; and with the field set two-to-one, Teddy met Hye-Jin as if she were an opponent. 'Where's Al?' asked Teddy. 'Do you know this man?'

'Ah,' she said, pushing past the man assuredly. 'I didn't expect to see you here.'

'Has he not told you that I run this place in his absence?'

'Only when he's absent,' Hye-Jin answered curtly. Teddy's

teeth tightened in irritation. If Alaric wasn't absent, why wasn't he at the shop with them? Hye-Jin had said it so matter-of-factly that it made Teddy feel like a fool, even if there was no evidence of Alaric's presence.

Teddy gestured to the man belligerently. 'And you are?'

With his hand held to his chest, he began, 'Sorry, I'm—'

'A friend of ours,' Hye-Jin interjected, ignoring Teddy's tight-lipped frown in favour of the unnamed guest. She placed her hand on his shoulder and gave it a firm, warning squeeze. 'Might be in your best interest to find him.'

Something long forgotten and ignored resurfaced in Teddy's mind. 'You're Carmichael, aren't you?'

The recognition was clear. The man looked past Hye-Jin's figure and swallowed nervously. Another witch, Teddy reasoned. Why else would he be allowed to pass through the caretaker's rooms at all? Teddy could only speculate as to why Alaric wouldn't let him pass through too.

'So, he's told you about me?' the man, Carmichael, asked.

Hye-Jin snapped back to Teddy, wondering the same, but it'd been her mouth from which the name initially slipped out, and she'd been silenced by Alaric promptly afterwards.

The remembrance made her uneasy. Teddy's mind was thrumming with a hundred thoughts that weren't his own – thoughts from Hye-Jin and Carmichael, of fear and hesitation. Hye-Jin moved herself between them, approaching Teddy with a needless caution as if he might launch himself at her like a violent dog.

He took a step backwards, his hands grasping one another for stillness.

Begrudgingly, Hye-Jin noted, 'Alaric was meant to be the one to talk to you.'

'What discussion was there to have?' Teddy's skin prickled, and he couldn't tell whose fear had triggered it. 'Where's Alaric?'

'Just behind us,' she said. 'Maybe, you could give us a second?'

Teddy peered over Hye-Jin's head, his gaze landing on the man's right sleeve. A spot of blood bloomed at his elbow, freckling his henley shirt. Following the boy's line of sight, Carmichael crossed his arms sheepishly, obscuring the spots from view.

'He's *bleeding,*' Teddy whispered. 'Why is he bleeding?'

'We were running some tests,' Hye-Jin answered. 'A matter of medicine.'

'You're taking witch's blood?'

Schwartz's steps were heavy outside the shop, and Teddy caught her shape in the glare of the dust-covered window; a pause to adjust the cuff of her jeans, then a mildly inconvenienced curse beneath her breath. Teddy took his eyes off Hye-Jin to meet her at the door, but the caretaker of Namwon acted fast.

One misstep cast him straight into the library, where a lamp clipped his knee hard. The shop door and the girl standing behind it disappeared, with only the muffled sound of her footsteps entering the shop leaking through the transportive enchantment.

Teddy staggered back defensively, facing the others with rage written plain on his face. Beyond the tall shelves of the library, he saw Alaric rise from a crouch and race towards them as he doubled over and clutched his kneecap.

'What are you doing here?' Alaric demanded.

'What am *I* doing here? Manning your fucking shop, that's what,' Teddy said, shrugging off Alaric's outstretched hand. 'Why's your friend bleeding?'

The caretaker's face drained of its colour. His dark eyes widened at the sight of Carmichael, but he said nothing.

He reached for Teddy again, softening at the edges; but if Hye-Jin reached for him in fear, Alaric did it with pity. Neither was enjoyable.

'You're all so damn cagey about everything,' Teddy hissed. 'You tell me nothing and treat me like an intruder.'

'What happened?'

Teddy swatted his hand away again. 'You tell me. Who is he? Hye-Jin mentioned him last time and you never spoke a word of him again. Am I not supposed to wonder why he's shown up at your shop with blood on his arm and nothing to say?'

Alaric pulled him away roughly with a force befitting someone younger and more agile. The caretaker whispered to him gravely, out of the others' earshot. 'Understand me first, Teddy. There is no friend of mine that isn't a friend to you. I trust this man. I trust Hye-Jin. But there are things I prefer to tell you myself. I can explain if you just let me.'

Voices from this end of the portal were equally as unintelligible. Teddy could hear Schwartz entering the shop, but that place had been sealed behind a locked door, a drawn curtain.

'She came for Meredith's letter,' Teddy explained.

'She's here?' Alaric's expression hardened once more. 'Now?'

'If you have some issue with us being here, let me at least give her the letter and send her off.' Teddy wasn't sure if that option was the better of the two he had in his mind, but it was something. What he wanted was for Alaric to get his hands off him, for he held him like a punished child, the boy once made to kneel in the chapel and atone. 'I'll leave you and your friends to whatever fun I just interrupted.'

Alaric grabbed him again, this time around his wrists.

The bangles closed around him; and after the sum of all their energy fell away, Teddy was left baffled and furious.

'Calm yourself.'

'Take these off me.'

'You're not thinking clearly. We need to talk first.'

Teddy ripped his hands from the caretaker's grasp. 'In these?' he shouted. 'You and your *dear* council . . . Do any of you talk before you resort to this?'

'Teddy, this is Carmichael Sum,' Alaric said then. 'You might recall meeting his wife a while ago.'

At that, the man beside Hye-Jin stiffened, offering them a benevolent smile. Teddy's eyes darted to the spot on his arm, thrust back into that room of the Tate Modern.

The knifepoint in his vein.

Leona's arm, laced in black. *He wants me dead,* she'd said. Just before she'd thrown her knife into Teddy's wings.

Through his clenched jaw, Teddy hissed, 'Why is he here? Giving you his blood?'

'It isn't what you think.'

'Tell me what you think that is, Friedman. Should I be relieved to see him here? After everything Leona put us through? Could you be any more shameless than to bring him here after what she did to us?'

'Do you remember what I said to you the other day?' Teddy didn't need his magic to know that Alaric was desperate for him to understand. 'About the fact that our kind is facing imminent extinction. I can't stress to you enough how dire the circumstances have become, but we're searching for solutions everywhere we can possibly find them.'

'And you think Leona Sum had the right answer.'

Carmichael answered first, his voice wavering with uncertainty. 'Lee's ethics and mine are completely incomparable, but that doesn't mean we didn't want the same thing at some point. We wanted *children*. We wanted them to have a future where they could flourish and thrive without the need to tread so lightly. In most cases, witches like us are allowed one misstep; and if it's large enough, we wind up dead. Or alone. You grow up believing that humans and us are mostly one and the same until you light a fire for someone without a match on a cold night and they never speak to you again. That terrifies me.'

'I didn't ask you,' Teddy said.

Alaric grabbed Teddy's face and turned it toward him. He pronounced every word severely, his fingers tight around Teddy's jaw. 'He is trying to help us.'

As if Teddy didn't know what it was like to be cast away like vermin. As if he hadn't seen it from both angles . . . The day that Louisa's bullies had pushed her to a breaking point, her teacher had found her locked inside a classroom closet, skirt wetted through from the sheer hours that had passed where no teacher had come to use that room. Teddy had excused himself from a lecture to take the call from her school and left shortly after. He spent the drive rehearsing every point he'd make to Gemma about having a phone of her own and being accessible to her daughter, but seeing Lou in a change of loaned clothing, walking to his car with swollen eyes and a splotchy red face covered that urge completely. She'd been six years old then, already shunned by her peers over something so trivial and meaningless.

And what she needed wasn't his anger. It was safety – *community*. A warm hug. She cried in the car while he drove her home and fell asleep in his arms as he carried her up the hill; and when Gemma opened the door to them, stunned by their untimely presence, he said nothing for Louisa's sake. She deserved a pleasant dream. A quiet house.

Deep down, Teddy knew he wouldn't have been such a fucked-up teenager if he had grown up with magical parents. If there had been more guidance, more answers. He had been messing up massively and searching for ways to make amends, but nothing ever seemed sufficient; and so, he relied on the few witches he knew to grant him forgiveness for the things he'd done. It was hard enough to ask Gemma to forgive him for her son's death without knowing that no one else ever would. *Look what they did to Lou*, he would think, whose magic would leave only a fraction of the impression that his did.

Alaric cleared his throat. 'I have never doubted your capacity for understanding, but you must see now why I didn't tell you about this before.'

Carmichael toyed with his sleeve nervously. 'This work is important to me,' he added. 'And unlike my wife, I want to conduct it as ethically as possible.'

'She didn't know, did she?' asked Teddy. 'That you can't take witch's blood without consent or else it'd be corrupted.'

The shapeshifter nodded. 'I caught her malevolent streak after it was too late. Telling her then wouldn't have killed her longing for magic. It would have only made her more effective. But I think about it every day – what might have happened if she knew better. Maybe she wouldn't have succumbed to the influence of poisoned magic.'

Teddy shook his head, more aware of the bronze bangles around his wrists than ever. They weighed him down, and he felt a low vibration all the way in his bones from the suppression of his magic. What was there, begging to be set loose? He knew it was likely to be his empathetic gift, yearning to reach the shapeshifter and weigh the validity of his answer, but the ever-present fear of death magic was still there. He'd never know. *That* terrified him.

'I'm sure you're grieving,' said Teddy, 'but I have no interest in humouring wishful thoughts about the woman who threatened my family and friends' safety. Whatever she was at first is not what I saw. And I will never forgive her for putting my loved ones at risk.'

Carmichael nodded once, keeping his eyes on the ground between them. 'I know.'

'I think it's best that I leave.'

Alaric's jaw tensed beneath his stubble. He pushed his glasses up his nose with his knuckle and mumbled, 'Right. I'll see you out. Just a second.' The caretaker's hand shot out to Teddy's wrist and clasped it over the bangle. The contact burned him like a flint sparking in the breeze.

Alaric led him into a room in the back of the library, in which an assortment of scientific notes was scattered across tabletops and discarded into bins. Alaric flipped the lock on the door without touching it, and whorled on Teddy in a way that the boy's mouth tasted like iron.

'You don't need to shove me out so quickly,' Teddy said through gritted teeth. 'I'm not a time bomb. Nor am I a child. I can use restraint.' He pried the bangles open with his fingers and thrust them into Alaric's hand.

'You're not above needing these on,' the caretaker said. 'The proper trigger can push any witch into releasing something they aren't prepared for. It's not about you. It's about your magic.'

'Because I am not more than my magic,' Teddy answered searingly. 'Because despite everything I've made of myself and everything I've done to take care of Lou, I'll never be more than a reaper. Is that it?'

Perhaps they were still too close to the others to be heard, even behind this door. Alaric sent the shop shelves up in a burst of magic behind them. Teddy flinched in spite of himself at the thunderous crack of wood, at the sudden exile from Alaric's library. He was in the shop again. More importantly, he wasn't faced with Alaric's secretive companions any more.

At the shop counter, Alaric slammed the bangles down, and the culmination of the caretaker's frustration swarmed him instantaneously.

Schwartz trotted out from behind a shelf, two books in her hand and an unsuspecting ambivalence in her smile.

Teddy averted his gaze. 'Give me the letter.'

The caretaker sighed and turned ruefully towards the basement to retrieve it.

Schwartz's hand curled around the top of his shoulder where Hye-Jin had grabbed him earlier; and although her touch was impossibly soft, Teddy couldn't help but twitch.

'Everything OK?' Schwartz asked.

He looked at the books in her hands so he wouldn't have to face her when he lied. 'Smashing.'

Her frown carved itself deep. The caretaker returned with an envelope in his hand, which Teddy took wordlessly and stuffed into his pocket.

'Can we talk about this sometime?' Alaric asked. 'Privately?'

Teddy grabbed Schwartz's hand and made them indivisible. 'You should have talked to me at the beginning. You forget who's been doing all your housekeeping, Friedman.'

'Not everything is about you.'

'And that gives you an excuse to exclude me altogether?' Teddy pressed. 'Come up with something better in the meantime. I'm going home.'

Schwartz didn't speak to him. She'd blanched at the mere mention of Leona's cohorts in their midst, and though she hid it admirably, she couldn't shake the dread that filled her body. He could see her looking for the words, for the courage, for reassurance that her nightmares were still just nightmares and that Leona would not find her again.

She looked but found nothing.

Teddy asked Lou for help with dinner to ease the strain emanating off Schwartz while she was left to consider. 'Cut these for me.'

Lou did as he asked; and though Schwartz had said nothing aloud to either of them about it, Lou looked over her shoulder at the girl sitting on the steps after every second slice.

'Careful, Lou.'

'Sorry,' she said, returning her attention to the halved yellow potatoes. 'Can we have a dessert tonight too?'

'What would you like?'

'Some ice cream, maybe – *Ow!*'

Teddy saw the blade slip fast and raced to seize it from her hands. Schwartz's head swivelled at the exclamation, poised to leave her seat at the step.

'Christ, Lou,' Teddy hissed. 'What did I just tell you?' The knife clattered across the tile countertop. He grasped her hand before she could bring it to her mouth and seal the wound with her spit. She'd hardly nicked herself; a spot of blood bloomed in the crease between her thumb and her palm that would be likely to close on its own within minutes. Behind their clasped hands, Lou stared up at him timidly. If anything could scare her, it was his intensity.

He loosened his grip in a silent apology just as Schwartz made her way to the kitchen and asked them to trade: a hand for a hand. He relinquished it wordlessly. Schwartz examined the mark, wiping it clean with a folded napkin before muttering a word beneath her breath that fixed the skin back together. 'Just a scratch.'

She pinned Teddy with a glare that levelled him in seconds. He made an effort to unclench his jaw, turning towards the ingredients on the hob for a distraction.

Schwartz retreated to the steps without another word, leaving Lou in the kitchen without anything else to do.

What was he thinking, giving her a knife like that? He could lose sight of her age and her limitations so easily – who else would tell him he was wrong? 'Go and wait downstairs for me, little bug.'

'Are you mad at me?'

He shook his head. 'Of course not. Everything's fine if you're fine, all right? Take this.'

Her faint brows tightened at the sight of the salt and pepper shakers. She snatched them from his hand begrudgingly, turning them over while she passed Schwartz on the top step.

He heard her whisper something to Schwartz under her breath and eyed them both in his periphery. Schwartz made herself receptive, straightening her back and pushing her hair behind her ears like clockwork; he'd seen her spring to life from the corner of the lecture hall whenever a fact caught her fancy.

Lou granted her a secret with her whisper that Teddy wasn't allowed to know. He stirred his pan of vegetables with his tongue pressed to his cheek, wishing he knew, painfully aware of the bright smile that Lou had planted on Schwartz's face.

Jealousy, he knew, wouldn't give him satisfaction, but that never deterred any mind from wondering. He'd spent months repairing their peace to a durable state, but Lou's smile was still a sparse uncertainty. She gave it so freely to Schwartz and

Alaric that Teddy wondered what more he could've done to earn it too.

Haven't I done enough?

He should be grateful. How much of that joy would Schwartz take with her when she left – not just from Lou but from himself?

He couldn't carry the weight with half a heart.

CHAPTER FIFTEEN

Carmichael Sum had been plagued by a similar thought long before his wife had died. She'd crushed the stolen piece of his heart with the first kill – the first step towards her vicious demise. Could he have asked for it back if he'd known earlier how cruel she would become? Would it have made anything easier?

The price of her stolen magic was temporality. Her health dwindled in small increments every day, leaking from her like air in a punctured raft. She'd plucked the spoiled fruit and now its rottenness blackened her mouth. What was left at the end resembled a monster.

Ji Hye-Jin cleared her throat, willing the other caretaker to speak once he'd returned to the library, but no one cared to press him further. Carmichael lifted his sleeve where a small bandage had been soaked through. His blood didn't clot easily; he cursed it for more reasons than that though. Hye-Jin clucked her tongue and left to retrieve a small jar of terracotta orange salve from a room upstairs. Carmichael bit his tongue and left Alaric Friedman to his pondering.

It hadn't occurred to him that Leona's victims would know his name.

He assumed they had all been murdered.

Of course, the leftovers – the witnesses – would live on with her image scarred into their minds, but who was he except another victim? The woman he'd once loved had become his tyrant – Carmichael, the mere gum beneath her shoe. He had given so much to her, both willingly and by force. More than his heart, but his dreams and his care.

No one would have understood it before Alaric Friedman, for he had been the first to listen, and consequently the first he'd asked for forgiveness. Could he blame any of them for where their minds wandered first? How could you punish a tyrant who'd once offered you their heart? Let you eat from their hands, wind your fists around their hair – given you everything?

He knew he couldn't blame the boy, but the hatred in his eyes struck him with an unprecedented force.

When Hye-Jin returned, she removed his bandage, swiped her fingers through the familiar salve, and spread it over the wound. 'I should remember by now,' she said as a means of an apology. This was the third sample they'd asked him for, the third time Hye-Jin left the salve out of reach while his wound struggled to close. Carmichael smiled timidly, trying to shake the fear festering in the back of his mind.

Theodore Ingram was only a boy. Not much older than he'd been on the day Leona had met him. Had it been his fault back then, when they were still young and driven by a great dream? Had they been doomed from the beginning?

Hye-Jin rolled the sleeve back over his arm. Alaric stalked forward, his footsteps noiseless and light. 'Give him time.'

Hye-Jin turned to where he stood above them. 'We don't have time.'

'We have enough,' Alaric said, scanning Carmichael's slouched figure intensely. 'You'll have to forgive him. He's rash, but he means well.'

'Leash him, if you have to,' scorned Hye-Jin. 'He's got the temper of an unfixed cat, not the makings of—'

'Gemma's disappearance rattled us all,' Alaric said sharply. 'And I haven't been gentle enough with him lately.'

Hye-Jin gave a displeased *hmph* and rose from the couch to grab her apothecary satchel, where a small vial of Carmichael's magical blood was secured under a wide leather strap. 'Our days are scarcer than ever, Friedman. It'd serve us all well for him to at least *try* to get along with Carmichael. Otherwise, what's the point? Save our skins just so someone else can flay them? I'm going home now. I have enough on my plate without him to worry about. Goodnight, Al. *Carmichael.*'

'Goodnight,' Carmichael answered.

Alaric pressed his lips together in disdain, scraping his stubble with a sun-spotted hand. Only after Hye-Jin closed the portal door to her collection behind her did Alaric's gaze shift to Carmichael.

They looked at each other for what felt like minutes, waiting for the other to speak. Not unlike the first time they'd met. The caretaker had found him on the floor in his flat, half-conscious and choking on his own saliva, minutes away but still too far from death. Carmichael had reached for his arm, unable to speak; and to his surprise, the stranger in his flat had reached back.

He'd looked like an angel. Carmichael didn't know if the stranger had come to save his life or lead him to his judgement. By then, he didn't know what the gods would make of him. They would have seen his silence and his passivity as a weapon just as fatal as his wife's blade and damned him to eternal suffering.

If only he'd been allowed to die.

'I *am* sorry,' Carmichael offered. 'I never wanted to see her go so far.'

'I know,' said Alaric.

'I didn't think I would be able to forgive myself if I'd been the one to stop her.'

To kill her.

The option had certainly come to mind.

No, he couldn't have killed his partner. Couldn't bring the pillow to her mouth while she slept to cease the torment. She had loved him once; and when they spoke of a world where witches like themselves lived freely, they'd traded their dreams in loving whispers, fitted beside each other in a shared bed.

No, he couldn't have been the one to kill her.

Alaric tapped the underside of Carmichael's chin with his hooked forefinger. 'What's done is done. Can't fix it if you're preoccupied with feeling guilty.'

'What if we can't fix it? What if some ignorance is unforgivable?'

Alaric's hand lingered between them, and Carmichael surrendered to the urge to tilt his head against it, repentant. Carmichael assured himself time and time again that he was, at least, a *better* man for letting Leona destroy herself instead of doing it for her. It was pointless, delusional, and altogether unimportant in the wake of her death, but he might have been able to forgive himself if he believed it.

For Alaric's sake, he needed to convince the boy of it too.

CHAPTER SIXTEEN

Schwartz folded her mother's letter into a small rectangle, then unfolded it, ignoring the book that rested in the bend of her stomach. 'She asked if I was safe?' Her head shifted in his lap. Teddy released the strand of her hair that he'd been toying with and let it crest her cheek.

'Among other things,' he said, though she didn't ask what those things were. *Is she loved?* Earnestly, he thought, even if he'd never told her. His thumb followed the curl along her cheek, coming to rest beside her jaw. 'Are you doubtful?'

She sighed, turning her cheek into his lap again. 'I don't see why she cares. All these years and she hasn't given a shit until now. It's insulting.'

He didn't bother reiterating that the version of Meredith he'd spoken to was made of paper. She lacked maternal comfort without flesh and blood. If anything, the creature that bloomed from the words in her letter was nightmarish and predatory. Her creases were the sharpest he'd ever seen.

'If she was so concerned, she should have told me herself,' Schwartz muttered. 'I've given up more than enough time to grieve for her. For what? To be your runner-up? Why should she trust *you*?'

Resentment dripped from every word. Teddy hadn't asked to see Meredith. He could only speculate as to what she latched onto when they'd first opened the letter in the basement. He'd shared some of Schwartz's grief but not in any capacity to which hers was comparable. Aside from Kenny, most of his grief took the form of a question mark.

She pushed herself from his lap, sitting upright beside his knees. 'Sorry,' she muttered, almost begrudgingly. 'I shouldn't have said that.'

Teddy wondered if he'd misheard. A timid, apologetic Aurelia Schwartz was a sight out of what used to be his wildest dreams – where her rage was an uncontrolled flame in need of dousing, and her words were needlessly cruel.

In any other circumstance, he might have cared less. He might have even breathed a sigh of relief to know she cared about his feelings.

He capped a pen in his other hand and discarded it onto the table. Schwartz watched him through the slits of her fingers while she kneaded her brows. Meredith's passing had smothered her spark so completely that she crumpled like a cigarette beneath one's boot.

They'd spent the past few days cycling through comfort and estrangement, with touches that lingered much longer than they should have, until they were forced to face the question, 'What's next?' And they would slither back to a safe distance from one another, one that hurt less to break apart when the inevitable separation came. Tonight, with her head in his lap, the question loomed like a taunt. How could he touch her? How much could he say to ease the strain without saying something that damned them?

'If I were you,' he began, 'I'd feel just as angry. It angers me anyway . . . All this speculation. These *questions*. I'd like for someone to give me a proper answer, just once, instead of giving me a riddle.'

She sat close enough to kiss, her shoulder against his, her eyes flickering to his mouth. He felt the feeling surge up inside of her then get smothered down. She tilted her forehead onto his shoulder. 'I wish it was just anger. Half the time, I don't know what to feel. How can I miss her so much if I don't even remember her?'

'You mourn the possibility,' he said.

'It'd be easier if she hadn't thought of me at all,' Schwartz said. The tip of her nose grazed the place where her brow had just laid, burning through his shirt and skin and all the way to his bones. 'If we'd just stayed strangers.'

But would Meredith's warning still prove necessary? Schwartz had gone to the burning anyway, stood beside her sister and Julia Chaplain, and inadvertently made herself a target. Whatever curse her mother had passed down still hung like a noose around Schwartz's neck.

If anything, Meredith needed to say more.

'Did you check the envelope?' Schwartz asked. 'He gave us Gem's letter too.'

Teddy's chest squeezed. 'Did he now . . .'

She grabbed it from the table and extracted another page. Under Alaric's care, the ink had smeared in new places. Had he looked at it often, searching for a new mark as vehemently as

Teddy had? How many corners could one overturn in a single page? They'd exhausted each possible clue.

And still, *nothing*.

Teddy took the page and turned it in his hands, deep in consideration. As if she could see the clockwork ticking in his mind, Schwartz added, 'We should wait for him.'

He traced the augur's words, the blurred blue patches of ink. 'I am so tired of waiting.'

For Gemma, for Alaric, for *her*.

The possibility of his life was passing him by with every second of inaction.

'We should try,' he said.

'And if nothing happens?' Schwartz kept her gaze steady, withholding any optimism from him, but he could feel her wanting – her hope. As much as he wanted to bring Gemma home for her daughter's sake, he wanted to prove to Aurelia Schwartz that the affirmation he'd given her was true.

We're allowed to have the things we want.

'Then we keep trying,' Teddy said. 'What's the worst that could happen? I'll lose nothing but a little of my pride. I'm already here with Lou. I can't undo anything that's already been done. But if I can just . . . I dunno. If there's a chance that I can bring Gem home, I'm going to take it. It's worth the effort.'

For all the undeserved grace that Gemma had given him, Teddy couldn't say with certainty that she would have made the same effort had he been the one to disappear. He suspected, thinking back to the character she'd made of him within her old grimoires, that Gemma might have even been relieved to have him gone. Then, she wouldn't have to wonder how long it'd be until he showed up unannounced again, polluting her sterile home with human ideology and dark, untethered magic.

But maybe, just maybe, they'd surpassed a need for his repentance. Had he not made himself obedient enough? Had he not surrendered enough of his devotion to her words that she wouldn't wait for him to make things right before deciding on her own that leaving was the answer? He could see her watching from the steps of her front door, hands braced on her hips, a smile growing on her face at the realization that he'd arrived. That he had found his way back home. And Teddy clung to that hope just like all the others – out of desperation.

She always faded like another spirit passing through.

Schwartz took the letter from his hand as if it were already a bird; delicate like a chick, tender like a beating heart. 'I don't think you'll ever stop bewildering me, y'know.'

'I'm quite straightforward.'

She snorted softly. 'Not really. You have, at least, one direct line to whatever it is I'm feeling. I have none. You're less readable than you think.'

'I do wonder how bad your assumptions of me must have been if I keep bewildering you so much,' he said, keeping his eyes on the ink beneath her thumb. After absorbing the particularities of Gemma's handwriting, it was all too clear that the words on the page were Gemma's and not Leona's. If only he'd seen it earlier . . . How much trouble would they have spurned?

Schwartz gave it one last look before giving it to Teddy.

He folded it solemnly, imbuing each sharp crease with a wish of his own: *Come home, Gem. Come back to us.* As he neared the final folds, Schwartz's attention moved to him. He kept his expression vacant out of habit. He'd grown so accustomed to the cautious manner with which Alaric looked at him, like he was a cracked window doomed to break, that he found himself dry-mouthed and embarrassed when all Schwartz gave him was admiration.

He wished he could love his sense of hope the way Schwartz did. But, as if touched and tainted by the magic that made him, he cursed it instead. What good ever came of unrewarded expectation? If the universe was doling out a lesson, it would not be kind enough for Teddy to forgive all the trouble he'd brought back to Townsend. It wouldn't make his losses any easier. It wouldn't grant Louisa Eakley the guardian that she deserved.

Teddy placed the bird on the table in front of them and scratched the nape of his neck. 'When we were working with your mother's letter, Al recited an incantation. I wish I could remember what it was. You might have known it.'

'Did you not?'

'No. Hye-Jin said it was an old language. One I couldn't place.' Casting her a sidelong glance, he added, 'I figured you would know its name, if it had one. You were always quite good at finding my faults. If I didn't know something myself, I could guarantee that you did.'

Schwartz rolled her eyes. 'Are you saying I had to scrounge for your scraps to pull myself ahead?'

'I wouldn't say that,' Teddy answered. 'That implies you were ever truly ahead of me. I believe we were tragically well suited for one another, which lent us first to competition before it ever led us here.'

She laughed, leaning into his side, and he watched a whisper of the word begin and end with her lips: *Tragically.* What was more tragic, he thought, than loving something impermanent – or someone? He'd spent so much time trying to peel himself from her trap that he'd denied himself the sweetness, the decadence that made him stray in the first place. He had her now for the briefest of moments, and all he could see was her loveliness, dreading the inevitable moment when it would all be stripped away.

He couldn't be close enough. He could have unfastened all the buttons of her blouse, wound her limbs around his body, finished with his mouth against her throat, still asking for more.

'Should we—'

Teddy pressed his lips together and nodded. The bird. The *spell.* He couldn't cast it without a clear mind, but he also couldn't shed the last of his desire. Whatever came after this . . . he didn't know. People lived and grew and died without him, while Townsend always seemed to stay the same. Everything before Schwartz's return blurred together in his mind. She was the punctuation that gave his days an end and a beginning. For both their sakes, he could only ask her for so much, but he looked at her often. He loved her intensely. And he thought to himself without cease, *Stay with me. Stay with me. I can't lose you too.*

'Are you sure you don't want to wait for Alaric?' Schwartz asked.

'I've spent so much time waiting for Alaric,' said Teddy, 'that I often wonder why he comes back at all.'

'Why are you always so hard on him?'

Teddy did not answer, but the words dealt a sharp blow. 'I want to do this myself. Like I said . . . nothing to lose.'

He pinched the tail and pulled. The wings shifted incrementally.

Schwartz had done this twice. Twice to cement the intention, twice to give it a full cycle of breath. Inhale. Exhale.

In. And out.

His own breath stalled as the bird began to move, the tips of its paper wings reaching for the wood like claws. Were it not for the befuddlement of Schwartz's expression, he would have assumed that the bird's tentative learning was what she expected to happen. The first few wobbly steps of a newborn, long before it ever learned to fly.

But the anatomy failed it. It puffed out a breath and sputtered back to stillness within seconds. The limitations of its construction rendered it lifeless.

His lips formed the word 'No,' but the sound never came.

Schwartz swallowed nervously, her gaze flitting from the object to his hands. 'Maybe it needs another—'

Teddy lunged forward for the bird and tugged its tail twice more for good measure, imbuing it with another cycle of breath; but whatever life he hoped he might wring from it was gone. The bird was merely paper and ink. It twitched, less like a muscle and more like a whisper of wind whipping a blade of starched grass. Teddy stared at it for some promising sign of life and found nothing.

Schwartz's hand pressed the back of his shoulder blades. He forced himself to breathe but couldn't force it to be even.

'Nothing to lose,' he said. 'Nothing's changed.'

Rising abruptly, he snatched the bird from the table and began to unfold it rather unceremoniously, cursing every sharp edge. What good was all this hope if nothing came of it? It promised never-ending heartbreak; and yet, the point of it was not to outgrow it, but to hold it close even as it wounded him, like a blade inserted between his ribs. He had to keep it in. Keep holding on. Even if he wanted to cast it away and curse it.

What was crueller than a torture you had to choose?

Gemma's scrawl greeted him again as he stood with the open-faced page in his hands. She had to be alive, but where? Why couldn't she have shared her plan with him? With Lou? Teddy crushed the piece of paper into an amorphous lump. Behind him, Schwartz's breath hitched, and she demanded, 'What are you doing?'

He shook his head, articulating a slow response. 'We tried, Schwartz. There's no point in keeping it. No use in having it if all it does is remind us.'

'This means nothing,' she said. 'She's still out there.'

'And we're still just as far from bringing her home. This letter isn't going to give us what we want. It won't bring Gemma back. Let's just forget this ever happened. We tried.'

Teddy lowered his head, avoiding her scrutiny. He felt her gaze inching over him like a warm breath, but the intensity was unshakeable. What more did she want from him? He had never been able to make himself impervious to her feelings. His boundary, like the wards of the cottage, had once been less defined to witches, but he could feel her presence like no other. A pestilence, a steadiness, an anchor. At best, Schwartz was his

North Star. But at the worst of times, which was where Teddy Ingram often found himself stuck, her presence was ruthless. She'd never let him rest.

'Have you asked Lou what she wants?' Schwartz asked carefully.

'We don't talk about Gem as much these days,' Teddy said. 'Got too difficult. There's only so much I can do for her that doesn't remind her of the way things were with Gem. There's only so much more I can give her.'

'But she's happier now, isn't she? I can see it, Ingram. At some point, the bad days stopped outweighing the good days as much. She started getting excited about things again, and started spending more of her time away from this place. I remember how much she loved you then . . . Even if Gemma came back now, Lou needs you.'

'As it stands, I'm not the guardian she needs. Or the one she deserves. She needs her mother,' he said, compressing the ball even tighter. 'I don't know what I'm doing here. I'm not her parent. I'm not equipped to raise her if her mother doesn't come back. I want to do right by her, but I find myself falling into all the same fears that made Gemma into such a recluse, thinking the only way to keep Lou safe is to keep her tied to me. God, I'm trying to be better about it than she was, but I don't know how I'm supposed to live with myself if something happens to her.' His mouth hung open with the pretence of another thought, but nothing came. He felt as if a decade's worth of pressure had fallen from his body, a secret that he'd been forced to carry ever since he met Kenny Eakley. He could never repair the damage from what he'd done to the boy he loved, but he tried his best to shelter the rest of them from it. He wanted to carry them all even if the weight wore him down.

His best efforts, he found though, were not always enough. Try as he might, he didn't know how to raise a kid. He should have been back at Pembroke, wooing the old fellows with his work, making dinner for one at his flat. He should have been wrapped around Aurelia Schwartz in her bedroom, flush-faced and half-dressed, whispering sweet nothings in her ear. Focusing on his studies. Making mistakes with smaller consequences. He should have had the chance to explore that life before Gemma swept it out from under him without warning.

That wasn't something he had ever said aloud. Not to Schwartz, or Alaric. It certainly wasn't something he'd ever said to Lou.

Schwartz picked at her nails until Teddy could feel it, only coming to the realization after he'd met her worried stare. She wiped her palms on the front of her jeans, smoothing away the clamminess. If he didn't know her so well, he would have thought she looked timid. Demure, even. The sharp edge of her voice could snap anyone out of a deep haze, could break a rose-tinted glass. 'You wallow unlike anyone I've ever met, y'know. It's not good for you.'

'*I* wallow,' he echoed bitterly. 'You are quite literally the angriest person I've ever known, Schwartz.'

'I never said you were angry,' she replied. 'I think you lack the kind of anger one would expect given everything that's happened. If anything, I feel like you're slipping away, disappearing somewhere I won't always be able to reach you. And that scares the shit out of me.'

Schwartz crossed to him and tugged the ball of paper from his hands, laying it on the table behind her. With nothing left between his body and hers, save for their inhibitions, she tucked her head beneath his chin and placed her hands on the sides of his hips. Her nose grazed his clavicle, and through the fabric he felt her breath moving steadily, tension dissolving from her face. For once, he wondered if she could sense his longing the way he sensed hers, if she pitied him for it.

He lifted his hands and tilted her face upwards. 'I have always been here. Right where you left me.'

'Yet you feel further away than ever. I have this horrible fear that if I let you go now, I'll wake up tomorrow with no memory of this place or how to come back. And where will you be but right here? Exactly where we left each other. Now, what do *you* want?'

He closed his eyes and sighed, touching his brow to hers. 'So many things,' he muttered.

'Name one.'

Everything he settled on reeked of shame. Of pride and greed and *lust*. He wanted to return to Cambridge, basking in the former glory of his work, to rewrite everything that brought him here and stripped him of his acclaim. When Schwartz's hands were on his skin, his mind went back to old fantasies, ones where she touched him and *owned* him. She was right there, asking to be touched, and yet it felt more like a cruel joke than a true chance at happiness. A light he could never reach.

When he didn't speak, she twisted his sweater around her fingers and whispered, 'You want to keep her safe, don't you?'

He nodded, steeling his expression.

'And you want to keep *me* safe?'

'I do. I could take such good care of you, Schwartz.'

'I think,' she started, as he slid his fingers beneath the collar of her cardigan, 'we're on the same page then. Equal footing.'

The cream-coloured knit drooped from Schwartz's shoulder, exposing the end of her tattoo. Teddy gave it more consideration, now that he was of slightly clearer mind and wearing more of his clothes. A ribbon bound the stems of lavender at the bottom of the bulbs, cinching them together in a vague X shape over the line of her scar. He wanted to ask how much time had passed before she got the tattoo, if she told the artist about the first instrument that pierced those inches of her flesh.

She shrugged the cardigan off and tossed it aside. 'I've been . . . ruminating on this idea of equality. Of worth. How much power could you really give me if it's meant to stay dormant and unused?'

At her peripheral mention of his offer, he found himself at the edge of the wards again, cleaved open and vulnerable, watched by the moon's omnipresent yellow eye. He asked, bracing himself for rejection, 'Have you come to any conclusions?'

'I'm finding that magic is much harder to quantify than I thought. But we're both missing something crucial: a sense of security. That's why you brought it up. I don't know if you're still considering it—'

'Have *you* considered it?' Teddy took in a deep sigh, measuring his breath before it could tangle with hers and lose clarity.

Schwartz turned her wrist nervously, rubbing her thumb down to the hard heel of her hand delicately. 'It took you mentioning Ryan for me to consider it. I thought, "Why would you give me something so strong? Something so dangerous? How could you settle for something as safe as my gift in exchange for something as exacting and volatile as yours?" But I get it now. There's no price too large for the ones we love. There's nothing I wouldn't give to keep Ryan safe, the same way you want to keep Lou safe. When I think about it that way, the oath stops feeling like a gamble and starts feeling like the only feasible solution for both of us to walk away feeling a little more . . .' She waved her final words away like a tendril of smoke. 'At ease.'

Teddy scratched the back of his neck nervously and said, 'I wasn't trying to take something from you, Schwartz.'

She folded her arms across her chest, raising a questioning brow. 'Blood oaths are inherently transactional. You must have considered that at some point.'

'Would you believe it if I said I was acting out of passion? That it was purely selfless.'

Her eyes narrowed at him with a light-hearted accusation. *What happened to the person I used to know? Whose wants were driven by a blind desire to prove himself?*

He's still here, Teddy wanted to say. *Proving himself to someone else.* To Lou. To Gemma. They all saw someone completely different when they looked at him; and from those versions of himself, he failed to find a common thread.

Sometimes he wondered, whenever Schwartz looked at him long enough, whether or not she had already figured him out. But if he was right in his intuition, in tune with his empathetic magic enough to know how she felt, he had deduced that she was already in love with him; and why could she not tell him? What did she see in him that kept her from admitting it?

He was only waiting for her to ask for something. Waiting to prove himself to her too.

Whatever she wanted – he could be that.

Slowly, Teddy shoved the sleeve of his jumper up his wrist and bared his palm to her. 'The offer stands. It's yours if you want it.'

She studied him like a fraudulent text. Something to deconstruct and find faults in. Maybe she saw him just as everyone else had: as an extension of his magic, of bad blood and the offspring of greed. Maybe, if he and his magic were so inextricable from each other, she could not take one without the other.

She stepped forward and laced her fingers between his. 'How do you want to do this?'

Maybe that was why she agreed.

Ceremonial magic implied a certain degree of pageantry. A circle of shrouded witnesses, carefully rehearsed vows, a blessed instrument of execution. Even in the darkness of the Tanks in the Tate Modern, Leona Sum had unearthed an athame from her hip, a blade with pure intentions.

The kitchen knife between them paled in comparison. It glinted with the light of the standing lamp, but the edge, Teddy knew, was hardly as sharp as it should have been, catching on halved apple cores and the skins of potatoes whenever he used it.

He also knew that, somewhere in this house, Gemma kept a ritual athame of her own, a blade worthy of enacting rituals like this one, but he had never seen it. He followed her unspoken rules and kept his hands to himself, internalizing her principles of secrecy. *Guard your knowledge, your blood, your heart.* He never went looking for it. Still, he had expected to come across it at some point in his search for other things.

Teddy left the knife untouched between their folded knees on the rug. If he moved too quickly, reached before she did, he thought he might frighten her. Spells – *promises* – with that kind of weight were made with delicacy. As if the occasion didn't have his hair standing already, Schwartz was masterfully concealing a frantic, nervous energy inside of herself that Teddy only felt in the shaking of his hands.

She wrapped her fingers around the handle, pulling it towards her with a soft scrape against the rug. She turned it once, assessing it with her particular brand of scholarship. It was almost awe-inspiring how she could afford such meagre things their due weight with a simple look.

This was alchemy, he thought. The creation of gold. It shouldn't have surprised him – he knew she could just as easily sanctify something with her touch.

She inched forward until their knees were touching, unfurling her hand in their negative space. She pressed the knife tip to her palm, then adjusted her grip. Only then did he find hesitation on her end; and he opened his mouth to reassure her but stopped abruptly as she pushed the blade into her skin with a soft hiss through her teeth.

Teddy averted his gaze instinctively. Fear caught in his throat; this time, it was entirely his own. He'd been squeamish at fifteen, almost ill at the sight of Kenny Eakley's incised hand, for the boy's wound had been far deeper. Schwartz was meticulous, engrossed in it, drawing just enough blood to pinpoint their target.

He gave the knife right back to her once she'd wiped it and relinquished it to him, folding her fingers around the handle instead. 'I trust you.'

A grave declaration. Mostly, he didn't trust his hands not to shake.

Schwartz swallowed and rolled the sleeve methodically up the length of his forearm. She eyed the bluish veins beneath his pale, lamplit flesh with reverence, her gaze tracing them down to his wrists. With her bleeding hand, she opened his palm to the ceiling.

He readied himself for the sting of the blade. She raised his hand to her lips and kissed his open palm. Heat fled to his face as her thumb dragged along the back of his knuckles.

Schwartz closed her eyes for a moment and remained oblivious to all of it.

'You're certain?' she asked again, whispering her words into his hand. The knife tip lowered to the map of his palm, balancing on the end of his lifeline. He nodded in return, but her hands remained still. 'You have to tell me, Ingram. Before it's too late.'

'Yes.'

She pierced through his skin, cradling his hand with a tenderness that outweighed the flash of pain. A dark bead of crimson emerged first. Then, the split seam.

'And you?' Teddy asked. 'Is this what you want?'

For a moment, her incised palm hovered over his, mere

centimetres from marrying magic to blood. He felt his magic reaching for her, rising from the wound with a grip of its own.

But hers – where was it? She looked at him with her knitted brows and crooked frown, saying nothing, and Teddy wondered if he'd lost her confidence, if the intention had slithered back from where it came. She laid the knife beside her legs, leaning forward so that their folded knees crossed each other's. He felt naked under her unwavering scrutiny, his hand still bleeding and unheld.

The ritual incomplete.

He began to speak but fell short as she kissed the corner of his mouth, holding his chin like an open book. Her fingers smelt of iron, leaving a faint dash of discoloration beneath his jaw.

'I want this,' she said, the low rasp of her voice laden with desire. Schwartz's nose pressed the side of his own, her lips parting his for a kiss that was more taste than touch, more craving and hunger than he knew what to do with. Their fingers locked one by one between their bodies, then came the slow press of slitted palm against palm.

God forgive me, he thought, *for how much I love.*

But as the threadlike gold tether of magic wound around their hands, Teddy knew there was more inside of him than magic that she was capable of extracting, and he prayed that she would let him keep some of it. That she would not ask for it all and leave him empty when she left.

CHAPTER SEVENTEEN

In his dreams, he took a thousand different shapes: the boy, the bird, the lover. Sometimes he stood in the chapel, staring up at his stepmother like she wore the righteous hand of God, and he was the son.

In this one, he was naked, bone-thin and white as chalk. His gaunt face was the first thing he found in the mirrors that cradled him. His ribs were carved like marble. Colourless wings dragged lifelessly behind him.

He turned to gauge his surroundings.

More mirrors. More of himself. They towered around him, stretching his body into an infinite blank slate.

He tried to wrap his wings around himself to cover up against the assault of an icy wind.

Wake up. Wake up.

He knew where he was in the waking world, and that was what mattered; Schwartz slept beside him and the wards around the house were practically impenetrable. The logical part in his brain assured him that he would wake soon.

But it couldn't stop the voice he heard within.

Vide cor tuum. Behold thy heart.

He turned to see Schwartz in the reflection, poised behind

him. He pulled his wings around his midsection, obscuring his concave stomach and shrivelled genitals.

She strung her arms around his neck, and he surrendered willingly to her touch. Even if she wasn't real, she was the warmest thing there. The softest hand. His bright star. Teddy's knees hit the ground, aching and bruised. His eyes fluttered shut as she pressed her lips to his ear and kissed it.

'I wish you didn't have to see me like this,' he said.

Her hand trailed down his protruding collarbone, splaying like a star over his heart. 'I am the only one who sees you. I am thy master. *Ego dominus tuus.*'

With a sharp split, his chest opened beneath her hand. He lurched forward, pitching himself onto the floor in agony. Like a wounded doe, he whined and writhed, stripped of whatever warmth remained inside of him. He knew how the story went; she would take his burning heart and leave him in Love's servitude – his Beatrice. He'd read it a hundred times and laughed at Dante's impossible naivete.

But in her hand was the paper bird folded from Gemma's note. A much easier thing to set aflame.

I am thy master.

Behold thy heart.

With a snap of her fingers, the bird ignited. Schwartz tipped it back into her open mouth and devoured it whole.

His obvious fear was that she'd seen everything; he'd seen plenty from the other end of the empathetic tether.

His magic wouldn't have fused in her so quickly. Such severe witchcraft required more than a night to settle, maybe even *days.* He remembered little from his first transference, except for the terror.

It had come for him in a dream.

To his remorse, Schwartz was already awake by the time he'd come to. After blinking the strain of midnight from his eyes, he sat up and found her sitting on the side of the bed, hunched over her knees with her head in her hands.

The bed creaked as he pushed himself up onto his elbows. She sniffled quietly, tidying her hair and wiping her face in one clunky motion. 'Didn't mean to wake you up.'

He couldn't help but sag with relief. Of course, she saw nothing. No paper wings, no tower of mirrors, no origami bird on fire.

Which meant she'd been crying for some other reason.

Teddy lifted the curls from her neck, his fingers skimming down the start of her spine. 'It's all right. Couldn't sleep anyway.'

Nodding, she said, 'I'm going to make some tea.'

'It'll wake you up.'

She shrugged, picking her already-too-short nails. 'I can't stop thinking about her. At least if I'm awake, I can try to think about other things too.'

He didn't know if Schwartz was talking about Leona or her mother, but he didn't have the heart to ask. 'Come back to bed. I'll tell you a story.'

She scoffed quietly. 'Like I'm a child.'

'Like it's a distraction,' he responded, weaselling his fingers between hers. With a gentle tug, she surrendered to the pillow beside him. 'Escapism is most effective when it's shared.'

'The same could be said for delusion,' Schwartz murmured.

'Folie à deux.' But she withheld her protest after that, fitting her cheek to the place above his heart. How easy it'd be, he thought, for her to reach in and take it, to weigh it in her hand like the paper bird and swallow it.

He pressed his lips against her hair and recounted one of the lesser-known Sir Gawain romances until he felt her heartbeat level and her breath calm; but he did not sleep.

A whisper beneath his mattress kept him awake.

CHAPTER EIGHTEEN

It might have been Meredith, but Teddy was fairly certain that it was Kenny Eakley who came to torment him that night. *Do you remember how we lay like that? Beneath the magnolia trees at the park by school?*

Of course, Teddy never forgot. He remembered the coarse red hair tickling his nose when Kenny ducked his head against his chest. He remembered squinting in the light that passed through the trees to take in the shape of the boy's freckles, the merging pink forming images like a moving cloud. Like tea leaves plastered to the bottom of his cup.

More than anything, he remembered looking over his shoulder at every sudden noise. The crunch of leaves beneath boots, however distant, made him wary. No one he knew ever noticed them. He suspected no passer-by had ever so much as glanced in their direction. But it could have been his mother too, and he wouldn't know unless he looked.

So he looked, always. Perhaps even more than he had looked at Kenny.

When Teddy hauled himself out of bed, Schwartz was nowhere to be found. He checked each room twice over, as if he could've somehow misplaced a sentient adult upon first glance.

Lou's door creaked open. She rubbed her eyes, though she'd been awake for some time; her clothes were newly put on, and her hair was neatly braided.

'Why are you up so early?'

''S not early,' she said. 'I'm just tired.'

Teddy passed his hand down the nape of his neck, idling in the doorway across from hers. 'You wouldn't happen to know where Schwartz went?'

'Aurelia?' Lou shrugged and made her way towards the kitchen, where she felt a few tangerines before choosing one to peel. 'I didn't know she'd left.'

His heart sank. Returning to his bedroom, he clicked through his phone for a message.

Wouldn't have come through anyway, he reasoned.

His nightstand drawer was empty, though Schwartz's hairpins still sat on its surface. Schwartz had a handful of different ways to tell him she was gone, so why hadn't she? His mind wandered to the worst of things: Louisa's cry, Gemma's note, months without resolution.

The most likely answer was that she'd realized what a grave mistake she'd made, and left to rectify it. Whether that was sleeping in his bed or swearing the oath, he couldn't say. It wouldn't have been out of character. She had no reason to make him an exception.

He was only different from anyone else in the worst ways.

'She's probably at Petro's!' Lou sang from the kitchen counter.

Teddy poked his head into the hallway and asked, 'What makes you say that?'

'She did my hair this morning,' Lou explained. 'I mean, I don't think she would have gone back home without telling us. She seemed stressed though. I saw her looking through the tea cabinets before I went back in to change.'

He breathed a heavy sigh of relief, shaking his head to himself. The tea cupboards were as barren as his nightstand drawers. Teddy had planned to fill them before she came back, but lost sight of the task amidst everything else. He changed in a rush, switching his pyjamas for the usual turtleneck and dark tweed, layering the scent of toothpaste with a spritz of his near-empty bottle of cologne.

'What are you all dressed up for?' asked Lou.

Teddy flattened the fold of his turtleneck neatly in front of the bathroom mirror. 'I always wear this.'

'You haven't worn those trousers in a while,' she said.

Blame it on the heat, he thought. It was still warm enough outside to worsen the itch against his neck, but he could weather it. Schwartz possessed the strange and enviable quality of knowing the perfect method for keeping warm. She donned the proper jumpers when the temperature dropped, and she kept her arms bare during the summer, leaving them perfectly sun-kissed and evenly bronzed.

Teddy Ingram wanted to cover up at any cost. He never gave much weight to the principle of his own modesty, but there was probably something staunch and Catholic behind his proclivity for long sleeves. He missed wearing them, the clean cut, the dark silhouette. He missed having someone to *see* him.

He kissed Lou's forehead while she gnawed on the last piece of her tangerine. 'Lock the doors.'

'I know.'

'I'll be back in a minute. Do whatever Agatha tells you, OK?'

The front of the house seemed to stir with spectral approval.

Teddy sped out the door and through the wards of the hill. He needed something to change – and soon.

Schwartz looked up from her seat at the table beside the window. She wiggled her fingers, discarding the pages of a printed document onto the table, and mouthed, *Hi.*

Her back straightened as Teddy bypassed the counter to take the seat across from her. She returned her attention to the stapled pages, scribbling through a long line of text with a red gel pen. 'Wanted to get some work done,' was all she said.

'I thought you'd left.'

Gnawing on her lip with a fleeting remembrance, she responded, 'Slipped my mind to leave a note.'

Between them sat a half-drunk teacup which Teddy eyed with interest.

'It's Assam,' Schwartz told him, 'if you want some.'

Teddy lifted it to his mouth and blew to cool it, but by then it was already cold. He closed his lips around the mauve print of hers and drank until the only thing left in her cup was the dark run-off plastered to the bottom. The familiar shade had all been wiped from her mouth, but he found it deep within the creases while she shaped her words.

The corners of her lips twitched as if she could feel it. Maybe she could.

Damn tether.

Schwartz's curiosity got the better of her. Over the edge of her papers, she asked, 'Is it good?'

He positioned the cup between them with a gentle *clink*. 'Rich. Are you working on something?'

'Trying to,' she corrected. 'I haven't been able to focus this morning. I needed a distraction – something to keep busy.'

'The first day's the hardest,' he said. 'Staying inside won't do you any good. Much as this place shelters us by keeping everything out, it does an equally grand job of preserving everything that's already inside. Everything I've felt for the past eight or nine years is still trapped between Gem's walls, it seems.'

Or under his bed. In Meredith's letter.

'Let's go somewhere. It's a beautiful day. The birds are out . . . It'll be nice to get out of Townsend for a few hours.'

Her cup scraped the tabletop as she rotated it mindlessly. 'Where?'

'Wherever you want,' he murmured, trailing off before he could add, *just not home.*

Schwartz's gaze fixed on the spinning cup. 'I figured I'd give Ryan a call while I was here and make use of the cell service, but they aren't answering. It's probably nothing, I know, but it makes me nervous. They're usually awake by now.'

The scrape of the teacup intensified. Teddy reached over his half of the round table and layered his fingers on top of hers. She'd spoken from the other side of a thick daze and snapped free of it at his touch.

'I can take you,' he said.

She grazed the sides of his fingers with a feather-light

touch, tracing the fine hair on his knuckles and the grooves in his skin. Her hand slipped into his, fitting to the curve of his palm.

Slowly, he heard the metronome of her heart quieting. She pushed a petulant curl behind her ear, exposing a cloud of flushing skin.

'You, um . . .' Teddy rifled through his pocket for the pins she'd left on his nightstand. 'You forgot these.'

Schwartz took one, prying apart the prongs like an open jaw. The yellow cafe light gleamed on its teeth, and her brows furrowed – the pin, transfixing her.

She was fading again.

Teddy knew he should leave her alone. He should give her time. Let her catalogue all the feelings she was currently juggling without the interference of his own. They held the tether from both ends now.

He shouldn't have questioned where she went. And yet—

'Schwartz,' he whispered. Her demeanour darkened, and though she acknowledged her name, she was captivated by the simple barrette.

'Can you get into the library? I think I just figured something out.'

Before Teddy could answer, Schwartz kicked her chair back and gathered her things: her bag, her papers, and both of her pins. She kept her cardigan on, set on a short walk to Alaric's shop instead of a journey up the hill. 'Come on, Ingram. Today would be nice.'

*

'I can't get into the library without Al,' Teddy explained, fitting his key into the shop door. 'Trust me, I'd like to, but—'

'*Alaric!*' Her voice rang through the silence that followed, raising all the hairs on Teddy's covered neck.

'Christ,' he whispered. She could wake dust mites shouting like that. Normally, opening up shop involved raising the blinds, but he kept them pulled over the windows now, for whatever illicit activities Schwartz was trying to cultivate. Her pulse was rapid, her skin set aflame with adrenaline.

'I don't know how I never thought of this before,' Schwartz rushed.

'Thought of *what?*'

She braced her hands on the edge of the front desk, her expression pinched tight. 'Do you remember that day when I delivered Gemma's letter to Alaric? Right after she went missing.'

Viscerally. He remembered an inconsolable child, an ache in his hard-set jaw, and Schwartz returning to the cottage soaked to the bone in sleet.

But he didn't want to talk about it. Seeing Schwartz in the cafe, nose buried in her work in an attempt to undo the strain of their circumstances, made him keen on a distraction. One day, which would have been the first in months, where he didn't have to think of Gemma.

'Schwartz,' he murmured, kneading the bridge of his nose, 'this is exhausting.'

She paused before her reply, stealing a moment to breathe. 'I know. I wouldn't bring it up if I didn't think it could mean something.'

Teddy sighed. 'Go on.'

'We were in the library at the time, talking about locator spells and navigator gifts. He proposed the idea that Gemma might have taken something with her, and that this *thing* would make it easier to find her.'

'But we never figured out what that'd be,' Teddy noted.

'Right. Until just now,' Schwartz replied. 'Lou has a little piece of hair at the front that doesn't want to stay tucked into her braid. I had to pin it back, so she left to grab this barrette with a frog on it—'

'She loves that one.'

'But she used to have this gold pin.'

It had been waiting in a dusty corner of his mind for someone to acknowledge it. The gold pin, Gemma's tracker – why *hadn't* they considered it before? It had been inconsequential enough to forget in the grand scheme of things, but it fitted so perfectly into the empty space of their puzzle that he should have never been able to ignore it.

Teddy's palms dampened.

'She couldn't find it?' His tongue was dry. The words tasted of gravel.

'It could be nothing,' she said pre-emptively. Her cardigan puffed out like pastry dough as she folded her arms over her chest. 'I didn't look for it myself, but I asked Lou – just on a whim. She hasn't seen it in almost a year.'

'You're joking.'

'I don't know how well she keeps track of her hairpins, Ingram. She's, like, *seven*.'

'Kid's a mess but somehow she keeps track of everything.

Her memory's a marvel, honestly. I don't know why I never thought of that. Jesus.'

'It seemed like a long shot to even ask her, but the fact that she could remember the last time she saw it struck me as equally strange. You don't normally keep a close eye on something you're not expecting to lose. Something that isn't valuable.'

'But it *was* valuable,' he said. 'Even if Lou didn't find the value in it herself, she was of her mother's making. Gemma was adamant that she keep it safe, and that gave it weight.'

'Enough weight?'

He couldn't deny how badly he wanted Schwartz's point to bleed through. If anything resulted from the theory . . .

No. It wasn't enough to theorise. What mattered in the end was Gemma's return. Until the augur found her way back to the cottage, by her own method or theirs, the theory was only another hope around which to stretch himself. A wishful thought and nothing more.

'I'd always assumed Gemma could just enchant another pin if Lou lost the first one,' Teddy said.

Schwartz's lips pressed firmly together. 'She would have had to fashion a new pair of wandering eyes altogether. That hairpin will always be tied to the same counterpart.'

'A twin,' he said.

'Could be,' Schwartz said, mentally flipping through the book Alaric had given her. 'Eyes were usually made with two complementary objects, which meant, more often than not, that they weren't identical. Do you know what its counterpart was?'

Over the years, Teddy had been beleaguered by its very existence more than he questioned its making, the way one considered the privacy invasion of baby monitors or hidden cameras more than whoever was on the other end watching them. He didn't give much thought to its creation. Like Schwartz, he was rifling through the memory of book pages – Gemma's numerous grimoires – for a salvaged scratch of ink that he'd retained.

It was an unlikely prospect, and one that proved fruitless. Most of what he remembered were the birds. Teddy hadn't the faintest idea of what Lou's hairpin would've been tied to. The fact that it'd taken Schwartz's return and all that lost time to make the connection pricked him with a twinge of bitterness.

'I could ask her,' Teddy offered. 'It's possible she still doesn't know. I can't imagine Gem told her everything that the pin was capable of.'

The veil parted behind them with a shimmer. Schwartz pivoted, bright and eager to see the caretaker again.

Teddy braced himself for a tense reunion.

They both sagged at the sight of Hye-Jin. 'I thought I heard voices.'

Schwartz gathered her composure in front of the unfamiliar caretaker. 'We were just looking for Alaric.'

'He's not in right now.'

Teddy grimaced in spite of himself. 'Of course not.'

'You were talking about the eye?' asked Hye-Jin. 'It has moved.'

Schwartz opened her mouth to question how Hye-Jin could possibly know, but Teddy couldn't risk losing the caretaker's train of thought.

'You mean the one Leona sent us?'

'Mhmm.'

Teddy's teeth ground together. 'Where?'

Carmichael must have moved it. He was in good faith with the caretakers and knew more about their work than Teddy himself was allowed. He was, potentially, the only one there who knew where to find both ends of the enchantment: theirs and Leona's.

Teddy thought of the mysterious breach of Hye-Jin's collection. Alaric never specified when it had happened or what had been taken, if anything, but it'd be easier to steal from a place you'd been invited into. You were less of an intruder, less of a suspect.

Hye-Jin said nothing of the breach – at least, not directly. After all, Teddy shouldn't have known about it. 'The eye is still in my care,' she answered. 'The other end has since been moved. Has Alaric not told you this?'

Of course not. Schwartz slipped into the shadow of their conversation, causing no distraction, making no noise. She let them talk, absorbing every word with her academic astuteness.

'Like I said . . . *Cagey.*' Teddy cleared his throat. 'I don't suppose you know where it's gone?'

Hye-Jin's gaze fluttered across every nook in the dark bookshop. 'You're welcome to look for the eye's other end. It's possible that you recognize something I don't.'

It wasn't what they'd come for. Teddy cast a questioning glance to Schwartz, who prodded him forward wordlessly. His former preoccupations slipped to the back of his mind; now, all Teddy Ingram wanted was an answer to justify the effort.

'We'll take anything at this point,' Schwartz muttered. Teddy searched her face for reassurance before tearing his gaze away abruptly. Schwartz was never one to coddle. Her encouragements were hidden behind scathing nicknames and a perpetual expression of distaste.

He'd sorely missed it. Maybe, all he needed after months of slow, unexpectant living was a hard kick in the ass.

'It doesn't hurt to try.'

It would hurt to fail, though. Seeing as Gemma was still missing, he knew the sinking weight of failure intimately by now. His thoughts cycled through the usual platitudes of self-loathing as Hye-Jin opened a door – a portal – to her collection in Namwon.

It's probably nothing.

This means nothing.

Sometimes, he thought he'd been made to spiral. To self-destruct. His stepmother would have certainly corroborated it; despite his mission to prove her wrong, he couldn't say there wasn't any truth to her judgement of misery.

It became harder each time to listen to the small voice interwoven with the rest that asked, *What if?*

What if you can still find her?

What if she's alive?

He did not ask about the disarray of Hye-Jin's collection. She looked to him in question, his silence an answer equally as telling. He knew. Of course he knew about the breach, otherwise he would have raised at least one innocuous question over it.

She raised no questions of her own, and she laid the wooden

box that held the eye on a low table before them. 'Sit,' Hye-Jin ordered. Then, more lightly, 'Make yourselves comfortable.'

Schwartz reined in her curiosity, centring her focus on the contents of the box. Alaric had swaddled the eye in fabric, which he'd then tied up with string like a parcel. Teddy would have laughed if there was anything less ominous tucked within those layers.

'It could be nothing.'

As he said it aloud, the others could tell he didn't mean it. He wanted a result. He wanted an answer. He wanted someone to throw him a bone, and he was so desperate at this point that he didn't care which bone it was. He'd take the scraps. Anything at all.

The smooth, gold surface gleamed back at him in his palm. Teddy held his breath as it departed for the empty space above it, spinning like a coin.

Ah. My old torment.

Schwartz shuffled closer beside him to match his view.

'Do you see something?' Hye-Jin asked from above them. She wiped her hands clean of dust, which Teddy hadn't noticed before, streaking a faded rag with the grey remains of her collection.

'I do,' Schwartz said. 'But I can't tell where it is.'

'It's moving,' Teddy said.

At once, the rag in Hye-Jin's grip went still. 'Do you recognize it?'

What the eye's size and shape offered in portability, it lacked in clarity. Teddy made out the nondescript shape of stone and the contrast of sunlight.

He nodded. 'I think so.' There was a particular slant of light in the spinning image that caught his eye, digging up a long-since buried memory; and with the light came the shape of Kenny's freckles.

Summer and first love and crippling paranoia.

It could be anything.

But for once, it wasn't *nothing*.

CHAPTER NINETEEN

'What did you tell him?' By the time Schwartz posed the question, they were already in the car, and Alaric had returned to assume the last-minute responsibility of watching over Louisa.

Teddy had been in the bookshop far longer than he'd expected and told the caretaker everything. 'Everything, except what comes next,' he said.

Schwartz sagged into the seat beside him, trying in spite of the unpaved road and her own anxieties to relax for the long drive. 'So he knows about the coven and Chaplain?'

'Mhmm.'

'And Gemma.'

A pause while the car hopped over a pothole. 'He's hazy on the details.'

A curve crept up the corner of her lips, undoubtedly questioning his audacity. 'So, what does he think we're doing tonight?'

'Carnal things,' Teddy said, with too convincing a deadpan on his face. He cleared his throat. 'I told him I'm driving you back to Cambridge. He can make of that whatever he wants.'

'You don't think he'll notice my bags sitting by the stairs?'

Teddy ran his tongue along his teeth, considering the

trouble Alaric would make for him whenever they returned. Secrets between them usually only ran one way; Teddy had been honest with him, so painfully honest that Alaric could have cleaved a path straight through his heart over a hundred times in his lifetime if he'd wanted to.

He didn't want *this* to be the thread that snapped between them.

'You're keeping a change of clothes here,' he explained. 'You intend to visit soon – for Lou's birthday.'

With a jerky nod, they'd agreed on a cover, though neither could come up with a reason why a cover was necessary. They'd done nothing wrong, and as far as they knew, nothing was *going* to go wrong where they were heading.

When he glanced at her for reassurance, Schwartz's tight-knit expression had begun to unravel into something less composed. 'You never mentioned her birthday was coming up.'

He hadn't even thought to. Schwartz was busy and Lou was soft. He wouldn't have blamed Schwartz for having other arrangements, but he wouldn't be able to forgive himself if Lou expected company only to be left with *him*.

'It's the tenth of October,' he said. 'You're welcome to come. So's Ryan, if that helps.'

'Helps what, exactly? You could just ask me, Ingram. I wouldn't say no.'

He felt her analysing him from the passenger seat, disappointed by what she saw. Then, a twinge of embarrassment. As if she should know better than to wait for him to ask.

As if she should know better than to be so willing.

Deep down, he knew the answer might be different without

Louisa to account for. If all that Townsend had to offer was a quick getaway and an old, reclusive rival, why would she ever come?

But she wouldn't disappoint Lou. As long as Schwartz knew the girl was waiting here for a friend, she could justify dropping everything to be with her; and Teddy was mostly grateful for that. Still he wondered, with his fingers twitching around the steering wheel, if his heart – and his patience – weighed *less*.

It certainly weighed less in Alaric's scale.

With that in mind, his small lie seemed a lot less heinous.

Schwartz tucked her knees across her chest like a seatbelt. It never failed to confound him how small she could become, twisted like a cat in sunlight. She was large to him, unavoidable. Try as she might to slip beneath one's focus, she filled every space Teddy found himself in.

She fumbled with the stereo knob for a while, before surrendering to the quiet. The drive would be short; half their journey would be by train. For the time being, Teddy relished her closeness, her ceaseless white noise, ignoring the silence altogether. It wasn't until they were at a station, shoulders grazing against each other in the crowd, that she asked how he knew where to take them.

About an hour north of London lay a graveyard, one whose grounds were never disturbed for new burials. As Teddy spoke of the ruins of the old chapel that remained fixed to its eastern corner, its stones cobbled together in his mind, and his memory turned to full colour.

He painted it as a relic of the past. A place where things had died and could no longer live. Nowadays, it hosted the occasional tourist group. Sometimes, locals from the towns around it would hike through the hills before returning to their habitable communities for coffee and a salmon bun. There were two informational plaques recounting the site's history, but the folks buried beneath those hills were neither ruthless enough nor legendary enough to garner much attention.

Truthfully, the graveyard and the chapel remnants were a landmark of one moment in Teddy's life where he'd felt most alive.

Memory served to ruin it.

By the time they'd reached the footpaths, Teddy was twisting the fabric from his neck with a hooked finger, trying to pull the evening's cool breeze into his fitted clothes. Schwartz panted softly at his side, masking the loud thrum of her pulse. 'Fuck these hills,' she whispered, fluffing her cardigan out at her sides.

A laugh hissed through Teddy's teeth.

He urged her on with a jerk of his head. 'We're not far. Best see what we can find before it gets too dark.'

She followed his footsteps, cautious as if she could rouse the dead beneath from their eternal sleep. *Maybe at one point*, he thought. Whoever was buried here would've had centuries to make peace with the grounds. No one was new. Their inquiries towards the reaper traversing the hills were passive and curious.

Specifically, the *first* reaper: Teddy Ingram. The one who was, at least, familiar with what it felt like to have one foot beyond the veil of death.

Schwartz needed more time to acclimatize to the porous

boundary of her new, destructive gift. She itched. She shed her cardigan, then put it back on, unable to make herself comfortable. Her pace quickened until Teddy was no longer required to cut his steps short for her sake. He knew time had forced these ghosts into complacency. Realistically, there was no better place for Schwartz to realize such side effects of her newfound magic.

'It'll pass,' he murmured. The ruins of the chapel rose like daylight over the horizon. He half expected to hear Kenny's laughter among the whispers, but if he did, he dismissed it as the cruel conjuring of his mind – not Kenny's ghost.

'They're leering,' she noted spitefully.

'Ignore them,' Teddy said. 'I imagine they leer at any woman wearing trousers.'

She rolled her eyes. 'How old *is* this place?'

'I'm sure some of these gents predate the Norman conquest, but that's when most accessible documentation on burials was drafted. Officially,' Teddy emphasized, 'the churchyard was recognized in 1780. Earlier than most, if you could believe it.'

Had the medievalist not been struggling to breathe, she would have remarked on it with great enthusiasm. Instead, her mouth formed a noiseless '*Riveting*.'

Ivy engulfed the chapel and its abandoned iron plaque. The moon peered between open stone jaws, its light pooling into the ruins like God. Back then, Teddy hadn't felt the faith pressing him as much, but it smothered him now, the way his stepmother's gaze did. Back then, all he'd seen was the boy, bathed in daylight and smiling back at him.

He pulled out the phone from his pocket, using it for extra light.

'How do you think it got here?' Schwartz asked.

Teddy kicked aside a cluster of foliage with his boot in the place he thought the eye would have been. 'Haven't the faintest,' he mumbled. It was also completely and entirely possible that he'd mistaken his view from the wandering eye for this when it was actually somewhere far away, foreign to him. He lowered himself to his knees and yanked at the stubborn roots until they gave way to reveal the stone beneath. 'I don't even know what we're looking for. If they were twin pieces, it wouldn't feel so impossible.'

Schwartz's footsteps quieted as she ventured to the eastern quadrant, where sat several tombs. At one time, they'd bracketed an altar; Teddy couldn't recall what year the altar had been rendered to debris by the ripple of an old bomb, but the nearby townsfolk believed the dead within those tombs to have been spared by miracle. By God's merciful hand.

She pressed her fingers to a sun-bleached tomb, swiping through dust. Moonlight ribboned her skin, cresting above the jagged edge of an old window. Teddy's search ceased as he studied her, his expression softened by awe. She murmured something to herself which he couldn't hear from the northern quadrant – something about the dust. The decay. He'd done the same thing when he was younger, before he learned what dark stains death left in the lines of his hands.

Descending the weathered dais, Schwartz wiped her hands clean and came to join him. 'I'd kill to have seen this place in its prime. It's almost the perfect time capsule.'

Teddy smiled to himself. 'I've seen this chapel in most of its seasons. "*All ripens and rots that rose up at first*",' he said, a recitation of Sir Gawain.

'I'd like to come back someday,' she stated. Crouching beside him, she began to unwind the mess of vines he'd made in his survey.

'I should like to come with you,' Teddy said.

They searched, never once knowing what they were searching for, until an hour had passed and every inch of the chapel, save for the tombs, had been overturned. A swell of disappointment took refuge between his ribs. He shook a spider from the edge of his boot and reclined against the dais in the dark.

Wiping the cool sweat from his brow, he broke the delicate silence, asking, 'What did you write to me?'

'Lots of things,' Schwartz answered, collapsing next to his shoulders with resignation.

He arched a brow. 'Important things?'

'Things best left on paper. Nothing you have to think too hard about.' She turned to him, her eyes flickering to his cheek like it'd been smeared in dust. Teddy drew his thumb across it, brushing a long strand of hair behind his ear. Schwartz's fingers followed its path seconds after.

He closed his eyes, left to wonder.

'I don't know if I have it in me to keep looking if Lou doesn't know what the pin is linked to.' He confessed to it like a sin. 'It's not like giving up is the easy way out. I'm so tired, Schwartz.'

Her only response was the continuous drag of her fingertips, an exploration through his hair. The words hung between them like laundry on a wire. *All this effort for nothing,* he thought. *I'll have burned my bridge to Alaric, lost my darling rival, and all without Gemma to tell me it was worth it.*

'Let's go back,' Schwartz said.

Teddy's head lolled against her calf. 'This wouldn't be the worst place for a nap. I could stay here and let the moss swallow me up.'

'Moss makes a poor blanket,' she pointed out. 'And stone won't facilitate a full night of sleep.'

'Yes, but Catholicism facilitates my self-flagellation so beautifully. If I stay here, Alaric will never have to hear my bitching and moaning again.'

Schwartz's mouth twisted above him. He would pick himself up for Lou and his home, but he couldn't deny how much harder it got each time.

'I would miss you,' she said solemnly.

You could stay, too. The thought crossed his mind as easily as if they were children taking shelter beneath the playground slide. *Let's bury ourselves in the overgrowth like the lovers in Pompeii.*

'I would never be too far.'

A burst of light in the western end sent them stumbling to their feet. All the dust they'd disturbed lifted from the surface of stones like violin bows.

'What the hell is that?'

'Could the eye do that?' he asked.

Schwartz shook her head. 'I-I don't think so.'

A shape hovered, black and devouring, ringed in a pulsating gold. Teddy could see through it if he faced it head on. Slats of wood, streaked in yellow light, made up the unformidable walls of a shack. Heat poured from the opening.

A portal. They joined in the answer. Schwartz's hand twitched between them, teeming with new magic. Teddy seized it at once.

'You didn't . . .?'

Teddy shook his head. 'Of course not. Portal magic is beyond me.' He wondered if a wandering eye could take this shape; the portal sat precisely where the eye had been – or where he thought the eye had been. Approaching it warily, Teddy studied the portal's innards, the heart of the illusion.

He recognized nothing.

But Schwartz found something in the portal to run from. 'It's Chaplain,' she hissed. Teddy heeded her order, tucking himself behind a fallen piece of roofing.

Hiding proved pointless. She'd already seen them somehow. With the portal hovering above him, Teddy caught a glimpse of the coven leader Schwartz had warned him about. Blonde hair spiralled neatly into a bun at the crown of her head, the soles of her shoes as fleshy as a palm. Her head snapped to the noise in the chapel.

'I didn't know if I'd find you again,' she said, trudging over the portal's bottom curve. 'You make it so difficult.'

Schwartz's teeth clenched. 'You couldn't have gathered that I don't *want* to be found? I told you you've got the wrong impression about me.'

Julia Chaplain smiled. The portal collapsed into itself behind her. '*You lied to me,*' she sang. 'You didn't think I would piece it together at Meredith's burning, but I did.'

'I don't know what you're talking about.'

The lid of a tomb split behind them. Teddy cursed to himself, shaken to his core. He inched between Schwartz and the sound, guarding her back.

'Don't play dumb with me. You thought I wouldn't look

deeper. That you could come and go without raising any suspicion. You should have been honest with me, Aurelia.'

'*Honest?*' Schwartz had to laugh. 'About what! Meredith didn't tell me anything. She wasn't even there to raise me. Why the fuck do you think I never had anything to do with her besides turning up at her funeral?'

Teddy felt the pressure rise in her throat. He'd shifted too far to reach backwards for her hand, but he hoped she felt the understanding.

At Chaplain's silence, he paused and turned his chin over his shoulder to find her closer than before to the girl. The high priestess's rage simmered down to amusement, and Schwartz, rooted stubbornly to the ground, let Chaplain lay her hand on her shoulder, almost comfortingly.

'So, this is where the trouble starts. That's all you had to say, you know. I can be understanding with a little openness.'

He couldn't keep his eyes on her, for the stones above them split again. Schwartz jolted, but kept her focus entwined with Julia Chaplain's. *Keep looking,* he thought. *Don't let her slip.*

Schwartz shrugged Chaplain's hand away.

'I can't tell you anything you want to hear. My m— *Meredith* wouldn't have told me. I don't want anything to do with her any more.'

'Why were you at the funeral?'

With fingers twitching restlessly around the hems of her sleeves, Schwartz pulled herself out of Chaplain's grasp. 'I don't know. To cut ties, maybe. Grief's a funny thing.'

'It's twisted,' conferred Chaplain. 'You thought it might

have been your last chance to see her. But I haven't lost all hope. You see, Aurelia, she asked for you.'

A hard gulp, and Schwartz asked, 'Did she?'

'Mm.'

Teddy assessed the sound with his back to her, but at the slightest peripheral glance saw Chaplain closing the distance between herself and Aurelia Schwartz; her hand floating towards the girl's face, smoothing back a curl with the flat of her palm. 'Afterward. If it pleases you to know, she is still around. We have our means of calling on her. Death is less permanent than you'd think.'

It isn't permanent.

They won't let me rest.

They'd called her from the dead.

Teddy cleared his throat, moving to Schwartz's side instantly. 'She won't help you.'

Schwartz was fearful that he'd broken the delicate moment she made with Chaplain, the one that guaranteed her safety in exchange for the illusion of passivity. He continued, before she tried to excuse the outburst for him, 'She's not a necromancer.'

Chaplain's disdain burned through his sweater. 'She can speak for herself.'

'Necromancy?' Schwartz shook her head. 'He's right. That's not me.'

'It doesn't have to be! But you're the key to making *mine* work, and then you could see her . . . *Talk* to her. Give her a proper goodbye, just like you wanted.'

From here, Teddy could fold Schwartz's hand in his, a spark igniting between them. *Think, Schwartz. This isn't what you want.*

It wasn't what Meredith wanted either.

They were all too close to one another, his eyes catching on the deep lines within Chaplain's face. At some point, all the ways to escape a discomforting situation dwindled to one; Teddy prayed they wouldn't get that far, that Chaplain – for some strange, yet incontestable reason – would step back through her portal and lock herself in.

'I can't do it myself,' Chaplain said. 'I'm missing something. They're never quite as they should be, but if I had a healer – someone who could return *life* to their bodies after I've woken them up . . . Someone who can help me bridge the gap between death and resurrection. Meredith told me things, but it wasn't enough. I know she has more inside her. Wouldn't you like to know what it is?'

She circled hungrily. She left like a tide, and Teddy braced himself for the eventual return, but she kept walking. East, to the crumbling window over the altar. The tombs lurched, stone crushing stone with a deafening screech.

'Look for yourself.'

CHAPTER TWENTY

Teddy lowered his mouth to Schwartz's ear. 'Run.'

She was transfixed by the coven leader's movements with a morbid curiosity, but she nodded slowly. Or maybe, he dreamed it. She didn't move an inch.

'You Brits have such neat characters,' said Chaplain.

Teddy kissed his teeth. 'Ones better left for dead.'

He'd assumed, up until this point, that the noise came from debris thrown by her spell or a general, earthen upheaval of discomfort at her presence. Until the last shadow of humour fell from the coven leader's face, and she thrust her hand over the tomb, he held onto the hope that it was only something striking the tomb from *outside* – and not from within.

'I thought you'd be more interested,' Chaplain mused to herself. The tomb lurched with the flex of her hand. Schwartz retreated on her haunches, keeping herself hidden beneath the level of the broken stone walls. 'It doesn't even interest you? That you could ask for guidance from anyone – any witch – we didn't burn? Ask for answers?'

'I prefer to leave the dead exactly where they are.'

'Even your mother?' The audacity to play with Schwartz's

loss struck Teddy with a dangerously unbidden sense of anger. 'You wouldn't give anything to see her again?'

He curled his fingers around Schwartz's wrist. *Don't listen to her.* What pressed more urgently upon them was the corpse clawing its freedom from the tomb. With every inch the cover of the tomb slipped away, the agitation of dust and decayed skin floating upwards.

Schwartz's hand shot to her stomach to settle it. 'That thing in the tomb isn't who it used to be, Chaplain. And neither is my mother.'

'You don't know that. I knew who she was, who she is, and I know now what she could be if you'd just try. I don't know why I try with you. I'm being so patient.'

She wasn't, but they were in no place to argue, standing beneath the altar of a risen corpse. The handle of a rusted blade was secured in its bone grip. Its fingers flexed, each bone strung together with delicate, sinewy threads of golden magic.

Bodies were not made to be resurrected. Certainly, none that had been rotting in a box for centuries.

Schwartz murmured something out of Teddy's earshot. Almost certainly a spell, one he couldn't predict. One that planted an advantageous seed of deceit in his mind. 'Not yet,' he whispered. Then, to Chaplain: 'She can't heal something that isn't alive – you need a true necromancer. Someone with access to the other side.'

Chaplain didn't need to know that Schwartz already had it. If she could rein in her offence, they could buy time instead of resorting to magic that would inevitably destroy more of their surroundings than she intended.

Schwartz's lips drew a severe line across her face, but she relented.

If Chaplain caught on, her expression didn't spoil it. It hardened into steel – unyielding, unforgiving. 'The good thing about these,' she added, stepping off the dais with a reverent gaze toward the corpse, 'is that you can't kill a thing that's dead, either.'

The body gripped the rusted sword at its belly and heaved it up in its arms. The body in the nearest tomb sprung with more vigour from its resting place.

Anything was fair game.

Teddy willed a fatal spell like a whip through the distance between them, where it struck an empty space. Chaplain vanished, reappearing in the north quadrant effortlessly. A portal, shut and closed in less than a breath.

Schwartz ducked at the foot of the dais as the corpses dragged themselves and their weapons forward, her fingers pressed to the ground above a deep crevice. 'I'm so fucking done with her,' she said.

'What are you doing?'

'What does it look like I'm doing, Ingram?'

Making a mistake. Chaplain turned her back to them, pitching her torso through a window to the churchyard. Two corpses were two too many. If she tried for the ones buried outside . . . The damage, the consequences, would be irreparable.

Schwartz would kill her. This much he knew. What he didn't know was how firm of a grasp she would have of new magic, and were it not successful, it would tell Chaplain everything he'd wanted to hide about her abilities.

'Move,' Teddy whispered. 'Tell me what to do.'

'It might not even work,' said Schwartz.

'It's worth a shot. Take my hand.'

She positioned her fingers over his and pushed them to the ground in her former place. 'There's a series of cracks on the ground that lead to where she's standing. If you're delicate enough, I think we can weave one of your spells through it without drawing attention . . . Grab her with it before she can figure out what we've done.'

'It *will* kill her,' he articulated, for death, even for the worst, weighed heavily on one's heart.

She nodded, squeezing his shoulder with her free hand. Forgiving herself was a problem for future-Schwartz. 'I know. And if we spend our time trying to tear this thing apart, she'll raise another twenty to do the dirty work of killing us first.'

Teddy gathered just as much; he would've forgiven her in a heartbeat anyway.

The scrape of the undead knight's blade drew nearer with each second.

The last time he hesitated, a witch had driven her knife through his wings and pressed her claws through Schwartz's skin. The memory alone should have been enough to kill the last of his apprehension, but it lived, virulent and unruly, to thwart him. Calling him a coward. Or virtuous. Maybe the only thing that separated the two was whose side he fought for.

He watched the undead knight stagger towards them, raise its sword, and bear it down upon the empty tomb nearest theirs;

and then, Teddy pressed his palm flat to the ground and sent the whisper of a killing spell through the cracks. The delicacy of it made it seem all the more sinister. It searched through the arteries of stone toward the dark heart that was Julia Chaplain in the window. It explored each passage deliberately, and even with the knight's blade scraping towards them, it was always aimed at the high priestess.

He'd never used reaper magic so deliberately. Even in Leona Sum's presence, it was Schwartz's safety that bled his magic from him, not a violent streak. A last-ditch effort at self-preservation.

He began to lift his palm to rescind the intention.

I can't forgive myself.

Julia Chaplain brought her hand above her face slowly, over the crest of a crumbling wall, as if raising a chalice in a blessing. Schwartz yanked him by the arm as another ghastly warrior swung his axe over Teddy's shoulder.

The spell severed. In his panic, he'd let more of it slip through the cracks, and the ancient stones parted with a heavy exhale.

'Are you done fucking around, Ingram?' Schwartz whispered.

The axe-wielder swung again, lodging its rusted weapon in a tangle of old roots. Teddy wound his arms around the corpse's neck, feeling its bones shifting at the slightest touch; but it felt none of the pain. Suffered none of the blows. Teddy pressed his palms to the knight's head as it attempted to shake him off like a dog shaking water from its fur. A spell rattled the corpse through its skull, reducing it to ash.

He couldn't kill a thing that wasn't dead – at least, not if it was simply a matter of life and death. But Teddy Ingram had known ruin all his life. Like Schwartz mending leaves and assembling tea for each ailment, Teddy's reaper magic knew death as *destruction*. As levelling art galleries and gnarled tree trunks just as it stopped heartbeats.

Sure, he couldn't kill a corpse, but weapons worked through more than a magic-woven stitch of bones. Whatever worked, he'd make it quick.

Schwartz leveraged the axe from the vines with a grunt and thrusted it toward the other knight. The blow knocked ribs loose, a dark, wretched sluice of rot within the corpse spilling from the frail pockets of skeletal frame. Teddy expected a scream or a grunt, but nothing came. They moved like puppets. No breath, no human noise rung from their chests.

Others sprouted from outside the walls. The other tombs.

'Grab her,' Schwartz gritted. 'Or I will.'

Chaplain moved from behind her shelter, a flash of blonde and white behind the haze of blackened limbs swinging in front of them. Teddy shook ashes from his body, sending another streak of magic towards her.

Dodged, again.

The lines beside Chaplain's lips deepened. 'Stay out of this.'

Metal rang behind him. The sword skittered across the stones. She pulled it back, committed to the weapon without death magic at her call. If Teddy couldn't finish it now—

A portal opened. Chaplain ducked, and then she was gone. Completely gone. He hadn't even blinked.

Schwartz screamed, and the clang of steel echoed throughout

the crypt, leaving her weaponless. She fumbled in the dim light. They were too far now, and the knight too close. Outside, Teddy could see the bodies rising, the ground breaking, the sea of rotten faces moving towards them like iron dust to magnetic poles.

They'd have to wait.

He summoned the sword. He'd been both an ineffective shield and a brittle sword thus far. Something to regret later on when they were gone; in the library, perhaps, with Alaric telling him off for his secrecy – but not now. Schwartz kicked the headless knight off her. It fell squarely on her knees while she kicked from her place on the hard ground, reaching and fumbling for her limbs in the dark; and as Teddy drove the blade through the first knight, he could hear her breath catch in a shriek.

He dragged the sword from the first knight's chest and impaled it again. In its stomach, through his ribs, severing the ghost of fabric that hung from its skeletal frame. Dismantling it was another kind of death – the one reserved for witches. You burned a dead witch to kill the last remaining threads of magic, and you tore apart the bone cage of an undead knight to release it from the enchantment within. You treated it with a violence that you'd never touch a living person with.

You became unspeakably cruel.

It didn't matter. The headless knight moved with a purpose in pursuit of his weapon, and with it, he'd enact the will of someone crueller than the two desperate young witches. He would ground Schwartz without a second – or first – thought, bruise her with the stiffness of his bones, all for the promise of his axe.

Teddy reached for her. She dug her fingers into his arm and

let him drag her out from beneath the jittering corpse. He pressed his heel to the headless knight's shoulders and drove the sword clean through his ribs.

He clipped through the axeman's knees. His elbows. His hands. Teddy's heartbeat pounded through his ears, in his temples; and it hurt, feeling so angry and vicious, knowing he could have stopped it all with magic if it hadn't been for his bloody *conscience*. The rattle of steel reverberated through him, and sparks scraped across the rocks.

Their assaulters were dead. Or rather, they'd been dead for hundreds of years, but they would never come back. Whatever dark resurrectionist magic that Julia Chaplain placed within their tombs and in their bodies had nothing left to infect.

The screeching of rock echoed like a church organ in the chapel.

'Get out first,' he said. 'I'll take care of it.'

'But she's gone,' Schwartz said. 'Why are they still coming?'

Chaplain had raised a goddam army before vanishing. It'd take a blast to stop them now. Teddy would have to raze the ruins into more ruined ruins. Make himself a *bomb*.

'I don't know. It doesn't matter. Find a way out and stay clear.'

'I'm not leaving without you,' she hissed.

'I'm not about to let you martyr yourself with some undead buggers either, Schwartz. The blast'll reach you too.'

Two undead soldiers lurched forwards, their newer remains dripping off their bones like tar. A dead man's teeth sunk into his arm, cutting him short. Teddy shouldered him off, crushing his boot into the corpse's neck.

Bodies surrounded them. Encased in decay like sap, Teddy felt as if the rot had claimed him.

The only way out was up.

'There's a gap in the stone that's only covered by tarp,' he gritted out. A cold, thin trickle of blood spilled down Teddy's arm from the bite. The clang of rusted steel on brittle bone deafened him, and he looked to Schwartz's puzzled face in a quick moment of stillness.

'What if it doesn't work?' she rushed. 'What if I can't shift all the way?'

'Then I'll carry you. If you stay, I stay; and that means we're both fucked. We have to try.'

They'd exhausted every other option. Schwartz twisted to kiss him clumsily against his half-shut, grimacing mouth, grabbing his shoulder with an aimless hand.

'Tell me where to go.'

She forced the transformation before the next corpse lunged.

Teddy hovered over her moulting form, the sword in his hand outstretched to form a faulty cage. Wings fluttered in his periphery. He expected the iridescent sheen of black raven's feathers, but they looked nothing like his, boasting shades of blue and white.

Then she was gone.

Gold burst from the epicentre of Teddy Ingram like petals, crushing everything in his wake.

He reared back on his heels and leaped upward, feeling his bones shift and settle into place. He bit his tongue hard, before soft mouth became beak and fabric became feathers. Before the fiery, sharp pain of having his physicality remoulded like clay dulled to nothing.

Outside, Teddy fell to the grass, shaking a bit of bone dust off his feathers. Schwartz found him quickly, urging him on. They were still too close. The town beneath them stirred with intrigue. Lights from houses switched on. Shapes of bodies emerged from their front doors.

No one will forgive me, he thought, not for destroying a house of God, of all things.

Then, they were airborne. The building collapsed beneath them. Teddy opened his beak and screeched a command that he wasn't sure Schwartz would understand in this form. Whether or not she did, he never found out; she followed the path of black wings, because there was nothing else around to follow. He shook the water from his wings, glancing past his tail to keep her small, avian form in his sight.

His gift had conjured a creature much less monstrous out of Schwartz. She was no crow, carrying the brunt of bad omens like he did. His blood had made her a magpie. A collector.

From the graveyard below, they were both shadows passing in the night. He led her to the only place they could feasibly reach before their small, thrumming hearts gave out completely.

Her wings gave out above the river.

She plummeted into the water before Teddy knew what was happening.

They were low already, descending towards the lampposts underneath Blackfriars Bridge. Teddy dived for her.

The Thames' surface buried her first. He felt her pulse

pattering unevenly, and then there was burning. Stretching. Her colour-drained face emerged within seconds, gasping for air; the magpie was gone.

She lugged herself out of the water, heaving and coughing. Teddy scrambled up beside her, his throat burning from the water in Schwartz's lungs; and once his feathers reformed to clothes, he took the jacket from his shoulders and laid it around her shoulders.

'It hurts,' she gasped.

'Where? Where does it hurt?'

'Everywhere. God, I feel like I'm dying.'

'I know.'

Her body racked with sobs, but the noise never came. She spat water, and coughed until her throat burned raw, turning her face into his shirt. 'I'm so cold.' She said it in every way, with words, with violent shivers, and a bloodless, quivering touch. She curled her knees into her chest, closing his jacket tight around her body. The pungent smell of the river tainted her hair, but he pressed his cheek to it anyway as he held her on the rocks beneath the bridge.

'I've got you. I'm right here.'

He clutched her hard to his chest. So hard that it probably hurt; they were already bruised and battered. One could tolerate this sort of pain, he thought. Dealt like a promise by someone you trusted enough to let go after they'd had their fill. Sealed together until traces of her were inseparable from him, soldered like wire to his skin and bones.

'Does it always feel like this?' she asked. 'Does it always hurt so much?'

He nodded, closing his eyes against the watchful gaze of a familiar purple light across the river. 'Every time.'

Schwartz had never seemed so small. 'I want to go home,' she whispered.

He answered, even if he wasn't sure what it meant. Even if he wasn't sure that home was a place he went to. Or if she wanted him there. But he had to make this right. He had an answer, which was more than he could say an hour ago – even if he hated the idea of it.

The last time he hesitated, here in London with Leona Sum at their throats, Schwartz had fortified her rage around him like a shield in the back seat of his parents' car; and underneath the pain of his torn flesh, he'd loved her for it. Her sharp tongue and fierce devotion. Her resilience beneath his staggering weight.

'I know,' he whispered. 'We're going home, Schwartz. I'm taking you home.'

He shut his eyes, and that purple light across the river chased him into the dark.

Teddy Ingram had a favour to repay.

CHAPTER TWENTY-ONE

He had almost forgotten that Schwartz had called Celia a cunt. The reminder of his stepmother's tight-lipped, sour expression would have made him laugh if they hadn't been recently attacked by a swarm of resurrected English Catholics.

As he stood on the unfamiliar steps of his parents' home, Teddy wasn't even sure that Celia remembered Schwartz's face. It was hardly the first thing one noticed when they found a sickly, shivering girl in ill-fitting clothing on their doorstep.

Teddy, on the other hand, had a face that Celia could never forget, no matter how much he knew she wanted to. The feeling was mutual, but evidently he was the only one left feeling the dread.

She didn't think of him much if she didn't have to.

'What have you done?' Celia asked.

He shook his head, holding onto Schwartz for comfort. 'I didn't know where else to go. I need to see my father.'

Celia looked at the girl beside him, maybe recognizing her now. Even if she did, the version of Aurelia Schwartz that faced her was a shadow of the one from the back seat of her car. Her fire had burned out, and all that it left Schwartz with was a blackened, ashen hearth, a sallow and shivering echo of what she had looked like before.

'Come inside. He should be home soon.'

As he passed, he gave Celia a curt nod, and mouthed, 'Thank you.'

'You haven't come home in a while. And I've lost track of how many times you've come to us with your problems. Or with new people to fix.'

Schwartz's retching cut Celia short. She doubled over, bracing herself on a nearby table with her weak forearms. He knew she was trying to right herself. To seem stronger and unfixable. Teddy pinned his stepmother with a stern glare and said, 'I'm short on options right now, OK? The least you could do is be civil while she's narrowly curbing death.'

'Forgive me, Theodore, if I'm apprehensive of what kind of trouble you get into when you're away so long. Why are you wet? Is she sick?'

Schwartz covered her mouth, but she held in her coughing. Was it from the water left over in her lungs or the wind caught in her soaked hair? She wasn't sick yet, but she would be. That kind of answer only led to more questions, for which Teddy lacked the energy.

'I don't know,' he answered. 'She might be. We can leave by morning, though. We won't be any trouble.'

'I didn't say I was rushing you out now, did I? I know your father will want you to stay.'

'And what about you? If you tell him you want us out, I'm sure he'd take your word as law.'

The clench of her jaw was uncomfortably visible. 'I just need you to tell me what's happening.'

Alaric's was the voice in Teddy's mind striking her down. Telling her no. Hoarding his secrets until they were spilling unceremoniously from loose seams.

Guilt centred in Teddy's body. This must have been what it was like to face Teddy in the shop, knowing he had to be civil, and being silent instead. Slipping the cuffs off his wrists, knowing what kind of questions came with magic like that.

'I'll explain everything later,' Teddy said, and it wasn't a lie. Schwartz swept the sinewy hair from her eyes and looked at him inquisitively. Once they had a moment to themselves to settle in, she would say that the truth wasn't something they talked about with humans, certainly not ones with such hostile demeanours and fraught relationships, but what she failed to grasp time and time again was that Teddy Ingram did not lie to people often. He simply kept much of the truth inside.

Celia placed a cold, unwavering hand on Teddy's arm and led them both up a dark, polished staircase.

'There is a bedroom on the left that you can use for the night. I'll have to ask Harry for help with new linens – he insists on keeping them out of my reach for some reason.' Celia then squared her shoulders to Schwartz and gave her a tight-lipped smile. How someone could look so intimidating in cotton pyjamas was unfortunate. 'The bath's through this door. I'll send Theodore up with some towels. My soaps are all on the back ledge, but they're obviously not made for curls. Use whichever you like.'

'Thank you,' Schwartz murmured.

'I could be more accommodating with a little heads up, you know.'

Teddy sighed. Somehow this was the easiest conversation they'd had in years. 'I wasn't exactly anticipating things to devolve into shit. Next time, maybe.'

'Hmm.'

Schwartz's weight bore into his side, quivering from the night air. He nudged the bathroom door open with his knee and hoisted her inside. 'Come on, Schwartz, stay with me. I've got you.'

Celia trailed behind them like a shadow. The bathroom was too crowded. Schwartz lowered herself onto the closed seat of the toilet while Teddy ran the bath.

'I don't suppose you have any of my old things boxed up somewhere? Some of my old clothes, maybe?'

'I doubt any of them would fit you any more,' Celia replied.

'It hasn't been *that* long.'

'Yes. It has.'

Teddy did his best to ignore the ire in her words. Three little words that could upheave his composure. He blamed it on the events of the evening, his tentative nerves, the residual illness overtaking Schwartz's body. Anything but believing that Celia Ingram could hurt him so easily, could find his core and cut into it with a single strike.

No one else understood how time moved differently in his quiet little town. Sometimes it was a standstill, but mostly it was a blur. An amorphous shape that he couldn't grasp. He measured it mostly by all the things he could have been doing in Cambridge, by thesis research he couldn't do, familiar restaurants he couldn't dine at. He missed playing a spontaneous game of football with Lawrence and his pals near the college. With all the time that seemed to pass without him here in London, why had nothing changed? Celia's pale brows took the same furious slant. Her mouth was always pulled into a grimace.

Maybe that was unfair. She had made it clear over the years that having him to look after was hard enough. Trouble followed him everywhere, sewed to his clothing in decorative stitching like designer labels. Even if it wasn't so dire, Celia made it into something mountainous and unending, never failing to remind him that they'd be better off without the trouble he tracked in on his boots.

Teddy swallowed the phantom taste of river water as the bath filled beside him. He perched on the edge, avoiding Schwartz's inquisition like the eyes of Medusa. 'Can I take these off?'

She nodded, removing her sweater with a visible jerk. Teddy kneaded her calf and got to work easing off her Chelsea boots. To Celia, he asked, 'Do you have anything then? Something I can lend her for the night?'

Celia appraised the shape of Aurelia Schwartz without her layers, her eyes catching on the tattoo ink at her shoulder. 'I'm sure I have something.'

The door shut behind her. The bathroom seemed to grow to three times its size.

He met Celia downstairs in the kitchen where she tugged red grapes from their stem and popped them into her mouth leisurely. Her hip pressed into the edge of the marble countertop, her hair loosened from around a strategically placed ribbon ever so slightly by a pillow she had been resting upon that silvery blonde threads brushed her neck. She kept her eyes on her bowl, leaving him unacknowledged. What did he have to say? He was a proper adult who couldn't shake the adolescent feeling of having his mother's pointed finger in front of his face.

'I left a change of clothes for her underneath the banister. Whatever's happened, I'm sure the silk will feel nice on her skin.'

'Thank you.' He said it aloud this time, and those two words were just enough to give away the wrongness of how it sounded.

Celia gave a single nod. Teddy didn't care much for small talk, but whenever Schwartz accused him of being too quiet or saying too little, he'd give in just so he didn't have to feel like he was Celia, giving him the cold shoulder. Chances are he had learned it from her in the first place.

'You said my father will be home soon?'

'Any minute now. He was catching up with some old friends this evening. I'm sure he'll want to talk to you tonight, too, but you have to send him to bed. He has a surgery tomorrow.'

'Sounds like he might be too tired for me.'

Almost scornfully, she muttered, 'He always has time for you, Theodore. He doesn't say it often, but I see how much he misses you.'

'Does he?'

Celia gritted her teeth. 'Don't be stupid. I'll show you all the things of yours that he's kept. It takes up too much space in the closets, and I'm sure you won't need it any more. If you've gone this long without it, I figure you won't come back for it later.'

It was a strange thought to him, because, aside from his teenage wardrobe, there were out-of-print copies of the first short story he ever got published and old books he used to love so much that their pages had fingerprint smudges of ink. Sure, he didn't *need* those things any more, but there were few happy moments in his childhood that Teddy could only preserve in the knowledge that those items were still safe somewhere. Be it in a box in his parents' new home or underneath his mattress in Townsend. They were colourful marks made over years of angry teenage rebellion that remained in his heart by an anchor's weight.

Teddy had been forced to consider his own sentimentality after Kenny Eakley died. He never understood Celia. He had felt her resentment long before he accepted Kenny's empathetic gift but never found out what he'd done to earn it. Whatever it was, she made it clear it was his fault. Few people were as scornful as Celia Ingram without good reason.

Still, after he'd delivered the folded stack of her silk pyjamas, he found her downstairs in front of a packed closet, mulling over his things, and told her, 'I'm sorry. For not coming home.'

His stepmother curled her fingers around her chin thoughtfully before turning to him. 'I never expected you to think of this place as home. I'm not sure what you consider home now, but I always knew it wasn't going to be our place by Vicky park. Too many bad memories hanging around the garden. We thought we would find something better here. Or at least, something new.'

'It's beautiful here,' he said, meaning it. 'I'm glad Dad found a place for his favourite tapestry.'

'I always hated that thing. It doesn't go with anything.'

Teddy smiled. His gaze wandered to a cardboard box that his name was written on. Even enlarged, Teddy recognized his father's handwriting. Harry Ingram's H's were always taller, and he had a jagged, doctor's penmanship.

'I think that's where he keeps your old school jumpers. You see what I mean? You don't need those any more. And Lord knows if you'll ever have kids to dress in them.'

'Good point.'

'Do you ever think about it? Children? You've been seeing that girl a while now, haven't you? I thought she looked familiar.'

'We aren't—'

'I believe she told me I was a cunt.'

Teddy groaned, wiping his hand over his eyes. 'It's complicated.'

'Why? Is she pregnant?'

'Christ, Mum, she's not pregnant.'

Celia rolled her eyes and pointed to a box above her head. Teddy silently fetched a stepladder from an alcove of the garage and grabbed it for her.

'You've been claiming things are complicated for as long as I've known you, Theodore; and I'm betting that things are far simpler than you think.'

With a sigh, he opened the box and rifled through it for clothes that might still fit him. 'Now, why would I do that to myself?'

'I don't pretend to understand why you are the way you are, but it's true, isn't it? Half the things you call complicated are quite simple when you step back and see the big picture, but you involve yourself so deeply that it's hard to look away. You invest too much of yourself into things you shouldn't worry about, and it ages you greatly. I know you care. I know you care so much it feels unfair sometimes. But I also know how easy it is to crash and burn when you've got your eyes on a different target. Watch where you're going. Take care of yourself. We've done enough of that for you already.'

Teddy said nothing. He lowered his head and found a pair of black joggers that could fit him passably.

It was only for the night, anyway.

One night was all Schwartz asked of him the first time he brought her to London, and it was all he allowed himself now. If she got sick, he would find them somewhere else to stay nearby and take her back to Cambridge at the week's end.

This was always a last resort. At best, Celia and Harry gave them a place to catch their breath, but around every corner was an argument waiting to break or a wound waiting to be reopened.

Celia grabbed his elbow and squeezed lightly. Her voice lowered to a whisper, smooth and even like cursive script though each word was a sharp scratch of ink.

'He will be so happy to see you again.'

Teddy felt compelled to ask, *And you? Are you happy?* But the words sank back down his throat, and he swallowed them hard.

It was a different house, yet the memories were all the same. All just as poignant, as unavoidable. Hidden in each stark alcove was the possibility of being discovered by Celia's wandering gaze, her steel grip. No matter how it began, it would end in shame, with a boy curled around his pillow, wishing he were anywhere else.

If Teddy Ingram were *not* Teddy Ingram, he wouldn't think of the house across the river as the worst place to be stuck. It was tidy and large enough to give their belongings the space to breathe without seeming too vacant. Impressive to anyone else, if a bit sterile. Teddy approached the closed bathroom door, feeling like the smallest thing there.

He knocked gently. Schwartz should have come out by now. She'd taken the towels and twisted the lock behind her. Teddy might have been worried if he couldn't feel the steady rhythm of her pulse on the other side, keeping time with his.

'You all right, Schwartz?'

She sniffed softly but said nothing. His eyelids lowered. He touched his forehead to the door, wishing he could undo the past twenty-four hours. He wanted to ask, *Are you cold? Come here and let me fix it. Are you shaking? I could hold you still.*

'Rory,' he said, but couldn't finish it. He had too many questions and a tone that was just too sharp despite his efforts to be gentle. Celia had retired to her bedroom already, so Teddy lowered himself to the ground, his back slunk against the door, trying his hand at patience.

What was a few more minutes of waiting for someone in eternal anticipation? For now, he measured the time by the weight of her breath, staying alert to the sound of the front door.

Schwartz cleared her throat. 'You should sleep.'

Teddy closed his eyes. 'As should you.'

A pause. 'You first.'

'It might be very difficult without you next to me.'

With a shuffle, he felt her weight pushing back against the door. Her voice was hoarse, barely audible through the wood. 'Is it always difficult?'

It didn't usually give him trouble, but curiosity kept his mind racing against its will. He couldn't fathom falling asleep without having at least one question answered. 'Did you mean to dive into the river?'

'I'll be out soon,' she said evasively. 'Go to bed.'

'I wouldn't blame you,' Teddy whispered.

'It was a long flight. I didn't mean to hit the water; I was just so tired.'

'You handled it better than I did my first time.'

He thought of the moonlight on her wings, the blue, silken tips of her feathers. All of her pocketed, unbroken leaves, her dandelion stems. Was there anything left in her pockets now? Had it all been washed away in the Thames?

If he made himself small enough, she might pluck him from the ground and add him to her collection of pretty things. He'd mind it less than he minded being under his parents' roof.

Silence dragged between them, moving them apart; and Teddy felt himself drifting, the exhaustion catching up. He could fall asleep here, waiting for her to speak.

A dog, he thought. A dead bird. He reeked just as badly as a dog with a dead thing; he was desperate for a shower, but it'd have to wait.

Minutes passed before she spoke again, until she could tell herself that he'd fallen asleep or that he'd left. 'When I was falling, I kept thinking of my mother. I saw her in a dream a few nights ago. She opened her mouth like she had something to tell me, but Chaplain never let her. It makes me think she's not just a puppet. That there's a chance she still has agency.'

'Chaplain is baiting you,' Teddy said.

'Knowing that doesn't make it any easier. Just makes it hurt more, thinking about how she could have been kind, in spite of everything. I kept seeing her face while I was over the city, wanting to talk to me; and I thought if I could reach into the river, she'd be on the other side reaching for me too. I didn't mean to fall in. I just . . . don't think I cared enough to stop it.'

Teddy pressed his lips together. 'I wouldn't let anything happen to you. What you're saying, it's just—'

'It happens to the best of us, Ingram. Your magic is no more dangerous than a knife or a bullet. I'm not dead,' she explained. 'Nor do I intend to be any time soon. But it overwhelms me. Weighs me down at the worst of times.'

He pressed his lips together firmly, wary of becoming another person with an open mouth and no words; but he'd given her his magic knowing it made unforgivable mistakes, and he couldn't help but think of what might happen if she gave in.

Again.

Schwartz told him, 'I didn't mean to scare you.'

'You terrify me,' Teddy replied through the door. 'I don't know what I would have done if you didn't shift all the way. Brought the whole place to the ground, I guess. Buried us with all those resurrected bodies.'

'I'd kill you for that. Even if you were dead, I'd kill you again.'

A curious thump sounded in his ribcage. He shifted against the door. 'What the hell are you doing in there, Schwartz?'

'Testing something. Do you feel that?'

He stilled his nerves. His ribs thumped again. 'Are you trying to kill me *now?* It's dishonourable.'

Schwartz laughed, and Teddy revelled in it like the bird-song of a rare and fabled species. He thought of her hands knotting into his mangled feathers, the innocent curiosity with which she drew them along his gashes. They were twined together now, linked by the magic in their veins. He pictured them spiralling towards the earth together like eagles with interlocked talons, veering just before she could take him down with her.

'Trust me,' Schwartz said. 'You would know.'

CHAPTER TWENTY-TWO

He was too tired to dream. That's what Teddy Ingram believed, but, at best, it was a half-truth. He dreamed of Kenny beneath the magnolia trees, stretched out in the sunlight with his jumper riding up his stomach. He felt the pressure of Celia's hand on his back – so solid that he wondered if she was truly there.

He shed the memory like sheets with the first light of morning. It streamed through the gauzy curtains and drenched the room in a dry haze.

Teddy listened to the call of birds in the garden. Mostly pigeons, though he heard the occasional bleat of crows too. There were always crows. Gingerly, he lifted the covers from his body and detached himself from Schwartz's back. A sliver of skin peered out from the layers of Celia's silk pyjamas, which he traced with his fingers. Damp with sweat, she shivered violently, the tight knot of her body rattling like a stone. He pulled the duvet up to her chin and secured it around her.

Her eyelids fluttered restlessly. She opened her mouth, trapped somewhere between sleep and waking, and did nothing more than breathe; but still, he waited.

With a shudder, she asked, 'Where are you going?'

He pulled the sticky, damp curls from the back of her neck, grinning to himself. 'You'd be angry if I told you. Go back to sleep. I'll bring you some water before I go.'

As he rose, he lifted the back of his knuckles to her temple. There was no point to the act. He could have known simply as an empath that she was running a fever. It didn't soothe the aching muscles and compression in her chest. He felt it all, worse now that he was so close.

'You're lucky I'm bedridden then,' she told him. 'Don't tell me. I don't want to know.'

Teddy flashed her a thin smile. 'Perfect.'

He left his coat at the edge of the bed but re-dressed in his other clothes, which were still damp from the river. He flexed his shoulders, then his toes, feeling the weight of the crypt hanging on his body. Those cold, skeletal fingers left bruises on his arms that had been covered up by his shirt. The mark of the first corpse's rotten teeth left indents on his bicep, red and tender to the touch.

He discarded the old pair of joggers he'd slept in and a shirt that was just a tad too tight. His shoes were stiff and cold, and he bent his ankles side to side to wear them back into their usual state of flexibility. Schwartz said little, neither probing him with questions nor objecting to his departure, her eyes red and ringed in dark, puffy flesh.

Tugging his belt through the loops of his trousers, Teddy was acutely aware of her gaze on his back even while he faced away. It crept up his spine like a chill.

'How old were those?' she asked.

'No fucking clue.'

'I've never pegged you for a sweatpants kind of guy.'

'Not even for pyjamas? They're comfortable.' He raised his brows quizzically. 'What kind of guy do I look like?'

She shrugged. 'Every time I think I have you figured out, you surprise me. To this day, your neck remains elusive.'

'Chasing the thrill of an open throat, I see.'

'It's a bit nunnish, honestly.'

The intimacy of watching someone dress had always felt scrutinous. Seeing how they built themselves up every morning from the blank slate, the marble slab refined. Schwartz had her reasons for refusing to keep her dates around for the morning, but Teddy found it humanizing, often to his chagrin. His past partners would watch him pull his jumpers on and tuck his shirt into the waistband of his trousers, and get too confident assuming things from the visibility of his ribs or the blankness of his stomach – like they were now the keepers of secrets he never intended to grant. They knew him in bed or in passing, in a pub or across the court, but not about his family or his passions, so he'd go about his week feeling guilty for ignoring their expectant messages.

They knew the person he wanted them to know, each one a different face – whatever they found charming the previous evening. A face shrouded in magenta club lighting, or a well-versed poet, armed with Romantic sonnets. He could be anything except himself, and they would think they had a key.

He wouldn't have let anyone touch his scars if he'd been brave enough to date after the events of the previous winter. It was only because Schwartz was so stubborn and incapable of failure that she managed to find herself in his good humour time and time again – and find him so willing to be touched.

Avoiding Celia in the kitchen, Teddy poured a glass of water and took it upstairs, placing it on the nightstand near Schwartz's head. 'You'll be OK while I'm out, yeah?'

She drank slowly and said, 'Can't be much worse.'

'As much as I hate proving you wrong, you absolutely can,' said Teddy. 'If Celia tries to talk to you, say nothing.'

'You think I'll come up with something meaner than "cunt" this time around? I swear I can be nice, Ingram.'

'I know you can. When people deserve it. I'm mostly worried that she'll say something that upsets you. I just need you to stay put until I get back.' Teddy reached for her hand and squeezed it gently. 'Then, you're going to let me take care of you. All right?'

She covered her mouth with her other arm to cough and said, 'I'm not dying. I'll be fine.'

'I don't care. It's just what we do. Be good.'

He stood to leave her bedside, but she grasped his hand and held him firmly in place. For several seconds, Schwartz said nothing. Her thumb grazed the tops of his knuckles slowly, raising gooseflesh all the way up his arms. She leaned forward and kissed them. 'Be safe,' she whispered into his skin. 'Whatever you're doing.'

A blush crept into his face. He nodded, omitting that he only meant to run to a Primark or the nearest equivalent shop to replace her tattered clothing. 'I know. I'll be back soon.'

Downstairs, Celia was transfixed by the television. He heard it in passing as he eyed some of his father's books in the hall. A historic burial ground, desecrated. Early investigations leading nowhere. Bodies that weren't simply thrashed but missing from their graves altogether.

Celia sat at the edge of a neat, cream-coloured sofa, hunched over her crossed legs.

Teddy couldn't help himself from lingering. What did people see in the aftermath? The result of an unsuccessful grave robbery? What evidence had they left? Hundreds passed through that cemetery daily, and the crypt was a particular point of intrigue. Fingerprints and loose hairs were endless. Blood, on the other hand, wasn't something you found regularly in a place like that.

Schwartz had come here scuffed, roughened up and bruised. Had any of the reanimated corpses broken through skin? Teddy had a mark on his arm in the shape of teeth, but the blood loss was minimal. It welled in the half-moon divots on his skin, branding him as a vandal.

That couldn't be enough to incriminate him, could it? They'd have to find him first. To know who he was . . . His clothes had been washed, but he checked each garment for signs of wear. Minimal, if anything, he determined. Schwartz's clothing hadn't been so lucky.

Celia cleared her throat, turning to where he stood in the doorway. 'You've heard of this, haven't you? I don't suppose you're here for the sake of family bonding.'

Teddy rolled his eyes. 'Wouldn't you say we're overdue for that?'

'I thought you'd be more interested, as a medievalist.'

'Former medievalist,' he corrected. 'I caught wind of it.'

'We'll have to talk about that too, won't we? Your schooling.'

'I don't want to talk about it.'

'All that tuition money,' she mused. 'None of which you paid.'

'I'm aware.'

Celia glared at him over her lenses sternly. 'You've made your point. You're going back to Pembroke. You and I both know it's best you keep this soul-search to a year and return next term.'

'Louisa needs to be looked after by someone she knows,' he explained. 'And she needs that person to stick around, not to jump ship at the next best opportunity.'

'There are systems in place for orphaned children. You are not her father or her brother. You're impersonating the man of the house for a family that you aren't even a part of. The real world is waiting for you,' she said. 'If you don't acknowledge it, it'll leave without you.'

He opened his mouth, but his throat had become threateningly small and tight, so nothing came. He shut it promptly, lowering his head. Anger bubbled up in his chest. He suppressed it again, as he always did, washing it over with gentler thoughts like sorrow or defeat.

This was nothing. Hardly the worst thing Celia had ever said to him, especially not in private like this. Still, he couldn't help feeling smaller in his stepmother's vicinity, reduced to a vulnerable sense of helplessness.

I'm waiting on the platform, watching everyone leave. Schwartz will leave even if she loves you. She'll leave especially *if she loves you.*

Teddy envied her strong will. He would have folded at the first ask, if she'd truly wanted him to stay.

Even so: 'I'm not leaving Lou. If that means I find a way to reimburse the tuition money and prolong my gap year into a permanent leave, then that's what I'm doing. I'm taking care of things.'

Celia raised the remote and paused the segment while the woman at the crime scene was in the middle of speaking, rendering her face in an unfavourable expression. 'Theodore,' his stepmother murmured musically. Since he was a child, he knew that specific tone came right before she'd deliver the cruellest words he'd heard thus far in his life. 'I don't think you understand how much patience we grant you in times like these. More often than we'd like to, I should add. Do you think Margaret Westfield's son shows up to their flat in the dead of night with a sick girlfriend on his arm and tries to hide their former whereabouts?'

'Eric Westfield was expelled from Imperial College on several counts of sexual harassment,' Teddy said. 'Our offences are completely incomparable.'

'You know what I mean,' Celia said, but Teddy's patience had been wearing thin since the moment she'd greeted him on her doorstep.

He sighed to himself, moving towards the front door to unlock it. Midday had sprung on him viciously. He squinted his eyes from the sunlight, and said, 'No, Mother. I don't think I do. I'll be back soon.'

*

The ringing sounded in the payphone's receiver. That he could remember Alaric's number was a miracle after the number of years he'd spent clicking on his name to send him anything. The caretaker didn't answer for several rings, and when he did, he sounded more his age than ever before – gruff and a touch lazy.

'It's almost noon,' Teddy said, unamused.

'And? I'm tired. I waited for you to call last night. Where have you been?'

'It's bad,' he explained. 'Have you seen the news?'

Silence trickled into the phone line. 'What happened?'

'Chaplain doesn't know how to resurrect the dead – not the way she wants to, at least.'

'She's doing necromancy?' Alaric asked.

Teddy peered through the glass of the telephone box for lingering tourists before continuing. 'I actually think she's a portal witch, but she's managed it. They're like puppets when they resurrect; they're not acting with agency of their own.'

'That's not unusual,' said Alaric. 'Not necessarily a sign of failed necromancy.'

'But you can't swear a willing blood oath if the other party is acting under coercion. Right?'

'Right.'

Teddy sucked his gums. 'Chaplain's a coven leader. She would know that. She's smarter than Leona Sum was – operating with more information.'

Alaric sighed on the other end. 'You're assuming that she wants witch's blood like Leona did. We can't know that. That isn't a popular opinion among witches. You'd be surprised to know how many consider the act almost taboo.'

'How else would she be raising witches from the dead? And why? Not for the company, I imagine.' Teddy checked his watch and saw that it was full of water. That, he could probably repair, but the river had damaged his phone beyond that, and he'd have to get a new one soon.

He might have had five contacts to add to it after the Thames flushed his first phone clean. Five, if he could remember them, including Alaric and Aurelia. He could hold onto that fraying thread of hope to which his old friends from Pembroke were still tied, but six months without their contact had given him reason to loosen his hold too.

Maybe he could return after all this time, and they'd carry on uninterrupted. He'd never forget how much half a year spent in silence weighed on him, how much their indifference stuck in his psyche.

The caretaker ignored Teddy's question and asked, 'Where are you right now? Where's Aurelia?'

'We're in London,' Teddy answered, wondering if the caretaker knew, despite the omission of his parents' names, that they would have had nowhere else to go – no one else to turn to. 'I think she's sick.'

'How sick?'

'A nasty cold, at least. Could be worse. I'll explain everything I can when I get back.'

'Teddy,' Alaric sang softly. It lacked the threat that his mother's words held and smothered him in a warm, familiar comfort. 'Are you coming back soon? Should I ask Hye-Jin for help?'

'I can handle it,' Teddy answered. Even if he wasn't sure, even if he didn't know, he'd figured out how to look after Lou, and a child came with far more strings attached than a partner. Together, they would figure something out.

Alaric remained silent for a while, waiting to be called. Waiting to be needed. Somehow, Teddy felt like he'd been in conversation with himself. If he couldn't speak, they'd keep each other on the line forever.

Nothing else came to mind – nothing except for what his mother had said, and Teddy didn't feel like divulging her words. It would accomplish nothing and make everyone miserable.

Before wishing the caretaker goodbye, Teddy added, 'Thank you, Al. For looking after them.'

He heard a small shuffle on Alaric's end before he received a response. 'You know, they're important to me too.'

'It isn't much, but I thought it'd help a little.'

She smiled faintly, moving aside to make room for him on the edge of the bed expectantly. 'Now, why would I have been upset about soup? Is it awful?' she asked as he popped the lid of the bowl off for her. 'Are you poisoning me?'

'The soup's fine,' he said, hiding a smile. 'Not poisoned to my knowledge. But some of your clothing from last night has seen better days. I had to find you something else.'

Teddy handed her a spoon, and she stirred while keeping her eyes locked on his. His chest tightened in response to hers, and he couldn't justify it quickly enough that it didn't fill him with guilt.

Schwartz cleared her throat, though the friction in her voice lingered. 'What do you mean?'

'I mean, that cardigan, which you doused in the Thames

last night, is shredded. Jeans are mostly unscathed, but your shirt is a little threadbare also. I knew you'd object to me getting you something new, but it was a necessity this time.'

She sighed, then promptly devolved into another cough. Teddy placed his hand between her shoulder blades as she pitched forward, stroking her back in lazy circles. Whatever illness she'd acquired from breathing in river water had festered in her lungs; and with the cough came the choking. With all that came the restless sleep. Teddy had slept with his arm around her stomach and her back to his chest, steadying her while she shook and groaned and sputtered.

'Honestly,' Schwartz said now, 'that shirt's been threadbare for years. I'm pissed about the cardigan though. I liked that one.'

Teddy's hand lifted with the slow rise and fall of her back. She held the heel of her hand to her forehead, pressing hard.

'I'm sorry,' he said, not knowing if it was the wrong thing to say. She shrugged. After another moment, he added, 'Alaric is worried about you.'

'You called him?'

'He's taking care of Lou right now,' he explained. 'I had to.'

Schwartz looked away, dropping her head. 'I know, I just – I'll be fine, Ingram. I don't want him worrying about me.'

'I wasn't going to keep it from him,' he argued. 'He asks about you frequently. Cares about you a great deal. He wouldn't have let me off the phone if I didn't give him a little assurance that you were OK too.' Although she busied herself in an attempt to appear indifferent, Teddy knew that the caretaker's concern weighed on her chest as painfully as her affliction.

'Besides,' he added, 'I told him I'd handle things. All that said, I know he doesn't need to concern himself with more than what's going on with Chaplain. If we're here, I can manage on my own.'

She shook her head, prodding the vegetables in her soup with her spoon. 'I don't want you to worry about me either. It's not fair.'

'You keep talking about fair like I'm going to serve you an IOU one day for all the things I didn't get back. That's not how this works. There's no debt between us. You know this.'

He left her side and took the wrapped piece of sourdough from where he'd left it on the nightstand, tearing a piece off for her.

He took the rest for himself.

'Your dad came in a little while ago.'

'Did he.' The curtness of those small words bit the response from Schwartz's tongue.

'To see how I was feeling,' she said. 'And for you.'

Biting into the chewy crust, he scanned the perimeter of the spare room, eyeing the bookshelves and the abstract art prints Celia had undoubtedly taken from the Tate Modern's gift shop.

'Apparently, Celia told him not to bother anyway.'

'Figures,' Teddy mumbled, mostly to himself. 'Can't even keep her nose out of a goodwill outreach.'

Behind him, Schwartz picked at her bread, tearing it into smaller, doughier shreds. The cold grip of her stare was absent from his figure, leaving him to twiddle his thumbs or tug at his hair – whatever mindless action tied the first glance and the next a little faster.

He didn't really know what to do with himself if someone wasn't looking. When it wasn't the other researchers at Pembroke – Lawrence looking at him over a gaming controller in his flat, or Carney from behind his office desk – it was Gemma and Lou. Who was he when he wasn't a friend, or a student? A brother, a burden? A word one couldn't quite pin down and left his tongue tied and clumsy.

His Cambridge flat had been vacant, almost sterile. There, he slept and dressed and cooked the occasional meal for himself, but he preferred being anywhere else if he could help it. He couldn't remember the last person he had invited in before Aurelia Schwartz came for dinner. But he remembered the diligent way that she had studied his bare walls and his stray papers. He remembered the sudden insecurity of having it take shape in her presence, having it become real. He'd never felt so bothered by it before she was there, studying it – studying *him*. Until then, he'd been switched off, carrying out his household tasks outside of himself, not really caring about anything.

It was easy to fall back into that mindlessness when he found himself alone. Easy to lose himself if no one else was there for his magic to feed from. His eyes moved over the spines of Celia's and Harry's books without reading them. He scanned them again, trying to remain present without Schwartz grounding him. They were the oddities, the outliers to all the carefully curated shelves downstairs in the living room, shunned to this private room upstairs to take up space and collect dust.

His shoulders sagged in relief as soon as her gaze returned.

'He offered to write a prescription for some antibiotics for me. He's nice . . . I mean, I knew that from the Tate. How'd he end up with your mom, again?'

'She's not really my mother.'

'Right. I knew that.'

'It's also not important. What matters is that I'm quite literally reaping the consequences of having her for a parent as opposed to whatever witch gave me my magic. There's a sharp, black rock where her heart's supposed to be.'

'Maybe she tricked him.' Schwartz cleared her throat with a scratch. 'Maybe it's blackmail.'

'My guess is as good as yours. I don't try to understand it, and I doubt Celia really cares if I do. Sometimes, I think things would be easier if I just believed in something. She believes in the Catholic Christian god, and that grants her an unprecedented vindication in everything she does – or says.'

'Hence the nunnish-ness.'

Teddy's lips twitched at the corners. 'Maybe the personal modesty trickled down. That, and the inimitable shame. But I was doomed from the start. If I had any chance of becoming more than my gift, it died in the church every Sunday while she was breathing down my neck. There is no hope for someone who is born wicked. I was never going to be good, even if I'd tried.'

Schwartz considered her bowl of soup while he came to and began considering her.

A pleasant jolt of surprise ran through him at the number of books on the shelf that had belonged to him. His eyes fell on a familiar title, the text flipped from that on the spines adjacent to it. He pulled it out with a dry 'Ha.'

Schwartz eyed him curiously over a dripping spoonful as Teddy held up the cover. *Poésies de Marie de France: Lais.*

'Is that yours?'

'Mhmm.' He pressed his lips together, thumbing through the pages. 'After I'd grown out of au pairs, Celia thought I'd lose my French, so she'd insist on me using French copies of most of my books.'

'Au pairs,' Schwartz echoed scathingly. 'Just when I start to think you're not as posh as you seem.'

'Product of my circumstances, unfortunately,' he said, collapsing into the large leather chair across the room from her. His annotations in the margins were all in English, his younger self's penmanship tidier than the current's.

The mattress creaked under her shifting weight. 'Which lai did you read that reminded you of me?'

Pink crept into his cheeks. He had said that, hadn't he?

There were lines, not lais, that made him think of her. If he had found a tale that'd tell him how their time would end, he would have followed it to the letter; but his feelings for Schwartz were unprecedented. He was still struggling to find his own words for what they were, cobbling a creature together out of parts from more reflective minds.

It was probably a complete coincidence that the most suitable words came from holy men. The mythical Sir Gawain with the Virgin Mary on his shield, chasing an opponent that would surely end him. To Teddy Ingram, faith was good for one thing: courage.

He shuddered to think he had almost been too late finding his faith in her. If he hadn't followed her to London that first time. Or folded his wings around her in the Tanks.

'None of them,' he admitted. 'More a collection of little things.'

She grinned into her bowl, tipping it back to sip the broth. 'Damn.'

'Sorry.'

Replacing the bowl on the nightstand, she asked, 'Did you always know you wanted to go into translation?'

He closed the book over a line that had made him think of her profoundly. From 'Lanval'. He balanced his right ankle over his left knee, sinking into the plush, packed leather. 'I did.'

She wiped her nose, glaring at him for the unsatisfying reply. 'Why?'

'Aside from the fact that I grew up idolizing Tolkien, I found people difficult to understand. There was a lot of disconnect in my home, if you could imagine. I used to wonder, why keep a child just to hate it? Why take him to church if you thought he would never know God's love? Everyone around me was always saying one thing and meaning something else. And after Kenny left me with his magic, I had this other layer of misunderstanding to account for – people feeling things that they didn't express. Sure, it's a matter of context, but there's so much that gets lost in everyday conversation. If I thought about it for more than a few minutes, translation seemed like the perfect way to apply myself. We lose something when we translate. Words in one language that have no equivalent or direct translation in another get distilled for the sake of consumption. I always loved translations that were less direct. There are so many ways to tell the same story, but I always loved the ones where you kept the intention, even if you lost the exactness. I dunno. I want to know how it felt to hear those stories for the first time. Before all we had left of the experience was a manuscript. I want to be in conversation with them. I want to understand them. That feeling is the facet I'm missing. I want to preserve it.'

'That's . . .' She nodded, trailing off. 'That's nice. It's a nice answer.'

'You wanted one,' he said, keeping the next confined to fewer words. Long-winded explanations wrung him for his energy.

'I mean, it's good,' Schwartz said. 'You act so steely with people, but you're annoyingly well intentioned. I don't know why you do it.'

'Do what?'

'Pretend you're so awful. If anyone else knew you as well as I do, they wouldn't believe it either.' She gave him a little smile. 'I meant it, you know. When I said you were a good person. It wasn't some pre-emptive attempt at self-preservation, like I thought you might punish me for thinking otherwise.'

'Theory doesn't make good people,' Teddy said.

'But you try,' Schwartz responded. 'That's more than most people can say about themselves, and it counts for a lot.'

Not enough, he thought. As much as he tried to absolve himself of the sin, his wrongdoing could never be undone. It'd never bring back Gemma's son. It wouldn't cleanse him of the dark magic that tainted his blood.

'Hey,' said Schwartz. 'You can't be too bad if you're bringing me soup and sourdough while I'm sick. I've been told I'm not exactly an easy person to take care of. "Too stubborn for my own good."'

Teddy's eyes traced the grooves in the floorboard. His fingernails scraped at the fading letters stamped into the cover of his book. 'Yeah. I guess not.'

CHAPTER TWENTY-THREE

What Schwartz didn't tell him until after he'd showered and changed into a newly purchased set of clothing was that Harry Ingram knew about her magic.

Teddy hadn't realized his father was still in the house. His absence thus far wasn't something Teddy cared to question. Teddy refilled Schwartz's glass with water and found Harry perched at her bedside when he returned, having popped in from the upstairs room with the deftness of a hunting dog.

'I hope I didn't interrupt anything.' Harry Ingram's intrusion shook them from their companionable silence. Teddy went to the chair to retrieve his book, clapping it shut like it withheld a dangerous secret.

'He was waxing poetic to me just now, actually,' Schwartz said.

Teddy rolled his eyes. 'Her cold is making her delirious.'

'"Some poets dare to be obscure,"' Schwartz lamented, pulling from the lais themselves, before a cough overtook her body. Swiftly she averted her face away from where Harry Ingram sat. Teddy pushed the glass onto the nightstand beside her and squeezed in-between them – two tall, observant birds on a wire.

'Did you need something?' Teddy asked his father.

'I was asked to be here,' Harry said. 'She said you could heal.'

'*What?*'

Schwartz's fingers curled over his wrist. She scraped her nails against the hem of his sleeve. 'Call it academic curiosity. It's worth a shot.'

Teddy's face hardened, his jaw setting so firmly he thought it might crack. 'He's never seen me like that, Schwartz.'

'But he knows,' she whispered back. Teddy couldn't lie to her now. Of course, his father knew that he and his son were not the same, that something outside of him had granted Teddy an inhuman, unnatural ability unlike anything he'd seen before. Harry knew that his boy was made of more than just his own flesh and blood; something and someone he wanted to be rid of. Teddy had garnered more than enough reasons in his lifetime to keep his father from seeing that side of him.

But that was before he'd sworn the oath with Kenny Eakley, before he'd accepted not only Kenny's empathy but a lifetime of accountability and unpaid debt. When Teddy was still more rotten than trustworthy, and his hands were dirtied by an impulse to steal and break. Long before he'd met Aurelia Schwartz, and even longer before she'd made him a healer, which – unlike his born magical gift – was inherently good.

'Is that what you want?' Teddy asked her. In the presence of his father, Schwartz brushed a strand of his hair from his forehead and said nothing else. 'OK,' he said. 'All right.'

Harry followed each of his jerky movements, studying each twitch in his son's fingers. 'I wasn't quite sure if I should believe it. My son, a healer.'

It was a horrible, doomed idea. Teddy's skin prickled at the overt scepticism in his father's voice. Schwartz swallowed, steadying him with a gaze too sure. How the thought of it didn't give her pause was a mystery to him.

Faith, he thought. She must have had a reason. Teddy wanted to trust her, to know what she knew when she decided to spill. To see what she saw in Teddy Ingram that made her so confident in confessing.

Maybe, just maybe, he was working himself up over nothing. Harry Ingram had always been kinder than Celia. Even now, noting the twitch in Teddy's hand, Harry was offering him an out.

'Perhaps,' Harry said, 'we ought to talk about this somewhere else.'

'Why?' Schwartz asked. 'If he can do it, why shouldn't he?'

'But magic . . . Logically, it can't be a more viable solution than medicine.'

'With all due respect, I've done things through magic that you couldn't even imagine,' she said.

'What does she mean by that?' Harry asked.

'You always knew I was different,' Teddy answered. 'You didn't really assume I was the only person like that, did you?'

From the bewildered expression on his father's face, Teddy wondered if that was exactly what he'd assumed: that his son was an anomaly, a singularly cursed child to keep their lead fastened tightly around. It made sense with the way they'd attempted to rein him in, but it hurt, nonetheless. The realization rippled across Harry's features like a drop in still water.

'I-I didn't know. I hadn't met anyone like that.'

'For good reason,' Teddy said. 'If you can imagine, witches aren't treated very kindly. We don't advertise ourselves if we can help it.'

Teddy aided Schwartz forward, sitting her upright at the edge of the bed. He didn't know if it made a difference, but it felt right. His gaze trained on her, avoiding the careful, contemplative gaze of his father who moved aside, during the shuffle, to watch.

'So, you *can* heal her?' Harry asked. Schwartz awaited his answer, turning her head infinitesimally to the side.

Teddy responded, 'Either that, or I kill her.'

Her hand shot up to cover her mouth before a snort rushed out. Harry met them both with horror.

'Nasty cough there,' Teddy explained. He placed his hands in the centre of her shoulder blades, simply because it felt like the correct place to lay them. Her chest heaved under his palms. If they were both nervous, grasping for a half-decent idea, it wouldn't terrify him as much; but it was probably just the tightness in her lungs and the swelling of her throat.

Still, he whispered words of encouragement against her hair. 'Believe me, I'm perfectly aware that you would have liked to repay the favour tenfold a year ago. You OK?'

She cleared her throat and bit her lip to keep another chuckle from spilling out. 'I think so.'

'And you trust me?'

'It worked for as little as one of Ryan's bad hangovers. Either it works for me now, or I'm dead.'

'I shouldn't have said that.'

Schwartz grinned at him in spite of herself. The quiver in his hands vanished.

He waited for one heavy breath to pass underneath his hands. In. And out.

Then another. In. And out.

He felt it curling around his fingers, the colour bright and inescapable. Whether or not his father saw it too came second to the enigmatic pull of it. But Teddy saw it leave his body and enter hers with the next rise and fall of her chest.

I can fix it. I can make it better.

Then, Schwartz pitched herself forward and tried not to vomit on his shoes.

She made it to the bathroom next door before it spilled out of her completely. Teddy followed after her, lingering just outside the thrown-open door. Schwartz spat out what she could into the toilet bowl, closing the lid over it promptly, then wiping her mouth.

'How are you feeling?' He shouldn't have been so hasty to ask. She was still crouched in front of the bowl, fingers still fastened around her frontmost stray hairs. The suddenness of his question wasn't lost on her.

'For a second there, I thought you might actually kill me,' she said, flushing the evidence of her soup down the drain. 'After the fact, I feel . . .' She cleared her throat again, massaging her neck with her fingers. 'Mostly normal.'

'Mostly,' Teddy echoed, wondering if he hadn't given her enough.

'I'm just tired,' she said as she pushed herself to her feet, 'but when am I not tired, you know?'

His hands buzzed at his sides, the final, stringy output of

magic trying to find a home. He flexed them, letting himself breathe.

In. And out.

He looked to his father behind him, standing with his gaze towards his shoes and his chin in the grip of his fingers. Teddy's gut was turning. He didn't know if it'd be easier to face his father or to face his father's indifference like this. A sudden, seemingly supernatural healing would warrant questions, but so had all the other uncommon occurrences that followed Theodore Ingram's footsteps, and Harry never liked to ask about those. He simply allowed Celia Ingram to stow them away and shut them up, like a schoolteacher swatting away left-handedness. He raised no objections to the mould she fitted the boy to, to the parts of him she broke off to keep him in line.

As long as Teddy didn't stir too much attention. Kept his head down, got good marks at school. If he made any fuss, it was none of their business.

Schwartz's shoulder brushed his sleeve, a stem from the tattooed lavender bunch peering out from underneath her pyjamas.

'You OK?' he asked quietly.

She looked up at him with the full expanse of her dark, moony irises and asked, 'Are you?'

Harry hid his face in his hand, kneading his brow thoughtfully while he started to pace.

Teddy couldn't answer – he didn't know.

He scratched the back of his neck and said, 'Your clothes are in the brown bag. Give me a minute.'

Schwartz's lips flattened. 'Oh.'

He bristled in anticipation of another disappointed stare that didn't actually come.

'OK.'

When he left to locate a linen closet or a spare rag, Harry followed like a shadow, saying nothing until they'd shut the bedroom door behind them again. Teddy kneeled with his dampened rag to wipe the small sheen of vomit from the floor. He kept himself closed as strictly as he could, but a second of straying thought exposed him to the whirr of his father's confusion. Teddy's teeth gritted as he wiped the spot again, and he would have continued wiping that same spot until Harry Ingram said something or until his rag scrubbed through the floorboards – whichever came first.

Say something, he thought. *Or leave me alone.* If Harry didn't want to talk, Teddy certainly wouldn't make him, but Teddy felt his father balancing a weight on each of his arms like the scales of justice: his concern and his regret.

Something needed to break. The tension, or the scale. The silence, before anything else.

'How is she?' Harry then asked lowly.

'Fine,' said Teddy. 'Cheerful.'

'How did you do it? Whatever you just did.'

Teddy hoisted himself onto the edge of the bed again, leaving the rag at his feet. From Harry's mouth, it sounded like an accusation. Witchcraft, or whisper of it, carried such negative connotations when spoken from human tongues. True understanding – true grace – always sat out of reach from those who were not within the clutches of magic.

Explaining it to Harry would prove more difficult than explaining things to Lou, for a barrier more cumbersome than age was otherness. There were things that a child born of magic would accept, and a man-made ego would require eternities to tear down.

'I'm not sure if I can explain it. It isn't something I've had for long either,' he added, like it was a virus.

'But she's better now?'

Teddy nodded, propping his chin on his closed hands. 'I think so.'

'Hmm.'

For a second, Teddy thought he'd evaded a more serious conversation with his father. Everything worth saying had already been said: *Is she safe? She's fine.*

Under his breath, Harry Ingram swore and said, 'Just like that . . .'

Teddy nodded, withholding his gaze.

'Have you ever considered the implications of . . . of magic like that in medical practice? Why wouldn't you have told me this sooner?'

'It's not mine,' Teddy responded. The words rushed free defensively as if he'd been caught with dirty magazines or stolen cigarettes after class.

'You must have learned it from somewhere,' Harry said. 'You must be able to teach people. This thing you have – it's near miraculous, and you can share that with others. Think about how much time I've spent in the practice, memorizing the ins and outs of the body just to prescribe something or execute a procedure that has a chance of going wrong. To heal someone so instantaneously . . .'

Teddy shook his head. 'I couldn't share it even if I wanted to.'

'Why not?'

That was the root of his problems, wasn't it? That Harry and Celia raised him without understanding that his identity and his nature was irrefutably detached from theirs. They would never understand how it felt to live alongside something explosive and dangerous, treading through life with caution in every step. He could never fully detach himself from his magic the way they could shed their uniforms and hairpins; and beneath the garments they clothed him in, he was still a monster.

Not even a good one, at that. Not a wolf in sheep's clothing but a sickly, bone-thin dog, begging for the scraps of someone else's meal.

How could he begin trying to explain something that was so deeply ingrained in his being?

Teddy perched his chin on his knuckles and told him, 'You can't learn magic the way you learn science. It takes more than an understanding of principles to write a spell or heal a body. Those things mean nothing if you're human.'

'Theodore,' Harry said softly. 'Look at yourself. You're my son. How could you be anything more or less than human?'

Teddy wished he could forget that vital difference. Everyone else did. But his gift had already made him the bearer of bad things; what was another to keep holding over his parents' heads?

'You're not even attempting to help me understand,' said his father.

'You've had twenty-four years to understand, but if I remember correctly, you never listened. Every oddity I showed you, every abnormality, was a problem for you to fix – not something to understand. I tried so hard to be perfect for you and Celia, but I was bending and breaking to do that, and you never once tried to meet me in the middle.'

'That's not fair. I couldn't have known that,' Harry said, hissing through his teeth, although Teddy knew Schwartz could hear them. The sink had stopped running. The floor had stopped creaking under her weight. Were he not bound to her through the tether, Teddy would have been convinced that he and his father were the only two left in the house.

'It's a property of my blood,' Teddy said sharply, 'that's incompatible with everyone that doesn't match my type. You understand blood types, don't you?'

Harry Ingram lifted his hand to his face and kneaded his white brows. Teddy hadn't given any thought to its premature whiteness before, but now he counted the years in his mind since he'd last seen his father with colour, without his wrinkles, without such dark bags beneath his olive green eyes. One day, Teddy would look just like him. The resemblance Teddy had found in Harry Ingram's old photographs would follow him to the very end; what had once been in a smile or a pestilent strand of hair was now in a weathered, defeated expression. The thought of filling his father's shoes used to give him hope, but it terrified him now.

He could not end up like his father. He had to be better.

'Then you,' said Harry. 'You could help.'

'I couldn't publicly declare myself as a magical healer and see anything but ridicule. It would benefit us both for me to keep quiet.'

'If you showed folks what you showed me, they would believe you.'

Teddy covered his face with his hands and sighed. 'You have so much faith in the belief of humankind for someone who didn't believe their son until he was in his mid-twenties. I needed *you* to believe me.'

Schwartz cleared her throat, leaning in the doorway behind Harry's figure with folded arms. Harry bowed his head and stepped aside, but she stared at him, unmoving, with so much conviction that Teddy felt less afraid. Less like a nervous teenager again.

'Is it not enough to say that I believe you now?'

Only because Schwartz was standing there, proud and unwavering, did Teddy answer, 'I don't know any more. Maybe.'

Downstairs, the lock to the front door clicked into place. Harry straightened his back, lowered his voice, and leaned in close. 'You don't have to go so soon, you know. Stay a few nights. We should talk.'

'I . . . um . . .'

'Dinner at least. Celia will be happy to have you.'

Teddy doubted that. He heard her shuffling through the ground floor, flipping on the television; he couldn't rid himself of her accusatory stare even if he closed his eyes.

He should have declined the offer. Lou was waiting for him in Townsend. Over Harry's shoulder, Schwartz waited for his expression to break into something more telling. Teddy was waiting too, pleading wordlessly with her to answer for him.

He relented, at last. 'Dinner, and that's it. I'd hate to push a good thing too far.'

*

He lingered beside the telephone box, leaning against the white wall of a storefront, while Schwartz dialled her housemate. Through the glass, he could see her lips moving fast, an irritable expression plastered on her face. She emerged quickly and said, 'Had to leave a voicemail.'

'Did you say when you'd be back?' Teddy asked.

'Soon,' she told him. 'But that could mean anything, really.'

It didn't, but she had offered that to comfort him, reaching out to thread her fingers between his while they walked in a way that felt familiar, even if he could tell that she was nervous. He squeezed her hand softly in reassurance, then said, 'Not really.'

'What would you rather have me say?'

That you're coming home with me instead, he thought. *Don't wait up.*

He shrugged. 'You'll have to call me when you're home. Let me know you're all right.'

'And if the call won't go through?' she asked.

He didn't want to think about the consequences of something like that in the worst of situations.

'You have my email,' he said, rubbing his eyes.

Harry and Celia hadn't arrived yet. The restaurant sat within walking distance of the Tate Modern, Celia's place of work. Teddy checked his watch again – waterlogged – and panic built in his chest. They were punctual. Exacting. That is, unless they were driving with company.

Schwartz's eyes flickered to the closing doors of the Tate warily. He should have asked Celia to go anywhere else.

He shouldn't have agreed to this in the first place. One civil discussion over dinner wouldn't quash his misplaced feeling of indebtedness. Civility was miraculous in its own right.

Family aside, he was itching for more time alone with Schwartz. Even in the aftermath of Julia Chaplain's failed necromancy, arms aching from the weight of the sword, he'd woken up with Schwartz's back pressed to his chest and a hard-on tucked between her thighs. Out of some adolescent, pious Catholic embarrassment, he couldn't bring himself to relieve it in his parents' bathroom, so he'd taken a strenuous piss and completed his morning errand with a sore pelvis.

He wondered, while stomach to stomach with her on the tube, if she could feel it through the tether. The thought drew his gaze to the overhead advertisements instead of her hair, which still smelled like Celia's expensive shampoo. Her arm circled loosely around his waist, gripping the nearby pole for support, and thwarted the best of his efforts.

'And Alaric is really all right with watching Lou for the rest of the night?' Her eyes had been level with the sagging neck of his T-shirt, traipsing curiously over the rarely seen expanse of his throat.

Some of the crowd dispersed from the carriage at the next stop, but she remained close, relishing the same scene that was making the predicament in his pelvic region infinitely worse.

'Not like he has much of a choice,' Teddy said. 'If I'm not there, he's all she has.'

He could have said no, anyway; Alaric's private council matters always seemed to supersede his responsibilities to the family. Then again, maybe Teddy expected too much from him. He and Alaric both loved Lou dearly, but neither of them was her father or her relative. If Teddy was managing on his own, why would Alaric stay?

Teddy had voiced plenty of traitorous desires to Schwartz in the past weeks, but one more traitorous than all still sat unspoken in the back of his mind: that he was jealous of Alaric's freedom. The caretaker had an out: Teddy Ingram's unwavering devotion to the Eakley family, a devotion born of his guilt and nurtured by his love. His guilt was a lead, a noose around his neck, tightening with the growing desire to prove himself. Alaric couldn't see it – free as he was to go elsewhere. He could turn his nose to other things and lose sight of the boy bound to the cottage, to the Eakleys, and of the weight balanced on his back.

They were a short distance from the Tate, at the place where his parents said they would meet them. Teddy turned his attention to the river below.

Having Schwartz nearby gave him something else to focus on that wasn't his father's words. Words could haunt him as well as ghosts did, and those words were fresh – a sharpened knife in a just-made wound. Focusing on her kept Teddy from envisioning skeletal faces on the bodies of passing Londoners, helped him ignore some of the pain in his arms.

Schwartz cast her line of sight into the distance when he looked at her, and it fell into the water like a baited hook.

'It's funny,' he said, 'that after all the time I've wasted in Townsend, twenty-four hours here makes me want to crawl back to it.'

'At least we'll eat first.'

'It's good you can eat,' he said. 'Seeing as you've just heaved up the contents of your stomach and all. This place makes me sick.'

She swayed into his side. Their arms pressed together like tightly shelved book covers.

'You're going back to Cambridge after this, aren't you?'

Meekly, she responded, 'I should.' A skip in her pulse betrayed her, but Teddy couldn't say if her hesitation was warranted or not. When the Londoners were brushing his shoulders as they passed, with their heads down and thoughts to themselves, he couldn't keep himself from picturing the dead knights' bony hands. The stench of undead bodies still hung on the tip of his nose; and not even the cafes along the streets could overtake it. Julia Chaplain had her ways of corralling them into her own personal playing field, her chess board, as long as she knew where to find them. If Schwartz left for Cambridge without him, he couldn't look out for her. Sure, a few hours of travel wouldn't make a difference to everyone else, but it had kept them apart long enough. If she needed him now, he didn't know if he'd reach her fast enough.

I should. Of course, she should. Teddy had dropped everything to look after Lou himself because he loved her; and he knew that Aurelia Schwartz loved her housemate profoundly. With Teddy's magic in her blood and a cunning witch clinging to their shadows, she needed to look after Ryan. And while he dealt with his own responsibilities, Teddy had to trust that Schwartz would look after herself too.

'God, this is miserable, Schwartz. You being there while I'm stuck in Townsend. I hate it.'

'Come with me, then.'

He felt as if he'd been waiting decades for her to offer. He liked to think he had more discipline now, but perhaps he'd simply acclimatized to the weight of familial dread on his chest. 'You know I can't do that.'

'So? Let's pretend for a minute that the option is there. What would you do?'

'Must we keep pretending with each other?' Teddy grumbled.

'Humour me,' Schwartz said. 'What do you *really* want, when all is said and done?'

It was the closest he'd ever gotten to asking, 'What are we?' which seemed, amidst all their unspoken agreements, like forbidden territory.

To put a name to something was inherently limiting. If that thing existed only as an idea, it could be anything, *everything* . . . It could be as lovely as heaven itself.

This, too, felt traitorous to indulge in. Even the most inconsequential conversations had a sharpness when it came to the care and keeping of Louisa Eakley. The girl was a constant, invariable factor in his life, one he appraised above all others.

Though Teddy said nothing about his drawback, Schwartz gave him a knowing, tantalizing look and squeezed his hand in reassurance. 'I've been trying to get comfortable with how unquantifiable we are,' she said. 'It's hard to entertain the idea of it when you're bound to end up alone. I do think about it, though. More than what's logically good for me. The way I see it, I can't lose something that I don't have, so I just keep pretending I'm OK with this unnamed thing between us. But I can't fucking stand it.'

'If it eases your conscience, you're not alone,' Teddy said. 'You'd laugh if you knew how much I wonder.'

Of course, she knew it already. For once, Schwartz knew him precisely as well as he knew her: wanton, hungry, and forced to hold the forbidden fruit but never taste it. Such desire was too cruel to share with someone else. *Touch me, but do not hold me. Kiss me, even if you cannot keep me.*

'But aside from the obvious?' he began. 'For how much I want, you'll find that my aspirations are quite tame. I was . . . content in my flat. I had a well-stocked bookcase, ample kitchen space. I wasn't far from the arboretum or a Tesco. Everything I needed, I already had.'

His words hung between them, his answer unfinished. The pace of her pulse quickened with every second that passed wherein he withheld an elaboration, but he hadn't cobbled one together. Half the world's poetry was written for love – its pursuit, its loss, its existence – and yet, all of it escaped him. Left to his own words, Teddy felt . . . insufficient.

'Have you ever been to one of Tricia's dinner parties?' he asked suddenly.

Schwartz shook her head, but a bemused grin crept across her face. 'She's never invited me.'

'She never *invites* anyone,' Teddy said. 'You just show up. Either way, I don't blame you. I've gone maybe twice and left with headaches from the sheer amount of smoke that trickles in from her back garden. But aside from that, they were wonderful. It's awfully humanizing to see where someone makes their dinner. See how they organize their films and decorate their bathroom. It's easy to forget that we're all wasting minutes over deciding what to eat every day when we're not furiously jotting down lecture notes. Maybe it's just the lighting, but it's hard not to be a little in love with everyone in that situation. You should go sometime, Schwartz. They won't bite.'

The tether around them grew taut from her feigned ambivalence. 'So, it's the people that you miss?'

'You'd miss them too,' he answered carefully, 'if you'd spent half your life feeling like a monster. You'd want to be good; and who else could tell you that you were? I couldn't convince myself of it. But if my peers liked me . . . If someone else could look at me and tell me I was good, I might believe it. I would have done anything to be good in their eyes.'

She slipped her fingers through his, tucking her body against his side as if there was a bite in the air she needed shelter from. Her closeness had fazed him lots before, but the publicity of it roused every bump on his skin. Behind closed doors, they could be anything: witches, lovers, confidants. Schwartz was probably more aware of it than anyone, which was why she held him like a secret.

Slowly, Teddy pressed his lips to her hair. 'You've been awfully touchy lately.' Each unacknowledged, furthering motion proved just how much he didn't mind it. His arms crept tentatively around her waist. Her back melted into his chest. He wanted her closer, to make her indisputably his to the strangers around them.

'And?' Schwartz turned her face ever so slightly. Her eyes dropped to his lips. 'After all you did to win my favour, you expect me to let you go?'

Her mouth stretched into a lopsided smile. This one, she

didn't bite into. She sunk back into him, surrendering herself to his grasp. Teddy answered with a worshipful whisper in her ear, 'Of course not. Keep me forever.'

'I didn't think we'd actually come back,' she mused. 'I wanted to, though. I wished it wasn't so terrifying now.'

'I wish we'd never gone inside.' This he whispered close to her ear, because nothing felt more heretical than wishing he could undo that tangle of fate.

I wish I could have been the one to kiss you.

Schwartz eyed the museum disapprovingly and folded her arms over her chest. 'Half the time, I'm in the gallery when Leona gets me,' she said. 'The other half, I'm back at King's.'

They had spent few nights under the same roof since the first time Teddy had brought her to the cottage, but he'd spent them unfurling her clenched fists while she slept, lacing his fingers through her hair after the all-too-familiar nightmare startled her awake. And though she'd eventually slip back into bed beside him, she wore the same dark circles around her eyes every morning – always tired, always ready to snap with the first unexpected sound.

'I'm sorry.' Teddy scratched his wrist beneath his sleeve, thinking of the pleas penned in Gemma's grimoires. *Does it ever get easier?*

As if unending torment wasn't enough to afflict one person with, it wanted everything and everyone in Teddy's close proximity. It had sunk its teeth into Gemma and Lou, and it'd do the same to Schwartz if she stood too close.

'I've been meaning to ask you something . . . Or at least, I've been wondering about this ever since you picked me up from Heathrow.'

'Hmm?'

Her chest heaved in time with his. 'Well, by design, empathy has a reactive quality; like you said, it always needs something to feed from. The last time we were here, and then again in the car park at Heathrow, you managed to calm me down without saying anything at all. I guess my question is: do you think it works the other way?'

'You're asking if I gave that feeling to you.'

'Strangely enough, I always feel a little calmer when you're around. Safer,' she murmured. 'I figured you were probably doing something about it.'

Teddy pressed his lips together firmly, watching the realization simmer through her. He would have figured out how to use magic like that by now if he had it. Lou would have been happier, and Alaric wouldn't have dreaded the mornings where he expected to meet Teddy at the shop.

Telling Schwartz that his magic had no influence over her feelings gave her all the credit – or the blame – for what she felt. He almost did, just to prove a point: *I can be useful. I can help.* She'd been too reluctant to ask for it, but he was dying for a chance to prove himself.

He could be more than his magic. He could be good, and all she had to do was let him.

The moment strung between them was so taut that he knew any wrong word or sharp tone could sever it like a blade. If his answer scared her, would she run back to the impenetrable safety of her armour?

They both remained quiet for the sake of keeping the moment intact, Teddy revelling in the familiar way she leaned into him. But the taste – the possibility – of her affection melted like sugar on his tongue: sweet, promising and dangerous all at once.

His name sounded in the distance, relentless in Celia's mouth.

That familiar thump reverberated in his chest again – a heartbeat, reassurance. The only thing that could dissuade him from running as fast and as far away as he could from the shadow of the Tate Modern.

CHAPTER TWENTY-FOUR

Teddy was, as Schwartz had suspected, a hit with single moms. Margaret Westfield harboured a particular fondness for Teddy Ingram that he couldn't help feeling somewhat responsible for – by being charming, or tall, or aloof in the way that also piqued the interest of curious children. He was someone who didn't give anything personal away of his own accord, someone who one could imagine themselves assembling from scratch.

Mothers loved him, except for his own. In that regard, Celia was as much of an anomaly as he was.

'Oh, he's awfully handsome now, isn't he, Celia? How many years has it been? Five? Six?'

'Three,' Teddy replied. Margaret swept him into a humble embrace. He returned the favour with a light tap between her shoulder blades.

Behind her strolled her son, Eric Westfield III. Impressive enough on paper, if one could ignore the glaring truth of the person who stood in front of them; the discrepancies were endless. Teddy hadn't foreseen just how many people would turn a blind eye to it. At some point, he thought, Eric would meet his match against any person who possessed a spine, but those must have been in short supply. Eric worked in a cushy, upper-crust job in central London, ascending the ranks with a speed motivated by nepotism. He and his mother shared the same pink button nose, but Eric had his father's knifelike grin, and it carved out the word *trouble.*

Celia drew Schwartz in by the elbow to introduce them to one another.

'I didn't realize I was crashing your dinner with friends,' Teddy said.

Celia's French-tipped nails scraped down his sleeve. 'Neither did I.'

'Nonsense,' Margaret exalted. 'The more the merrier.'

Terrible fucking idea.

Over their heads, Harry offered his son a sympathetic smile.

'So.' Celia sent the word across the expanse of the round table, smoothing a napkin across her lap. At her sharp command, they settled into place; Schwartz sandwiched between Teddy and his father, Eric between Celia and Margaret. Teddy inhaled the warm mix of steamed vegetables and braised meat wafting up around him. His stomach roiled in response. To his left, Schwartz challenged his lax posture with a straight back, toying with the fold of her napkin beneath the others' lines of sight.

'So,' echoed Eric. 'What brings you back to London, Theodore?'

A black-clad waiter filled their glasses with water. Teddy twisted his glass into the tablecloth gingerly and answered, 'I was in the area. Figured I'd say hello.'

'And what good news for us!' Margaret added, jovial. 'How long are you staying?'

'He's just passing through,' Celia said. Her jaw worked irritably, and her gaze flickered to Harry Ingram's wristwatch, which only made her jaw work *more* irritably. As if Teddy couldn't leave soon enough.

'Ah, back to Cambridge so soon?' Eric adjusted the crisp collar of his shirt with a slight tilt in his brows. 'What is it you study again? History?'

'Medieval literature.'

'How fruitful is the field of medieval literature? Financially, that is. I can't imagine there's much competition for' – Westfield waved inexactly – 'whatever it is you do.'

'He's taken a brief sabbatical from his studies,' Harry said, to the dismay of everyone but Eric.

Teddy met Eric Westfield's interrogative stare across the table, pinning him with a slow, heavy downing of his water. 'Is that so?'

His teeth clenched. 'Yes.'

'Well, I think that's marvellous, darling,' said Margaret. 'Young people and their strides to reinvent their new adulthood. I actually know a few folks your age who are taking time to travel. To broaden their horizons. It's such a positive trend, don't you think, Celia?'

'I suppose.'

'Eric has been considering a bit of time off for himself as well. You see, his firm has been going through a big organizational staffing change recently, and the promotions aren't quite what we'd expected. He's such a valuable player, though, it seems only right to remind them of that. It'd falter without him.'

'Is something funny?' Eric said.

All eyes gravitated to Schwartz, who twisted her head to find the perpetrator herself. 'Did I say something?'

'You have a look about you.'

She scoffed. 'A look?'

'You know,' Eric added, trailing off until the blanks filled themselves in, but no one seemed to catch on. 'What is it you do, then?'

The infinitesimal toss of her hair wasn't lost to Teddy, nor was the defiant jut of her chin. He peered at her from his periphery, pretending to skim the menu.

'Papers,' she said. 'Lots of them.'

'Anything that'd interest me?'

'Doubtful.'

'Are you sure? I please easily.'

Celia cleared her throat. 'You were saying, Margaret?'

She spoke long enough, loudly enough, that Teddy could spare a whispered remark to Schwartz without drawing any attention. He leaned back in his chair, lifted his fingers, and brushed her hair behind her ear. 'You're practically vibrating. Take my hand.'

'I don't think that'll help.'

'Suit yourself,' he said. Before long, while Margaret was plying Celia with congratulations on her latest exhibit, Schwartz's hand slid between their chairs, splayed open for him to take. Teddy grazed the outer edge of her pinkie. Traced the ridge of her heartline with his middle finger. His hand crept to her thigh and settled on top of the sprawl of her fingers.

'Theodore,' Margaret sang. 'Perhaps you'd like to come with us?'

'Hmm?'

'To Verona? In the spring. We were just discussing our plans for after the holidays.'

'Pay attention,' Celia demanded.

With a dry huff, Eric Westfield said, 'It seems Theodore's mind is elsewhere.' His fingers tapped restlessly at the glass, his eyes sidling up the curve of Schwartz's neck expectantly. 'You should know all about that: "Fair Verona, where we lay our scene."'

'That's Elizabethan,' Schwartz said.

'Come again?'

She released an uninhibitedly deep sigh, which caught the table's focus once again. 'Shakespeare's not medieval. He's Elizabethan. Jacobean. There are literally at least a hundred years between what any basic European history class will tell you is the end of the medieval period and the beginning of the Elizabethan era.'

'So, you're a medievalist too then?' Eric's eyes flashed with a devious glint.

Teddy bit his tongue, until he heard Celia make a quiet addition to Harry alone. '—Fussing over a silly little misquote . . . don't know why you let them come . . .'

Schwartz's hand tightened around his protectively.

What had he been thinking? He shouldn't have agreed to this. When the time came to venture back to Townsend, he didn't want to be mulling over dinner with the Westfields when there were more pressing, more important matters to worry about. He had a missing person to find, bruises to tend to from a makeshift army of the undead, and yet, more fearsome than all of it was his stepmother.

As if sensing his resignation, Margaret grabbed his bicep delicately, her fingers adorned with colourful rings that covered her knuckles. 'Will you pour me some wine?'

'Of course.'

He did as he was told. Hated himself for it. He put his head down whenever Celia looked his way. Kept his mouth shut when she had a bone to pick with him. Sometimes, he was quiet for the sake of listening in. Sometimes, he simply failed to say anything at all.

'Ooh!' Margaret squealed. 'That's a bit much. What are you trying to do with all this wine?'

'Stop it,' Eric said. 'You're embarrassing yourself.'

'I have no idea what you're talking about.'

Again, Celia intervened. 'Verona. This spring. How long?'

Eric collapsed into the back of his seat. Margaret righted herself from the path she was chasing into Teddy Ingram's personal space. 'A month, maybe? We haven't quite ironed out all the details, but we'll have the villa to ourselves. Me, Eric, the lot of you. It should be great fun. Giorgio, our tenant, loves to cook for us whenever we're in. He's a local, so he knows all the best markets to buy from. What do you say, Theodore?'

Their stares pressed him from every angle, like the tower of mirrors from his dream ascending over him. When all of them wanted him to say something different, what could he say? He wanted to tell Harry that he'd made a mistake coming here tonight; he should have been on a train heading towards the churchyard station already. He wanted to tell Eric Westfield to quit leering at his girlfriend, and to ignore his mother completely.

And Schwartz – what did she want from him? To talk to his father? It was too much, too harrowing. He wanted to skip over this night like an unretained chapter and forget that this ever happened. He wanted to rewrite the narrative completely until his stepmother was no longer wicked like those in the fairy tales and he was as valiant as a knight. *Be brave,* he thought. *It's just dinner with your family.*

It shouldn't have been this difficult to get through. And yet—

'He'll be back in his classes by then, Margaret. It's only temporary. I'm sure this trend of withdrawal from higher education is right for some, but if he knows what's good for him, he'll be back at Pembroke by Lent.'

'Why does it bother you so much that he's taken some time off?' Schwartz hissed.

'Excuse me?'

'Your priorities,' Schwartz articulated, 'are twisted beyond reason, given everything that's going on.'

'Do you think *you* know what's best for him then? I suppose this isn't the first time you've inserted yourself into a conversation you don't belong in.'

Schwartz shoved her chair back with a screech and ripped her hand from Teddy's grasp. Teddy opened his mouth, but she was going before he could call her name, manoeuvring angrily through the path of hosts and their affluent parties.

Harry Ingram blinked as if doubting what he'd seen, but Schwartz was gone from her seat, gone from Teddy's side. Celia swallowed the last of her wine and sucked her teeth, seething.

Teddy balled the napkin and tossed it onto his empty plate. 'I'm done with this. Enjoy your dinner.'

'Sit. Down.'

'Are you proud of yourself, Celia?' His voice was even, but his words were marred by grit and tight teeth. 'You have managed to tarnish every good thing I've ever been allowed, and I'm sick of it. Go to hell.'

He cut her off with the angle of his body. It gave her nothing: no face, no notice, no threads of kindness. He felt alive with the adrenaline in his veins, the courage to cut his ties with her once and for all.

Teddy paused in reconsideration. He had forgotten something.

He turned on his heels, bracing himself over the expanse of the table, and fixed Eric Westfield with a pointed finger. 'Look at her like that again, and you'll be lucky to leave with all your teeth.'

He felt as if he might combust with the speed of his heartbeat. His skin was smattered in a patchy flush. The city looked new. Before now, Teddy Ingram would have assumed he'd seen every colour that streaked the skyline, but he must have missed a few. The Tate, with its lighted sign and colourful windows, was dazzling and opulent. Schwartz paced at the edge of the walkway, silhouetted in the spill of magenta, looking brighter than ever.

She spotted him, wiped her face with the inside of her wrist, and shook her head. 'I don't know what I was thinking, letting you come here; she's horrible, Ingram. I should have made you come back with me. I should have told her to go fuck herself – come up with something meaner than cunt!' She couldn't stop moving. Rage had set her body aflame, and she was shaking it off to the best of her abilities, but it kept spilling out of her. 'How are you just going to let them talk to you like that? She treats you like shit, and you just take it like it's what you deserve; but you're better than that, Ingram, and you know it. You're the smartest person I know, and she talks to you like a goddam child!'

Teddy captured her wrists and stilled her against his chest. 'Stop talking.'

'But your mother, she's—'

Teddy silenced her with his mouth. His hands slid to the back of her neck, the small of her waist. His body arched over hers. He pulled her flush to the curve of his body, plastering overeager kisses to her lips while she tried to finish her complaint.

His name in her mouth was a grievance the first time. A mumbled curse against his kiss. The plane between her brows possessed a sharp crease when she pulled away to look at him.

'I don't want to think about them right now,' Teddy groaned, moving his lips to her jaw. She said his name again, laden with pity, which did nothing but send a rush of blood to his pelvis. 'I'm not my parents. *We* aren't our parents. I'm not going to let them, or any bloody portal witch take this away from us, OK?' He pulled her closer. Never, never close enough. 'Can I just—'

Schwartz's lips parted in a bewildered gasp as his hands slid lower, lower, lower towards her hips and gripped hard.

'I shouldn't have said yes to this stupid dinner,' he told her, punctuating every sentence with a starved kiss. His hands grabbed at whatever they could, never twisting into one place for too long, as if each part of her would disappear little by little the moment that he stopped touching her. 'I should have kissed you the first time we were here. I should have never left.'

Despairingly, she whispered, 'Teddy . . .'

What would you do? she'd asked, wanting him to grant her his truth even if it killed him. Even if he could not have it.

'Christ, Schwartz, *this* is what I want. I want to be better than my parents. I want to live my life without looking over my shoulder to see if they're still behind me. I want to kiss you in a moment that isn't rushed. I just . . . I want—'

So much, he thought. *I want so much.*

Teddy felt delirious. Blabbering like a fool. Courage swelled in his chest, and he held her like the last breath of air while he was drowning.

Or the first, once he'd broken free.

Her fingers raked through his hair, and she pulled away to study him, panting. 'I want that too.'

What did she see? Not the bright-eyed scholar he had been in Cambridge. Not the docile, dedicated caregiver that living with Lou had forced him to become. He knew that when he looked at her, sick and wet, wiping her nose with the inside of her wrist, she looked as beautiful as ever, which seemed completely unfair. Now, with her hair mussed from the clench of his fist, her lips swollen from his kiss, she looked like she could be *his*.

He couldn't remember what made the wanting so shameful. When he looked at her, he knew exactly what drove Leona Sum and Julia Chaplain past the point of no return. No measure was too much for the people you loved. The first bite of sin was saccharine, red and ripe like a lover's mouth. They'd been blind to the monsters that they would become, but he was already a monster. Trying to be good, trying to make things right. Was he not allowed anything beautiful too?

His thumb grazed the peach fuzz at the top of her cheek. 'You're so lovely.'

Teddy knew better than to place her on a pedestal, better than to beg for crumbs. He never wanted to be Dante, weeping at Beatrice's feet with the light of God at her back – he wanted to be Virgil, with all the answers on the tip of his tongue. Virgil, who served a purpose and had a place.

But there had to be some worship in love. They shared the same, overwhelming sense of devotion. Schwartz met his line of sight and reached up to brush a lock of his hair. The unguarded awe in her eyes was something he'd only dreamed of before now, like Troilus's spirit dreaming of Criseyde.

During Teddy's years of scholarship, he came across plenty of texts that remained nothing more than classwork – than necessity; more than one of which was written by Chaucer. But there were words he'd never felt the weight of without an experience to tie to it. Words that were only words until they erupted, like the birth of a universe, into something more: 'Blessed be love that can convert people like this.'

'Please don't ever ask me to come back here,' he said.

Her lips slanted into one of her rare, toothy smiles. 'Never.'

'I mean it. I'd rather pitch myself into the Thames than have to sit through another dinner like that.'

'You didn't even eat.'

'I know. I'm famished,' he said, taking her hand. 'Do you like dumplings?'

She followed his lead, looking everywhere but to him, like he was as bright as the sun. He'd been so many things to her before that he was itching to try something new, to be someone else.

He could be the one who harboured all her secrets. The one who fixed her tea every morning. Maybe all she needed was a distraction from the complete and utter calamity that was the portal witch's proposition.

At that moment, Teddy didn't really care. He would become anything she wanted.

They ate without speaking. Schwartz poured herself a cup of green tea from the small white pot once she'd had her fill of iced water, and Teddy found himself serving spoonful after spoonful of green beans, sating his hunger like a temperamental animal. A group to their left dressed in suit jackets and clean polo shirts drew his attention as he cleaned his plate again; and Teddy thought of his father at that dinner with Celia to his right. Celia, commanding the focus of the others with her stern yet seductive manner of speech, where each word possessed intrigue.

Teddy's father, saying nothing. Teddy reasoned he would never even tell her about Schwartz's rapid, glowing health. Would she care?

Schwartz eyed him from over the table, wiping the corners of her mouth with a napkin. Her legs were crossed beneath the table, and she nudged his leg with the side of her boot to break him from his stupor. A silent question: *What are you thinking?*

He made himself impervious to it, stolid. *Nothing worth discussing.*

But his mind raced with thoughts of his father, of Lou, and Alaric. If Harry had been there for him when he was young and opened himself up to the possibility of magic, what would Teddy have told him? How much difference would it have made when his father was only one man and the world was a devouring sea? In the end, Harry Ingram would always float, and Teddy would still have to learn to swim.

He expected Schwartz to ask aloud, to press him for an answer the way she'd done so many times before. He would have told her, 'You. I'm thinking about you,' and he wouldn't have been lying. Her pulse, a soft, perpetual thrumming in the back of his mind, kept him tied to the present with the lightest hold. He grounded himself by the rampant flicker of her eyes, the fluttering of her lashes.

Instead, she turned to the mother eating beside her with her children and asked, 'Do you know what time it is?'

'Eight thirty.'

'Thanks.' Schwartz shifted in her seat with another question in her eyes. *Do you want to get out of here?*

He smiled, brushing her ankle beneath the table with his leg. 'I'll get the bill.'

He found it unlikely that Harry and Celia would still be out by now. It wasn't worth the effort to go back for their tattered old clothes. Facing them spelled trouble that he didn't have the patience – or the heart – to deal with, and he shed the responsibility of owing them a goodbye. But they were close enough. After this, Celia would surely toss his things and rid their white box gallery home of his intrusion. He wanted to spare the old copy of Marie de France's lais, mark every line that made him think of Schwartz, and give it to her instead.

He didn't *need* it. He already owned a paperback copy in the shelf behind his bed that was in decent condition, wherein every usable margin had been defaced with his notes. Teddy simply had too much to say and not enough ways of his own to say it. He wanted to line her shelves with copies of all the books he loved, the stories and passages and poems that made him think of her; and soon enough, she'd be surrounded by declarations of his love, housed in it when he couldn't be there to love her face to face.

They approached his parents' place warily, checking each window to see which lights had been left on. He closed the gate behind him without making a sound.

The kitchen light beckoned them in. The pair exchanged a questioning glance as if to say, *Did you leave them on? Do you remember?*

Schwartz gave herself a moment to explore the kitchen and

the living room downstairs, rooms she'd only seen in her periphery last night. Teddy thought of his mother, cross-legged on the couch picking through her breakfast with bone-thin, talon-like fingers. The room was elegant but sterile, just as she was. He could almost hear the news anchor from the morning, airing their dirty laundry to the British public as if she had any idea about what the hell was going on.

'They don't have any pictures of you,' Schwartz noted irritably. 'That's kind of fucked up.'

'To be fair, they don't have many photos at all.'

Celia had dressed up the empty wall space with art of amorphous shapes that probably cost a term's worth of tuition fees. Pity, he thought, to spend so much money on something so visually uninteresting. Still, Schwartz couldn't ignore the deliberateness of the wall hangings the way Teddy could. She squinted, frowning, into the unlit shelf spaces and found them occupied with small, sculptural pieces instead of picture frames.

'I doubt I'd like to see any of my old school photos on display.'

Schwartz studied a small, bronze sculpture, then replaced it on its shelf with a sigh. 'My dad has maybe ten photos of me and Annie scattered throughout the living room alone. It's nice in theory. You'd never forget he has kids. But I was the only one who had to wear braces, so I'm practically glowing with the silver light of my teeth, while Annie looks perfectly normal and straight-toothed. It's so unfair.'

He smiled. 'Don't get too comfortable.'

Rolling her eyes, she replied, 'I would never.'

*

She stole away into the backyard garden while Teddy went upstairs to collect the last of his belongings, which was where the ambush happened. Celia's throat cleared as Teddy passed her room. He paused, pressing his shoulder to the doorframe, his book tucked beneath his arm.

Her voice was soft in the way that made him cower. 'Where were you?'

'Had to eat,' he said simply.

'Ah.'

Avoidantly, she set to folding her laundry. The bedroom was as vacant as she was, with a dresser, two nightstands and a small desk in the same bluish shade of dark brown that looked like harsh shadows in the daylight.

She kept her edges beautifully neat, as she did with her conversations, and Teddy knew he could not leave yet. She could keep him waiting for hours, and he might never flinch.

Her silence needled excuses from him.

'Are you done now?' she asked.

Done with what? Had she assumed whatever trouble followed them here would come and pass so easily? Teddy pressed his lips together, hanging his head. 'I'm fine, Celia.'

'Spoke your mind at the table, and now you have nothing left to say,' she muttered, torturing the pile of folded towels into neatness. 'Come inside.'

His view of his parents' bedroom depended solely on the lamp beside her pillow. It buzzed quietly. Celia took her towels from the bedroom and organized them into a closet elsewhere.

Teddy parted the slats at the window. His father was deep in a conversation with Schwartz over the stalk bent into his hand, charming – or appeasing – her with his enthusiasm and the crooked curve of his mouth, which Teddy had thankfully inherited. One of the only positive contributions that the Ingram bloodline made to him. One that must have made Celia's blood boil.

Celia returned and gestured him to her side. He folded obediently, perched on the edge of his parents' bed while she cocked her head to the side and read his expression. Low as a hum, she told him, taking his chin in her hand, 'You're a cause for worry these days. You're disobedient. Crude. Lazy. I don't know what you said to your father earlier, but you could do without burning the last bridges you have left to your name.'

'I don't know what you're talking about.'

'It worries me, how you've turned out.'

It was not his fault being born into a family without magic. It was not his fault that they couldn't understand him, no matter how long they dismissed his needs for outbursts.

'I've grown up.'

Her lips thinned. 'I pray for you sometimes. Though I shouldn't. I don't even know if you believe in God any more.'

Anger burned underneath his ribs. She knew a hundred different ways to tell him he was wicked. That he'd been cast out of God's love long ago, and that she was righteous for asking Him to take Teddy Ingram back. Since his first Sunday mass, where she cradled him in her arms with less warmth than his nannies did, Celia had imposed the idea of an infallible God on him. Teddy lost days transfixed by the crucifix behind the altar, the shifting colour cast from stained-glass windows. He felt the weight of Celia's hand pressed on his shoulders as she did when they kneeled for prayer.

It might have been soothing with anyone else. Celia's hand was a reminder, an assignment of guilt and the sin needing to be absolved.

He was born unholy and grew up knowing it. The very nature of reapers was antithetical to God's decree. Every flower in his father's gardens turned their face from him, inching further from his path each day. His magic, his mother and his faith assured him he was unworthy of grace, of beauty. Naturally, it was only a matter of time before he refused it.

He wondered often, in the loneliness that re-emerged when Kenny died, if God had made him so wretched and cursed him to destroy him later on. Perhaps he'd been born a cautionary tale, an example to be made.

Celia Ingram – follower, believer – would never love him like Gemma loved her children. How could she? He didn't think twice about asking himself that question, or pretend he was worthy like everyone else of forgiveness. She could accept her failure as a mother if it meant she was not complicit in raising something that defied her God. She gave him pity instead of warmth, ignorance instead of guidance. She cast it to him in passing glances, as if he were the shadow of a starving alley cat to feed once, then promptly forget.

How merciful she was when no one had to feed him at all. It made him sick. Depraved.

She looked at him now like a lost cause, sighing through her nose. 'Your hair is too long,' she said – her closing statement.

Teddy rose from his seat, departing with a face full of heat and shame.

'Cut it soon.'

He left with the book in a grip so tight that all the blood fled from his fingertips.

He shut the door and didn't look back.

CHAPTER TWENTY-FIVE

Schwartz toyed with the weave of her new cardigan, unsteady in her seat.

'Does it itch?'

At once, her fingers ceased their torment. 'Is it distracting you?'

A little. Not that Teddy minded. Few things managed to tear him from Celia's words and the crumbling chapel. Were it not for the incessant, inaudible scratch of her nails through knit, he would lose himself in it all, wallowing into catatonia behind the wheel of his car. He asked her what his father had said. She told him she'd never seen such a well-kept garden that hadn't seen some magical intervention. The way he kept his garden and nourished his treasures was, perhaps, the one similarity Teddy prided himself in, but he was more like his father than he cared to admit.

He didn't tell her that Harry Ingram's first flower had been his son.

The radio's infrequent buzz helped a little too. Every few minutes, Schwartz would lean into the middle and toy with the knob, though they were nearing Townsend now, where nothing reached and no one could find them for the indiscretion in the chapel. In his clouded state, he couldn't decide which indiscretion was worse: the destruction or the desire.

The destruction, he thought. *But there are plenty of ways to defile a house of God, some which could still preserve the sanctity – or the structure.*

The town approached, killing Schwartz's final attempt to get the radio working. The sun glared through the crevices in his sun visor, heat permeating the glass, his skin, his throat. They'd left London in a quiet rush, slipping out with their few belongings and a washed, threadbare set of clothes in a manner they'd only known through one-night stands. She spent the journey in silence, and he wondered if this was the first time she'd ever left and dragged someone out with her.

Teddy parked the car behind the shop, where its previous stagnancy had forced the weeds to grow up through cobblestones in twists around the wheels. He needed a drink, some food, something else to do. The shop door was locked, which Teddy didn't think twice about; if Alaric was busy (of course, he'd be busy) and Lou was still in his care, it'd be safer and ultimately more convenient to keep her in the library, where the wards were unlike anything a common witch could craft.

You're thinking too hard. Teddy cursed himself for jumping to that conclusion. His waxing paranoia brought him closer to Gemma in one way he hoped he'd never need to be; but it was the truth, perhaps the only truth Teddy returned to again and again through all his months as Louisa's guardian.

Townsend would keep them safe.

Louisa shouldn't have to hide forever.

Soon enough, she would be enrolled in school again, and

she would learn exactly the kind of friendship a girl her age was deserving of.

Teddy left the lights off, calling the caretaker's name into shadow. Something shifted in the library, across the veil. Teddy registered another witch but knew, in some inexplicable, bone-deep way, that Alaric wasn't there.

Hye-Jin, probably. Teddy kneaded the nape of his neck, curling his fingers over the place where she'd gripped his shoulder the last time they'd seen each other; and recognized that, despite his knee-jerk reaction to soothe a phantom pain, he harboured no ill will towards the caretaker. She hadn't expected to be the one to tell him about Carmichael Sum. Hye-Jin shared Teddy's baseline expectation for Alaric to be honest, which said more about her than it did about Alaric. One expected him to be cagey, stand-offish. Hye-Jin had a vice grip around her concept of morality, of truth and fairness; and Teddy could appreciate it, even as he worked out the vice grip of her hand on his shoulder.

It could be Carmichael, though. Schwartz kept her head down and her senses sharp for another shift in the atmosphere.

'I'll be done here soon,' Teddy said. He removed the wallet from his pocket and a card from its sleeve, handing it to her. 'I can meet you at Petro's in a few. Grab something to eat.'

'You know,' she muttered, turning the card between her fingers, 'I should leave soon.'

'Have something small, at least. Too much travel on an empty stomach does no one any favours.'

Breakfast was the least of their concerns. He didn't have the heart to say what truly plagued him, that the thought of

Schwartz leaving after not one, but two fruitless attempts to find Gemma Eakley made his heart burrow to the floor of his stomach until he felt sick.

Sick of failure, sick with regret. Sick with wanting and hollow from all the lives that God had spooned out of him. Their feelings, laid out in the open, couldn't surmount the truth that was his duty. He couldn't leave loose ends with Alaric. The logistics of leaving the cottage had yet to be determined; it was thrilling, and so terrifying that he wasn't convinced of its plausibility, like an impossible dream just vivid enough to believe.

Whichever outcome he chased, he was bound to lose something. The girl, the house, the memories. What if it wasn't worth it to take the jump and return? What if he couldn't fall back into the rhythm of Cambridge as easily as he'd hoped?

Schwartz asked, 'Help me pack?'

Teddy nodded, unable to speak. The chapel was gone and with it went the memory of his head beside her leg, her fingers in his too-long hair, and his dream of planting himself in the ground beside her like trees with tangled roots.

She left for the cafe without another word. Teddy waited in the shop for someone – *anyone,* at this point – to come through and receive him, but for once, he didn't mind the silence. His elbows perched on the front desk, holding up his weight while the feeling, the sickness, swelled into his body until he felt like he'd drowned in it.

It was Carmichael who came blustering through the veil. His steps were hesitant, as if he knew any sudden movement might paint him as a threat. He pushed his sleeves up to his elbows. 'Hello.'

Teddy greeted him with a small jerk of his chin. 'They've left you here?'

'N-no. Hye-Jin has her hands full with something in the library. A breakthrough, really. She'll be pleased to hear it's *you* here. There's much to show you, once you're settled back in—'

'And Alaric?'

Carmichael's dark eyelashes fluttered like crows' wings as he blinked away his confusion. 'He's at the house now.'

He'd said it as if there was no other place Teddy could have expected him to be. 'The house?' Teddy's jaw worked into a hard edge.

Carmichael nodded slowly. 'Yeah, with Louisa. He said he tried to call you, or maybe that was Aurelia. Did you not hear what happened?'

Teddy's breath laced tight underneath his ribs. 'Hear *what,* Sum?'

A kind-hearted smile tugged at Carmichael Sum's full lips, but the effect couldn't have been more opposite.

'It's Gemma,' he said. 'She got back this morning.'

Over half a year had passed since he'd last seen Gemma Eakley. It was enough time for him to have turned twenty-four, enough time to have missed two terms at Pembroke, become a guardian, and forsake his family for good. It'd been long enough to lose all hope that Gemma would ever return. Long enough to not wait another minute.

He ignored the familiar twinge of pain in his leg and the ache in his muscles as he bounded through the grass. The wards around the cottage turned him away, whispering discouraging platitudes with each step he took.

Don't come. Turn back. There's nothing on this hill for you.

There is everything, he told himself. *Everything and more.*

The wards ripped apart to let him through, their silence a reward of its own. He could feel the others now: three heartbeats in conversation behind the closed door, a song of witch's blood carried on wings. Teddy brought his hand to the doorknob, and it swung open in anticipation.

The house seemed to rattle at his entry, as if his presence and his magic roused it from a peaceful sleep. At the counter stood Alaric Friedman, stripped of his glasses and his usual gruff expression. His emotions were unguarded. Teddy couldn't save himself from the flood. Didn't even know if he wanted to.

Behind him stood Gemma Eakley. Her hair fell in thick strands down her back, her silvery streaks hidden behind its dark curtain. She looked up at him, more stunned than anything. Something about her look was more familiar than her smile. She'd always acted surprised to see him when he would show up for holidays, as if it were something she couldn't – or hadn't – foreseen.

'It's you. It's really *you*,' he said uselessly.

Lou emerged from the basement steps, her face dappled in red. She threw her arms around his hips. Alaric mumbled Teddy's name in a warning tone.

'I would have come sooner,' Teddy said. 'I swear, I didn't . . . I had no idea.'

'Where were you?' Gemma's voice was coated in sand, shot from crying or shouting – Teddy didn't know which. He pried himself free from Louisa's firm embrace, then from the barrier Alaric made of himself in front of Gemma.

Teddy walked through him like a door. *To hell with him.* He threw his arms around Gemma Eakley.

Flesh and blood and *breathing*. He fell apart at the confirmation, thinking she would hold him.

Finally, finally.

Gemma flinched in pain.

'*Teddy.*' Alaric's tone was heavier this time, his fingers twisted in the boy's shirt like the scruff of a cat's neck.

Stumbling backwards into the caretaker's chest, Teddy felt the whisper in his hair.

'She's injured.'

Judging by the way Alaric's gaze shifted to Lou, Teddy decided not to ask while she was there. Gemma's arm twisted over her midsection, the ache echoing into his own ribs. It was deeper than skin, muscle and bone. *God,* he thought, *how deep does it go?*

'It's all right, Al. I – *ah* – don't have the energy to talk about it,' Gem said. 'Can you sit me down, maybe?'

With a sharp jut of his chin, Alaric shooed Teddy out of his path to walk the woman towards the sun-bleached sofa. The unevenness in her gait appeared to stem from something in her midsection rather than her legs – an unwillingness to twist too much or let her arms fall naturally to her sides. With Alaric's help, she lowered herself to the cushion, and asked again, 'So, where were you, then? I thought you would be here.'

Teddy scoffed a little at the question, hands braced on his

hips. 'Well, I went to the churchyard the other night and then to London, after a small incident.'

'The churchyard?' Gemma asked, just as Alaric asked, 'Incident?'

Gemma knew about the churchyard. Kenny had never told her about what they'd done there, but he'd told her everything else. She knew it well enough, at least by reputation, to let Kenny keep going.

But Teddy could see from the steadfastness of her stare that she *had* been there. Triumph swelled in his chest until it had no room left for breath. 'You were there, weren't you? I knew it was you. Carrying the eye. Do you have it?'

'Teddy,' Alaric muttered. 'I think it's best that you talk tomorrow. She's had a hell of a journey back.'

'It's been eight months,' Teddy interjected. 'I think after eight months, I'm allowed some answers.'

'And you'll get them. *Tomorrow.*'

Gemma nodded. Her fingers, which had curled around Alaric's for support, tightened with gratitude. Teddy didn't know why it bothered him so much. What was a day to eight months?

Well, it was unnecessary.

'But, Gemma—'

'What is it about you that makes it so difficult to exercise some patience?' Alaric hissed. 'Go on a fucking walk, if you can't keep your questions to yourself right now. Take Lou out for an errand or something.'

'Not Lou,' Gemma said. Then quieter, as if Teddy did not need to hear it, 'She stays here with me. I need to see her.'

Alaric nodded obediently. 'Of course. Slip of the tongue.'

It was then Teddy noticed the evidence of his small betrayals littered across the floor of the kitchen. There were diary entries penned in Louisa's large, looping script pried neatly from the glue of their binding. Teddy had never read them, but it was obvious what they were. And what they *said* . . .

Still on the counter, having not yet fallen to the floor beside the other papers, were copies of the forms he'd filled out for Louisa's new schooling. He didn't think he would ever have this conversation with Gemma.

He swept her diary entries up one by one, realizing the girl had stayed tucked behind the counter herself. She wiped her face, snatching the pages from his hands possessively. 'You guys weren't supposed to read them.'

Crouching down, he asked, 'Lou darling, I would never. Did you tear these out?'

She shook her head, and he could see faint streaks of tears still wet upon her inflamed cheeks. Abruptly, she stormed past him and the others, stomping towards her room where the door slammed shut behind her and she began to cry.

'She's not going to that school,' Gemma said. 'What were you even thinking, trying to enrol her?'

'Did you read her diary?' Teddy demanded. 'You got back home and – what? Decided to rip apart her diary? Why?'

'That's enough,' said Alaric.

'How could you do that to her? Do you understand how much it hurt her to lose you? How hard it was to figure out how to move forward without you – only for you to come back and keep your secrets and *rip apart her diary.* All you had to do was ask how she felt, and she would have told you.'

Gemma's lip curled with disdain. Another thick strand of grey had begun to streak through the front of her hair. She seemed *dirty,* among other things like weary and not entirely present. As if she hadn't showered in over a week and desperately needed to sleep.

'You knew how I felt about her schooling, Teddy. This house was meant to protect her. *You* were supposed to protect her. I've told you it's not safe for her out there. Not in Cambridge, not in London, but *here.*'

He shook his head with an indignant scoff. 'Jesus Christ, Gem. How can you say that? Where were you? Where were you when I was looking after your kid?'

'It's a fair point,' Alaric interjected. '*I* didn't expect you to be gone as long as you were; I had to tell the Syrian caretaker to wait on a request he had for me, because you hadn't come back yet.'

Teddy didn't know what to say to that. After months of uninterrupted childcare, he had been stupid to think he was owed, or at least deserved, a bit of time to recover while Louisa was in Alaric's care. He hadn't considered the repercussions of another day away.

But he could only feel so bad about it when Gemma added, 'It's not about a night or two. It's about the future, and what you're throwing Lou into. You'll feed her to the wolves.'

'Wolves,' Teddy repeated belligerently. 'They're *people.* Human beings, no better or worse than we are.'

'To each other, maybe. Not to a witch. You've got so complacent over the years trying not to be a witch that you've forgotten just how dangerous they can be. I can't let Louisa experience that. I'm unsettled you would even consider it.'

To this, Alaric said nothing. It was a diplomatic avoidance he'd picked up in his role on the council. It made Teddy's teeth clench and ache.

'You don't get to tell me I endangered Lou by letting her off your lead when you left her completely. I just wanted her to have a normal life. I gave up everything for her. I suppose Al didn't care to mention that I left university for this. I abandoned my studies and my flat and dropped everything to make sure she was provided for when you didn't.'

Was it true? Had Teddy been an afterthought? Had he ever been more than a bandage for the wound that Gemma had left, an ellipsis between her disappearance and her return? As long as Gemma eventually came home, it didn't matter what he'd gone through on his own. All that mattered was how much he'd disrupted her belongings.

Teddy wrung his hair through a tight fist, tugging in frustration. He turned from Gemma's irate stare and shut his eyes.

'I had my reasons for holding her so close, Teddy,' she said, folding her arms over her chest. 'After what they did to me . . . After what they did to my son. I will not let the same things happen to her.'

'But I was here too, Gemma. She was never going to be alone the way that Kenny was – she had *me*.'

'Then why weren't you here when I came home? What is that on your arm?'

His arms were mostly covered by long sleeves, but a bruise peered out from his wrist. 'It's nothing.'

'Don't lie to me. You're covered in them. Look at you,' she hissed. 'I couldn't have trusted you not to find trouble with my daughter in your care, could I? Risk an injury while Louisa was waiting at home?'

'Are you . . .' Teddy didn't finish. A disbelieving huff shot out of him. 'You're serious right now.'

She said nothing but touched her fingers to her side and sucked in a sharp, pained breath. Teddy felt the echo of tenderness against his ribs when she did, a screaming phantom pain. Alaric's hand lifted away. He stood and pushed his glasses up with his knuckle, looking Teddy squarely in the eyes. 'Come outside.'

'But Louisa—'

Alaric made a flourish with his hand, and the front door swung open. '*Now.*'

There were others outside the cottage. Every ghost he'd ever seen, save for Agatha, who must have been with Louisa in her room. Teddy shoved Alaric's grip off as it came around his elbow. He was being cast out like all the ghosts, forced to relinquish reign of the hillside now that Gemma had returned.

The door shut behind them, and the caretaker turned the boy by the shoulder to face him. 'Look at me when I say this, Teddy: she's wounded, exhausted, and she's pissed as all hell right now. It doesn't matter what you've done for Louisa since she's been gone or why you ended up in London, because she won't listen. And I'm trying to save you from a proper offence right now, because she's saying things she doesn't mean, but you've got to fucking cooperate with me, OK?'

'Like what?' Teddy folded his arms together, unconvinced.

Alaric shook his head.

'It's about Kenny, isn't it? She blamed me for him just like she blames me for this.'

'She'll drop it before the week's over.'

The lie was pale. Teddy knew Alaric wasn't so naive as to think Gemma would forgive him now if she hadn't already. 'It's been *years*. I know what she thinks of me. I'm the reason he's dead; she thinks I defiled him.'

When Alaric didn't respond, Teddy's eyes flared with heat. Teddy had seen the words Gemma wrote in her grimoires. It was pointless to deny it. He had carried that regret on his back every day, letting it flood back in out of self-flagellation whenever his conviction started to turn.

His magic killed Kenny Eakley, and that guilt buried him deeper than any of Gemma's beliefs possibly could. But when he had given Kenny the blade, he'd given it to him with the handle first, posturing himself at the end like a sacrifice. It was never his choice to turn it. It was never his wish to be the weapon when he could be the shield.

He turned away, covering his face with his hands. 'You didn't even try to defend me. You think me unreasonable.'

'You don't know what I think,' Alaric said. 'Look, Teddy . . . why don't you get out of here for a night or two. Stay at the shop, or with Aurelia. It'd be better for everyone if you just kept your distance.'

The lack of specificity sent Teddy's heart galloping: not just Gemma, but *everyone*. 'And then what? Come back when she's ready? I waited eight months for a sign that she was alive.'

'I know—'

'Eight months cleaning up a mess, and after what Leona did to us—'

'I know it isn't what you expected—'

'This is exactly like what happened the first time,' said Teddy. His words were frenzied, slipping into one another almost incoherently. 'She boxed me out and gave me all the blame when Kenny died. You saw it. But I would never, *ever* have done something I thought would hurt Lou. I know better now—'

'Calm down—'

'I did my best.' Teddy's voice broke at the final word. 'Lou doesn't deserve to be locked away in this house. She deserves a proper childhood.'

'This isn't the time, Teddy.'

'This is exactly the time! She needs to grow, to meet kids her own age!'

'Why can't you understand, that's not your decision to make?'

'Just talk to her, Al. You can't let Gemma cage Lou in this house forever. You have to *do something!*'

A thunderous clap struck him seemingly from within, like a sonic blast concentrated between his lungs. Then, for a second, Teddy was weightless. Everything around him a blur.

The wards split open at his back before he fell hard into the packed earth.

He felt the scrape of broken grass against his cheeks, then the pain blooming across his back before he knew what had happened. His head throbbed from the impact.

He'd been thrown. *Tossed* like a feather-light ragdoll.

Sitting up, he saw he hadn't travelled far, but it was enough to place the caretaker on one side of the wards and him on the other. Alaric lingered motionless, hands twitching from the involuntary expulsion of magic. His eyes widened, as if he had committed the act from outside his body and had only just returned to it.

'I . . . I didn't . . .'

Teddy could see the shape of Alaric faintly from his side of the ward, spindly as a tree and weathered like old bark. Rather than force himself to complete the sentence, Alaric pivoted on his heel and disappeared completely. Teddy heard the door click shut – and something in his heart breaking.

There was a numbness between his ears, a strange heat on the back of his head where it had struck the ground. Teddy lifted his fingers to the nape of his neck. No blood, he thought, just heat.

It was a terrible relief, one that spoiled in his gut as soon as it'd appeared. Alaric had, quite literally, cast him out from the magical boundaries of the only home he had. Whether the caretaker meant to was beside the point; they were on two different sides of a wall now, and Teddy couldn't see from his side if the caretaker was going to welcome him back in.

Gemma's face felt like a misremembered dream. How was it possible that he had looked at her again and yet she still didn't seem real. That there was anything still keeping them apart made his stomach twist.

Perhaps, it was just the impact. He pushed himself to his feet, reeling and uneasy. The world tilted and slowed in front of him.

Schwartz was nearing the bottom of the hillside, no larger in his sights than a smudge of ink on the pad of his thumb. She would want to know. Even if their interrogation of Gemma's note had yielded no results, Aurelia was invested in Gemma's return too. What would he tell her? That Gemma was back but couldn't be bothered, or that his formerly inescapable duty as Louisa's guardian had come to a sudden and unforeseen end?

She must have been too far when it happened to feel the echoes of emotion through the tether; Teddy pulled at it in his mind and found only a pleasant, unknowing calm inside of her. He stepped towards it. Towards her. This was right. Nothing else but *this* was right.

A disturbance shuddered through the surface of the ward: Schwartz's backpack, levitating through the shimmer before dropping swiftly at his feet. He hoisted it up, bowing under its weight. Alaric must have added something. Teddy unzipped the topmost edge and saw a change of his own clothes peering through, and the white of his toothbrush. There was something almost thoughtful about the gesture, like he'd been packed an overnight bag to spend the night at his childhood friend's house.

Then, through the ward, Louisa collided with Teddy's hip, toppling over the bag. Her arms flung around him.

'You can't go. You just got back.'

'Louisa,' her mother called. It sounded like sand on the other side of the ward, sifting through the metal prongs of a fork. 'Come here, darling.'

The girl looked up at Teddy. Her features scrunched up in the centre of her face, her chin wobbling like a bird. Her eyes were glossy with fresh tears.

'Please?' she mouthed out of her mother's earshot. 'You could take me with you.'

He weighed that option treacherously. Maybe he could. Maybe, with more time, they could have started something new, something beautiful and limitless, far from the cottage where the ghosts constantly reminded them of unfinished business. Maybe he should have done more to show her the world before her mother came home to steal her away from it again.

'I'm sorry, Lou. I need you to move.'

'Where are you going?'

He didn't know. Cambridge was the obvious choice, but he didn't have a flat any more. His resting ground was entirely conditional on Schwartz and her housemate, and the thought made him feel like less of a person.

'Nowhere,' he said, 'I won't be far. Just—'

Not here.

'What's going on?' Schwartz met him halfway up the hill, her brows upturned as she registered a pain she couldn't place.

'Tell him he can't leave!' Louisa said, trying her luck with Schwartz. Aurelia nearly dropped both drinks as the girl struck her with unprecedented force.

She didn't have the parts to piece together, but Teddy knew she was trying. He wanted to tell her not to pry, that everything would pass and nullify the effort – so why bother?

'What's going on?' she asked the girl.

Teddy interjected with a sharp whisper over the girl's head. 'It's not Lou. I don't know what I was thinking, trying to hold things together here. I thought we were doing well.'

'Is it Alaric?' Her eyes widened with realization when he didn't respond. 'Is it Gemma?'

Teddy continued onwards, driving past Schwartz towards the bottom of the hill.

She placed herself in his path again, unyielding to his stubborn gait even with the girl stuck to her hip. 'Ingram, look at me. *Please.*'

He adjusted the backpack on his shoulders and the puckers of his coat that formed beneath the straps. 'I think we should leave. Let go, Lou,'

'Wait a second,' Schwartz said. 'Can we just talk this through? You and me.'

Louisa tugged at the open flaps of his jacket. 'Please don't go. She won't be mad forever. I can talk to her. Please?'

'There's nothing I can do if she doesn't want me there.' He articulated each word but his voice still bled. 'You have to go inside. You're only going to make things worse.'

Schwartz slid onto her knees in the grass beside Lou, peeling strands of the girl's unbraided hair from her wet cheeks. Louisa stared at him over Schwartz's shoulder, pleading with large, glistening eyes for an assurance that Teddy couldn't give.

'I could tell her the truth!' Louisa cried. 'She's wrong! All I have to do is show her, and she'll see. I swear!'

If he let the girl think there was a chance, she'd follow in his footsteps and make herself a wall, and she was too young for that. Still so small and susceptible to heavy blows. She'd topple at the first harsh word, and then that wound, like his own, would grow and leave her bitter. He couldn't let her do that. The thought of her trying in vain to shield him from her mother made his blood run cold.

He said nothing, except to Schwartz. 'I'll meet you at the car.'

Lou's sob felt like a fist against his ribs. The air rushed out of him, his lungs porous like a crumbling dam. He turned, just halfway. Enough to see that the girl was folded into Aurelia's arms, mucus dribbling onto her shoulder, and that his lover was wearing perhaps the most scornful expression he had ever seen in all his years of knowing her.

Her head fell with utter disgrace, and she pressed her lips to Louisa's hair, whispering what looked like an incantation but was probably more of a sweet nothing.

He shrugged the strap of his bag up his shoulder and started towards the bottom of the hill, thinking of Schwartz's question by the Thames, wondering if there was truth to it that he'd been too stupid to realize.

If I could give you a feeling, I would, Little Bug. If I could give you the world, I would bleed myself dry for it.

But Teddy felt and couldn't give, and always more than was good for him. Schwartz met him at the bottom of the hill and said nothing as the car took them from Townsend, both of their paper cups discarded before either had been drunk from.

CHAPTER TWENTY-SIX

Silence permeated the walls of Schwartz's house. She laid her bags at the foot of the staircase, twisting her hair behind her ears before she shut the door behind him. The lock clicked into place with a flick of her fingers; she couldn't be bothered to attend to it herself, her mind flooded with a plethora of other things.

'Give me a minute.'

Teddy lowered his head, forcing a knot down his throat. They'd hardly spoken to each other in the car. His face held the heat of the ache in his spine, then the heat of a fluster. His jaw ached from the tight clench of his teeth. He knew Schwartz had plenty to say to him, but she spent longer unravelling the morality of chastising a just-hurt boy than she did acting on her anger. Teddy had braced himself all the way through her front door for her to resurrect her old offences and hurl them his way.

Go fuck yourself, Ingram.

You're too proud to be good for anyone else.

He couldn't have blamed her for it; at present, Teddy felt like an utter failure to everyone he loved. His swift departure had hit a nerve that wasn't tied to Gemma or Lou but to *Meredith.*

She could see her mother for the first time walking out on her, the years of waiting and living without. Meredith, disappearing without a promise that she would someday come back.

When she had eventually found the words, they were unembellished and backed by unfiltered disappointment. 'You're a prick, you know that?'

'What was I supposed to do?' he'd asked. 'You didn't see the way they looked at me.'

'No. I didn't. All I saw was the way Louisa looked at you when you turned your back on her. For all your talk of putting her first, you left without more than a second thought.'

'That was *not* easy for me, Schwartz.'

Then, she'd gone quiet, favouring the taste of her fingernails to another harsh word. A great divide stretched between them – a cliff, a grave, where all their animosity went to die. When they were stopped in Cambridgeshire traffic, Teddy let his gaze wander to her profile. He'd spent so long asking her to see him as a friend that, by the time he might have become something more, he was practically desperate for her not to rescind her affection. He was reaching for her through that tether, asking her to understand him and give him grace.

After a while, Schwartz had reached for him in a physical sense. Their fingers had woven together on the console between their seats.

She left him at the bottom of the staircase, leaning against the banister like a wet umbrella.

Not much had changed since the last time Teddy Ingram stepped foot into her house except that there was a different witch searching for them. Her housemate's signs of life were fresh around the kitchen: rinsed dishes in the sink, the lingering scent of cinnamon above the hob, a sticky spot of jam that hadn't yet dried on the tiles. The kettle was still warm to the touch. They'd left only minutes ago.

Schwartz slipped into the kitchen soundlessly behind him. 'Would you believe it if I said it's usually messier?'

The strain in Teddy's face eased as Schwartz's comment ushered in a hope for less complicated conversation. The folly of it all forced the feeling up to his head in a blind rush. 'You must hate me now for what I've done,' he added quietly.

Schwartz folded her arms around her body. 'A little.'

'I've been trying to forgive myself for what happened to Kenny, but maybe it's true – it's no one's fault other than mine. If I thought Gem could ever forgive me, that feeling is gone now. It's clear I'm a liability to her.'

In the dark veil of his covered eyes, he saw the podium of the church where Celia made him kneel, the emaciated saviour behind it, and he imagined Gemma Eakley in the robes instead. Passing her judgement on him, laying out the terms of his redemption like beads on a rosary.

'I was a terrible son. To my parents, and to Gem. But God, I tried to be better for Lou. I did everything I could.'

He traced the outline of the jam smear meticulously, until he could close his eyes and make its shape. Schwartz's hand smoothed around his waist. Her cheek found the hollow between his shoulder blades. He counted her breaths.

One. Two.

Six, until she pressed her nose to the edge of his scar and kissed it through the fabric. 'That's a commitment, though, to be better. You have to *keep* being better. Promise me you'll go back for her.'

The world was an impossible gift to give; it belonged to no one, least of all a witch cursed with reaper magic. Lou, of all children, wouldn't know what to do with a world so big. She might not even want it.

But Teddy could give her his word, cities away, through a promise to someone else: *I'll always come back to you.*

You and I are indefinite.

Translation, as Teddy believed, was a matter of connection, of bridging a gap. Schwartz could hardly keep the meaning of a thing consistent within herself, which made him wonder time and time again if she meant to burn the bridge with him.

He used to think she was fickle, back in the early days of their university rivalry, but that word didn't encompass nearly everything it was supposed to. He'd settled on the word *unanswerable* later on, and it hadn't failed him yet. An answer implied a question, an uncertainty, a possibility. Teddy never quite knew where he stood with her, and so he carried all of it with him, everywhere he went.

Now, she was ushering him towards the art gallery in rushed strides. The air was still thick with the unsaid words that trailed off the end of their last conversation. He couldn't help wondering if Schwartz resented him for what had happened. If she carried him around like a burden. They could only go so far in silence before letting something rotten fester between them, but it was clear she didn't know how to talk to him with the wound so fresh. She needed a walk, and to see her housemate.

Through the glass, Teddy saw the recognition catch in Ryan Jena's expression. Their head turned, and with a quick adjustment of their glasses, they excused themselves from the company of a white-haired gallery patron and met their housemate at the open door.

Ryan swept Schwartz into a hug that lifted her onto her toes. 'There you are. Better late than never.'

'Is everything still here?'

They nodded, face obscured in part by the mop of Schwartz's curls. 'Nothing'll come down until the end of the month. It's all been purchased though. That guy's actually a buyer.' A grin stretched across their face as they pulled away, shifting the dark, rectangular lenses incrementally up their cheeks. Ryan's hair had been a bleach-yellow blond the first time Teddy met them, but it was shorn close to the scalp now and coloured like beetroot. They raised two fingers triumphantly and whispered. 'Two pieces. He's not even my highest buyer.'

'We're not interrupting, are we?'

Ryan shook their head. 'I hoped you would. I've been waiting for you to see.'

Schwartz stepped into the building. Teddy lingered for a moment, salvaging his hair from the warm whisper of a summer's-end breeze weaving through the trees. Despite his best efforts, it proved uncooperative.

Ryan's mouth twitched into a larger, conspiratorial grin as Teddy passed through. 'Ah, yes, if it isn't the fabled Theodore Ingram. I always wondered when you'd come back around.'

Schwartz pulled Ryan's arm into the loop of her own. Teddy thought of Celia's sharp heels clicking through the emptied

Tate Modern before an exhibition went public. Her sterile sense of scrutiny, scrubbing the white box from floor to ceiling with her ice-cold stare. She was always quick to place a box around illustration. She would have perused a gallery like this with an upturned nose, her heels snapping the linoleum floor with a deliberate evenness. She might have called it quaint. *Cute.*

Ryan gestured for him to join them as they continued down the narrow passage of the gallery. Midday promised them a mostly empty playground in which to gaze at their preferred pace. Schwartz crooned praises like a proud mother as Ryan recounted the news of the opening they'd missed. She laid her head on their shoulder, stopping in front of a familiar pyjama-clad figure in the kitchen.

She had shown Teddy this painting outside the Tate Modern, shrunken down on her phone screen. 'I didn't realize it was so big,' he said.

More than half his height, in fact. Ryan shrunk into themselves, lowering their head as if threatened by some unspoken implication. Teddy meant nothing by it, certainly not an accusation; if Ryan made her a muse for their work out of buried love, who could blame them? Part of what made it so unfair to love Aurelia Schwartz was how easily you could do it.

More unfair was the fact that she kept that love so guarded.

She raised a brow at Teddy, her eyes flashing with a dare. 'Weird to think I'll be making breakfast in some stranger's flat for the rest of eternity.'

'Or until it fades,' Ryan said. 'Archival-quality supplies are stupidly expensive, you know.'

'Impermanence and rarity never devalued a piece of art,'

Schwartz assured them. 'Anyway, no one needs to know if it looks this good now. They can cross that bridge when they get to it.'

He could spend years unravelling the look she gave him, decades to find a word for it. Teddy sidled up to join them, Schwartz's closeness a dizzying spell. Her sidelong gaze fixed him from beneath a curtain of dark, curled lashes. Reciting for her alone, Teddy swept back the hair hanging over her ear and whispered a note of praise from the Faerie Queen that seemed better suited for her. '"So hard a workemanship adventure darre, for fear through want of words her excellence to marre."'

Ryan, from over Schwartz's head, gave him a small, flushed smile. Teddy couldn't discern what quality he found most compelling about Ryan, but he considered that smile invaluable. It took a different, elevated sort of understanding to capture the light above Schwartz's image, one that Teddy was still trying to pinpoint.

He thought he would have to make peace with the unattainable nature of her charm until now – what good were his questions when she was there in front of him: captivating, lovely, his bright star?

But Ryan had done it. Pinpointed the thing he had most wanted to discover for himself. He could have been jealous that Ryan found what he wasn't worthy to. Mostly, he found himself leaning into Ryan the way Schwartz did, another victim to their charm, hoping he could be understood so beautifully.

The bell above the gallery's door drew Teddy's attention to the front, to the university students passing the window. He caught a familiar mop of chestnut hair and a hearty laugh from a boy in a green jumper. Teddy gave Schwartz's hand a gentle squeeze and said, 'I'll be right back.'

Lawrence had reached the exterior of another shopfront by the time Teddy Ingram stepped outside.

'Kressler,' Teddy shouted, summoning a bewildered look from the boy in his band of friends.

'Is that who I think it is?' Lawrence's face broke into an exuberant grin as he pushed his way forward to meet him with open arms. 'God, Theo, where the hell have you been? I thought you'd fled the country or something.'

Teddy's hand clapped Lawrence's shoulder enthusiastically, his cheek pressed to the other medievalist's ear. Vaguely, he replied, 'I was needed elsewhere. You look well.'

Lawrence studied him briefly. 'I can't believe you're here. I texted you loads of times.'

Teddy instinctively reached for his ruined mobile. 'I never got anything. I figured I'd faded from the general consciousness of Pembroke's medieval department.'

'Of course not. We talk about you all the time.' Lawrence's cheeks dimpled slightly, faint lines like whiskers etched beneath his eyes.

The joy on his face pulled at Teddy's chest. Why had he never received Lawrence's messages? What else had he missed within all that lost time?

'Are you here for a while? We'll have to catch up. I'm having dinner with my mates from Christ's tonight if you'd like to come.'

Lawrence waved his friends along without him. Teddy knew he shouldn't dawdle, that Schwartz was waiting for him here and Lou waiting for him in Townsend. But a wishful curiosity plagued him to know what shape he took when wasn't there. Who was it that they spoke of in his absence? Surely, it couldn't have been the same person that was taking care of Lou in Townsend. He'd left a hollow shell of himself behind like an over-starched garment.

Presumably, it'd done a fine job of keeping his place while he was gone.

He looked back at the gallery door expectantly. Lawrence caught his line of sight, mumbling a soft, 'Strange,' before he could answer.

'What's strange?' Teddy asked.

'Just . . . You two never really got on. Is it weird running into each other while you're back in town?'

Schwartz's head was tilted onto Ryan Jena's shoulder, their hands clasped between their sides; and though she appeared entirely unsuspecting of his conversation, Teddy wondered if she felt his gaze on her the way he'd felt hers so many times before.

He could have told Lawrence the truth – that outside of his studies at Pembroke, there was a world moving without him – just to know what it felt like on the other side. In hindsight, it didn't matter to Teddy that he'd missed out on so much; he was here *now*. Even though his hair was longer, his image less stark and polished, he could fall back into the natural state of things easily, and don that old shape like a coat.

From the gallery, Schwartz gave him a small smile through the window.

Is it weird? Lawrence had asked.

Sometimes, Teddy couldn't fathom how Schwartz was anything more than a dream. That they could exist here simultaneously and be not bitter but bound to one another made far less sense than the things he'd imagined after a glass of Alaric's witch liquor.

Who is the person for whom you are so destroyed by Love?

Unlike Chaucer, Teddy had an answer. Not a lie, nor a full truth.

'No. It's not weird at all.'

CHAPTER TWENTY-SEVEN

Aurelia could see her mother at the edge of the bed, reaching for the curl on her cheek to smooth it back. *What a cruel, cruel nightmare,* she thought, *that made itself so inviting to grieving girls.* Meredith was warm beside Aurelia's furled body, the honey shade of her palm etched with deep lines. She smiled, lips chapped and unpainted.

With her cheek tucked into the pillow, Aurelia smiled back and mouthed, *Hi.*

Aurelia felt the warmth of skin on her face, but the curl remained unmoved on her cheek. This must have been the uncanny vision that visited Teddy Ingram in the night, whose lips could move even when her chest didn't rise with breath.

I don't know what to do, she told her mother.

Who says you have to do anything?

It's not that simple. Because of you.

It didn't count as 'speaking ill of the dead' if she didn't say it aloud. Even if the thought was truer and backed by years of anger. She had a right to it, didn't she?

She wished Meredith could hear her now; if not in the flesh, as a ghost. Aurelia could give a voice to this unmanageable curse Meredith left her with – the *resentment.*

But like the undead knights in the chapel, Aurelia couldn't hurt something that couldn't feel. She couldn't ask for an apology from a woman without a beating heart.

I wish you'd been there, she said.

Meredith stared at her blankly.

You're not even sorry, are you? You thought this was the right thing to do.

Aurelia shut her eyes, forcing a tense breath. The newfound tether between herself and those around her had been ceaseless to an impossible fault. She'd been so eager to manage it, but if she could reach her mother with her new gift and ask Meredith why she had done it, Aurelia would.

Again and again.

Let me understand, Aurelia pleaded. *Tell me what to do.*

Meredith cocked her head. Her curls grazed her shoulder the way her daughter's did. Aurelia wondered at which point her father made the discovery that she looked more like Meredith than she looked like him.

It hurt less to say she missed him in her dreams.

She watched her mother lean forward, bracing for the touch of skin and flesh – human body – though nothing came. Meredith's hand, still wearing her wedding ring, floated through her hair and onto the pillow beside Aurelia's face.

Breath seized in Aurelia's throat. She bit down on her lip to keep an uncharitable sound of heartbreak from slipping out.

She closed her eyes again to the image of her mother placing a kiss upon her brow.

Wake up.

Wake up.

She lurched toward him like a magnet in the dark. Her fingers grasped his wrist. The room was swathed in darkness, slivers of residual lamplight falling onto the opposite wall, and Aurelia could feel his breath against the nape of her neck.

His arms were locked around her torso. Carefully, he eased her grip open. 'Just me.'

With a terse shudder, she sunk into the mattress. 'One bad dream for another,' she mumbled. 'Can't catch a fucking break.'

'Mhmm.'

The initial strike of fear fell off her like a shadow. Her pulse tempered. Everything in the dark shade of her bedroom was exactly where it was supposed to be.

Except maybe Ingram. It still came as a surprise to her each night she woke with him at her side. He could drive off nightmares with a little waking intent, but he slept straight through her general insomnia. His hair, which cost him so much time to tuck around his ears throughout the day, would fall across his cheek and curl around his jaw. His lips would be parted, the crease in his brow smoothed over. Unfairly, she always considered waking him up. He looked at her with such tactility, such certainty, that she would *know* she'd broken free of her mind.

She reoriented herself in his direction, studying the crease in his brow through muscle memory. 'Did I wake you?'

'I wasn't sleeping,' he mumbled. The shadow of his hand rose to her cheek. 'In fact, I'm failing miserably.'

'You should have kept me awake.'

'You needed the rest.'

'We could have made it a game,' she said. 'You probably knew I would win, though.'

Teddy smiled, half-hidden in Aurelia's pillow. Propping herself onto her elbow with a groan, she relented against the late hour. 'I'm up now. Maybe you could tell me a story.'

'You *do* enjoy my stories, then.'

'What can I say,' she sang softly. 'You have a knack for telling them.'

He hummed his thorough consideration once more, but his eyes had already lit with excitement over the prospect. With the gentle slip of his thumb, he charted her expression in the dark. It was soft under the cover of darkness, unguarded against the tether, but sheltered in every other visible way.

'Do you remember *La Vita Nuova?*' he asked.

'It's been a while. The Italian Renaissance is a bit late for me.'

'But you know it.' His thumb slid to the corner of her mouth. Then her chin.

'I wouldn't mind the recap.'

'It's not entirely useful for conversation's sake. There is a dream written in *La Vita Nuova* where Love comes to Dante and compels him to surrender. I think I had the dream recently. Not quite the way Dante penned it, but I haven't been able to shake it.'

'It amazes me that we sleep at all with all these terrors floating between us.'

'You weren't sleeping. Not when I woke up from it. I actually wondered if you'd seen it.'

At that, Aurelia withheld her quips and repaid the favour of his touch. Her hand found a home over the curve of his ribs, her fingers slotting over his bones like piano keys.

'I was a bird again. Chalk-white. Sickly. I saw myself in a room lined floor to ceiling with mirrors, and everything was cold. I can't remember the point you came to be. Had anything made sense, and were it not the nature of dreams, I would have seen you in the mirrors too; I could see myself in them a thousand times over. It felt like minutes. Could have been hours. You know, you're the only person besides Alaric who's ever seen me with my wings?'

Aurelia shook her head.

'Well, you are. And seeing you there, I remember feeling so safe . . . In *La Vita Nuova,* Dante dreams of Love personified feeding the poet's heart to Beatrice, and it's anything but comforting. His heart is on fire. It's literally *burning* as Love wakes Beatrice from her sleep and feeds it to her. It's ruthless and unrelenting and all powerful – so much that Dante writes, "Here is a god stronger than I, who comes to rule me." But there I was, half a monster and frail enough that you could have folded me like a page. And I *did* fold at the sight of you. When I woke up . . . like I said, I wondered if you'd seen it.'

'I would have remembered something like that.'

'Well, there was no heart in my dream,' Teddy noted, omitting the presence of Love altogether.

Cut from her sleep, Aurelia lacked the filter and the awareness to deny him a confession if he asked.

'You took something far more valuable from me.'

'I don't know if there's anything more valuable than a heart,' Aurelia said.

'There's plenty, if it's mine. "My body, but for your blood, is barren of worth."' He fell silent, watching her fingers tap and tug at the collar of his T-shirt like restless wingbeats. 'Somehow, I knew what you'd taken was Gemma's letter. It was folded into a bird already. Sentient enough. I watched you devour it in every mirror.'

Two nights had already passed since Ingram came to stay. Two nights skirting around mentions of Alaric, Gemma and the things they had said to him. Aurelia knew, regardless of the others' feelings toward him, that he was biding his time to return.

They spoke little of what would come next. They were still pondering the initial question they'd asked each other over eight months ago: *Must we keep pretending?*

She couldn't bear the thought of doing anything else, not when pretending was all that kept him here. Foolishly, she'd let herself lean into the impossible idea of waking up next to him morning after morning, as if permanence didn't go against every truth they'd established between them. She had her work, her steady life with Ryan, her shapeless mourning for her mother. Teddy had his devotion to Lou and his strange family in Townsend.

As long as they weren't dwelling on their duties, they could have each other too.

The delusion faded quickly. Aurelia sobered up enough to pull away, ridding his scent from her lungs with a sigh. 'For once, everything is so quiet to me, and yet my nerves won't let me rest.'

'One less person makes a hell of a difference,' Teddy pointed out. Sensing the immediate tension, he added, 'Ry left a note on the fridge. They're with someone named Ciannon tonight.'

Vaguely, she recalled her housemate's passing mentions of their long-time, non-committal fling, Ciannon, who never made it out from under pink club lighting and into the rest of Ryan's life. Their presence was limited to red lipstick prints stuck to the inside of Ryan's collar, which neither Ryan nor Aurelia could wash out for days. 'Ah, Ciannon.'

Her skin warmed enough that he must have felt it. His grip on the tether was remarkably steady. She wasn't jealous of her housemate. Maybe a little jealous of Ciannon. She had always been grossly possessive of the people she loved, even if she tried not to be. Theirs had been a rather romantic friendship, which hadn't changed for Teddy's expense, though she didn't know if it would change for somebody else's. Aurelia couldn't help wondering if she'd find Ryan Jena in the kitchen tomorrow, scrubbing at a red stain in their clothing, or if they were cosy enough with Ciannon to grab breakfast with them – lipstick stains and all.

Teddy looked at her with an unnerving sense of understanding. She wished he would ask about it, that he didn't know her so well, and they would never run out of reasons to speak to one another. *Ask me how I'm doing,* she thought. *Even if you already know.*

'It's going to feel like this forever, isn't it?' she mumbled.

'Don't tell me you've grown tired of me already.'

'I tired of you years ago,' she said. 'And still, you managed to make yourself comfortable in my room. In my bed.'

He grinned at her like he'd won something through her words. What was another impossible idea to someone who defied those odds?

'I don't know where to put all of this,' she said. 'I wish I could push it all into a corner or close it in a box and forget about it.'

'I've tried to push it beneath my bed, but it comes out at night when I least expect it. This magic *needs* perpetually. It starves.'

The empathy begged to be acknowledged in a way that his reaper gift would never match. 'For what?' asked Aurelia.

'For the living,' he said. 'Empathy and isolation don't make suitable partners. It's a gift that builds off others. You can feed it all your feeling, but you can never truly sate it. It needs a friend.'

'What a fucking leech,' she said. 'What happened next?'

'In the dream?'

Aurelia nodded. 'After I destroyed the bird, what did you do?'

His gaze descended the slope of her nose, the straight of her cheek, a look that translated into heat and satin. *Would it ever get easier?* she wondered. *To be read so closely?* He unravelled her fist and brought her palm to his mouth.

The scar of their oath had dissolved once their gifts had taken root, but the memory remained. Teddy kissed it once, letting it sear like a brand into her skin. He drew another kiss to her wrist. Her pulse point.

'Nothing,' he whispered. 'I just let you.'

CHAPTER TWENTY-EIGHT

Standing above the Thames, Schwartz had asked him what he wanted, and the answer was there in a swathe of different forms. He missed Cambridge for all its life and Pembroke for all its purpose. He wanted Gemma to come home and fill the gap her absence created.

At one point, he would have died for Gemma's forgiveness. Died for it or killed for it. Certainly, one weighed more than the other, but he hadn't discerned which yet. He knew there was love you could die for and love you could kill for, and both would lead him, sword in hand, to his knees in a plea of devotion.

Teddy wasn't betting on absolution any more. Not from Gemma or from Alaric.

He drew another kiss to the inside of Schwartz's forearm. Her word meant just as much, her decree an unwavering truth. Her touch holy.

'Come here,' Schwartz mouthed.

Her fingers grasped at the back of his neck, her arms winding like vines around his shoulders. Those two words ignited something dormant in him. He wanted to be needed. To be desired. He wanted someone to touch him, wanted to come alive with their belief, to feel their hands on his flesh as a reminder that he was not a ghost. He wanted someone to say his name and speak him into existence like a thought buried in the back of their minds.

Too much to ask from someone in the throes of grief. He could wait another night, another fifty nights, the whole damn year if he needed to, until her mind was clear and their time was abundant. He captured her roaming hands above the waist of his briefs. Their bodies were twisted around her sheets, caught in their haste. 'Is it too much?' he asked.

Those months on the hill stretched to impossible lengths, but he still knew the precise angle of her nose, the cupid's bow of her upper lip. What difference would it make to wait a while longer?

She brushed his nose with the cold tip of hers and whispered, 'It's perfect. *You're* perfect.' She met his lips, finding him receptive. Teddy obliged her fervently, hypersensitive to the path of her touch.

Because you made me, he thought. *I was all parts – fragmented and scattered – before you brought me to life.* With her hasty, tooth-addled kisses, Schwartz carved him out like a figure trapped in a marble slab. An artist. His creator. A master. If she was a promise, he would see it through – however long that took.

Though his fingers were patient and inquisitive, hers ravaged him like a blaze, raising the hair from his skin just to suppress it with a warm touch. He could be chivalrous and take his time, sure, but his inhibitions fled the moment she pulled his body flush to hers and mouthed the words, 'I need you.'

Her hold blossomed through the clutch of her thighs. After

the first garment came another, until they were mostly naked, and her sheets were kicked gracelessly down the length of the bed. She fumbled with the final layer of his briefs. Schwartz cursed as they caught at the bend in his hips.

'You know, for a while there,' Teddy said, 'I thought you might've said you missed me out of pity.'

In answer, she pushed him down onto the bed and pinned him beneath her weight like a moth in a frame. His head fell against her pillow, a vanquished groan rolling up from deep within his chest. There, with his body suppliant underneath her, she kissed the column of his throat. 'As if *I* could pity you. Pity is passive. I've never had a thought about you that made me want to sit still. Even before . . .'

'What?' It was only because he'd known her for so long that the question ever came to be. She'd hated him for little more than petty squabbling; and even if he knew she was ardent and tender at her core, she could be so inarguably indignant at the worst of times.

'It made me angry,' she confessed. 'God, you were infuriating. It'd keep me up sometimes, just thinking about the way you walked, and your stupid, confident posture. Then, I'd wonder what was wrong with me to be so bothered, and it'd make me even angrier. I couldn't stop thinking about you. Antagonizing you. Besting you. And nothing made me feel more alive, except maybe wanting you, which also felt so much worse.'

She took him into her hand, stroking him between their bodies. The feeling, for which there was no direct translation in her body, piqued a wicked but eager curiosity in her. Her fingers tightened around him. Her mouth bruised the hollow of his throat. She tested the pressure points of his body, buried a laugh into his skin and whispered, 'Oh, this is *so* unfair.'

Teddy lugged himself upright and brushed her hair back from her neck. Her smile thinned as she steeled herself to the exploration of his fingers. He knew where to touch to make her shiver. How to make her flush.

'I dream of you like this too,' he said. 'Of having you. Touching you.'

'I'm not always a paper-hungry beast?'

He trailed his fingertip down the centre of her ribcage, over her navel. She pressed herself closer just as he pulled, a delicious, frictional collision of his mouth and her skin. He bit. Tasted. An oft-dreamt dream of forbidden fruit, melting on his tongue.

His mouth closed around the peak of her breast, his eyes fluttering shut. 'You're so many things,' he whispered. 'Quick to anger. Hard to please. But I belong to you in every fantasy, and *you—*' *You possess me,* he meant to say, but he was certain she already knew that. He nuzzled the dip between her breasts and groaned, 'God, Aurelia. I feel fucking crazy right now.'

She gasped his name in response, pushing his cock against her entrance. She was slick, pliant around the test of his fingers at first, but as he eased his length between her thighs, he felt her body seize. Then, a whispered apology. 'It's been a while for me,' she admitted, resting her brow against his. 'I might need . . .'

He didn't move, only looking at her expectantly. 'I can stop, if you—'

She shook her head. 'Just, um. Just kiss me a little, yeah? Until it gets easier.'

He did as he was asked, and it was the easiest responsibility he'd ever borne. He kissed her mouth, her throat, her chin. In-between, he murmured confessions until her body grew languorous and soft, such as that he would think of her often when he was at the bookshop, he would think of the pre-emptive lift of pages around her fingers while she read, so deliciously eager to turn to something new. And the thought of her fingers, her hands, her *touch* made it impossible to think of sleeping with anyone. She had ruined everything for him. He wanted to rewrite the world for her.

Teddy didn't ask how long it'd been for her since the last time she'd had sex. It didn't really make a difference – she was here with him now, or better yet, Teddy was here with *her*, fingers laced in her hair, their hips canting together into a rhythm that became easier and easier as he lavished her with sweet nothings. Something in the tightness of her breath told him they'd been waiting for each other with equal desperation. And if something drew him away again, she would still possess him entirely. She had woven her magic into the threads of his veins.

The initial burst of pain gave way to pleasure as she adjusted to his size. Each noise from her mouth was a sweet temptation, and each kiss was a pardon for his sins. Up until then, they'd been kissing in places where the walls were thin or the privacy was precarious; the sound of his name uttered with the fine rasp of her voice threatened to unravel him. His fingers bit into her sides, his teeth into her earlobe. She braced herself on his shoulders, the headboard behind him, the pillow, his wing scars. Her breath laced through the shag of his hair, his name a drawn-out plea.

It took every morsel of Teddy's restraint not to come, but she felt it. Of course, she did. Pleasure amassed cyclically through the tether, strengthened by hers and then his again.

He felt the ache between *her* thighs as much as he felt his own; he couldn't bear it. He twisted them around, caging her beneath his limbs. Seeing her splayed open for him like the ripe petals of a flower, laid out by her desire, drew a dangerous word to the forefront of his mind: *mine*. It was a word she would tell him in every dream. She would trace it on his back or mumble it against his mouth. There was always a measure of belonging between them. *My rival. My torment. My lover.*

Schwartz tucked her fingers beneath his jaw, dragging him to her mouth the way she'd done with her bloody palm in his basement. She looked unfathomably beautiful. Otherworldly and divine, haloed in her curls. It never failed to catch him off guard, how painfully pretty she was. How much of his being was vested in her presence.

'Did I ever tell you how much I love your hair?' Schwartz asked, sparing him the intensity of admitting something so grave.

She toyed with the strands falling over his face. He hid his reddened complexion in her sternum. 'Wouldn't have guessed.'

'Mm.' Schwartz offered him a thin smile. 'A little longer and I could cut it just like mine.'

She guided Teddy back to her body, tracing his leftover bruises in the dark. It was easier this time and the pleasure manageable, though her rapt attention still made his skin burn. With his hand tucked beneath the small of her back, he traced the ridges of her spine studiously. He could feel her coming apart, surrendering to it all with him. Felt the fever beneath her skin spreading like wildfire from his words. Everything – he felt *everything*. He knew what she loved and what she loved less. He knew the threshold where her pleasure gave way to pain, so he kissed her hard and touched her gently.

He lowered his mouth to her neck and left a mark dark enough to be his name. 'I'm so close,' he whispered.

She took his face between her hands, nodding. 'I know. Me too.'

Not long after, she came with a sharp cry. Teddy's hand fisted into the pillow beside her face as he followed, his body slicked in sweat. He tucked his forehead beneath her jaw, blinded by the heat behind his eyelids.

'It's never going to be like this with anyone else,' she said breathlessly.

'Like what?' *Like ruination. Like heaven.*

She bit her lip. 'You called me Aurelia.'

Like I made your name another way of translating 'love'.

Teddy traced the constellation of dark freckles above her breasts. He kissed her shoulder. The end of her tattoo. The mark he'd left on her throat that he wished to make as indelible as ink.

'I actually think I called you *God*,' he replied.

She asked him, after they'd bathed and buried themselves under her sheets again, what he meant by it. It was late enough at that point that either of them could forget the question within seconds of his evasion; half his answers were hums and the other half he laboured through with a slack-jawed mumble. 'Am I a god you love or a god you fear?'

He placed another kiss beneath her eye on that beloved, soft patch of skin just before she drifted off to sleep beside him. 'The one I follow to the ends of the earth.'

'Sabotage,' Teddy hissed, tossing his controller to the couch beside Schwartz's feet. The devious glint in Ryan's eyes hid behind a technicolour reflection of a Coconut Mall race playing out on their glasses.

'I'm just too good,' Ryan said. 'Pure skill. Masterful drift. Sore loser, et cetera.'

'You kicked me.' Teddy rolled the knot in his neck out, letting his head fall back against the seat of the couch. Schwartz peered around the screen of her laptop and offered Teddy a split glimpse of the smile creeping onto her face. 'You saw it,' he mumbled. 'Call it, Schwartz.'

'I saw nothing of the sort.'

Ryan collected the discarded controller on the other side of Teddy's body, stretching over his lap. Shoving it back into his hands, Ryan twisted, bearing the full, uninhibited grin of a successful saboteur and mouthed, 'Get fucked.'

Teddy won the next race by a hairline margin, only because Schwartz set herself to removing the single, silver tooth earring grazing Ryan's neck during the final lap. Teddy swore he saw nothing.

'Give me that.' Ryan snatched the earring back from Schwartz's possession. She closed her laptop and manoeuvred out from behind their heads, leaving them to sift through other course maps in silence. Ryan kicked Teddy's ankle again, sweeping it out from underneath him.

Whatever Schwartz had disappeared to work on stirred a significant amount of brainpower. The hair on Teddy's exposed forearms stood attentively. Ryan was waiting for his decision on a map, but relevant thoughts were currently impossible. 'You all right there?'

'Give me a minute,' Teddy said. His body creaked in numerous places as he rose from the floor. What the hell was Schwartz doing? He made it to the hallway before she returned, her expression gathered into a tight knot of concern.

'You want to help me with something?'

Teddy ran his tongue across his gums. 'Possibly.'

She brushed past him, plucking at her cuticles restlessly. 'I should have done this months ago, but it slipped my mind. This house doesn't have any wards around it.'

'Wards,' Ryan mumbled, shifting their narrowed gaze from the screen.

'I haven't raised a ward before,' Teddy said.

'It's not hard. It just takes two to set.'

Ryan looked at Teddy with a question. Teddy remembered suddenly that perhaps he shouldn't be so comfortably discussing magical topics around Aurelia's human housemate. But it was harmless with Ryan. Their sense of trust, no matter how small and misplaced, made Teddy's cheeks alight with pink.

'Just an extra precaution,' she said. 'Please?'

He nodded. 'Where do you want me?'

Schwartz led him to the back of the living room where they were all gathered, past the point where it became Ryan's space alone, and their hanging clothes marked a private niche. Ryan's sofa bed was tucked into the furthest corner from the front door, against a wall with a back door that Schwartz had said 'leads nowhere'.

'I'll draw the frame starting here. Drag your fingers through it and pull it around the perimeter of the house like wet ink.'

'How far?' he asked.

'Until you reach me again,' she answered. 'Which should be toward the front. We'll move back to opposite sides when we raise it. Dip your fingertips into the border and pull upward. It should feel like ink. Pull hard enough that you can send it climbing on its own once it gets high enough. It needs to reach the upper floor.'

Teddy lowered his head dutifully. 'You'd make a wonderful teacher,' he said.

'I would, if I had the patience for children.' Quickly, she corrected, 'I mean, I love Lou, but my tolerance for kids as a general idea isn't great. I mostly tutor teenagers, and that's the most I can handle.'

He laughed. 'I get it. I'm not sold on the idea myself.'

Her face warmed with a treacherous thought. She cleared her throat, levelling her gaze on the ground where she marked the beginning of the ward's boundary. 'So, you don't want kids?'

Teddy leaned forward, pressing his fingers to the streak of gold she'd laid at the threshold of her back door. 'Not particularly. Looking after Lou is more than enough for me.'

Schwartz bit down on her lip. Had she anticipated a different answer? Teddy hardly expected the question himself; domesticity implied some level of permanence, and despite his longing, they were anything *but*.

'Do you?' he asked.

She shook her head. 'I'm perfectly happy with taking care of Annie's future kids from time to time. Or Ryan's. But there are too many things I want to do before I die to commit to a kid. I don't think I'd be a good mother. I don't know how to be the soft place for someone to land, you know? That's what I needed when I was a kid.'

That was what Teddy needed still, what she'd given him, even if she didn't know she'd done it; but they were in agreement, so he didn't press the point.

Sometimes, Teddy caught himself wondering why Gemma wanted another child after losing Kenny. She'd been pregnant at the time of his death, but not far along, and Teddy assumed, rather naively, that she loved the newborn so much to make up for all the love her son would never get. She certainly held Lou closer for that reason, raised her wards around the Townsend cottage to keep her daughter safe.

But Gem was stubborn. In the best of ways and the worst of ways. She loved her children no end, even if it poisoned them. Raising them in a world as cruel as theirs, even at a distance, was an act of courage in her eyes – to endure against all odds. Lou lived under the weight of all her mother's devotion as Gemma's personal *fuck you* to a world that stole her son.

Teddy drew the boundary around Ryan's bed and underneath the staircase, thinking of Gemma. For all their differences, they shared a strong disposition to take care of those around them. The root of their altercation was buried in the way they both loved, with conviction, with assurance.

Teddy never questioned whether or not he would forgive her; the answer was always yes. But would she meet him halfway? If he could not love Lou exactly the way that Gemma deemed fit, would she ignore the fact that he'd loved her at all?

According to Alaric, the witch race was damned anyway. Such trivial musings on love wouldn't save them from their imminent demise.

Ryan craned their head to steal a glimpse of the gold thread she wove around the couch behind them, blind to it by their human nature. Schwartz mouthed a quick *thank you* before she met Teddy at the front door, tying her line to his.

She straightened her back in front of him, swallowing nervously at the unexpected closeness. 'You want to take this side?'

He nodded and forced down his sudden inclination to kiss her. *Trivial, yes,* he thought, *but I love you anyway.* 'Tell me where I need to be.'

'Just—' She grabbed him by the shoulders, placing him outside the line. 'There. Give me ten seconds to get there, then pull up. Don't stop pulling until it reaches the top, OK?'

Ryan twisted into the hallway as Schwartz rushed to the back door again, striking Teddy with an inquisitive glare. 'What the hell are you getting up to?'

'Sorcery.' Teddy wiggled his fingers.

'Ready?' The question, a curiosity deeper than the lone word, flared through the tether unexpectedly. *Ready,* he thought with such intention that he hoped it was enough. It was embarrassing enough pulling up on a gold thread in front of Ryan that they couldn't actually see. He wasn't sure how useful an explanation was to Ryan Jena; it looked strange anyway.

Teddy pulled, willing the ward spell to his fingers. Gold marbled into a sheer film between himself and Schwartz's housemate. Up and up it climbed, until the room was swathed in gold and Teddy, standing on the outskirts of it, could only think of Gemma, Lou and Alaric behind the impermeable wards of the cottage. Did Gemma make herself a pot of tea that morning? Did she slide a plate of breakfast to her daughter and eat with her at the countertop as they'd done before?

Were they thinking of him, wanting him back?

CHAPTER TWENTY-NINE

Midnight was fast approaching when someone at the front door disrupted the wards.

Ryan reached it just before Teddy did, squinting through the peephole. 'Are you expecting someone?'

Schwartz's expression flattened, although her heart was still hammering. Teddy could see it in the half-second blip that she hadn't made that distinction yet, that witches and humans were strung on two different kinds of thread.

It was easier to feel a witch coming around, and damn near impossible to force them out.

Teddy took Ryan Jena's spot at the peephole, grumbling as he reached for the knob and turned to reveal a haggard, itching Alaric Friedman waiting on the step. 'What are you doing here?'

The caretaker straightened at once, flexing his hands at his sides. He had expected a softer greeting, more time to collect himself. He smiled meagrely at Ryan with the embarrassment of a boy caught pretending to be something else. A man, maybe even a father.

The smile faltered against Teddy's stern look of opposition. Alaric looked up to Schwartz, who had trailed down the steps behind Teddy. 'Eh, Carmichael told me you called.'

This was news to Teddy Ingram. Schwartz excused her housemate, whispering something to them that the others didn't catch. Replacing them at the entryway, she replied, 'Yeah, but I didn't think you'd show up out of the blue. It's a long ride to Cambridge.'

Alaric fussed with the dried leather cuffs of his bomber jacket. Schwartz ushered him inside, and as he passed the threshold, the ward shimmered gently around his frame. He eyed the open doorway and studied their handiwork before responding vaguely, 'I didn't take the train.'

Schwartz could be patient when she wanted to be. However, such joyous occasions came so infrequently that Teddy was almost aggravated when she asked the caretaker, 'Want some tea?'

'No, thank you,' Alaric said. 'I don't have much time anyway. As far as the other caretakers are concerned, I'm still in Townsend.'

'Are you not supposed to be here?' Schwartz asked.

'It was important to me that I got here as soon as I could,' Alaric explained. 'Unfortunately, it was also important to the council that we discuss the findings of another . . . I'll explain later. Technically, I'm in the deliberation hall with them right now, keeping my mouth shut. It won't be long before someone finds a flaw in that and pins my decoy with an inconvenient question.'

Schwartz's nostrils flared in a silent laugh. 'Carmichael helping you play hooky?'

'Just for a few minutes. I've got an old friend manning a portal nearby to make the jump back home before he's discovered.' To

Teddy, he said with an unprecedented gentleness, 'I needed to speak with you.'

Privately, he meant. The thought bothered Teddy more than it seemed to bother Schwartz, considering the caretaker had come into her house to request the audience. She turned swiftly, tucking her hair behind her ears, but not before pressing a kiss to the shoulder seam of Teddy's shirt for good measure. He tried not to blush at the small, affectionate gesture, but he couldn't remember the last time anyone had witnessed him at the mercy of such softness. Alaric looked more embarrassed than Teddy felt, and maybe, that was Schwartz's intention.

She left quietly in her housemate's direction, whispering a question to them to deter their curiosity. Teddy wondered if he'd been unfair in his bewilderment when Schwartz admitted to telling Ryan about their witchcraft. With everything else that she kept hidden from them, even magic seemed a small secret to withhold.

But Alaric's suspicion only grew. He watched after Schwartz with a puzzlement that Teddy could never place. He'd seen it first on the day they'd gone to London to find Leona, when the caretaker took him aside to list his many warnings. They were all trite musings, but his concern was genuine; he regarded her tentatively as if she – or her magic – was equally as devastating as Teddy.

Well, she was now. It was only fair that Teddy took back a few secrets of his own. And what Alaric didn't know couldn't hurt him.

Teddy cleared his throat. He didn't know if he should speak

first. If he had gone back to Townsend, he knew the conversation would have started much differently, with his head hung low and his words tucked between clenched teeth.

None of that mattered once the caretaker finally spoke. 'Are you OK?' he asked. His voice was even. Low and rich with compassion. 'I hurt you the other day. I hadn't meant to, but I did.'

It lacked all the indifference that Teddy had expected. The digs that Teddy had meant to make disappeared. His mouth quivered, and as he pressed his lips together to force the feeling away, Alaric stepped forward and enveloped him in the tightest embrace they'd ever shared. 'I don't know. Are you?' asked Teddy, whispering the words against the caretaker's greying curls.

'I'm fine,' Alaric said dismissively. 'Gem's fine and so is Lou.'

Teddy was grateful for once that he didn't have to ask. 'I was going to come back soon, to make things right. I should have been kinder to Louisa. I shouldn't have yelled.'

'You didn't know,' Alaric said. 'I wouldn't have been different in your shoes, and yet I wasn't any better to you about it.'

Teddy dreaded the release, the moment where he would have to face Alaric with his welling eyes and clenched jaw. Whether Alaric sensed it or *shared* it, Teddy was glad for the hold he kept around his shoulders. When his eyes shut, he couldn't keep the tears from trickling out.

Alaric pressed his palm to the nape of Teddy's neck, covering the stripe of bare skin that peered out from his overgrown locks. 'I should have explained it to you outside. In my head, it was as if she could still hear me from where she was. She wanted to tell you, Teddy, but seeing Louisa's school sent her into a bit of a tizzy. It wasn't fair. It shouldn't have reached that point.' The caretaker's thumb swayed along Teddy's hairline, his touch – his closeness – as much of an apology as his remorse was.

It was more of an apology than Teddy expected. More than what he would have accepted as apology too.

If only Harry Ingram could have seen his own faults as clearly. He was not a bad father, simply *ignorant*. He gave himself to his work while Celia gave herself to Teddy's rehabilitation. She broke him down, filled him with parables and misguided prayers, and Harry didn't question it. Was he not equally as liable for Teddy's upbringing as she was? Why had it taken him years to acknowledge his shortcomings as a father?

Even then, he had only apologized once he had something to gain.

Alaric pulled away, pressing his hands to Teddy's cheeks. 'We are fallible creatures, and we make mistakes. Mine was letting her think she could cast you out.'

'I tried, you know,' Teddy said, 'to make it work for Lou until Gemma came back. I always hoped it'd be a temporary fix, but I didn't think she'd just cage her in like that.'

The caretaker quieted him with a firm, consoling grip. 'You did everything you could. That was not your fault. I've talked to her about it – about all you've done. You did a good job, all right?'

Teddy had lost years waiting for someone to say those words to him. For Harry Ingram to soothe the sting of Celia's hand from his face. For Gemma to ease the burden of Kenny's death from his shoulders. For Schwartz—

Well, she had been the first to do it, to put their war to rest and lay down a new foundation. Something vibrant had bloomed in the barren war zone. A dream, a *what if?* Absolution was a forbidden fruit he sought to taste again, when he'd felt that the gates of Eden had long since closed to him. The others were still there in the garden, oblivious or unconcerned. They watched him passively as he begged to enter once more.

'What about Lou?' asked Teddy. 'Is she OK?'

Alaric studied him with an unwavering gaze. 'She's fine. Shaken and confused, but fine. It's been a gruelling couple of days for all of us. Had I not told Gem that I would find you, she would have left again to see you by herself. If she knew I had somewhere else to be right now, she still might have.'

'Why didn't she?'

'I told her not to,' Alaric said slowly. 'Things escalated much too fast for us to discuss what happened with her vanishing, but I thought it best that she stayed in Townsend for a while to recover. She's not . . . She's not quite well.'

Teddy fought with even breaths to subdue the dread creeping through his body. The heaviest hands came from those he loved the most. They knew precisely where to strike. They knew just how large a vacancy their absence would create.

'What happened to her, Al?' Teddy lowered his voice, but he suspected that Schwartz was listening in her own way, not with sound but through the tether.

Always a man of secrecy, Alaric Friedman didn't answer immediately. 'She'll want to tell you herself. And I should return to Townsend before my luck wears off . . .'

The bottom of the banister dug into Teddy's spine. Lowering his head, he answered with a conciliatory hum.

'There's no need for sulking,' said the caretaker. 'You said you were coming home soon anyway, yeah? I'll make sure she expects you.'

Teddy looked to the mouth of the hallway where Schwartz and Ryan were only half visible from the corner. They sat beside each other, Ryan with the controller in their lap and Schwartz watching the gameplay rapturously over their shoulder. For all the anxiety that festered beneath Schwartz's skin, she was comfortable with Ryan in a way that Teddy could only compare to what he felt whenever he returned to Townsend, melting into it like an embrace. Home was, for Aurelia Schwartz, a person instead of a place, one whose hold she could reciprocate. The cottage could embrace him in the way that he could swathe himself in its blankets and hide himself behind its doors, but it could not console him when he needed more. It couldn't keep the ghosts out.

It was always Gemma who held him, squeezing him tight on the stone step, fussing with his hair in the basement while he stole Lou's markers and pencils. He didn't know if they could reach that point again; perhaps, it had been born out of delusion or silence. With their true feelings in the open, Teddy's idea of home was more disconnected from Townsend than ever.

He'd been waiting too many months to find out where she was to waste another night with all these questions. As Schwartz shot a look through the doorway, Teddy gripped the railing and asked, 'Can the portal take me too?' His skin prickled with the weight of her stare. She found him in the narrow frame and did not look away.

Alaric nodded. 'Make it quick.'

His coat bunched around the bottom of the banister, heavy with his keys and the useless weight that was his phone. The hum of the microwave and the whistle of Schwartz's kettle met him at the bottom of the steps. Alaric idled on the other side of the open front door, glancing repeatedly at the watch tucked beneath his coat sleeve.

Inside the kitchenette, Schwartz asked, 'You sure you don't want some to take with you?' Teddy paused, sidestepping into the space to evade Alaric's impatient, wandering gaze.

'When I get back,' he told her. She poured a cup for herself and her housemate, teabags bobbing up to the brim.

As Alaric's figure disappeared from view, Teddy threaded his arms around her waist and pulled her flush to his body. She dropped her spoon into one of the cups, reaching up to his face as he littered her cheek and jaw with soft kisses. 'Be safe,' he whispered.

'Come back soon,' she said. She bit her tongue; there was more to the statement than what she gave. *Go, but come back to me. Go, but don't make me wait again.*

'Of course,' he said. 'I left things here.'

Schwartz wriggled free from his grasp just enough to turn and face him. 'You could leave a few more things here. If you wanted to. There's some space in my drawers for a few shirts or extra pairs of socks, y'know.' What few belongings Teddy had brought with him were sprawled out across Schwartz's room as if it were his own. He should have been more thoughtful, kept his things tucked inside his bag, but *she* had been the one to toss his jacket on the floor. To kick his shoes into place beside hers. He simply never protested.

He knew why he'd left Cambridge the first time. He knew, and he didn't regret it; but after the falling-out with Gemma and Alaric, Teddy thought with more wistfulness than ever about what could have been if only he'd never left. He'd lost some part of himself when he returned to Townsend. There were things he couldn't say in front of Lou, things that hurt to harbour, and just like Leona Sum's tainted magic, it chewed him up from the inside out, laying waste to him every day.

Schwartz paused at the staircase, turning him by the wrist to face her. 'You'll be good to her, won't you?'

Despite their habitual vagueness, Teddy didn't need to ask if she meant Gemma or Lou. The girl still occupied a delicate chamber in his heart, made of lilac and crooked-penned lines. In Louisa's heart, Teddy's shape was becoming a shadow. A vacancy.

'It pains me to think I've been anything else to her. I spent so many months doting on her, and I feel as if I've squandered it all.'

'I worried about her all the time, y'know,' Schwartz said. 'She asked me why I never came to visit, but I thought about it constantly.'

'I never blamed you. It's not always an easy place to go back to.'

'I tried so hard to remove myself from everything that happened there. I kept my head down, got a new job . . . Believe it or not, I got so much better at talking with the rest of our programme that Tricia Werner, of all people, has started texting me from time to time. But it's tiring to keep trying like that. Even now that you're here, I feel like I have to pretend I don't love it so much – but I *do*. I feel safe when you're around. It's easier to sleep.' Schwartz shut her eyes, warding herself off from his inquisitive stare. 'Sure, Leona's still there, but so are you. I don't think I realized just how bad it was until I saw you and Lou again in Townsend. I had this perpetual wonder waiting inside of me to see that the two of you were OK. I don't want to keep wondering.'

She tucked her head beneath his chin, obscuring her expression from view.

'Plus, Ryan likes you,' she said. 'Probably more than I do.'

'You couldn't let me have the moment, could you?'

She inclined her head and kissed him clumsily, her teeth stifling his laugh. He tasted a mumbled apology on her lips, the whisper of breath on his cheek. She was made from angles and hard, knobby joints, and he could tell that she made a deliberate effort not to hold him too hard or fit the sharper edges into him. All his life, he'd been a landmine, a tool of inevitable destruction around which to tread lightly, but he could break just as easily. Instead of flesh and bone, people saw dark magic and misplaced guilt.

No one else cared to treat him delicately.

Teddy pulled away and looked at her. She was beautiful and desirable, her lips swollen by the blunt of his teeth. Such harrowing assumptions of his magic made him cautious and restrained, but Schwartz kissed the way she fought – with fire and conviction. She kissed as if it would save her.

Alaric cleared his throat, the door whining on its hinges.

Schwartz wiped her mouth. 'Get out of my house. Before Al leaves you here.'

Teddy threw his coat over his arm and smiled. 'Ever the charmer, Schwartz.'

CHAPTER THIRTY

Ryan was the only one left paying attention to the screen. Aurelia's head rested on their shoulder, her eyes on the blurred words of her mother's letter. The fibres of the paper furred and split in spots from her incessant irritation.

Her housemate's occasional side-eye told her that the constant fidgeting was a great distraction.

'Give that to me,' Ryan said. Begrudgingly, Aurelia relinquished the letter. 'Where's your stress ball?'

'I'm not stressed,' Aurelia said.

'Well, you're something, and it's stressing me out.' The race paused abruptly.

'Can I ask you something?'

'Shoot.'

'Have I not grieved enough about my mom?'

Ryan blinked, then frowned as if they'd misheard. Slinking back against the couch, Aurelia explained, 'She came back for me, you know. After I went to Vancouver. Apparently, my grief didn't call to her as strongly as Teddy's did, which is why she found him instead of me.'

'You're talking about ghosts, yeah?'

Aurelia shrugged. She couldn't understand it either. Maybe

if Meredith had appeared to the correct person, she could have explained it better, but even in death, she remained out of Aurelia's reach. To manifest so clearly in response to Ingram's feeling . . . It made her wonder if hers could be insufficient.

'It's hard to explain.'

'I wish I could understand,' said Ryan.

'You understand better than most people,' Aurelia admitted. 'So much that I forget that we have such a fundamental difference between us. I swear I'd tell you if I could. I hate feeling this way.'

'Do you still want the stress ball?'

'I think I broke it.'

Ryan disappeared to search for the remains of the ball. 'How the hell did you break it? They're meant to withstand everything you throw at them.'

One day, Aurelia had pulled it too hard. It was a thick, gelatinous ball with beads inside of it that made a generous squelching noise whenever she compressed it in her hands; but somehow, while absorbed in a study of a new manuscript digitization, she'd discovered its limit, and the shape had spit out sixty hard beards that got lost in the hidden corners of her room. 'I'm incredibly capable,' Aurelia said.

Ryan opened an unlabelled drawer in the hallway to find a pool of loose beads rolling across Aurelia's shelved papers. 'Damn.'

She cast her spare blanket off, scooting to the edge of the couch cushions. 'I don't know how I'm supposed to feel. I can't help being pissed off about it. She removes herself from my life completely, and then what? Expects me to cry harder? As if I haven't cried enough?'

'Your anger is entirely valid too,' Ryan said, kicking their slippers back and forth underneath the coffee table.

'Not enough for her to give me the message herself. What if I never went back to Townsend to see Ingram?' Aurelia asked. 'Was she just going to die with her warning and make me piece it together on my own?'

'I don't pretend to know why your mum's the way she is,' Ryan mused. They kicked their left slipper out of reach, shoulders slumping into a sigh. They scanned the room for something else to occupy their restless body, settling on a page beside Aurelia's notebook. 'Ooh, a love letter.'

'What?' She tried to grab it at first glance, but Ryan Jena was quicker.

'Oh,' Ryan sang. 'Is love not the most delicious kind of distraction?'

'Give me that.' Aurelia swiped it from her housemate's hands, clutching it to her chest while they hounded her with a goofy, conniving grin.

It was hardly a love letter, she thought. Not nearly as forward as the one he'd tucked inside *Sir Gawain and the Green Knight*, at least. Save for the term of endearment at the top, nothing about it indicated any affection at all.

But that term of endearment alone could unravel the knot he'd tied in her chest. *Bright star.* It could cut damn right through the meat of it.

For all its lack of intrigue, she folded it in half carefully and guarded it against her stomach like it carried a multitude of their secrets. 'It's nothing,' she said, and wished she were smart enough to believe it. She tucked it inside her closed laptop again, sealing it away from her housemate's inquisitive gaze.

It would be easier to think with his letter out of sight. Easier to let the question pass through her lips without his affectionate nickname in the back of her mind: *bright star.*

My *bright star.*

She couldn't remember how the poem went. Keats was centuries too late for her to afford him more energy as an academic. She didn't want to think of Teddy Ingram jotting down poetry in her name, imparting a spell in his words for her to discover with a few calculated folds. She couldn't let his letter consume her – not with another malicious thought swimming in her mind waiting to devour it.

It would be easier to forgive herself for entertaining her morbid curiosity.

Her mother. This time, Aurelia wouldn't let the thought slip away.

Stealing back the page with her mother's faded words, she told Ryan, 'I want to try something.'

It was a long shot, but something she hadn't considered before. Maybe the new magic in her blood would bear enough resemblance to Teddy's to call her mother back to her. Maybe all she'd been missing was this ability to conspire with the dead, and she had it now, amassing in the map of her hands.

'Will you stay with me?' she asked her housemate.

Ryan, none the wiser and devoted to a fault, agreed without question.

CHAPTER THIRTY-ONE

There was a scar etched into Gemma's side from the collision that had grounded her. She theorized that another bird had swept into her, sunk its talons into her side to push (or pull) away; though she admitted it might have been an inanimate scrap of metal or glass pitched into the air by a storm. None of it mattered once she was tumbling from the sky. Nothing could have saved her.

The descent had happened slower than anyone would expect. She'd flapped desperately with a crushed left wing, past the hope of staying airborne and trying in vain to make the landing less brutal. Then, the impact had broken ribs. Her transformation, like Teddy's in the museum, couldn't finish without the proper alignment of parts. Just as a feather fallen from her wings would keep its form, her bones wouldn't change once they were dislodged. She lay in a field on the south border of the Surrey Hills, praying that whoever found her on their morning hike would not deem her too far gone and put her out of her misery.

When she explained this to Teddy Ingram, he asked, 'How long did it take?'

She told him, 'Three days.'

Twice a fox had come to lap at her small, winged form on the first night, deciding in some strange twist of fate that she wasn't fit for consumption. Something in her near-dead body had repulsed him. She'd held on to consciousness just long enough for a curious young boy to stumble across her during a walk with his family. He'd begged them to take her home.

From that moment, she could no longer be a person. She'd sung like a bird, ate from their hands like a bird, let them coddle her and squeeze too tight. She'd watched television from a clear tub on their dining room table which the family had padded with rags and grass leaves, and hoped that the birdsong of her pleas didn't aggravate them enough to do away with her fragile body like vermin.

'Yes, I was paranoid,' she said pre-emptively to Teddy. 'And I know that, perhaps, I am too paranoid for my own good.'

The boy, she said, saved her life. Had his parents found her in the grass without his accompaniment, they would have passed just like everyone else did, leaving her for the foxes to dissect when they inevitably became desperate and ravenous.

The boy collected his spare time like loose change and cashed it in at her makeshift bedside, staring wondrously at her feathers through the distorted clear plastic. He'd been convinced that she could understand him, though his parents laughed light-heartedly. She sang when he asked, taking from his small hands with a gentler bite than from his father's hand.

'Because he was right,' Gemma explained to Teddy. 'I could understand him. I wanted him to know that.'

She could not say it aloud as they tended to her wounds, just as she couldn't ask them to stop whenever they overextended her broken wing as a test.

Teddy let her explain with little interjection. He had always loved stories. They could assuage his stressors, take him somewhere else. It all sounded so fanciful when Gemma told it, like a fairy tale, that he almost forgot he was a part of it too. He and Lou were in the margins, as was Alaric with all his private attempts to find her.

'I couldn't see the fall,' she said, 'but I saw that everything else would click into place. I knew you would be safe. I knew Louisa would be safe. I knew Leona would die by your hand and you would all come home together. And in the end, that was all that mattered to me, so I didn't think to keep looking until it was already too late.'

Gemma's shoulder grazed Teddy's as she smoothed the dimples from her knuckles in meditation. 'You can't imagine the toll divination takes from you. How much it burdens you to know so much . . . I don't like knowing it all. That I have the power not to look so far is a gift that cost me eight months away from my home. It was never supposed to last this long,' she continued, keeping her gaze on her hands while his were on her profile. Beneath her palm, the edges of a note curled like wilting flower petals, hiding a message within. 'I didn't think of what I did as running away. To fulfil a prophecy – to bring it to fruition – the events leading up to it have to align in a particular, perfect order that leaves little to no room for divergence. Beginning with one decision, one choice, you're one step closer to securing that end result. God forbid you make the wrong one. And in this case, I saw leaving as a step towards your shapeshifter's demise.'

She gave him the note with quivering fingers. He wondered if he had seen her faltering so blatantly since Kenny died; the front she displayed to him was made of hard rubber and heavy brick. Based on what he'd seen in her grimoires, she tucked all signs of it away. Stubborn, impossible Gem, he thought. Was there no way to share in mourning without making it a conflict? Without exploiting his blame? It could have been so much easier to forgive himself if she'd just grieved with him.

For all the missed opportunities to see her with her defences stripped back, seeing it now reduced him to his teenage self, when Kenny's death was still ripe in his conscience. *Please, please,* he thought, *tell me what you're hiding in your mind.*

'This is how it should have gone,' Gemma said. 'That fate required such a tangled path of travel, but the promise of it was enough to sway my decision. And because I thought it would end with Leona, I didn't . . . I didn't—'

The woman stood from the bed where they sat beside each other and started pacing. She watched him read, her closed fist poised over her mouth. Whatever words followed her abrupt end fought to emerge, and Teddy wondered what could be so wrong that she'd rather keep it in.

My friend,

You have loved me enough to withhold your scepticism, and even if you say nothing, I know you will never know these fears like I do. Somewhere in the back of your mind, you may even think that I'm frail and lacking like the girl you loved twenty-five years ago. I have been so many things in my life that I'm sure you were right at some point.

But I can be strong with my love, the way you are strong with your word. It's because I love them that I'm leaving now. If Leona found us once, she will find us again. There is no other way to escape than to kill her, and that is a magic that I'm lucky enough not to have. It is a curse that I've known though, and were I faced with the woman who threatens our safety, it's one I would wield in a heartbeat.

Teddy would do the same. The boy is cursed with dark magic but blessed with his cunning, and he will find her. He will be her demise, and you must be his shield. You have to let him.

Protect him. Hide him. Let no one touch my children as long as I am gone. We won't be wholly safe as long as the second eye is still somewhere out there. I'm going to find it.

Gem

'It was for Alaric,' she said. 'I don't know if that was clear—'

'Clear enough,' Teddy replied.

'I knew you would find her on your own. That much, I was certain about,' Gemma added, rushing to salvage something he didn't quite know to be amiss. 'I saw you in a room. In the dark. I couldn't have told you where it was, but you made it there from what my divination told me. Somehow, you figured it out.'

Teddy skimmed through the message again, folded over his

knees. He'd fought back tears in this position on the couch in Alaric's library, the same couch on which Alaric and Schwartz had tended to his bloodstained back. The caretaker had looked him in the eye with complete sincerity and – what? Lied to him? Guarded the truth from him for the hundredth time? He couldn't recount how many times he had started his days at the shop with the question of Gemma, how many times Alaric greeted him with a severe indifference and said, 'I would tell you if I knew.'

Maybe it was muscle memory, but Teddy thought he might cry all over again. 'So, he knew the whole time.'

Quickly, the augur shook her head. 'He never found the letter. Or so he tells me. I was angrier at him than I was at you, for not looking for me. Trust me, I was.'

'You must have berated him too, then,' said Teddy. 'Unless it was something other than anger that drew you to treat me the way you did in front of Lou.'

For a while, Gemma stared at him, the creases beside her mouth deepening with the sharp, tight press of her lips. Save for her shaking fingers, she remained utterly motionless, not even rocking on her heels the way she often would while bored in her kitchen. Few things ever caught him off guard any more when it came to Gem. Even the deep-seated resentment she penned in her grimoires was less of a shock than it was an affirmation to the shame he'd harboured for years. But this . . .

He'd never expected her to send him away or behave just like his father, who said nothing in opposition to Celia's heavy-handed efforts but also never once raised his voice to his son. There were unspoken agreements made between parents and their children not to question the methods that kept them obedient.

Give him shelter and he must comply.

Behold thy master.

'I'm sorry,' Gemma whispered. 'I thought . . . . Well, I don't know what I was thinking.'

'Hmm.'

'Everything happened so quickly when I came back. Alaric was insistent on knowing everything, and I was still so weak. Teddy, I *am* still weak. You have to understand—'

'It's humiliating, being reduced by someone's vitriol in front of the person you're meant to be strong for. Lou shouldn't have seen that.'

She stepped forward warily. '*I* shouldn't have made you leave. I spent the evening wondering if you had a proper bed to sleep in, you know – worrying myself to death over you. It doesn't excuse what I did, but I'll do anything to make it better. It's not the same for us when you're not here. I reckon Lou is never happier than when you come home from uni.'

'I've left uni,' he murmured. 'I brought all my things here to look after her. We were comfortable, Gem. I took care of her.'

Gem surveyed the room to humour him, though the evidence of his uprooting was plain in every inch. The marks he had left in the room were still few and far between, but they were deep and irreparable; and until he had returned to Cambridge with Aurelia, he sometimes doubted that he existed on the other side of these doors. This was his place.

'And when you fell?' he asked, itching in the silence.

A heavy breath rattled out of her and she sat beside him

again. 'There are lasting injuries. I healed enough for the transformation to happen, but there was so much left to fix. I have a—'

Gemma twisted tentatively, giving Teddy the distinct impression that any sharper movement might wound her further. Lifting the hem of her oversized shirt, she revealed a mottled scar that stretched from the side of her chest to the bottom of her ribcage.

Teddy's breath stalled in his throat. 'Looks like mine,' he mumbled.

'Yours?'

He untangled his fingers from each other to untuck the hem of his own shirt, but he couldn't overcome the violent quiver. All at once, the swell of emotion in his body rushed to the surface, to his burning eyes and bitten lip.

Teddy sniffed, turning his face from view. He was past the point of return, but in a last-ditch effort he thought maybe – just maybe – shielding it from her could save him the shame. 'I'm sorry.'

'No,' she crooned, 'This is not your fault.'

She wound her arms around his shoulders, wincing as he relaxed into her embrace. Teddy thought to suggest it wasn't worth the pain; there would be time to reconcile this way. He could sit with her words for now, and that would be enough.

But Teddy always wanted more. For once, he allowed himself to have it.

He didn't intend to wake Louisa before he left, but deep down, he hoped she felt the weight of his hand in her sleep so exactly that she would recognize his presence. He combed through the unfastened tresses of her hair, arranging them on her pillow like rays of sunlight.

He could stay. That was what he'd intended to do. But there was now a possibility to leave too.

With all the tension spilling out between him and Gemma, he felt overworked, wrung for every ounce of empathetic magic festering inside him. Teddy penned Lou a note when she didn't wake, after her hair had been drawn out into the shape of the sun on her pillow, and her dreams had begun to take shape. Where there had been dragons were now birds, still colourful and free but far less fantastical; and Teddy wondered if she dreamed of flying away. If she, too, had wings, where would she go?

As far as they would take her, he knew. His aspirations were smaller, his dreams simple enough to reach out and grab, yet still so impossibly heavy. What was worse: to have such attainable desires slip through his fingers or to want the world, and have only a piece of it?

He wrote his apologies, his regrets, his secrets. He told Louisa he loved her and her mental compendium of bugs, though he hated all their spindly legs. He would take her to Heffer's soon, whether Gemma had to know about it or not, and buy her the last Chronicles of Narnia books for her to make her marks in.

One of these days, I will have the world to give you. The great, wide possibility of it. I gave you everything I could, but there's more out there to give, and I'll find it. I promise.

Teddy folded it into a swan and left it on her nightstand.

The light in Alaric's upstairs window drew him out from the cottage and into the night. Gemma watched him disappear through the wards, her exhaustion there and then gone from the tether with a few small steps. Teddy shook the remnants of it off like rain from a dog's fur. Clean paws meant the caretaker wouldn't think twice about letting him inside.

Teddy's key jammed at first but gave with a little shove. The shop was dark and expectedly vacant, the upstairs light left on by matter of forgetfulness.

It was too late to catch a train to Cambridge. Too difficult to sleep in a house brimming ceaselessly with emotion. The caretaker had rooms in both the shop and the library, and if he didn't return before the night was over, Teddy would take cover on the little mattress upstairs.

The shop room was furnished as sparsely as possible, with a twin-size mattress on a metal frame, a mostly empty nightstand and a flickering yellow lamp. Alaric kept it for the rare occasion of late nights in Townsend, for dinners at the cottage that left him too stuffed and lethargic to slip through the veil into the library. Teddy couldn't remember the last time they'd eaten together – all of them. Four bodies packed around a small wooden table, Alaric at Gemma's right, smiling out of the corner of his stubble. In all the years they'd known each other, Teddy never once saw the caretaker sporting a short, tidy haircut; and Gemma would reach out no less than three times each meal to push Alaric's curls from his forehead. Such affairs were so commonplace in the cottage that Teddy never questioned why Alaric and Gem didn't live together, or why they went no further than to tidy the other's stray curls. Dinner was always delicious, spirits remained high, and Alaric never cut his hair to a more manageable length. Challenging a good and lovely thing seemed pointless.

Teddy busied himself with each drawer, rifling through the caretaker's clothes and his old cassette tapes, always poised to stow them into place the second the veil parted to let Alaric back in. From the nightstand, Teddy unearthed a pile of photographs held together by two dried, crisscrossed rubber bands.

He took advantage of the silence down below.

Black dye and a hairless face. Leather and torn denim. Teddy leaned back on the mattress, grinning at a version of Alaric that looked no older than himself – ringed around the eyes in smudged silver makeup. A cigarette hung between his lips, an assortment of old friends or Gemma Eakley hanging off his shoulder.

And Kenny.

Kenneth Eakley, with all his freckles and his toothy smile, exactly as Teddy remembered him. His knees were tucked into his chest, a compact figure in an itchy sweater on an itchier couch. Gemma kissed his cheek. The faded garland on the window of her South London flat signalled Christmas.

Forcing his nerves down with a hard swallow, Teddy turned the photograph face down on the nightstand and searched for something else.

Does it ever get easier?

He'd written a hundred letters in his lifetime but Gemma's

words remained the clearest in his mind. Would he ever know? He could spend the rest of his life chasing an answer to that question.

By then, Teddy wasn't expecting Alaric to show. At the sound of footsteps, he hid the stack of photographs and moved to the edge of the mattress.

A warning edge cut through him. 'What are you doing here?'

Carmichael Sum crashed through the door in a hurry, leaping out of his skin at the sight of company. 'Jesus. What are *you* doing?'

Teddy made himself tall. His voice dropped to a whisper. 'I asked first.'

'An errand,' Carmichael answered, sliding through the cramped space. 'He asked me to grab something.'

'So, he's in the library.'

Carmichael's hesitation filled the tiny room until Teddy felt gagged by it. 'He's busy.'

'He can't possibly be busy. It's later in Luxembourg than it is here.'

'Can I—'

'You're lying, Sum.' With a flick of his fingers, the door locked them in together. He saw the knot work down Carmichael's throat, but to his credit, the man maintained his composure. He flexed his hand at his side to grab the boy's attention, but it lacked a gold spark. Teddy followed its path to the nightstand where a familiar pouch of salt lay shut beside the lamp.

Carmichael deposited it into his pocket slowly. 'No. I'm not.'

Teddy conceded. 'Why does he take to you? He must have had aversions, given everything Leona put us through.'

Carmichael's expression softened. He shook his head. 'I'm sure he would have preferred me if I wasn't attached to her. But he's not as keen on me as you'd think. I have something he wants and a willingness he appeals to. He's fair in spite of himself. I think he wishes he could hate me.'

'Makes two of us,' Teddy mumbled. 'So, what is it?'

'What?'

'You said he wants something. What is it? He doesn't tell me much.'

Carmichael's eyes flickered to the closed door.

'Has he got you under a vow of secrecy, too?'

'N-no.'

Teddy ran a hand through his hair, pausing to knead the nape of his neck. 'I don't know why I bother.'

'You said you were waiting for him, yeah?'

With a tight jaw, Teddy said, 'I did.'

'He's *busy*,' Carmichael reiterated, as if the tone alone would give something else away. All it managed to do was wring Teddy out a little more. 'You may as well make yourself at home and expect him tomorrow.'

'That's fine. Really.' Too late to push at a cause that wouldn't break. Teddy dragged his hand down his face. Carmichael had what he needed, yet he hovered beside the door with his hand on an unturned knob. 'What?'

The man opened his mouth. Then closed it. 'I know what it's like to live in the dark. More than that, I know what it feels like to be kept from a secret by someone who thinks it's for the greater good.'

Teddy raised a brow.

'He means well. I know he does,' Carmichael added. 'Friedman's got a strange but steady handle on fairness and whatever that means to him, but it doesn't really translate to others. Hye-Jin levels him out a bit, but they're two ends of a wide spectrum. She thinks . . . well, we both think he's a bit too careful with you.'

'Careful,' Teddy mumbled. 'As opposed to?'

'Honest.'

Teddy didn't even care that it was Carmichael who said it. Even Schwartz, who defended him honourably, wanted to justify the caretaker's behaviour more than she wanted to admit that he might just be a prick sometimes.

Carmichael whispered something to himself gravely, unearthing the pouch of salt. 'Here. He's waiting for me to bring it.'

'I'm forbidden from council matters.'

'Why do you think *I'm* going? This has nothing to do with the council. I'm sure he would have told you once he returned, but it's rather important you know now.' Carmichael pushed the salt into Teddy's hands. 'Truth is, I'm worried about him. He found your witch earlier today – the portal witch. Hye-Jin wanted him to bring the issue to the council, but he refused, and now he's going on his own. Go with him, please. There's an object portal in the basement that he's expecting me to use. I should have been back already. You should use it instead. Talk to him.'

'Why are you doing this?'

Carmichael was close, their hands brushing between their stomachs where they both held the pouch. 'He gave me a second chance. He had faith in me when I thought myself to be irredeemable. I owe him my life, but he's too good to take it.'

CHAPTER THIRTY-TWO

He'd read about small-object portals only once, but the one Alaric had sent was instantly recognisable to him. Hovering above the ground was a fissure in the universe, through which Teddy could see a sliver of somewhere else.

'You should not be here,' Alaric hissed. He turned on Teddy abruptly, the shop shrinking behind him.

Teddy's neck craned backwards as the caretaker seized fabric at the seam of his shirt, bowing away from the caretaker's warning breath. 'You should have told me,' he gushed. 'Let me help.'

From here, the scowl beneath Alaric's stubble was unignorable and, though coupled with a clench of his fist, boasted no fire. For a split second, he wondered if he should fear the same explosive anger from him that overcame Gemma, searching the caretaker's wide, darkening gaze for an answer. Teddy could forgive Gemma while the sting of her slap was still seared into his mind; the fear had endured long before and would endure long after.

But Alaric . . . Panic never came from his grip. Teddy had the feeling that Alaric's face would change with his own like a mirror, and with enough composure, Alaric would only be as fearsome as Teddy was in that moment. Teddy couldn't understand his mother's contempt as a boy, but as he grew into his *father's* shape, he could see why Harry kept his eyes to the ground. He saw enough to keep asking for second chances.

The caretaker did not inhibit his sharp edges the way Schwartz did. His love erred on the tougher side. His eyes were wide, his brow heavy, and his voice had preserved the grit of countless cigarettes smoked during his youth. Through his severe expression, Teddy still found concern in his warning. 'You've done enough. Go back and wait for me.'

Teddy's weight shifted to his heels as the caretaker released him. 'Tell me what you're doing.'

'It's not your business.'

The portal waxed and waned at Teddy's back. Alaric's gaze flickered between the portal and the boy during its final, fleeting moment with a growing aggravation, perhaps weighing the consequences of pushing Teddy into it.

'You're going to kill Julia Chaplain,' Teddy said.

'If I find her. Let's hope it doesn't come to that.'

I hope it does, Teddy thought. *I hope she never touches us again.*

The portal shrunk before his eyes, the golden ring collapsing to the size of the council's bronze suppressants. It hovered in place, burning like metal in forging fires, and once it had cooled enough to be taken from its invisible mount, Alaric unbuckled the band and secured it around his wrist with a sigh.

'That's Kenny's watch, isn't it?'

Alaric adjusted his glasses, moving swiftly towards a broken window in the creaky, dilapidated house. Light slipped through silvery clouds. It was warmer here than in Townsend, but not by much. Teddy shielded his eyes as he replaced Alaric in the frame, gazing over an expanse of what he assumed to be untended farmland. If they were still in England, Teddy couldn't tell. Wherever Alaric had gone, he wouldn't say.

When he didn't reply, Teddy added solemnly, 'I could make it quick.'

'You don't want to kill anyone,' Alaric mumbled under his breath, opening a fridge in the kitchen to numerous Kilner jars of pre-portioned foods. He turned a stalk of broccoli in his hands, discarding it at the sight of mould. It seemed evidence of his visitation didn't concern him. Knocked-over chairs and tilted frames were the makings of ghosts, and Alaric was a threat far from extinguished.

No, Teddy didn't want to kill anyone, not even witches like Leona Sum or Julia Chaplain. But denying his capability wouldn't make the caretaker's job any easier. Alaric hadn't seen what Chaplain was capable of. He couldn't attest to her precision and her cunning the way Teddy could. There were things he wouldn't understand until he came face to face with her, and at that point, with a duel in their sights, it became a matter of who struck first.

Teddy would do anything to ensure Alaric came back alive and unharmed, even if it meant enacting a spell dark enough to damn him. Besides, was he not damned already? 'I never wanted to kill the others either,' he said. 'But it happened. I can be useful to you.'

Alaric finished his rounds in the tiny shack, finding all its dusty crevices lacking. In the comfort of its vacancy, Alaric's gallant posture deflated with relief. 'You've given me everything

I needed, Teddy. You have enough weighing on your conscience. Luckily for us, it doesn't look like she's been here for at least a week.' He leaned over a tabletop beside the front door, fingering leisurely through old mail.

'How did you find this place?'

'The caretaker from Argentina is a portal witch,' Alaric said. 'Bastian. You'll meet him soon, I'm sure. He's the one who helped me close the gap between my father's library and Townsend back when I took up the mantle. Metaphorically speaking, he built the castle in which I reign.'

'Seems like a convenient friend to keep.'

'He once told me there were better candidates for my council seat dead under his shoe, but he's warmed up to me now. In his defence, I was an incorrigible twat back then.' Teddy permitted himself a thin smile. 'He deals with inventory on a larger scale than I do though. He's scrutinous with his belongings and impossible to take from. The day his ducks aren't in a row is the day all hell breaks loose in the world. That said, if I ask Bastian to find a witch that steps out of line and appears wherever she pleases, he finds her. *Some,*' Alaric added pointedly, 'more quickly than others . . . Gem's bird form obscured his methods. I've had him monitoring Julia Chaplain's movement for a few days now.'

'Did he rig that watch for you as well?'

Alaric paused to consider the wristwatch this time, allowing Teddy a glimpse of its face before the caretaker decided it wasn't worth the fuss of explaining, and unclasped it. It disappeared into his pocket, Teddy's underlying questions smothered against the dark fabric. 'Nifty, isn't it?'

'I suppose it'll take you back to Townsend after whatever . . .' Teddy gestured carelessly, which seemed to aggravate the caretaker even more.

'After nothing. Nothing is happening while you're here, understand?' Alaric's voice lowered and he said, like a solemn prayer, 'It'll take me home.'

Teddy hummed in response, shielding his gaze from Alaric's sudden gravity. 'Seems strange for Bastian to send you here if Chaplain hasn't been around in weeks.'

'She's only ever here for minutes at a time,' Alaric said. 'Just a blip on the map. Naturally, I assumed she was leaving things here. Or visiting someone.' He gathered the mail and handed it to Teddy in a no-nonsense way, defending his theory with a pointed finger.

Each letter was addressed to Meredith Albert. Mainly, they were bank notices and overdue bills marked by red, foreboding stamps and printer ink. The Schwartz surname drew Teddy's eye to one envelope in the stack, as did the singular mark of a person's messy penmanship and the fact that it was the only one that had been *opened*. The top edge was jagged, shredded by an urgent hand. In the skirmish, the sender's first name had been sacrificed, but it was short based on the point at which *Schwartz* began. Teddy was willing to bet on Aurelia's father, Tony.

Battleground, the envelope read. Teddy knew she'd probably kill him when she found out where he'd been, but he didn't quite know where that was or how to bring it up. Schwartz would want to see the letter, to tuck it into her books for safekeeping, and care for it like a silver family heirloom. He knew she should have been the one to discover what was inside or, even before that, to discover that Meredith still lived in Washington, what might have been less than an hour's drive from Vancouver.

Of all the things the sin of greed compelled him to take, Meredith's correspondence was hardly the worst.

As he unfolded it, he asked, 'Did you know about Gem's note?'

'When?' Alaric tugged a pouch of salt from his trouser pockets and took a large pinch from it.

'You know what I mean.'

The caretaker whispered an incantation under his breath, drawing a line along the perimeter of the room. Salt spilled through the slats in the floorboards and sunk into the grooves of the wood. Between the first words and the echoes of it that came afterwards, Alaric tilted his head up and replied, 'You're insinuating that I kept it from you. I don't know why you would think that.'

'Because you keep most things from me. The idea isn't that preposterous.'

Teddy attached himself to the caretaker's side, pretending to read although his mind was filled with the clockwork of Alaric's consideration. His footsteps were slow and even. Alaric nudged a moth-eaten lounge chair from the wall to keep the line of salt from breaking, and Teddy sputtered to a halt as the arm clipped his hips.

'I do it out of love, you know,' Alaric said. 'The kind of secrets I hide would keep you awake at night. You don't need to know them. You carry enough weight on your own to take more of mine.'

'I want to help you, Alaric. If we could just . . . talk to one another.'

'Let the worlds we carry on our backs be our own. When I need your help, I'll ask you for it. I promise.'

The same way he didn't fear Alaric, Teddy wanted to believe him but couldn't. He trusted him enough to, at least, let his mind stray from the topic of Gemma's note and back to Meredith's.

'Almost done,' Alaric murmured. 'You'll have to step outside with me before I can close it. The next time Chaplain lands here, we'll reroute her to us.'

'Us?'

'To the—'

The world went white as Teddy's head snapped from a sideways blow. He reached for nearby furniture but fell faster than he could catch himself. A wooden chair clattered to the ground beside him.

After a whirr of grey and pink behind his failing vision, Alaric slammed into the wall.

'You thought you could salt me in?' raged the voice of Julia Chaplain. 'Hasn't anyone ever told you to keep your nose out of things that don't concern you?'

Heat flooded to Teddy's cheek, his hand fumbling nervously around his jaw to assess the damage. 'Isn't even your house,' he slurred.

Chaplain's voice came from his other side, where only the wall existed. 'She is *my* practitioner, kid. What makes you think she'd want you here?'

He pushed himself upwards, kneading his eyes with a groan,

but Chaplain's training shoe swung like a club into his ribcage, grounding him instantly. Alaric stuttered unintelligibly. Chaplain struck him just as hard and hissed, 'Give me that.'

Teddy blinked until he could see Alaric's wrist pinned to the ground beneath Chaplain's heel, his fingers twitching with monumental effort. The man's head lolled to the side, and red trickled from his nose into his silver-flecked facial hair. His lips parted feebly. He doled out an instruction too quietly for Teddy to hear.

Silver, black, pink . . . The caretaker was made of so many vibrant colours, yet all Teddy could see was red. His fingers twitched with the weak flickering of a spell, producing less than a spark. Alaric shook his head as discreetly as possible. A warning.

Chaplain's gaze shot to the glimmer around Teddy's fingers like an arrow. Her mouth curled into a scowl. 'You kids have no fucking manners these days.'

Within the blink of an eye, she was towering above Teddy, her knee jutting into his chest as she crushed a vase over his hand. The glass fractured into his skin. He gritted his teeth, trying to shove her off with his other hand, but she evaded him expertly, like a gnat he could never catch. She appeared at his legs, then Alaric's side, behind the kitchen counter, around Teddy's throat. Blood trickled from the vein in his wrist, and he clutched it tightly with his other hand, letting the spell trickle back into his bloodstream.

Was it a deep enough cut?

He didn't know. He hadn't seen this much blood since the day Leona cut it from his wings, but that had happened in a blur, outside of himself. He'd been trapped in a dream and found it only when he came to consciousness again.

This time, his eyes were wide open. The colour trickling down his arm and Alaric's face were brighter than any golden shimmer.

The fear of death could revive even the faintest hint of magic.

Chaplain assessed the state of disarray she'd left him in – distracted enough to keep his hands to himself while she dealt with the caretaker – and she turned from the boy, visibly disgusted.

'Don't touch him,' Teddy said.

'You're trespassers,' she said. 'I'll deal with you as I see fit.'

Alaric fumbled for something in his pocket while the boy spoke. 'What does that make you then? Landlord? Thief? Does Meredith know you're—'

Another blink and she was inches from his face, yanking him to the ground by a fistful of his hair. 'You don't get to talk about Meredith to me!'

Alaric unearthed the wristwatch, his eyes trained on Chaplain's back.

She curved forward like a scythe's blade. Her breath danced through Teddy's hair as she seethed, 'You didn't know her. You didn't know what she was like. All the things she could have done to help us – to help *you*.'

Teddy drew in a deep breath, grimacing as the kick to his ribs manifested itself like wildfire all over his torso. Pacing out of his reach, Chaplain eyed him bemusedly, not like a threat but a plaything to snap and break within her jaws.

But if she was looking at him, she wouldn't see Alaric slip back into the portal. If Teddy could just hold her attention . . . if he could give Alaric a chance to get away, he could send his magic out like a bomb, levelling the place before Chaplain had become wise to what was happening.

The shack was as good as gone already. He had an address to show for it. Schwartz wasn't likely to have found anything worthwhile if she had come – just sun-bleached furniture and rotting food.

Surely she would forgive him for acting in self-preservation.

He reached for her ankle feebly, reaching only the tips of her shoes, which she kept still out of curiosity. 'You won't get far crawling,' she told him. 'Your best bet is to stick around and die in peace. Unless you want the birds to pick you clean. There's no one close enough to hear you crying.'

Alaric lifted the old wristwatch up to his mouth, and it was still only a watch, an unassuming piece of magic whose edges lacked the tell of shimmering gold. To it, he mouthed an incantation. Teddy watched it double in size, adopting its first gleam.

'I don't intend to die today,' Teddy said.

'That's a shame,' said Chaplain. 'You have good bones – hard to break. You could be useful to me if you behaved. Fresh-faced . . . Real enough. Maybe you could tell Meredith's daughter she's needed back home.'

'Can't,' he lied. 'We split.'

'*Figures,*' Chaplain grumbled. 'Was it bad enough to want revenge, or should I try something else?'

The caretaker placed the shining object on the ground and raised a silencing finger to his lips. Teddy watched his fingers flick methodically. Behind the closed door of Meredith's bedroom, something began to rumble: the effect of Alaric's wordless spell.

Chaplain's head pivoted towards the commotion. Then, she vanished, presumably to follow the noise.

Alaric looked pointedly to the opening portal and mouthed, 'Get in.'

Teddy stumbled, unable to mask the drag of his boots in his stupor. The shape stretched until it was large enough to swallow him – but *only* him.

He had already placed one shoe inside before the caretaker, who had risen onto his haunches in anticipation, began to close it around the boy's shape. He opened his mouth to protest but Alaric spoke first, his brows knitting intensely over his eyes; one of them had been split by the rough soles of Chaplain's shoes. 'When the portal closes, grab it from the other side.'

'What?' The room was spinning. The pieces of himself that the portal had already closed over like a coin purse felt weightless, pressed together by the immeasurable possibility of what was on the other side.

'Listen to me, Teddy. Grab the watch and keep it fastened.'

'I'm not leaving without you,' he gritted. 'I could deal with this if you just get in. I'll make it quick.'

Up close, even with the glaze in his vision, Teddy found more red spilling from the caretaker's face than he did before. He could see everything. *Feel* everything. The consideration, the fault in the caretaker's judgement.

Alaric shoved him into the portal and sealed it shut, leaving Teddy to feel only his own panic.

This must be what it feels like, Teddy thought, *when an astronaut leaves their spacecraft.*

He was weightless, suspended in the fold between one distant part of the world and the other. The portal had swallowed him. Teddy expected it to spit him back out just as quickly, but it kept him in its mouth like a chewed-up piece of gum.

He didn't realize it could trap him.

The bruises were still blooming at his side, the blood oozing from his hand. A shard of glass from one of Meredith's broken vases made the journey into the void with him, marking a wound in the centre of his palm that looked like a stigmata. Teddy couldn't stay out here much longer. To his knowledge, Alaric was still captive under Julia Chaplain's all-seeing eye. He had to get back, which he couldn't do if he didn't know where he was starting from.

Teddy had to find his footing first to figure out which way to turn.

Get to the end, he thought. *There has to be an end.*

He couldn't remember where the portal was supposed to take him – what Alaric had corrected him on – so, he lingered there suspended in the distance between possibility and what had already been.

It'll take you back to Townsend?

No, that wasn't right. He couldn't remember Alaric speaking those words, even though Teddy had asked them.

He plummeted in the darkness, lured by the gravitational pull of a place he couldn't yet see. The pain of his wounds was no longer dull and forgettable. It amplified until he was blinded by it, helpless in their throes.

Colours, shapes and unidentifiable sounds flew past him in overwhelming abundance. He reached with his injured hand for something to hold onto, but it burned as if he'd thrust his hand into an open flame.

So, he made himself small and held onto his own body. It had been possible before to disappear when no one was looking at him. Teddy could lose himself in the expanse of the unknown too.

He closed his eyes, folding in on himself until the exigent ache in his ribs debilitated him.

He would crash like a cannonball. Like a bomb. Teddy Ingram, who was made to self-destruct. Teddy Ingram, who was born to be broken.

Get to the end.

Where is the end?

CHAPTER THIRTY-THREE

A pungent cloth tickled Teddy's nose. He groaned, swatting it away before he opened his eyes and discovered it had come from a sock.

Above him, Ryan Jena grimaced, their face momentarily unrecognisable without their glasses. 'I fucking told her,' they hissed. 'She wanted to use a teabag, or something nice like that.'

'Where am I?'

'On my couch. Well, on our couch. You spawned in the hallway, and I nearly pissed myself, because I was standing' – Ryan gestured to the doorway – 'right there.'

Teddy wiped his nose with a hand that bore fresh scars instead of blood. They littered a once-blank slate from his knuckles to his lower forearm like translucent caterpillars travelling along his skin.

He pushed himself up from the couch, seething from the pain that still lurked in his torso. Ryan sank back into the plush beanbag behind them, watching him squirm into position. 'There's a massive bruise on your side,' they pointed out.

'Yeah, I feel it.'

'What happened?'

Teddy shook his head and arranged the cushions behind him to keep him upright. The wristwatch was gone. Teddy wasn't sure why he'd ended up here of all places. He could think only of Alaric.

'I need to get back,' Teddy muttered.

'Back where?'

He could still feel the stiffness of the envelope in his trouser pocket. With a strained twist, he took it out and handed it to Ryan for inspection. 'Wherever that is in Washington.'

'Jesus,' they whispered. 'How'd you get here so fast?'

The heavy sigh rolling out of him sparked a new burst of pain. 'I don't know. I wasn't trying to come back here at all. Alaric said . . .'

The rapid beating of footsteps overhead rendered them both silent. Schwartz emerged from the hallway with a vengeance, filled to her limit with an anxious buzz that Teddy thought he would never see the end of. At the sight of a living Teddy Ingram, it seemed to bubble over and pour out.

Ryan lifted their sock like a fisherman wielding their latest catch. 'It worked.'

Schwartz confiscated it just to toss it aside again. 'I'm not applauding you for that. God, I can smell it from here.'

'Desperate times call for desperate measures,' Ryan deadpanned. 'It needed to be gross.' They manoeuvred out of the beanbag, returning to the corner where their belongings were kept. Morning lurked behind them, taunting Teddy with harsh sunlight. Schwartz was still in her pyjamas, but Ryan had already changed, posturing in front of their mirror with a jar of pomade.

How much time had Teddy lost?

Where was Alaric?

Schwartz took a seat beside his thighs, balancing her small frame on the edge of the cushion to face him. 'How are you feeling?'

Teddy didn't know. Better than he'd felt on Meredith's dusty floor, although the colourful bruise on his side dampened his normal capabilities. Relieved to be in Schwartz's house, even if he didn't know why he'd ended up here.

Mostly, the thought of being so far from Alaric without any signs of life filled him with unparalleled dread. But where could he start?

'How long have I been here?' he asked.

'About five hours?' Schwartz estimated. 'You just sort of . . . appeared in the hallway around three o'clock in the morning. You were mostly unconscious at the time, but I got a few words out of you.'

The slow stream of his thoughts sped to life as he ran through the possibilities of what might happen to Alaric in that time. He'd offered the caretaker his magic to be used like a holstered weapon, but with the kind of ignorance Alaric always kept him swaddled in, Teddy hadn't the faintest clue as to what the caretaker was capable of on his own. Alaric was a councillor, one leg of the governing body of witches everywhere. Surely, he knew how to take care of himself in situations like that.

Teddy wanted to believe that. After the way Alaric sprung to action at Julia Chaplain's disappearance, Teddy could believe that he was more resilient than he made himself out to be – playing dead like a cornered possum so as not to draw attention.

Although Teddy remembered little of what Alaric said before, he remembered the urgency in the man's face and the blood marking the impact of Chaplain's shoes. It was harder to recognize things that were missing.

The absence of the wristwatch left a heaviness in Teddy's heart and mind that he couldn't shake.

Alaric had asked only one thing from him, and Teddy had let it slip through his fingers.

Schwartz's voice lowered as she leaned in and raked her hand through his hair. 'Tell me what happened. Who did this to you?'

'Chaplain,' Teddy answered plainly. 'Alaric located a house where she'd been reported to visit occasionally. He didn't tell me he was going, but Carmichael was worried about him. I crept into the portal behind him. Chaplain wasn't there yet. Al started to salt the place to ward it off from her, but she turned up just before he could finish. He sent me back through the portal before she could do something worse. I don't know why I resurfaced here. I asked him earlier if it'd take us back to Townsend, and he just said . . . he just . . .'

Schwartz took his hand, tracing the scars she'd sewn in his sleep. For someone who thought she didn't have enough to give, every scar on his body was a testament to the second, third, and fourth chances she gave him. When he was half-dead and unreceptive to the severity of his wounds, she'd found where he was lacking and brought him back to life.

Alaric's words returned to him as Schwartz drew her thumb across the scar on his wrist. *It'll take me home.* She shuffled forward, nestling her head on his shoulder while her arms circled his torso. Teddy gently eased her uncombed curls from his face, drawing in the familiar floral scent of her conditioner. The thumping of her heartbeat beneath his spell-sewn hand brought him comfort unlike anything else. He wondered if it was the oath that first tied them together, or if his magic simply knew, long before he knew it himself, that Aurelia Schwartz was his home.

She turned her face into the crook of his neck. 'You scared the shit out of me.' Teddy wasn't sure if he'd ever get used to the way her lips felt against his throat. There was a disjointed quality to the way she touched him that came from her cognizance of how hard her fingers were; the effort she made to be gentle was always at odds with how hard she wanted to seize him. Her lips remained soft, even when she was taking bites out of him.

'I have to go back,' he said.

'Tell me where.'

Teddy stumbled on a response. He hadn't expected her to be so willing, and the arguments died on his tongue. He gestured to the envelope Ryan left beside their seat.

In the reflection of the mirror, Ryan Jena was looking at it too. They unhooked the denim jacket from the back of their chair, casting it around their shoulders, and retrieved the note before Schwartz could stand and do it herself.

Her face steeled as she read. 'What is this?'

'The only piece of open mail in your mother's house.'

'I thought you were looking for Chaplain.'

Ryan's hand met the back of Schwartz's shoulder blades, fingers creeping over her shoulder like the horizon. Schwartz covered her mouth, staring at the page until she'd read her father's words three times over.

'Chaplain was there,' Teddy said. '*Constantly,* according to Al. For all I know, she's left Alaric there for dead.'

'And you went there?' He heard the accusation in her tone, but he couldn't take anything back now.

'I don't think Alaric knew it was her place before he got there. I would have told you if I'd known about it earlier,' Teddy said. 'I know how important it was to you that you found her.'

The thought hadn't occurred to him until he saw it melting across her face that she might have found her much earlier. Alaric had the tools, the capability of finding Meredith Albert, but would he have done it? If Schwartz had only asked him, could he justify the search?

'Rory,' her housemate said. 'Tell him what you saw.'

She shook her head.

'Tell me what?' asked Teddy. Ryan hummed to themselves, offering Schwartz a conciliatory squeeze before leaving for the kitchen. Being the only one in the room that was still oblivious to the matter made Teddy want to scream. 'What happened?'

'I tried to trigger the spell in my mom's note a little while after you left,' she said. 'Something just told me that she would be there if I tried again. One more time, y'know.' His tongue ran dry. She sat wilted beside him, as if preparing to deliver an answer he already knew. 'I only saw her in pieces.

She was . . . *flashing*. She sounded like she was stuck in-between stations, and I thought – maybe – that meant she was stuck between something else. I thought I could pull her out.'

'Did you?'

Schwartz frowned. 'Sort of.'

Ryan returned with a sealed storage container the size of an ottoman, extending it to them like it was a grenade without its pin. As Schwartz took it, something inside the container hissed.

'What the hell did you pull out?' Teddy asked.

'I don't know, OK?' Schwartz said.

Ryan added, 'I didn't see the thing she saw. She told me it was a heart. Like, a beating human heart.'

'*Not* a human heart,' corrected Schwartz.

'Whatever. A beating witch heart. Either way, what *I* saw is whatever's in that container right now. Does that seem like a vital organ to you?'

The creature inside the container hissed again, striking the inner walls so hard that Schwartz nearly dropped the container. 'It's definitely not a heart,' she said.

'Is it a snake?' Teddy asked and took the container from her hands.

Ryan nodded, still lurking behind her with their hands knotted nervously around the hem of their shirt. 'I think it's a north-western garter snake . . . I looked it up.'

'You must've taken a good look at it then,' Teddy murmured.

'Not exactly. More of a hunch. They're native to her area, but from what I gathered, they're usually much smaller, if that helps.'

Not at all, Teddy thought. He didn't know what to do with a snake, let alone one that wasn't *actually* a snake. Would he, too, see something different if he unhooked the lid? Was it wise to try? If he found something else within the container, it would prove only that the creature inside was enchanted by magic none of them were capable of breaking through. And if it was a snake—

What the fuck was he supposed to do with it?

'It's a demon,' Schwartz stated, shaking the last of her reservedness off.

The container jolted again. The snake's hiss steamed from the crevices under the lid like a doused flame. 'Fucking Christ.'

'Well, I obviously didn't know that when I grabbed it,' Schwartz said.

'Why are you getting defensive?'

Her nostrils flared once. 'I am *not* defensive.'

'How exactly did you come to this conclusion?'

Ryan barked a sharp '*Ha!*' then, mocking Schwartz's accent, said, 'She "read it in a book", if you can believe it.'

'What?' Schwartz asked. 'There's reputable, magical scholarship on the nature of demons.'

'What about what I saw from the note?' asked Teddy. 'Aside from getting properly blasted in the chest by spectral energy in the end, it talked to me like it knew you. Like it was your mum.'

Aurelia's mouth twisted discerningly. 'And it was, at the time. I'm sure it was. But a relic like this – something that holds memory so tangibly – can be corrupted. The fact that that I kept folding and unfolding it, hoping she might show herself to me again, made it into something unrecognizable.'

Ryan, who had been waiting patiently to make another quip

about the absurdity of demon manuals, went utterly quiet and grave, and Teddy wondered how much of that Schwartz had told them before he showed up.

Teddy needed to scratch his wrist, so he twisted and placed the container on the floor between them. Coincidentally, this was also the moment he remembered that he hadn't pissed in over ten hours. It was impossible to think about routine practices when there was a demon in his hands and a friend in need of rescue. 'I'll be right back.'

Ryan cleared their throat, toying with the chain that crested over their collarbone. They whispered a question to Schwartz. Teddy was gone before he could hear her reply.

Between Teddy's departure and return, Ryan Jena had gone and left the door locked behind them. Teddy caught the last glimpse of them in the kitchen window, speeding down the pavement with their hands buried in their jacket pockets.

Schwartz was exactly where he'd left her. Staring blankly at the container in front of her, she folded in around her knees, consolidating into a shape Teddy could scoop up into his arms. 'How's your side?' she asked, feigning nonchalance.

'I think you fixed a broken rib or two.'

'Good.' She nodded a little, lowering her gaze to her lap. Just then, Teddy caught the reflection of the phone screen in her hand. 'I called my sister to see if she could find that house. Then my dad and Gabrielle. Nobody answered.'

'It's probably nearing midnight over there, Schwartz.'

'Someone ought to be awake right now. It's hard to believe everyone I know goes to bed at a reasonable hour except me.'

'Look, Rory,' he began. Each syllable felt detached from every other, jumbled up in his mouth. 'I need to get back there. As far as I know, Alaric is still there.'

'You don't think he could make it back on his own?'

'No.' Then Teddy shook his head; what was he thinking? 'I mean, he's capable of finding his way back. Of course he is. But I left him in such a bloody state that I can't be sure he made it. If he's still there, I need to bring him home. Can you tell me how to get there with this?'

Schwartz read and reread the address on her father's letter. Each pass made a new revelation, like each layer of paint remade an image. 'We won't get there in time. Not unless we can go back the way you came. I'll call someone else. Maybe I can find a friend from high school who'll answer.'

'No other family?' he asked, to which she shook her head. Teddy nudged the container aside with his shin, slouching back into his seat. The snake – the demon – hissed in retaliation, and Teddy almost laughed thinking of how casually they sat together, as if they could turn on the television and play a game together. He'd have to kill the beast inside the box; the real outcome was much less amusing. 'I have to get there, Schwartz. He gave me a way back and I've lost it.'

'What do you mean?'

It was impossible to explain something he didn't fully understand. It'd taken him far too long to figure out why the watch had led him here instead of Townsend. Only Alaric could say whether it would take him back to that dingy shack in Washington; all Teddy could say was that the portal took him exactly where he needed to go at the point that he most needed it.

So he began, cautiously so as not to make himself sound too self-assured. At the best of times, this unwitting guise of self-assurance did little more than piss Schwartz off, but it could cost them a life now. He wouldn't be able to forgive himself for letting Alaric – like Gemma and Kenny – slip through his fingers.

'The portal he sent me through had been rigged into this wristwatch of his. He whispered something to it, and it grew just large enough to fit me inside of it. It was supposed to shrink back to its original size once I was on the other side of it. When it did, Alaric told me to grab it.' Teddy averted his gaze, lowering it to the container. 'I don't know where it went. I don't know where it is, but I think it could have taken me back.'

Schwartz worried her lip, writing her thoughts out in another one of her meticulous lists. She rose quickly and left without a response. Teddy shut his eyes, guilt-ridden, listening to the mouse-like scurry of her footsteps above his head. Her bedroom door shut behind her, rattling the frame and surely waking the neighbours. When she returned, her breath was rushed and shallow, and the band of the wristwatch was crushed in her hands.

'I took it,' Schwartz told him. 'It seems really stupid in hindsight to grab something under an unfamiliar enchantment, but I guess I was in a mood for grabbing strange things.'

Teddy rose again and held it to the light like a blanched communion wafer. 'You're a wonder, Schwartz,' he said.

'I know. I'm going with you.'

'Afterwards,' Teddy answered. 'I'm not giving Chaplain the opportunity to get her hands on you too.'

'I'm going now. I'm not arguing with you on this either.

That's my mother's house Chaplain is in right now, and Alaric is my friend. If you think you can get me to stay here and wait, don't try it. You promised me.'

In fairness, he'd promised her a lot of things: his magic, his heart, his safety. It was only because of her stubborn, unyielding determination that the last hadn't been broken twice now, first in Alaric's library and then on her housemate's couch.

Despite the fear that had overwritten the night of Gemma's disappearance, Teddy remembered much of it clearly. He remembered the way her hands felt on his chest and in his hair, how she'd asked him into her bed knowing, somehow, that he wanted to be held. He remembered passing through Gemma's door feeling small and powerless to the anger in Schwartz's eyes, and that she'd told him, 'Don't try that shit with me again.'

But that hadn't been a promise. As the seconds dragged on, she seemed to remember it too but wouldn't rectify her words on the off-chance that he believed it.

'Do you even know how to open the portal?' she asked, twitching with nervous energy. 'Because I do. If that watch is what you say it is, then I can get it to take us back to him.'

'And if I don't want you to come,' Teddy said, 'what will you do? Keep the portal closed? Let Chaplain have her way with your mother's house and leave Alaric there to die?'

'Chaplain's already had her way with my mother's corpse,' Schwartz said sternly. 'I know what happens if we don't get him. And *you* know what she's capable of, which is why you're going to let me come with you. You *need* me.'

The ache in Teddy's side left him an easy target on his own. Even with the wounds in his hand sealed, knuckles wiped clean of his blood, Chaplain would know where to find the tenderest flesh, the places that would hurt most. She had created them.

In theory, it shouldn't have got that far. His magic could level giants, leave the coven leader as nothing but ash and bone. But it was also merciless and all-devouring, uncontained like a forest fire feeding off summer brush. If he could not get them out before he burned, he ran the risk of taking his loved ones down with him.

More bodies, more risk. It took a stronger spell to kill a person than it took to destroy a tree. He wasn't sure if he could contain it well enough to leave both Aurelia *and* Alaric unscathed.

Short on time, he asked, 'You're not going to budge, are you?'

Schwartz took his hand, closing the wristwatch in a knot of their fingers. She lifted his hands to her mouth and kissed them softly. 'You are too principled for your own good,' she said. 'It's one of the reasons I love you so much. You're kind and gentle. But you're bound to your goodness and to impossible expectations. You hesitate too much, and it'll cost you if you aren't careful. Let me come with you. Let me do this, and you can live with a clearer conscience after it's done.'

In spite of the pressing matter, Teddy asked, 'You love me?'

She pushed her hair behind her ears, admitting, 'Well, *yeah*. I figured you already knew that.'

'I had a hunch.'

Her thumb traced the ridges of his knuckles with such attention that he thought she might be looking for a hint of blood, but she'd been thorough in wiping them clean. By the time Teddy had escaped to wash his hands, there was nothing left to scrub.

'We should take care of this,' Schwartz said. Teddy pried his fingers free, flexing them against his stomach. The demon in question quieted to defensive silence. 'Have any ideas?'

'I'm not exactly familiar with the practice of exorcizing demons.'

'Right.' The corners of her lips tugged into a severe frown.

'Don't suppose you'd have any moral hang-ups over destroying it.'

Schwartz shrugged, tangling a fist in her hair as the box travelled inch by inch beneath her. 'I wouldn't know. I'm pretty inexperienced on the demon front myself.' Nervously, she reached for the top of the lid. Her fingers splayed over its surface, hovering like an evening sun. They sparked with gold once, nothing more than a test that Teddy wasn't privy to. Whatever the spell was, the creature in the box wept for it.

Not a hiss, but a childlike cry. It devolved into a myriad of gut-wrenching, sorrow-inducing sounds like whining rabbits and human pleas. Whatever it took to elicit sympathy, it seemed. Whatever it took to keep itself alive.

'I'm just going to do it,' Schwartz said. 'Open the box and kill it.'

Teddy circled the container, levelling his gaze on her like a hammer. 'Whatever's inside will do anything to stay alive. It'll try to deceive you, Schwartz; don't believe it. I'll be right here. Just . . . try not to kill me too, yeah?'

She nodded again. Teddy curled his fingers around the lip of the lid, not yet unsnapping it.

'But in case you do,' he added, 'I love you. I probably should have told you earlier, but—'

'I'm not going to kill you, dumbass. Open the box and confess later.'

CHAPTER THIRTY-FOUR

SNAP.

Teddy pressed his weight over the lid, waiting for her approval. The sounds inside converged into a deafening crescendo of cries, whistles, and otherworldly growls. Schwartz made a sign, moistened her lips, and as the demon in the crate burst free, knocking Teddy and his lid backwards, she braced herself for its force, hands outstretched and twitching with the first tendrils of a spell.

It remained a mist, blackening their surroundings – untouchable, ungovernable, but sentient nonetheless. It studied her with an omniscient sense of knowledge, and in the darkness stretched a sharp-toothed, oil-sheened grin. It whispered something Teddy couldn't hear, settling over Schwartz like a warm breath, a loving promise.

Teddy's bruised side bloomed with pain as he cast the lid off him and rolled onto his knees. The demon looked at him, its untethered particles mimicking a shape, then deemed him useless.

He had too many fears for its liking, too many feelings. Only Schwartz had something worth extorting.

All at once, it collapsed into a body. Black mist turned to

rich, tan skin, wringing the shadows into light. The sound, which had become a chorus of desperation, dwindled to one voice – her mother's.

From where she stood, Schwartz couldn't see the unfinished tangle of congealed oil that was the demon's shortcomings. Tendrils of it fell from the back parts of Meredith only Teddy could see, writhing like small offspring of the snake they'd captured. Teddy's fingers buzzed with the impulse of his magic.

Kill it while its back is turned.

Something in Schwartz's hand gave him pause. A metallic gleam he didn't recall from thirty seconds ago.

Meredith fell to her knees, worming her arms unsuccessfully around her daughter's waist, murmuring, 'Please, please. I've been trying to break through.'

'Get off me.'

Meredith held her hands above her head, cowering. '*Please.*'

His darling rival, his bright star – she had made a weapon from the spark of gold toiling at her fingertips, a full-bodied axe akin to what she'd used to fend off the knights in the crypt. It was made of his dark magic, of burning black and starlight.

In one full swing, she sunk the blade into her mother's neck. It seared all the way through, then collapsed with a dark splatter into fluids around their heels.

For a moment, she simply stared at it, her chest stalling for breath; and they both waited for something new to appear in the sheen of oil like a prophecy. It shouldn't be so easy, he thought. Then again, he couldn't tell how hard it was for Schwartz to execute the shape of her mother while she was holding her breath so tightly.

Softly, he asked, 'Are you OK?'

Schwartz cast the weapon away, the matter dissolving into nothingness once it left her grip. She lifted her feet from the oil pooling on the ground and firmly pressed her quivering lips together. 'This is going to be a nightmare to clean.'

CHAPTER THIRTY-FIVE

The infinity between two ends of a portal was, Teddy concluded, simultaneously the most unpleasant and most convenient place to be trapped. On one hand, it adhered to the thin, malleable principles of magic that made it governable by intention; if he had a place in mind, extracted from the pull of all others, he could reach it in an instant. On the other hand, if he wasn't driven enough, or wasn't sure, he could lose himself to the terrors of the ether.

This was where he found himself again, just before Schwartz took his hand and pulled him through.

He wasn't thinking of the dingy little shack but of Alaric. Wherever the caretaker was came second to the fact that he was *somewhere*. Still alive, still breathing.

It wasn't enough to drive Teddy Ingram. The intention lacked clarity.

Schwartz turned to him with her hand still closed around his wrist, the golden, fractal light of the portal's other end shining at her back like the Empyrean. 'Come on,' she mouthed. 'Keep going.'

She'd never looked more beautiful.

More importantly, Schwartz knew where they were going, treading like a soldier to their trench. Even if he couldn't see where she was leading him, Teddy knew he would follow her anywhere: into battle, towards heaven, or hell. Luckily, she had enough direction for them both.

On impact, though, Teddy wasn't sure if she had the right one. His face hit cold dirt and crushed, wiry leaves of grass not unlike the kind that blanketed Townsend Hill. Seemingly nothing bordered the grass for miles save for a single, sputtering pickup truck on a road nearly obscured by a thick layer of trees. It came and went as he pushed himself to his feet. Schwartz paced past him, scouring the grass for the fallen wristwatch – the closing portal.

She groaned, sifting through the grass in a rush. 'This isn't . . . I don't understand. I asked it to take us to the address on the envelope.'

Perhaps it did. With the salt circle left incomplete, Julia Chaplain could still place a spell of her own within the boundaries of the house. What else could he expect from a skilled portal witch than a redirection as large as this?

Uselessly, he noted, 'None of this is familiar.'

'Because we're north-west of Vancouver right now. This is Clatskanie, Oregon.'

'You've been here before?'

Schwartz pointed to a harsh silhouette peering through the treeline. 'There are some large structures I recognize over there. A mile or two up that way, there's a cafe that my dad used to stop at whenever he'd drive us to the coast. He would insist driving through here even though it was a bit out of the way. Extremely rural. Eerily quiet.'

A fair observation. Aside from the trees and the distant, delicate lines of telephone wires sewn through them, all he found was dried brush and sparse litter tumbling onto his shoes. There were few places to hide. Few places to stow a body.

'Try it again,' Teddy said.

She fumbled over the incantation, but the watch ultimately stretched, glittering and gold. In its face was a reflection of their image, tracking each small movement and rushed breath. Faced with the uncanny, Teddy's blood ran cold.

'Shit,' she muttered.

The portal collapsed like a rubber band snapping off one's fingers. She seized the watch from the ground in a huff.

So, they were exactly where the portal had meant to take them.

Within the thick tangle of forest, a light flickered on. A window was illuminated, a cross between its panes like an omen.

Teddy's skin prickled coldly. His tongue was too large, too clumsy for coherent speech. 'We should go back.'

'*Quiet!*' The hiss came from within the grass like another snake. The source dragged Schwartz down beside it. A head of faded bubble-gum pink swivelled up above the cover of grass to Teddy, gesturing for him to follow. 'I think she's got someone in the house with her.'

Schwartz wrestled her arm free with a grunt. 'Who? Chaplain?'

'Of course that's who. You're here for her too, aren't you?'

The girl shifted her attention between the bonded pair, blue eyes wide and fearful.

With his voice low, Teddy asked, 'Are *you?*'

'N-no. Well, technically yes. I work for her.'

'Doing what?'

'Whatever she tells me to do. I don't really have a choice.'

Teddy should have been able to sense her. A pulse, a breath, or a feeling. Schwartz was overwhelming in the most platonic, unnerving way imaginable – as if the other person wasn't there at all.

'You're Meredith's daughter,' the girl mused. 'Julia was right. You look just like her.'

'What did she do to her?' Schwartz asked in spite of a knotted throat.

Before the girl could speak, Teddy reached between them and pressed his fingers to her wrist. No pulse. She averted her gaze in shame.

'I'm the only one that turned out so *normal,*' she replied. 'Everyone else Julia brought back ended up like your mom: unresponsive for the most part, not in control of their basic motor functions. Julia got me early, though, just after I died. I was fresh. My body had barely shut down.'

'How?' Schwartz knew the answer before Teddy did, before the girl could draft up an answer.

'It was an accident. A complicated spell gone awry. But Julia knows I waver in my faith. The next time she kills me, it will be intentional.'

Silhouetted by the light in the window, Chaplain paced back and forth, waiting for her younger companion to show.

They had no time to pry, to ask if the girl believed in the innocence of her death, or if she was capable of wondering otherwise. They asked for her name: *Rosie*. Then Schwartz asked, 'Who's in there, Rosie? Is it my mother?'

Rosie shook her head. 'She didn't last very long after the resurrection. Necromancy, especially the half-finished, ungifted kind that Julia works to perfect, will never bring someone back to their former self. They're a shell. A frame. Each day between your death and your resurrection is a step further from the person you used to be. There was no strength to put back in her and no point in keeping her sustained, you know? She collapsed about an hour after Julia got the answers she needed.'

'But you,' Teddy noted, 'function perfectly fine without her. No puppet master. No divine intervention.' The possibility that Rosie could be puppeteered now was grim, but the truth was still totally abysmal. Either Rosie was sentient and tied to Julia's side out of fear or – God forbid – loyalty, or she was a pawn pushed forth by Julia to wipe them off the board.

Julia didn't strike him as someone who doled out the duties of punishment. He suspected she would want to deal with them herself.

Still, Rosie could drop them both on Julia's doorstep like birds in the clamped jaw of a dog. He and Schwartz were either supplicants or gifts. They'd been sitting in the grass much longer than they'd wanted to be.

'I'd barely stopped breathing by the time she decided to act. Meredith had been dead for weeks. There are two steps to resurrection, we found. One to pull the deceased back to the point of their death, to the precise point where they are both alive and dead; and another to *heal.* To cement them into the realm of the living. You can't heal a thing that's dead, but if you can get them to that transient, half-dead state . . . you can get something like me. I think and I wonder and I *want,* but I can't feel the heat on my face as well any more or the rain on my skin. It rains all year here . . . I'm not dead, but it feels that way sometimes.

'Julia manages half of the resurrection process, but attempting both halves drains her. Even so, my body doesn't work the same way as it used to. I'll die soon unless she gets to me first. If she can't find a gifted necromancer, a healer is her next best bet – someone to complete the resurrections she begins. Meredith's secrecy gave her reason to believe you were something special. Maybe you are. I don't know. I try to know as little as possible.'

Schwartz laid her fingers over Rosie's in the grass. 'So, she's gone.'

'Gone for good.'

'Burned?' She asked with such ambivalence that Teddy's stomach twisted. He didn't know what Meredith wanted, but he knew what her daughter wanted: to give her magic back to the ground. He wondered briefly if it would change, now that her magic had taken a different shape. He wondered constantly if he had ruined her.

'I did it,' Rosie whispered. 'But she's untouchable now. She was good to me.'

Chaplain disappeared from the window. There and gone. Through a portal going to somewhere he could only hope was far away. Teddy inched forward on his haunches, leaving the others in solemn conversation.

Yes, he thought, *someone else is here.* Another witch's magic pulled him through the grass by the tether. He followed it like his shadow, never quite reaching it, but he was getting closer. He only knew because he recognized, upon losing sight of Schwartz, that it was Alaric's magical signature drawing him in like the familiar scent of home-cooked dinners through the window of an empty cottage. It shouldn't have been there. There was no good or promising reason that Alaric should have been there.

So, where did Julia Chaplain go? He called back to Rosie and asked. Slowly, she pushed herself up to her feet, scouring the field for a clue, and shrugged.

'The watch brought us back to Alaric,' Teddy said to Schwartz. 'He's alive. I feel him.'

Rosie's pale brows furrowed. 'You came to save him?'

'This stays between us.' Schwartz told her. 'It's too late for my mother, but it's not too late for him.'

'I think I saw him,' Rosie said. 'Just a little while ago. He's the reason I'm out here instead of in there. If he was coming to stop her, I couldn't be in his way.'

Let's hope it doesn't come to that. Teddy and Alaric had been talking about a more malevolent figure then. Teddy couldn't imagine the caretaker being anything other than fair if faced with Rosie – fearful, soft-syllabled Rosie. He thought of Carmichael fidgeting with the salt pouch in the doorway, how ardently he'd cared for Alaric's safety. Carmichael, whose wife had tried to kill them too. Alaric had the commendable, widely unfathomable ability to see the moral innards of a person and grant them mercy.

By now, he was likely to be hell-bent on retribution. If Rosie's distant examination of him proved correct, Teddy could at least be assured that they were all on the same page.

'Would you have let him kill her?' Teddy asked.

Rosie replied with a small jerk of her head. 'I'm going to look for him. Stay put.'

Quickly, Schwartz pulled him in by the stretch of his shirt and kissed him, sharp and urgent. His chance to touch her in any solid way came and went like the first clumsy flicker of a lighter. 'Just in case,' she whispered.

Teddy echoed, 'Just in case.'

As he walked, he heard the snake. The demon. A mutating, middling sound that started as a hiss but lost its shape like a beaten-up hat. He ducked low amidst the grass, following the faint pull of Alaric's magical signature, and wondered if he was leading the source of the sound to its next meal.

It had to be paranoia. There were animals in the woods and whispers floating between the two girls behind him, and he was willing to bet he wouldn't be encountering another demon anytime soon.

If he ignored the wind and the melodic hooting of owls in the trees, he found a hammer where his heart should have been. Teddy held his breath, but his pulse betrayed him. He fingered the weave of his jumper.

A head of dark curls emerged.

Alaric brought his finger to his mouth, barely visible in the offshoot of light leaking from the house. *Quiet.*

So, Alaric saw him. A shiver shot through him, worsened by the wind. He beckoned for Alaric to cross the bounds of the house, to come with him. With Alaric's help, surely they could configure a portal opening, through the watch, back to Townsend. Whether it took them all or left Teddy Ingram there to take care of unfinished business, it didn't matter.

This time, he wouldn't hesitate.

He'd said that before, and back then, Teddy had felt he had a better handle on the situation, even if the aftermath proved him entirely wrong. He thought back to the eruption at the Tate Modern, the cataclysm of his magic as a result of last-second desperation. He could have left the walls where they were, made less of a mess, if only he'd acted sooner. If only he hadn't hesitated.

Alaric raised the palm of his hand, giving Teddy pause.

I was supposed to be made for this, Teddy thought bitterly. *Wicked and violent, made to be broken like a mirror and used for my sharp edges. I was made to destroy.*

Sometimes a weapon and a shield were the same thing. If he could just get them home . . . If Alaric would listen to him and leave . . .

Teddy mouthed, 'Come here,' as if the caretaker could possibly see him as more than shadow. Teddy couldn't see the blood on Alaric's face, but he knew it was still there, dried and buried deep in the creases of his skin.

To hell with warnings. Teddy crept forward, leveraging the heavy soles of boots to keep quiet.

'I sent you away,' Alaric whispered. 'You were supposed to stay there.'

'I wouldn't have left you if I'd thought you wouldn't be right behind me.'

Alaric laid his hand on Teddy's shoulder, holding him undercover. His fingers caused an itch in the crook between the boy's neck and shoulder where a seam ran through the knit. Teddy's nerves calmed at the small gesture. 'I knew that,' Alaric said softly. 'Which is why I never told you anything, you know. You'd have rushed head first into trouble you're not prepared for. I care too much to see you hurt.'

'I can handle it.'

'I don't want you to handle it. I want you to keep quiet and lie low and not have this weighing on your conscience for the rest of eternity. There's more to life than this moment, I promise you. Did you bring the watch?'

'It's nearby.'

Alaric peered at Teddy over his smudged glasses. 'You should go back. This will be much easier if you leave.'

'It would be quicker if I stayed. I think you know that.'

Alaric's hand tightened on his back. 'You will send me straight to my grave, out of the goodness of your soul, you hear me?'

'Are you asking me to swear to it?'

'I'm making a declaration of truth and hoping that you will disprove me.'

Teddy sighed, prodding within his mind for the tether drawing him to Schwartz. He kept silent and tried to pull it. *You OK?* It was an estimation of the question; he couldn't really ask her from here. They'd found ways to understand one another without words – at least, *exact* words – and he knew they could do it again. Translation of a heartbeat was more intricate than any spoken language.

He listened, but the hiss permeated everything.

'Schwartz has the watch,' he murmured. 'There's a girl with her. She can tell you everything you want to know about Julia. She saw you come in.'

'I know.'

Teddy couldn't see them. It should have been a good thing to know they were so well hidden, but it unnerved him to look out and see only darkness. 'You didn't find her worth questioning.'

'There's a lot to learn in my line of work, if you make yourself open to it. Foul people take extreme measures to cover up their rottenness, and those with all their faults laid open to see in passing are usually harmless. I detect a sizeable mess and move on. I only saw her after she very audibly said "*shit*".'

'Ah.'

'That rhetoric serves me well most of the time. Quiet now.'

As if on cue, a gold ripple in the fabric of space split the front steps of the house, and Julia stepped through it.

Teddy dipped lower, his heart rising in his throat.

Alaric shifted away, bidding Teddy's stillness. Through the grass he crept like a fox, soft-footed and expert.

For once, Teddy did as he was told. The adrenaline drove his thoughts to unforeseen ideas, played out in quick succession like film slides. The demon, the destruction, the oil pooling around Schwartz's slippers. How she had harnessed a power that Teddy had always believed to be insurmountable and made it a blade. If he could concentrate it into matter like she did, he could work around the caretaker easily. Finish the job and leave no stain.

Reaper magic did not glow quite the same way empathy did or healer magic did. Like the warm glow of dying embers rather than a spark. He wondered if Julia would see it in the dark, if he could get away unseen with something small like a knife.

Again, Teddy found himself alone in the grass, searching.

Chaplain was too close. Too still. The perfect target, if he could will himself to take the shot.

Just then, Schwartz sent her reply through the tether – three sharp thumps against his rib cage. He'd forgotten how bruised it still was until a grunt slipped through his clenched teeth.

Teddy swore he saw Chaplain's lips slant into a grin before she closed herself into a portal and vanished once again.

Too late.

Another bash to his ribs split them apart again. Schwartz gasped out his name, reeling backwards clumsily. Teddy was on his back, snuffed out like a flame under Chaplain's boot, when Chaplain caught wind of the others and snapped to them too.

Teddy pushed himself up with a hand tucked to his sternum. Schwartz was hazy, and Alaric was a blur, sending out a spell like a bullet towards the witch nearby. A pulse of energy shoved Schwartz into the caretaker, and they both hit the ground with a thud. Teddy's legs forced him on, though the pain sought to ground him. He saw blue – never-ending, blurred-together blue – and he blinked it away urgently, just in time to see

Chaplain raise a furious, kicking Rosie into her arms and drag a knife across her throat.

He didn't feel it.

Alaric righted himself and barrelled towards Chaplain, half-stunned by the mere presence of Aurelia Schwartz, as if he didn't believe she was really there until she was pushing herself off him. She looked at him, then to Rosie in horror, her gaze landing on Teddy with unignorable rage.

Chaplain whispered something in the dying girl's ear, withdrawing the knife. Teddy caught a slice of moonlight on the blade, white like lightning. She threw it just as Leona Sum did months ago in the Tate Modern, mostly by means of a directional spell, into the open mouth of a golden portal where it disappeared and did not return.

Not for several, drawn-out seconds.

Teddy's magic burst free like a whip, wild and uncontained, but was held within his hand and bore a tangible weight.

Alaric ducked, cursing to himself. 'Watch it!'

Chaplain threw herself aside with a grunt. Her knife was nowhere, held inside a spell that kept her captive. Schwartz moved to Rosie's still body, reasoning with Death to give her back. As if she hadn't had more chances than the rest of the dead – just one more. How had Chaplain done it? Not on her own, but maybe she could.

Alaric leaped to his feet, moving on the downed coven leader with unprecedented urgency. No witch could cast two spells at once, and the knife was already occupying one of Julia Chaplain's.

But only for several, drawn-out seconds.

Desperate, unforgiving seconds.

Alaric had her pinned to the ground when the knife slashed through Teddy's shoulder, which would have wounded his heart if she'd had better aim. He was worthless to her, an impediment to the known healer. If she could dispose of Rosie with such little consideration, she would kill him without any question at all.

The force sent him staggering, but the knife didn't follow, stuck upright in the dirt behind him. The still moonlight was a white flag, surrender.

With a spell saved for herself, Chaplain passed straight through the caretaker like a chill. She emerged on the other side, his liver crushed in her hand.

CHAPTER THIRTY-SIX

This brought them all to a violent, stuttering halt. Schwartz pitched herself over the body of Rosie Starling, her arms twined around her stomach in pain. Her body lit up like a flare.

Teddy didn't compartmentalize it as easily; his arm was bleeding and his ribs were cracked. Bruises littered his body from Chaplain's last assault. He was hardly a picture of composure.

When he fell, he burst. The concentrated shape of his spell dissolved like feathers in a wreck, scattering through the field.

It was not enough to reach Chaplain or be useful for any matter. Chaplain puzzled over him smugly, though he couldn't tell if she knew how it hurt him. That it *did* hurt him was enough. One less thing to worry about, and two fewer witches to stand between herself and the healer.

Teddy's vision blurred at the corners. He picked himself up, dislodging the knife just to keep it in his reach. His thoughts were an endless cycle of the caretaker's name.

AlaricAlaricAlaric—

Chaplain squeezed the organ in her hands. Alaric screamed as if he could feel it in his body, though there would have been a cavity there now, welling with blood or waste – a critical vacancy.

He was nothing to the coven leader, nor was Teddy Ingram. So inconsequential and harmless to her in their wounded states that she took her eyes off them both in favour of Schwartz.

Teddy struck at that moment. It whipped around her ankles, a tendril of gold shooting through the dark. Her mouth had opened to speak, but a howl emerged. She wiped the dark imprint of the spell from her leg, but it had settled into her body like tattoo ink.

Upwards it crawled, digging deeper and deeper into her body. 'What is this?' Chaplain seethed.

Teddy didn't answer. He lugged himself upright, hand over his ribs, muttering a silent prayer to mend the bones.

Tripping over her ruined ankle, Chaplain fell backwards with a sharp cry. '*What did you do to me?*'

'I should have killed you the first time,' he said. 'I should have left you in the chapel to feed the rats.'

'You idiot! If he dies, you can't bring him back – not without me.' A portal she conjured opened its jaws, then snapped shut; the decay had begun to spread.

Already working diligently with unsteady hands to create something out of nothing in the caretaker's body, Schwartz did not stop Teddy from his pursuit. She couldn't make a missing piece, but she was trying desperately. The fear was blinding. They couldn't save him.

Chaplain shouted, '*Stop*.'

Teddy gritted his teeth as the cracks in his bones sealed. Ablaze with his fury, his new and old magic alike, he stalked towards the cowering witch.

'Please. Please, I can bring him back.'

Schwartz shook her head, muttering a chorus of '*No, no, no.*' Her spells wouldn't take. Alaric heaved, laid out under the canopy of stars, reaching for her gilded hands.

Chaplain's transportive magic flickered ineffectively.

Teddy pressed his foot into her chest in the exact place where she'd kicked him on Meredith's floor. It was solid beneath his boot. Her heart knocked against it, overworked, waiting to be freed.

You cannot hesitate.

'The gods won't forgive you for killing another witch,' Chaplain said. 'Never. Can you make peace with that?' Her eyes were large, stained red with fear. She faded in and out, but couldn't evade him any more, too weak and too uncontrollable. Like an image trying to find itself in the static of an old television, she broke apart and sewed herself back together again, all to no avail. Her hands shook. Her last breaths were stilted. Her hair fell free of its tight little knot, fraying around her head like a crown.

Teddy thought of Alaric's hair tickling his ears, his arms around the boy's shoulders. Gemma and her scar. Schwartz's letters piling up in her drawer. He thought of Leona Sum's plea for help in the final moments of her life. He'd been weak enough to fold then too, to fall for such desperation. What had kept him from intervening? It was never the knowledge that his magic couldn't be reversed. It was never the inability to salvage a life that he'd already infected. He would have tried, because he couldn't stand the noise, the pleas, the guilt.

'I don't need the gods to forgive me. Just *them*.'

He'd done it for love. The essence of his reaper magic

flooded to his hands, and just like Schwartz wielding the axe in the chapel, he moulded it into something.

This time, it would not be an untameable burst but a broad, heavy sword. It would strike true. He would not take it back.

'I will haunt you forever,' Chaplain hissed, cursing him.

Teddy closed his eyes, his chest throbbing with the weight of Alaric's wound.

Be the wicked thing.

Be the unholy beast.

God was never going to forgive you anyway.

CHAPTER THIRTY-SEVEN

Her hands were stained, though the exit wound of Julia Chaplain's body was remarkably small on Alaric Friedman's stomach. 'I'm trying,' Aurelia whispered. 'Why isn't it working?'

Alaric covered her hands with his. His eyelids fluttered as he fluctuated between her and the boy kneeling at her back. Was it worse that he knew, or better? There was nothing inside for her to heal, no organ to fuse back to the rest of him. Trying to call for an ambulance in the grasslands of Clatskanie was futile.

Teddy moved in closer behind her, his hands tangling in the nest of his own hair.

'There has to be someone,' he said. 'A nearby caretaker. Someone who'll know.'

Alaric almost smiled; all Aurelia could see was peppered stubble. Gently, he took her hand and gave it a very particular squeeze. 'Aurelia,' he mumbled.

Nothing followed. Carefully he raised two fingers and pantomimed cutting shears.

'What?' She shook her head. 'I don't know what you're—'

He did it again, then laid the shears against his chest. Aurelia remembered, through the fatigue of a night spent fearing for her life, what he'd sent to her in the library, standing in front of a crackling fire.

The beats of my life are knotted on a string of fate.

Cut it, he was saying now. *Cut it.*

'No,' she said.

Alaric nodded.

'How do we call a caretaker?' Teddy demanded. '*Tell me* what to do!'

Indignant bastard, Aurelia thought. She leaned forward as if it were possible, or even necessary, that they speak privately; in the end, it didn't matter who heard. She had always planned to take their conversation by the fireplace to her grave.

'You should have told me. This can't be how it happens.'

Impossibly quiet, he replied, 'You wouldn't have wanted to know.'

She brushed the curls from his forehead, away from the streak of blood stained in his skin. She pressed her lips to his temple, her hand to his chest, as was his final wish. Silently, she tripped over a prayer she'd long since forgotten from her father's faith, rare as his invitations were.

A frigid whisper laced through her hair, *be brave, be brave.*

She swore it was her mother.

CHAPTER THIRTY-EIGHT

TWO WEEKS EARLIER

Her father idled in the living room, his fingers dancing over Aurelia's rusting keychain. Summer was brutal in Vancouver; even with the shades slanted upward and the curtains drawn, sunlight managed to find its way inside, as did the heat. The house had two bedrooms: one for Tony and the other a converted office space, which went mostly unused until one of his daughters asked to stay.

Aurelia couldn't have avoided him. She didn't know why she even bothered. The sound of her keys digging through the grooves of the table alerted her to Tony's presence.

They were both rather small, unassuming, easy to miss at first glance if they wished to be. He'd been lingering there as quiet as a ghost for the past several minutes, likely turning a thought over in his mind to the rhythmic scrape of the keys.

She crossed to the kitchen, rummaging through the fridge for a spare peach-flavoured yoghurt.

'Did you sleep all right?' her father asked.

Aurelia moulded her gaze to the French Vanilla in her hand, attempting to dispel Tony's curiosity. The drive home from the procession might have calmed her if not for Gabrielle's intervention. She'd turned her words over, watching her sister's car disappear down the street that would lead her back to her own apartment, and had again later on as she'd twisted into the green striped sheets of her childhood bed. With all the things she had outgrown, her bed still fit the same – a twin-size that could feel like a monument when she was most heartbroken. It never got smaller, and she had never felt more *unwound*.

When she'd woken hours later, her body curled into a fist, the slats in her blinds had barely cast any light. Sweat had slicked her body, even though the sheets sat twisted at her feet. In the lingering dark, she'd reached for her phone on the nightstand, tapping to her email; but the distance was daunting, and she'd felt smaller than ever.

She'd been awake ever since, fighting off fatigue with a slew of teabags and a half-finished crossword puzzle that she'd found folded up on the coffee table. Tony must have overheard her stealing away to her bedroom.

'It's probably just jet lag.' The excuse was as flimsy as her half-drowned teabags; she'd been home for a week.

Her chin remained tucked, gaze averted out of self-preservation. When she was younger and much smaller, she would make a game out of hiding, testing the divide between seeing someone else and that person seeing you back. What could she shield? What would they ignore? At some point, with her face hidden from view, people would redirect to something else – her body or her voice or someone else entirely. Things were simpler outside of scrutiny, especially when you were made of magic.

But family didn't abide by those outlines. Aurelia had dragged in all her shitty flings and her slew of social inadequacies like an outdoor cat presenting its bloody night-time catch to the front porch. It was her father's job to see through them and Annette's job to talk sense into her. She couldn't make herself small enough for them to overlook.

He lifted the keys from the table, dropping them into a square dish alongside his. 'Did you go to her funeral?'

'What do you mean?' she asked. Her father used to say that she bore a striking resemblance to her mother, but she and Tony shared the same severe and undeniable look of disappointment; and she found his often whenever she tried to sneak small lies past him.

Tony cleared his throat. Once, Gabrielle said, he had been a constant cigarette smoker, only weaning from it for Annette's sake when their mother was first pregnant. Though she'd never caught him with cigarettes, Aurelia would catch a hint of tobacco on his things or a cough that never bloomed into a cold, and she would wonder whether or not he'd kicked the habit – if it was stress that caused him to relapse.

In retrospect, all her teenage fibs seemed completely insignificant. 'I'm sorry,' said Aurelia. 'I knew you'd tell me not to.'

Her father shook his head, a grim, downward curve building in his features. With years behind her since her last visit home, she found the age in Tony Schwartz's features to be undeniable. His eyes were ringed with dark bags, his brown hair tinged with silver. Though he was smaller in stature, knobby and clean cut, Aurelia saw a clear resemblance to Townsend's resident caretaker that made her love them both a little more.

With her hands held close to her chest, Aurelia worried her nails until they were red and aching. 'I'm sorry,' she said again. 'I just thought . . . y'know, since we didn't know each other. I didn't know if I would have another chance to say goodbye.'

Tony gave her his arm, which she tucked herself into, laying her head onto her father's hard shoulder. She squeezed his stomach, closing her eyes tighter and tighter until it hurt. The more it hurt, she thought, the less it would linger tomorrow. At that point, she could shed some of her grief like a snakeskin, grow out of it and move on.

She had recited those same naive affirmations to herself last week when she had first tucked herself into her childhood bed before burying a year's worth of tears into a fresh pillowcase, and it never got easier. Annette, who had somehow steeled herself to the absence of their mother with age, assured her it would pass, that grief would fall from the forefront of her mind. Running her fingers through Aurelia's hair, she told her, with a misguided sense of optimism that Aurelia could only dream of possessing, 'Look at all we've done, Jeanie Bear. All by ourselves. We couldn't have done a better job.'

Time, which had shaped them both into different people, pushing them onto separate paths, would also shape them into something larger than grief eventually. Aurelia simply had to pass this part first.

'It's OK,' Tony said. 'Hey, look at me. You need some tea.'

'If I have another mug, I'm going to *explode*, Dad.'

'Just a cup for reading, then.' He brushed her hair back from her face, his eyes glistening and bloodshot. She couldn't remember the last time he'd done something so sweet, so simple. Or the last time he'd done anything even remotely adjacent to magic in her presence.

He was no diviner, but he put away enough servings of tea that he often joked that he'd become one with the medium. A green witch with enough determination could learn enough from the shapes at the bottom of his cup to rival the laziest diviner, couldn't he? She would roll her eyes as he squinted and scratched his head. 'This doesn't look like anything,' he'd say. 'Maybe . . . maybe a heart?'

She sipped the oolong until a shallow sheen of it remained. They sat together in the living room, hunched over the coffee table where an assortment of finished crossword and sudoku puzzle books had been shoved aside. The cup clinked against its saucer as Tony twirled it, drops leaking from the gaps in the rim.

Aurelia eyed her cuticles. Gabrielle's salve left them with a repulsive, bitter taste. 'Has it ever gotten easier for you – missing her?'

His eyes flickered past the cup to her. 'Easier to forget sometimes. Easier for other things to take priority. It's never truly easy, Pumpkin. I miss her every day.'

'Oh.'

Tony reoriented the cup. His mouth twitched with something else to admit, but it never came. Aurelia had lived so long without knowing that she wondered if she could carry on like that a little longer, if the empty space her mother had left would eventually get covered up like height marks on a door frame beneath a fresh layer of paint.

Her shoulders fell. So did his.

'Annie was probably still too young to remember this, but there was a period following her disappearance when I'd given up all hope. I barely ate. I lost my job. The house was filthy, and Gabrielle was always furious at me. But I had to be a father, even if I couldn't be a husband any more. That was hard. I didn't know how to have a family once I'd lost such a great piece of it.'

The leaves settled at the bottom of the cup. Neither of them moved to inspect it.

She tried to picture him hopeless. Twenty years younger with all the age he had now. All her life, Tony had put up a strong front for them, with open arms and care that was never too heavy-handed. Always there in the periphery of his daughters' lives, waiting for them to say they were hungry so he could make dinner or for one of them to ask for help on schoolwork. When she was in Cambridge and Annie had moved out, he'd kept his distance out of what she had only ever assumed was exhaustion; almost thirty years of fatherhood warranted a moment of quietude. He'd busied himself inside the house with his puzzle books and drew himself out of it whenever Annie invited him to forage in the mornings. Never in her passing curiosity had Aurelia thought he was avoiding something, that he had been stretched out like a rubber band from the centre point of Meredith Albert and that their absence had caused him to snap right back.

She smothered the amassing guilt in her gut. Still, she wondered . . . 'Did you ever think it was my fault?'

Tony paused. 'I entertained the idea very briefly just before you turned one. I knew it was unfair. In my mind, *someone* needed to shoulder the blame for it, and her disappearance seemed like something that had happened *to* her rather than something she'd elected to do on her own; because, why would she? I couldn't fathom that. The thought didn't last more than a few days. You were a very good baby. Big eyes, full of sweetness. And you loved me very much. It's hard to be mad at something so small. Something that needs you. We were all suffering her loss together, but I could pick myself up, whereas you and Annie couldn't.'

Aurelia's fingers twitched instinctively toward the cup. Her hands were unoccupied, nails too bitter from Gabrielle's salve to chew. She could force herself to stomach another cup of tea if needed.

Tony adjusted the unbuttoned cuffs of his sleeves up his forearms. 'Let's see what the leaves have for us today. Something cheerful, I hope.'

Aurelia deadpanned, '*A great fortune will find you.*'

'Mm,' Tony murmured, 'or *a promising weather forecast grants you a safe journey home.*'

'Think big, Dad.'

'That *is* big,' he said. 'For me. I hate flying. Hate the little seats. I need room to stretch my legs.' Tony turned the cup in his hands, fitting his middle finger through the carved, dainty handle. Painted roses adorned the petaled lip, faded from years of infrequent use. Aurelia watched him patiently as if the next intrusion could be the one that reminded him of his general aversion to magic.

His brows furrowed at the puzzle before him, which was a litany of amorphous streaks and hills whose meanings would carry infinite potential in a diviner's hand but meant nothing to him. 'I believe . . . This is a pen. Or maybe an arrow.' He turned the cup toward her for a second opinion. Two non-diviners with as much expertise as the other.

'A snake?' offered Aurelia.

'I see it,' Tony said. The book beside him was not his grimoire; Aurelia couldn't remember the last time she saw her father stowing his life's magical practice into a box beneath his bed like illicit paraphernalia. If she asked now, would he show her? As he flipped through a cheap, hand-held spiral notebook for his notes, she decided not to push her luck.

She was rather enjoying the simplicity of the affair.

'Ah,' Tony said. 'Snakes spell bad omens. Or so the book tells me.'

'Figures.'

'I'm sure there are other readings of snakes that aren't as grim.'

Aurelia shook her head, pulling her arms around her body. Her thumb stroked mindlessly up and down her bicep, and it wasn't until she remembered the way Ingram had touched the tattoo just above it – the way his gaze kissed her skin – that she brought herself back to the tea leaves and the possibility of bad omens. Tony studied the other shapes, but they proved even less conclusive. He relinquished the cup to its saucer.

'Good thing I'm not a diviner then.' Tony offered her a smile.

She returned it thinly. 'Was probably an arrow anyway.'

CHAPTER THIRTY-NINE

Someone had pulled a cover over the skylight in the library. Teddy didn't ask who it was or *what* it was, but the darkness was palpable, and nothing within the walls could drive it away. He sat hunched over his knees on the couch where the Townsend Hill caretaker had washed his blood and tucked a pillow beneath his head after his collapse. He willed his knee to stop shaking, without success. At every creak, every incremental shift in the arrangement of floating dust, Teddy hoped Alaric would appear around a bookcase, etched with lines in a way only the living were capable of.

He never came.

Hye-Jin instructed him to sit while she retrieved something upstairs. As if stillness calmed him. As if this could possibly be easier than keeping himself busy. More likely, she was saving him from stumbling across a volatile spell while his mind was preoccupied. Alaric once told him that certain books in his collection were warded with spells of their own, and that Teddy should feel a warning before the spell laid waste to anything; but Teddy wasn't thinking straight. Perhaps Hye-Jin thought he might go looking for danger, or at least turning a blind eye to it.

She lumbered down the staircase, uneasy on her feet. She'd

been torn between her own collection and Alaric for the days following his death, split between time zones so that the other caretakers didn't encroach on the vacancy. She was drowning in fatigue. It pooled from her robe with every heavy step. Teddy measured her footsteps like the drip of a leaky tap.

'This place doesn't give up its secrets easily,' she remarked. Teddy rose from the couch to meet her, but she sent him back with a blunt, pointed finger. 'If I remember correctly, the will itself is rather short. He only had one person on it and few things to pass down.'

Teddy clasped his hands together on his knees, squeezing until the knuckles turned white. 'What about Gem? Or Lou?'

Hye-Jin sat across from him, pressing a leather folder flat on the table between them. 'It was my understanding that he wanted you to accept full responsibility over his estate. You're welcome to do with it as you please, whether you keep it all or break it up. He knows you'll think of them. I'm not sure he expected Gemma to return, anyway.'

'So, he was expecting this.'

'Everyone, at a certain age, should have a will,' Hye-Jin said. 'But there was a sense of urgency to its creation. This is quite different from what you'd see in a legal document. Easy to rewrite at a moment's notice but made binding through quick enchantments. He rewrote it just after Gemma's disappearance. Yes, the fourteenth of January. Says here. It's possible the last version left something to her.'

Teddy urged her on with a jerk of his chin.

Hye-Jin cleared her throat. '"My possessions, all but one, are hereby entrusted to Theodore Ingram. The shopfront property and all its revenue are hereby entrusted to Theodore Ingram."' The caretaker of Namwon prattled off a list of Alaric Friedman's possessions, each ending in the boy's name. It never sounded so much like a weapon until then, and it *had* before. Spoken by his mother, a rope. By Gemma, a branding iron. In Alaric's hand – the illegible scrawl of black ink – it was a knife twisting. 'My collection – its care and its keeping – are hereby entrusted to one *Theodore. Ingram.*'

He should have known it was coming. Or perhaps, Teddy was simply dreading it. 'He told me nothing about what the role entailed. He was so adamant about it too.'

Hye-Jin did not continue immediately. 'He was planning to eventually. I think we all had got too comfortable with the silence, and then the urgency . . . Well, I assumed he had more time. We all did.'

He thought back to what Schwartz said, though it'd been pulled from a chorus of choked sobs as she lay over his body. *You should have told me.* He had known. Alaric must have learned his prophecy from Gemma. Gemma, whose divination was non-specific at the worst of times, who bore a scar to back it up.

What did she tell him? Maybe that he would die on foreign soil, or beneath a twilit sky. Maybe, even more upsetting, that he would die by the hands of people he loved, or somewhere far away from her.

'You don't have to decide now,' Hye-Jin assured him, inching over the tabletop. 'But the rest – his assets – are yours. You have the bookshop, the cottage, the library, although much of the collection will need to be reshelved with a different caretaker should you not accept the council seat. Otherwise, do what you please with it.'

'What are you doing with the body?'

Hye-Jin sighed. 'Caretakers are burned in private rituals. As his replacement, you're allowed to attend, but the others—'

'They can't come?'

'I'll see if I can get them to bend. It's not very common for us to have families. They might make an exception if I ask nicely.'

He couldn't tell if this was Hye-Jin's attempt at humour; she didn't smile, though she wasn't insincere either. Teddy kneaded his brows. 'You said he gave all his possessions "but one"?'

Hye-Jin's lips pursed into a tight knot. 'His dog, Neil. Left to Carmichael Sum "to fend off isolation". A late addition to the will. Since it was added to the will after the enchantment, you're more than welcome to dispute it.'

'That's all right.'

'He loved you, you know?'

Teddy stared dumbfoundedly across the table until the words sunk in.

'What?'

'Alaric,' Hye-Jin said, as if that was the piece from which Teddy drew his confusion. 'He thought so highly of you. I can't say I understood it in the beginning. I chalked it up to his habit of adopting strays. But I see that goodness in you. You are grave, but you're good too, just like him. Not all caretakers appoint someone when they leave; not all of them can think of a person they trust enough to give that to. And he loved you very much.'

'Ah.'

From beneath the handwritten will, Hye-Jin slipped a kraft paper envelope bearing Teddy Ingram's name. Another with Gemma Eakley's.

'If you could give this to her . . .' Hye-Jin placed them both on the table in front of his knees. Teddy traced the thin lines of his name, barely visible against the brown grain. His pulse skipped. His lungs capsized in his ribs.

He'd been doing so well. Kept it in so beautifully. Everything rushed forward, the high tide of his emotion came to drown him at last.

'Is that it?' He stalled at the first word, but if Hye-Jin noticed it, she didn't say anything.

'That's everything. Consider the role, will you?'

Everything was too bright, he thought, locking the shop door behind him. Too fucking bright. Gemma cut herself short from a reply to a solemn Martin, their neighbour at the bottom of the hill, as Teddy stepped into the glaring sunlight. She bade the man a stunted goodbye.

Teddy was holding himself together by the loosest of knots, and her sudden attention hit him like an anvil.

She looped her arm through his, leading him towards the hill. 'How was it?'

Tight-lipped, he replied, 'Fine.'

'And Hye-Jin? Is she faring well?'

'As expected.'

Gemma made a quiet hum of disapproval, pressing him with silence he deigned not to fill. Her breaths cut shorter as she ascended the hill, the ache in her side permeating the tether. Teddy slowed and muttered, 'Gem,' but she gave him back his non-response. More urgently, '*Gem.*'

'It's this damn house,' she whispered. 'You remade the wards, and they're stronger now.' Without his arm, she tucked her hands in the mismatched denim pockets of her dress and stalked upwards in a huff.

'Ribs bothering you?' he asked.

'There's plenty bothering me at the moment. Come on, darling. Quickly.'

He discovered an equally daunting sensation on the other side of the wards. He wished he'd found, at least, the smallest give in the pressure bearing down on him once the wards were called off his back, but he wasn't so lucky. He returned to an eerily vacant house, and the ghosts that had always been so eager to swarm him were nowhere to be seen.

Now, you disappear. Right when I need you.

'Looks like she's boiled some more water,' Gemma noted, brushing past him into the kitchen. Louisa was with Martin's son at the bottom of the hill, but the house was still aflutter with the heartbeats of witches; quieter beneath the floorboards were Aurelia Schwartz's and her father, who had dragged himself through a portal of Hye-Jin's fashioning when he'd heard the news. He was a hair too similar to the late Townsend caretaker, despite being a head too small, for Teddy to spend more than a few minutes in the same room with him.

Gemma didn't seem to consider the resemblance. She left Tony and his daughter to their own devices in the basement, stopping in only to announce when she'd cut up some fruit or brewed a fresh pot of tea. Their hushed conversation crept through the floors, all hums and long pauses. Teddy traced the handle of the teacup Gemma set before him and poised himself to receive a pull from Schwartz through the tether. Nothing.

'So,' Teddy began gently, 'when did you know?'

Gemma scooped his teacup away, her gaze fixed on the steady pour. 'Know what, darling?'

'That Alaric was going to die?'

'Always,' she said. 'Everyone does, in the end.'

His tongue clicked against his teeth. 'That's it then? You're going to act like you didn't know?'

'I didn't. Not how you think. It's been years since he asked. Maybe decades. He's always been very severe . . . very intense,' she remarked wistfully. 'We were . . . how old? He went grey so early, it's hard to say. And with all that hair dye—'

'Gemma.'

'He asked me one night while he was feeling rather existential, if I would tell him how he died – if I knew. I told him he didn't really want to know. No one does. The feeling passes, and people wise up. I should have let it pass, but he was captivating. And saying no to him made me very sad. I didn't *really* know, though, darling. I knew magic would kill him, but I didn't know when. I knew he would die shrouded in gold, which pleased him, because he considered himself just and valiant; and I knew that a piece of him would be missing, which he thought was too abstract. But that's the thing about divination: so much of it is making the right interpretation of an abstraction. If I don't have the right pieces, or enough pieces, I could send someone chasing the wrong future, looking for the wrong outcomes.'

She covered her mouth abruptly, leaning back against the sink. Her chest heaved with a silent sob. 'You know why I had Kenny buried instead of burned?' she asked.

Teddy had thought nothing of it. It wasn't until he stood on the hillside with Schwartz last winter, with his hands in her hair and a spell on her tongue, that he discovered witch burning was the *normal* practice.

'A *phoenix* came to me. In a dream. You can assume—' Gemma hiccupped on the word. 'You were always so determined. I knew you would find a way to breach the veil and cheat death. Still, I didn't know when, but I . . . It's too late now, but I couldn't have known that then. Every day that passed, I lost hope that I would ever get my boy back. You see how divination can be very unfair sometimes, yes? I see everything in such quick succession; it's hard to tell how much time will pass and how much we'll lose by waiting.'

She lifted her wrist to her forehead. Then, also in quick succession, she retrieved a spoon and began to stir hurried little circles in their teacups. 'You like the oolong, don't you?'

His limbs were heavy, his chest hollow. He didn't want to tell her how bitter the oolong was, and he didn't feel like lying, so he gave a small, compliant nod. Gemma's eyes met his for the briefest moment as she set the cup in front of him, the first time all day. Possibly the first time since Alaric passed and Teddy returned home with only the watch in his hand.

Home.

It felt emptier without the caretaker nearby. Leaving was but one by-product of being present, and Alaric's presence had been faulty for a while. Why, then, did Teddy feel as if the caretaker took so much life, so much heart, from the cottage at the top of the hill – a place he barely went, a place he had long since forgotten how to love?

Teddy wanted to cry, but he'd been wrung for all his feelings. He watched Gemma pour into the mugs that Schwartz had chosen for herself and her father, the tea rising slowly as his lungs filled with breath.

He should have thanked Gemma for the tea. He downed it in front of her, the heat welling in his mouth until it burned. He drank and he drank until Gemma's shoulders collapsed in a sigh of relief, believing she'd soothed him in some small way.

God, it was bitter oolong.

His arrival prompted a lull in the steady murmur of Schwartz's conversation. Tony managed a smile in Teddy's direction, taking his cup with both hands. 'Thank you.'

Schwartz took hers with one and curled the other around his wrist.

Unlike Gemma, she had no problem with looking him in the eye. He almost wished she did; her eyes were large, reddened and raw. Her gaze chased him deep inside himself, because he couldn't meet her in the middle now. 'You can stay,' she whispered.

'Gemma's been wonderful,' Tony said as the boy settled in beside Schwartz. 'This place . . . It's beautiful here. I've never actually left the United States before.'

'It's quiet here,' was all Teddy said.

'This place is truly something else.'

Teddy nodded.

'Thank you for having me. For the portal. I'm sorry for everything else.'

Teddy considered the man thoroughly, taking in all the resemblance until he could no longer bear it. He wished there was none. He wished there was more. He wished, more than anything in the world, that Alaric Friedman was still alive and keeping his secrets. If he could take it all back, he would never bother him for answers again.

Schwartz laced her fingers through his, binding him to the moment, to the place they'd made their oath and she'd given him her faith. He forced a mild-mannered smile towards her father.

'I'm sorry too.'

CHAPTER FORTY

Carmichael handed Teddy his drink just as the barista at Petro's started to usher them out of the building. The day had passed quickly. Another twenty-four hours lost, spent wasting away in his mind. Schwartz and her father were going to Cambridge tomorrow, and Teddy knew he should go with them, if only to grab his car but also to start reconfiguring the pieces of his old life back together.

But with Hye-Jin's offer . . .

He didn't want to think about it. Luckily, Carmichael was riddled with his own dilemmas, so the conversation was brief. They paused outside the shop – Teddy, Carmichael, and Neil, toted along by a faded red lead. Teddy dug the keys out of his pocket, but they hovered unused in his hand.

Night encroached on the town, and in the upper-floor window, Alaric's bedroom light was still on.

Carmichael leaned back against the wall, his ankles crossed on the cobblestones. 'If there's anything remotely positive about what's happened, it's that I don't have to tell Alaric our idea didn't make it to a wider trial. The council doesn't see enough promise in it. That's what we were working on, you know. A solution for the population decline.'

'And it didn't work?'

The coffee was bitter, but the mocha syrup redeemed it somewhat. Teddy folded his arms over himself as he sipped, sidling up to Carmichael by the window. The glass at his back was still warm, though the temperature had dropped substantially. A stark comparison to the cold skin and clammy palms he'd been all too aware of for the past several days.

'It did. Mostly. It's a promising idea, and there's an uptick in interest from other council seats, but we're resting at a 74 per cent success rate right now. It's not enough for the council as a whole to approve wider testing. You can imagine how difficult it might be to rally up enough witches for that sort of thing in the first place.'

'What about the other 26 per cent?'

Carmichael sighed. 'There have been no adverse effects to the antibody injection, which is why the decision frustrates me. That remaining 26 per cent comes from total non-response from the body. Alaric had figured out that my blood, as a born shapeshifter, had a changeable property that could benefit witches with a wide variety of gifts. The properties of magic that exist within the blood are fragile and easily overcome by the influence of non-magical people. It's near impossible to create a medication that can protect every witch, but no one has been *harmed* from it either. The injection goes in to shield the magical properties of the blood from further decay or affecting viruses. And if it fails, well, nothing happens. The witches carry on unchanged, for the better and for the worse. But it's a substantial number, so the council is erring on the side of caution. I can't blame them.'

Teddy drank again and studied the mauve imprint of

Schwartz's mouth on the rim of the cup, wondering what she was drinking up at the cottage. Certainly, something less bitter than this. Less bitter than Gemma's favourite oolong.

'Be honest with me, Carmichael,' Teddy said. 'How much time do you think we have? Are we in as deep as Alaric seemed to think we were?'

'Depends on what kind of world you want to leave when you're no longer here to tend to it,' Carmichael answered. 'You and I will make it to old age. We keep our magic until we die. But after that . . . Think of Louisa. Has she met another witch her age?'

'She hasn't met much of anyone.'

'It's a miracle you found not one, but *two* other witches you'd consider swearing a vow with. That Gemma cares for you as much as she does, all things considering. Most of us don't have that kind of community. The isolation drives us to dangerous measures; when it's you against what seems like the entire world, you fight with all your power. It's how witches like Leona start spiralling into their desperation. She could have dragged me down with her if I were any less grounded.'

For the first time, Teddy felt a pang of sympathy for the witch who'd tried to kill them. It vanished quickly, but the existence of it, no matter how slight, led him to say, 'I'm sorry for what happened to her. For all of it.'

Carmichael sniffed, turning his face away. 'You're lucky, Theodore. Really lucky.'

'I know.'

'And you're a good kid. I don't want you to give up on them.'

Teddy felt his spine stiffen against the glass defensively.

'I've never once given up on them. It's possibly the only thing that gives me any sense of purpose any more.'

'Caring for them?'

Teddy sipped his bitter coffee again, humming in agreement.

'And who cares for you?'

That was hardly a reasonable question, Teddy thought. The consideration of which made his stomach turn with longing. He sensed in a way that he had never sensed before that there was one less person in the world who'd do that for him.

Carmichael returned the careful brush of shoulder against shoulder, tightening his fist around Neil's lead. 'I know there's . . . Well, I'm sensitive to all the animosity between us. I'm not sure if I can truly rectify all the wrongs Leona did before she died, but I'm hopeful I can rectify this one. Setting aside a potential work partnership, I rather enjoy having company.'

'*My* company?' Teddy asked, entertaining the thought as much as an impossible dream.

'It's not the most ideal of circumstances to bond over, but it might be easier to weather with a friend. Whatever you decide you want with the council, you know where to find me. I offered to help Hye-Jin with further trials, but it was Alaric who kept me around.'

Before Teddy could claim otherwise, Carmichael pulled a trifold wallet from his jeans pocket, and from the frontmost position, a shred of lined paper denoting his address and mobile number. Teddy took in every step, the twitch in Carmichael Sum's fingers as he pressed his notes back into place, the bob of the man's Adam's apple. The offer had raised his heart rate, placed the smallest of creases between his dark brows. 'You're not alone in this. Remember that.'

The echo of Carmichael's words was unshakeable. Teddy couldn't forget them even if he tried.

Hye-Jin left the first wandering eye in the top drawer of the shop desk. He couldn't remember if they'd discussed it or not, but when he spun it on the axis of his spell, all he saw was a pile of unfolded laundry in Gemma's room. He closed his hand around it, tucking it against the wood.

He nearly forgot it was a stolen artefact. It made no difference; Teddy wasn't planning to return it.

The shop did not speak for him as it usually did with its wooden croaks and eerie shudders. No longer did it look like a gateway to glory, or a disguise for more magical things. It was simply a dingy, washed-out shop on the corner of a tilting building in a town that was as good as *nowhere*.

The door handle wiggled, and before Teddy could grumble a response, Schwartz called out, 'I know you're in there. It's just me.'

The bell above the door rang softly, or so he thought. The shop ate everything, including the sound, and left only the clutter in its wake.

Teddy turned the lock again behind her. 'How's Tony doing?'

Schwartz idled by the door, rocking back onto her heels with her back to the glass panes. 'A bit out of his comfort zone in a house full of witches. I think I might have underestimated how much he acclimated to magic-avoidance since I left.'

'So, he doesn't like it.'

'No, he *loves* it,' Schwartz said. 'It's kind of endearing. He finds everything that Gemma does wildly fascinating. He also adores Lou. Keeps asking me if I remember being that old, telling me about things that Annie and I used to do when we were young.'

'She's easy to love.'

'He misses me a lot.'

'Well, you're easy to miss,' Teddy said. The usual tension in her brow had all but vanished – crying tended to wear one down to their barest face. Teddy had done plenty of it in his own time, but her eyes were still coated in a sheen of it that captured the white of the moon above them like starlight.

Schwartz closed the cardigan around her body, sealing herself off with the considerate tuck of her hand. Gently, as if it were possible to break him any more with the mere suggestion, she added, 'He wants me to come home for a little while.'

'How long?'

'I haven't decided. I figured I should talk to Ryan about it first, considering we split rent. Dad offered to take care of it, of course, but I don't want to ask him to do that for me.'

Teddy nodded, bracing himself against the front desk. He had a number of places to stay now, but the one place he truly wanted to be was with Schwartz. The library held too much of Alaric's essence, and the shop was too desolate to hold him while he was neck-deep in mourning. While his things still littered the spare room at the cottage, the feeling crowded him and made it impossible to breathe.

Gemma didn't seem to mind the absence he'd been taking. If he was there to suffer from her suffering too, she added to it by taking on blame, which did no good for anyone.

Such a fall from grace he'd seen since Schwartz had drawn him into her house. Did the offer still stand? It didn't feel right to let himself in while she was gone, and just as wrong to curl up in her doorway until she returned.

He nodded to himself for no reason other than to fill the space. 'It might be good for you. Get as much space as you can from this place for the time being.'

She leaned against the desk beside him, her grin askance and hidden by the low light. 'You're just saying that to even the academic playing field. Next you'll be telling me to stretch it out into a year. Then two.'

'Somehow, you're *still* thinking about your studies?' Teddy broke into a smile. 'Your dedication is a force to be reckoned with. I truly never had a chance.'

He took her hand – or perhaps, she took his. It was possible that they'd been linked to one another longer than that, but he couldn't remember. His thumb slid through the grooves of her knuckles one by one.

'Will you be there when I come back?' Her eyes were full and wide, her expression bared so unabashedly that Teddy couldn't help succumbing to it. How could anyone be so sure of themselves – so unafraid? If she could make him anything, she could make him brave.

'I will, if you'd like.'

'There were other letters, you know. I kept all the drafts in my desk drawer on the off-chance that you wrote me back. I spent a lot of time thinking about what to say. If you wanted to sift through them, I'd never know.'

She laid her temple against his shoulder. More deliberately, Teddy repeated, 'I can, if you'd like.'

'Do you think you'll keep running the shop now that he's gone?'

'I don't know. I'm definitely not selling it. He left me a multitude of decisions to iron out, and it's the last thing I want to do right now.'

'The light's on upstairs,' she noted.

A knot formed in Teddy's throat. 'He always kept it on. I don't know how he ever got any sleep.'

She scanned the shop indiscreetly, no doubt looking for Alaric, or a page of plausible deniability that he wasn't coming back. Her eyes flickered to dark corners, to faded spines. The most improbable of places. Although, Teddy thought, if you wanted to hide something, the shop was the most effective place to do it. Had he not been there to say goodbye, Teddy would've torn apart every shelf and turned over every floorboard to find the caretaker, convinced he'd stowed himself away like a photograph, eternally questioning, *Where is he? Where is he?*

'Were you looking for something here?' Schwartz asked.

Teddy didn't really know why he'd come to the shop except to think. He knew Alaric wasn't here, nor would he be just a few steps beyond the veil in Luxembourg.

Objectively, he knew.

But Townsend gave its ghosts the room to grow. Alaric's

spaces possessed as much of a soul as he did, and Teddy had a responsibility to nurture it, lest it mourn itself into dust.

'I could use a drink,' he told her.

'I think there's a parable out there about drinking a dead man's liquor.'

'You'd think,' said Teddy. 'I don't know if he kept anything here. The last time we had any, he fetched it from his room in the library.'

It went without saying that he couldn't stand the sight of the library just yet. Even with Schwartz at his side, he wouldn't dare to venture across the veil for more than what Hye-Jin or Bastian deemed business. Beneath their concern, they were still short a councillor. No matter how gently they prodded, the urgency struck him like a thorn in his side.

Upstairs, in the room where Alaric's light was still on, something heavy clinked onto the floor.

Their heads lifted to the ceiling. Schwartz took a silent, cautious step towards him. 'I thought you said—'

He lifted his finger to his lips. 'Wait here.'

Each step up to the attic he took slowly, holding his breath. He didn't know if the other caretakers had access to the bookshop, but Hye-Jin was always courteous enough to spawn in the basement.

Teddy pushed the bedroom door open and then stepped back as if he were merely a breeze.

A bottle rolled forward from an opened cabinet. He checked the other side of the door, the underside of the bed, where all he found were closed boxes and stacks of records.

Finding nothing else of interest in the room, Teddy halted

the bottle with his foot. A handwritten, crookedly pasted label curled upwards at the edges. Alaric had tied a narrow strip of paper around the neck, which, while turning the bottle over in his hand, Teddy discovered was a letter.

You bastard, he thought. *Never could say things to me in a more convenient way.*

He wiggled the cork free and brought it to his nose, confirming his suspicion. The absinthe scent made his eyes well again. 'Everything's fine up here.'

She held her breath, tightening Teddy's chest.

Teddy wiped his eyes before he returned to her. He unfurled the strip of paper from the rim of the bottle, granting it the barest pass before he pressed it between the flat of his palm and the curve of the bottle.

Don't drink too fast. Or alone. The kingdom is yours now.

'What was it?' she asked.

With a half-hearted brandish of the bottle, he replied, 'A parting gift.'

The first sip went down hard. The bottle sat between them where they both lay on the floor of the basement. Teddy flipped Alaric's copy of *Aladdin Sane* above his chest, watching the bolt on Bowie's face reappear over and over again. They were listening to something else – an unfamiliar record Schwartz had chosen from Alaric's disorganized stack – already through half the bottle, despite the putrid potency of it.

The room blurred at the edges. Teddy felt nothing but his

own body, and it was marvellous not to have to balance drunkenness and his empathetic magic. Schwartz did not say much as her dose of witch liquor took. She traced the speckles on the ceiling blankly, picking out shapes as if they were clouds, tea leaves, a loved one's freckles . . .

If Teddy looked up there too long, he'd start searching for answers. *Why did you take him from me? Why did he have to know?* What would the blank space give him? Nothing. Those were answers meant for diviners, written in black pools and on birds' tongues. If there were answers in the cracks, he couldn't understand them.

'What should I do, Schwartz?'

'Tonight?'

'Forever,' he said, losing the end of the word to his dry, hot tongue. 'What if it's always like this?'

Schwartz shuffled closer until their shoulders touched. 'It won't be. Even if this never gets easier, there's so much that *will*.'

'I want to believe you,' he said.

'You should. I'm right. And honest. Two things you used to hold against me so often.'

He'd been a fool for it back then. Saying the wrong things to her, burying himself deeper and deeper inside of a problem, until he was too far from the one thing that could save them.

Even now, he was searching for answers in all the wrong places. In layman's divination, in ceiling speckling. Teddy pushed himself up and took another large swig from the bottle before moving it to his side. Her gaze followed him astutely, and her fingers trailed up his wrist from where she lay.

'Do you think you're going to take the job?'

He nodded. 'He wanted me to have it. All things considered, I think I could be good at it.'

'And you could let me use the library.'

'Mhmm.'

He swallowed painfully. What he didn't tell her was how quickly Hye-Jin and Bastian expected an answer from him. He'd been waiting to break the news to her. It mattered a great deal to him what she made of the offer, and he'd been expecting a weightier response.

Maybe, this was better. Easier. She didn't try to dissuade him, though he knew she *would*, had she any reservations. He was grateful for the brevity. His heart couldn't handle any more blows.

'You know what Hye-Jin told me the other day, when she asked about a decision?' he asked. 'Half the things Alaric kept from me were unimportant. At any point, he could have let me in on what he was doing. He could have shown me how to navigate before he left me to fend for myself, but he kept me in the dark on everything. I want to be angry with him, but then I think about Lou, and I get why he did it. There's so much I don't want to tell her, things about Kenny and her mother and this bloody town; and I prayed I wouldn't have to be the one to do it, hoping to God that I could just weather it all for her instead. If I could absorb it all, then she wouldn't have to. I'd do it in a heartbeat.

'But I shouldn't,' he continued. 'I see that now. It's not fair to her to keep things like that to myself. I want her to be strong and unafraid and independent. I want her to love what she is and *who* she is, and embrace her magic before it's too late. I went about it the way that Alaric taught me, withholding the details and keeping her distracted. I figured, since it was better than Gem's way, it was the *best* way; but sometimes, the best you can do still isn't enough. Lou deserves to be happy – exactly as she is. Not human, not as a tempered-down version of herself, but as a witch. In spite of everything, I know Alaric did the best he could to keep us safe. I can do better now. I want her to know what a beautiful thing magic can be. It's . . . God, it's everything. I'm babbling, aren't I?' Teddy took in a restorative breath, his cheeks flooding with heat. 'Maybe this is my limit for witch liquor.'

Schwartz reached for the bottle over his body, stuffing the cork in it. 'I like it when you babble . . . Or when you talk so much that you get breathless. I like it when you don't think before you speak, because your sense of hope betrays you. *Downnn* goes that broody wall,' she sang.

Teddy laughed to himself. 'And to think, you wouldn't have liked me if I wasn't a witch. I would have missed out on all your secret, romantic notions.'

'*I'm* not the one writing poetry into all my notes,' she said, equally flushed. 'Not that I mind it. I'm becoming a sucker for romance. Y'know, Alaric told me something that night we made new wards around the cottage, about how you could only change so much before you killed the former version of yourself. Sometimes, I think you killed her.'

'I didn't mean to,' he whispered. 'I would have loved you as you were. As you *are*.' He tucked his hand beneath her jaw and drew their twisted figures flush against each other. She lifted her fingers to his face and trailed them down his lips. He wanted to tell her that he could take care of her too. That everything made sense when he looked at her, so he stopped looking for answers. He wanted to tell her that every spell he'd learned was to make her proud, and all his courage came from knowing she'd be waiting.

Except, he could wait a while longer, too. Teddy would tell her all of it when she'd returned from Washington, when they were no longer inebriated, and when he knew what to do with the shop. He would take some of his things to her flat, read her letters, and see what they still had left to say.

For now, he kissed her softly, slowly, waiting for the needle of the record player to reach the centre groove; and when he left to change the record for another, she wiped her mouth and said, 'This is really strong stuff.'

Thank God for it, too. It'd granted him an unquantifiable relief from what was possibly the worst pain Teddy had ever endured. He smiled to himself, sliding the record back into its sleeve. 'I think I'm a bit drunk,' he admitted.

'Genuinely?' Schwartz's eyebrows raised incrementally.

Teddy stretched out beside her again, enfolding her like a cocoon. He nodded into her hair and traded the lingering scent of liquor for her conditioner, humming his response for good measure. 'I don't have to pretend when I'm with you.'

EPILOGUE

The walls spit up a multitude of Alaric Friedman's treasures over time. In the beginning, Teddy finds folded slips of paper lying in corners he knows he's already dusted, and upon consideration, they bear the caretaker's words of encouragement – or sometimes, vague threats from beyond the grave.

> Please do a routine check of the books in the library to make sure everything is where it's supposed to be. Some of the books have a temper when placed too close to other books, and not all caretakers are as religious about sorting as I am after they're done.
>
> I only made enough of this witch liquor for a year, so don't overdo it. My recipe for it won't appear to you for months.
>
> If you sell any of my records, I'll know. I can't tell you how, but I'll know.

Then, presumably because he'd hidden those notes around the shop long before he thought to give his dog to Carmichael Sum:

Make sure to give my dog a few treats today. No more than four small ones, or two larger ones. Remember you can have a treat too.

The first makes him cry. The shop is closed. The till is empty, as usual. His mind is elsewhere, expertly dissociating itself from his grief, when the wad of paper tumbles out of the cash drawer like a weak spitball. Inconsolable, Teddy slides to his knees to make himself as small as possible. It's just the first of many reminders of Alaric Friedman he is faced with following his death, and it's the worst punishment imaginable.

He tells no one about it and falls asleep wrapped around his pillow in the room above the shop where the light is sometimes on and sometimes off now. There's no one waiting for him anywhere. Teddy's barely there himself.

But then, trinkets appear at the threshold between doors. Photographs between closed books. A bracelet with spikes on the basement step. On rare occasions where he lacks the energy to erect the library entrance and cross through the veil, he makes for the bedroom, removes his belt and his shoes, and then he turns them over in the morning to see if the walls of the room have regurgitated something into them while he slept.

Alaric's gifts come infrequently, unexpectedly, and rarely from the same place twice. Teddy found a marble in his shoe once, but now, if he's lucky enough to catch it, he'll shake a spider out before it gets too comfortable where his toes should be.

His lips tilt upwards at the corners as he collects a giraffe figurine from the library shelf holding DaVinci's prophecies. A recipe for witch liquor unfurls behind the mirror once he drains the first bottle.

A year later, Teddy will laugh at them like he's bantering with the postman, and the truth will feel less like a heavy stone rattling in his stomach. He'll wonder if Alaric knew Teddy would hate him for it at first. That he would only think of Alaric stowing his treasures away, counting down the days until his untimely death. How miserable it must have been to face death head on, knowing he could not conquer him.

Teddy doesn't spend much time at the shop, except for with Lou; Gemma runs it as an exercise in modern conversational skills, reacquainting herself with humanity at the bottom of her warded hill. Most of his conversations take place in the library with Hye-Jin or one of the other council members, at whatever hour makes the most sense for all parties to be awake simultaneously. He loses track of the time. Some of their words escape the lexicon of his brain, but he's doing better with time. Retaining more of their council-speak and translating more of their intentions. Bastian helps him enchant a door in the upstairs hallway of the library to lead to Schwartz's Cambridge house where he sleeps most of the time. Bastian takes to Teddy Ingram far easier than he took to Alaric Friedman, and in turn, Teddy responds by being a purposeful nuisance to him.

He's not sure if the walls are capable of passive aggression, but he wouldn't put it past them, especially if they're a product of Alaric's petty magic.

Schwartz is usually still awake when he comes home, either working on a paper at her desk or wringing her hair dry from an evening shower. Teddy steps through the door leading to

Cambridge, shuts it behind him, and remarks how cluttered the room is, though half the clothing on the ground is his. Her stomach growls as a result of her forgetfulness, so he slogs to the kitchen and fashions a quick fix. Eggs and buttered toast with whatever fruit they have ready to cut into; Teddy saves new recipes for when he has uninterrupted evenings in Cambridge, when Ryan is awake to share their unfiltered opinion on the level of seasoning. Schwartz usually protests when he replaces the emptied mug on her desk with a plate of food, but she picks through it all minute by minute. 'You don't have to do that,' she says with a fond exasperation.

His fingers lace through her hair, tipping her head back against his stomach. 'You should have eaten, then.'

She smiles often and brightly. It's gotten easier to digest and doesn't leave him wondering if she's laid a trap out in front of him to fall into. She smiles at him over Ryan Jena's head while the artist immortalises him in the bright glow of the television. It curves into the dip between his shoulder blades as he nudges a stir-fry around a blackened pan when everyone else in Cambridge is asleep. It endures all the tedium of domesticity. He places the hundredth mug of tea on her desk, and she tries to hide it, tracing the string of the teabag around the loop of the handle like it's a ribbon-wrapped gift.

It's his favourite thing – Aurelia Schwartz's smile. Beautiful and abundant and utterly ruinous. He's used to it now, but it's just as lovely as it was in their rare beginnings. There's wonder in the curve of her lips, endless potential. He wants to spend the rest of his life finding a perfect translation for each one. An impossible task that keeps him busy when he's bored in the shop.

But some things, Teddy knows, he will never get used to. Gemma's cottage never feels quite as full, like a belly that's always craving one more bite. There's a vacancy that can only be filled by Alaric Friedman, right next to the one housing Kenny Eakley's memory. The walls make room for others: for Aurelia, Tony, and eventually Ryan Jena when Gemma relents and tears down the wards and erects new ones. They are forgiving wards that leave Ryan's mind unperturbed by morbid fascinations.

Teddy will never get used to the shop's silence. Each time he opens up, he expects to hear Alaric's muffled voice in the basement or through the veil. At the worst of times, he imagines the clink of Neil's collar and lead jingling in the old caretaker's hands.

One day he won't be able to make that jump down. And at some point, neither will I.

Grief is a great devourer. It laves everything in its path, every inconsequential facet of life until nothing can be divorced from it. It's eaten the shop, the library, the cottage, every single door that Teddy passes through. It eats the spare flesh beneath his cheekbones and under his sternum, but it's gracious enough to give it back later on. It fixes him in a never-ending battle.

It is also proven to relent.

He'll never get used to the way Lou lights up when they're all together, how her laughter solidifies into the warmest hugs Teddy will ever receive. He'll never get used to the glint of silver around Schwartz's ring finger. It catches in the sunlight while they're laid out underneath the white sun with a book to shield their eyes. A recent instalment. Another gift from the shop, offered up by the tap of the bathroom one evening.

He'll never understand why she agreed to it, until he remembers that she didn't *really* agree to it. Not aloud. Teddy pocketed the ring at first, repocketing it into every pair of trousers he wore from the point of its appearance, until he mustered up the courage to ask; except it wasn't really a question at all. It was a declaration with the moon at his back, the grass tickling his knees, when they were both groggy and stuffed full of Gemma's best stew. They were talking about the future which, prior to that, had always seemed like an impossibly distant concept, one they could never reach. One where witches like Leona Sum and Julia Chaplain were not driven to desperate measures and made to fear the imminent demise of the witch race. One where Gemma was less afraid to visit the flat in Cambridge, and their nightmares were assuredly nothing more than nightmares.

It's daunting. Teddy doesn't know if it will ever happen, but he wants it more than ever when he's looking at Schwartz.

He kissed her beyond the wards, and the grass lurched towards them with an unseen magnetic force. He told her all of this. She laughed, because he was always so intense, but his intensity was a feature she loved about him. One that Teddy, underneath all his frustration, loved about Alaric Friedman. Teddy showed her the ring. She stared dumbfoundedly for what felt like forever, let him slide it on her finger, and clasped his hand. And since there was no question, she gave no answer except a bleary-eyed, 'After I get my PhD, OK?'

He nodded. She kissed him. Again and again and again. They kissed until she could hardly breathe and he felt like he could die. Her mouth was swollen and red, and his face was smeared with the mauve of her favourite lipstick.

She tastes like honeydew. Like summer and rich tea. Kissing her is all he wants, and somehow it's still never enough.

He learns that grief is only a devourer because love was hungry before him; and before love, it's *hope*, bright and promising, rife with the possibility of love to be made. Hope is the headiest knot on the string of fate, one that Teddy has only ever known one person to cut. It's the moment just before he shows Aurelia Schwartz the ring, where the future is still only hypothetical. It's the hesitation just before Alaric wraps his arms around him in the threshold of the Cambridge flat. It's a beautiful, magnificent and harrowing uncertainty.

Love is the litany of things in-between, from the cups that litter Schwartz's desk to the scratch of Lou's pencil in the margins of his loaned books. It touches everything, leaves the colour of the world a little rosier. He feels it in the softness of the ground when he joins Gemma for dinner, the flush in Schwartz's cheeks when he kisses her neck. It's tangible, ineffable. Worth every spat he's ever had with them.

Teddy knows he can be difficult. Schwartz still tells him he's proud and Gemma tells him he's afraid. But grief is yet another stain over the world, and it overwhelms him to see through many people's obfuscation at once. To look at the ring on Schwartz's finger, knowing Alaric will never see him get married. To feel each knot lodged in the channel of his throat simultaneously so that he cannot breathe. Grief is a ghost beneath his bed, the memory of sun-drawn freckles, and a boy caught in eternal youth. A bookshop accruing dust without someone to care for it.

Love, everlasting.

If there is a name for this peculiar amalgamation, Teddy doesn't know it. No word he has found thus far feels large enough to encapsulate it all. He thumbs through the pages of his favourite stories, clinging to others' words for strength. To the Gawain poet, to Chaucer, and to Dante.

Here is a god stronger than I, who comes to rule over me.

If anyone had wished to know love, he might have done so by looking at my glistening eyes.

In the evenings, he slips onto the bed beside Schwartz. He smiles into her collarbone or her curls and says, 'I'm sorry I took so long.' Her fingers rake through his hair. Her legs stretch out at his side. When she thinks of him, the buzz of her mind lowers to nothing. She whispers something in his ear that he is often too tired to remember in the morning, but the sound of her voice soothes him like a lullaby. 'You're here now. That's all that matters.'

The world is quiet when his head is nestled in the bow of her stomach. Her thumb grazes his cheek, and as it lulls him to sleep, he swears he has found the right word. The word that carries all of his staggering weight. He chases it down like a white rabbit, falling, falling.

By morning, it is gone.

ACKNOWLEDGEMENTS

There are infinite ways to grieve someone or something. In writing this book, which explored grief in many forms, I lost someone who was very dear to me, the person to whom my first book was dedicated. I lost someone else very recently as well. It's interesting how grief reinvents itself once you think you've gotten used to it.

This is a heavy topic to explore, much less to build a romantic fantasy novel around. During this process, I've relied on the support and love of so many people, all of whom are invaluable to me. I simply cannot imagine a life that doesn't involve you in some way. There are pieces of you that I carry with me, whether I realize it or not.

For my distant friends: Sophia S, Andrea C, Grace A, Sarah U, Ania P, Ellie T, Colby D, Ryan A, Teagan K, Angela V, Anne E, Bri B, Yves D and Harvey B. I think of you all the time, even when you're not around.

For my local friends: Kelsea Y, Courtney G, Rosiee T, Emma H and Gabrielle M. I treasure all my time with you. Thank you for putting up with me in person.

For my agent, Sheyla. May we succeed in our slow efforts to

take over the world with kissing books. It's also because of you that I now have Cody and Kat in my life. Mwahaha.

For the team at Tor UK. Thank you for giving this series a home. I never intended for more than twenty-five people to read it, maybe, ever.

For the coffee shops and various third spaces that have given me a safe place to write and work: Relevant Coffee, Honey Latte Café, Portal Tea Company and Archive Coffee. Please stay open later.

For every artist who has felt inspired by my books to create something of their own. You amaze me. I love you, I love you, I love you. Your creativity and persistence in the ugly face of sinister GenAI overlords (looking at you Midjourney) is impressive and beautiful. You deserve so much respect for all you do. I would especially love to shout out Mia Minnis, Little Chmura, Briar Boehm, Mitra Katsuyoshi and Bea (capuchinhoslibrary) for their stunning contributions to the *Modern Divination* universe.

This year, I've met so many new people within this industry who have lined the rough path forward with moments of much-needed relief. I know that I will miss some if I try to recall them all, so I am not going to try. If you've grabbed a meal with me in the UK, chatted with me at the Seattle Convention Center, or split an order of steak bites with me post-event in Portland, this includes you.

This also includes my cat, Mossie, and my family.

It is, perhaps, a sad fact that the world will, one day, lack you. You are inextricable parts of my life, which can only mean that something miraculous has happened to put us all on earth at the same time. More than this book is about grief, it is about love, and the abundant, immortal nature of love. Share that love as much as you can.

MODERN DIVINATION

Go back to where it all began with the thrilling
first novel in the Spells for Life and Death duology.